WANDER IN THE DARK

BOOKS BY JUMATA EMILL

The Black Queen

Wander in the Dark

JUMATA EMILL

DELACORTE PRESS

This is a work of fiction. Names, characters, places, and incidents either are the product of the author's imagination or are used fictitiously. Any resemblance to actual persons, living or dead, events, or locales is entirely coincidental.

Visit us on the Web! GetUnderlined.com

Educators and librarians, for a variety of teaching tools, visit us at RHTeachersLibrarians.com

Library of Congress Cataloging-in-Publication Data is available upon request.
ISBN 978-0-593-65185-8 (trade)—ISBN 978-0-593-65186-5 (lib. bdg.)—
ISBN 978-0-593-65187-2 (ebook)

The text of this book is set in 11-point Warnock Pro Light.
Interior design by Cathy Bobak

Printed in the United States of America
10 9 8 7 6 5 4 3 2 1
First Edition

This one is for you, Dad.

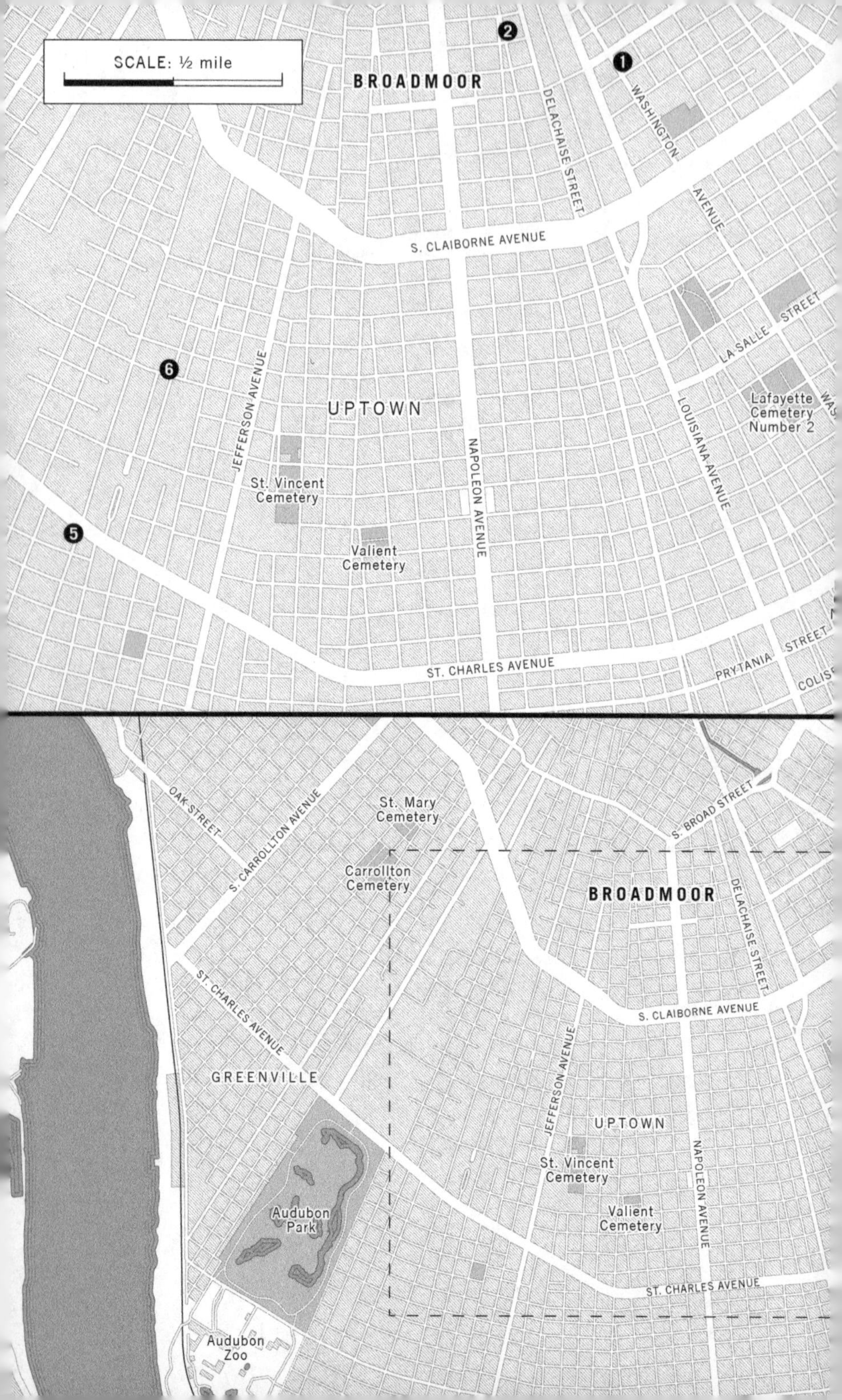
SCALE: ½ mile
BROADMOOR
WASHINGTON AVENUE
DELACHAISE STREET
S. CLAIBORNE AVENUE
LA SALLE STREET
Lafayette Cemetery Number 2
JEFFERSON AVENUE
UPTOWN
LOUISIANA AVENUE
St. Vincent Cemetery
NAPOLEON AVENUE
Valient Cemetery
ST. CHARLES AVENUE
PRYTANIA STREET
OAK STREET
S. CARROLLTON AVENUE
St. Mary Cemetery
Carrollton Cemetery
S. BROAD STREET
BROADMOOR
DELACHAISE STREET
S. CLAIBORNE AVENUE
ST. CHARLES AVENUE
GREENVILLE
JEFFERSON AVENUE
UPTOWN
St. Vincent Cemetery
NAPOLEON AVENUE
Valient Cemetery
Audubon Park
ST. CHARLES AVENUE
Audubon Zoo

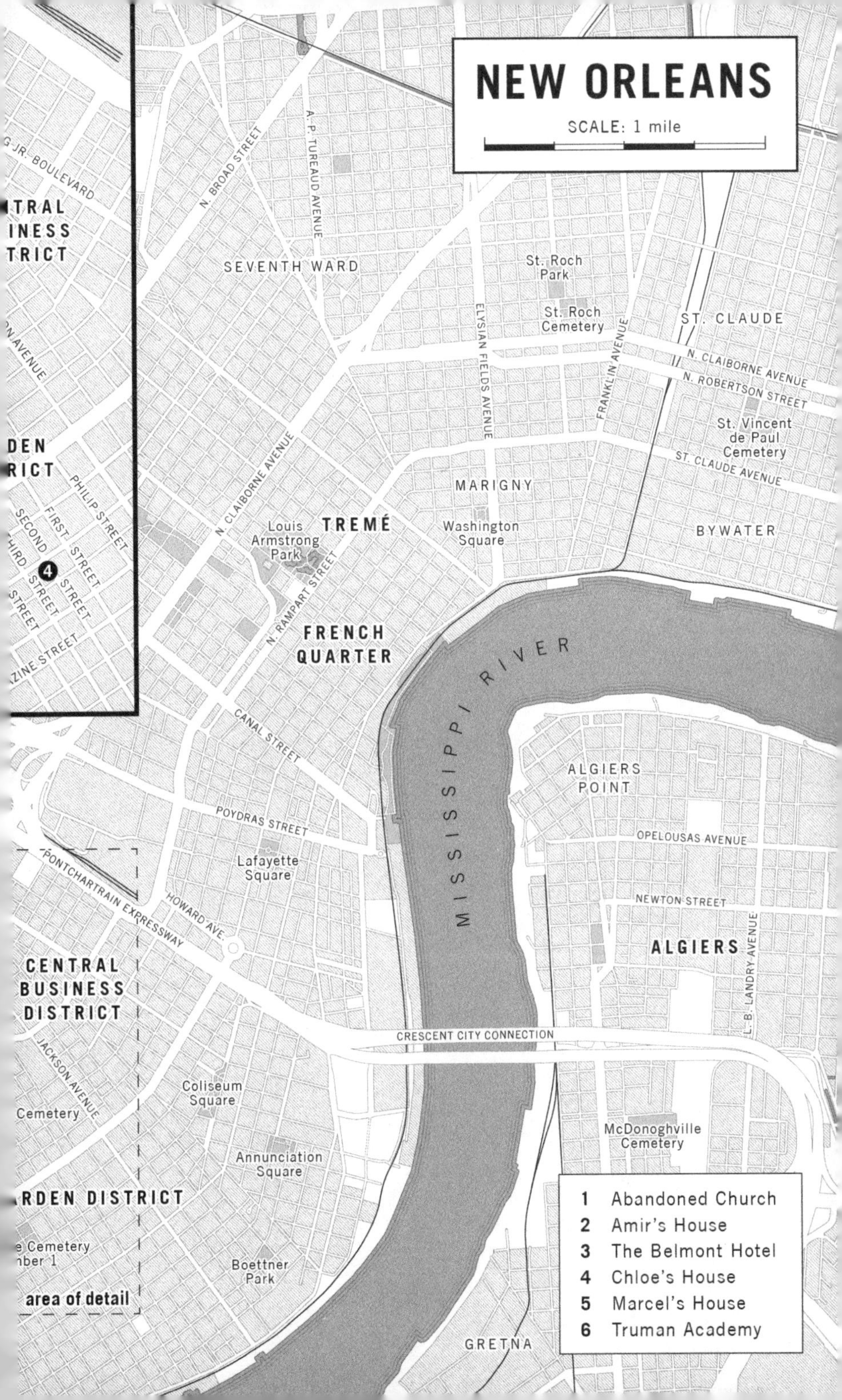
NEW ORLEANS
SCALE: 1 mile
SEVENTH WARD
N. BROAD STREET
A. P. TUREAUD AVENUE
St. Roch Park
St. Roch Cemetery
ST. CLAUDE
ELYSIAN FIELDS AVENUE
FRANKLIN AVENUE
N. CLAIBORNE AVENUE
N. ROBERTSON STREET
St. Vincent de Paul Cemetery
ST. CLAUDE AVENUE
MARIGNY
Washington Square
BYWATER
N. CLAIBORNE AVENUE
Louis Armstrong Park
TREMÉ
N. RAMPART STREET
FRENCH QUARTER
MISSISSIPPI RIVER
CANAL STREET
ALGIERS POINT
POYDRAS STREET
OPELOUSAS AVENUE
Lafayette Square
NEWTON STREET
PONTCHARTRAIN EXPRESSWAY
HOWARD AVE.
ALGIERS
L. B. LANDRY AVENUE
CENTRAL BUSINESS DISTRICT
CRESCENT CITY CONNECTION
JACKSON AVENUE
Coliseum Square
Cemetery
McDonoghville Cemetery
Annunciation Square
RDEN DISTRICT
Boettner Park
area of detail
GRETNA
TRAL
INESS
TRICT
G JR. BOULEVARD
DEN
RICT
PHILIP STREET
FIRST STREET
SECOND STREET
THIRD STREET
4
1 Abandoned Church
2 Amir's House
3 The Belmont Hotel
4 Chloe's House
5 Marcel's House
6 Truman Academy

1

Amir

Why did I come to this party?

I'm standing in the crowded hallway, surrounded by a bunch of drunk kids I don't even like. But annoyed more with myself than with them, 'cause I know the answer to that question. It's Chloe Danvers.

She texted me, out the blue, an hour ago.

You should be at this party, it said.

Who dis? was my immediate response. I didn't recognize the number.

Chloe.

That's all she had to say. There's only one Chloe I know. Well, sorta know. She's one of the P&Ps at my new school. P&P = Pretty and Popular girls. She's a junior, so we don't have any classes together or hang in the same social circle, but I see her a lot because she dates Trey Winslow. Trey is a senior, like me, and one of the less than a dozen Black dudes who attend

Truman Academy—also, like me. Chloe used to wait for him in the hall after a few of the classes Trey and I have together—that's when I'd see her.

I heard they broke up this week. Have no idea why. I don't really be socializing with any of the pretentious kids I go to school with. Her randomly hitting me up tonight has me doing the very thing I wanted to avoid—being at this party. But Chloe's got a tight li'l body, even for a white girl. I'd be lying if I said I'm not curious to find out if the text is her way of shooting her shot at me. I swear I caught her checking me out a few times as I was walking by.

The right side of my mouth curls as I stand against the wall, rereading the rest of our brief text thread.

How'd you get my number? Marcel?

Does it matter?
U coming or not?

Wasn't planning on it.

What's up wit dat face? 😹

Wanted to see you.
Finally hang 😉

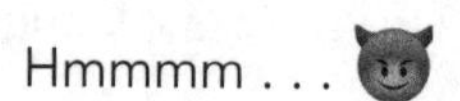

She had to get my number from Marcel.

It looks like he invited everyone from our school to his

sixteenth birthday party, meaning there are enough people here, and this house is big enough, that I'll be able to avoid him. Haven't run into him yet, but I'm sure it's only a matter of time. I don't want me showing up tonight to give him the wrong idea. Fool him into thinking things are good between us. They're not. And never will be. I don't care if he *is* my half brother.

"Hey, we good?" my best friend, Quincy, says after tapping me on the shoulder.

I look up from my phone, pursing my lips at him. "Bruh, don't even. Not after going behind my back and telling Buster and Nick about this party. So, no. We not good."

Quincy was at my house two weeks ago when I threw Marcel's invitation in the trash. He knows the backstory. Knows all the wounds being here opens up for me. Which is why I'm still trying to process why he suggested we come when we were looking for something else to do tonight. Of course Buster and Nick jumped at the chance to visit the two-story Greek Revival mansion my dad lives in with his new family on St. Charles Avenue. Ever since Buster and Nick found out the man *Food & Wine* magazine recently crowned one of this city's most accomplished chefs and restaurateurs is my dad, they can't stop asking why I don't visit or ever talk about him.

My homeboys don't know about Chloe's text. I've let them think they've talked me into being here.

"Bruh, I'm not being the opp," Quincy leans in and yells over the music that's vibrating in my chest. "But what went down between y'all—"

"Mannn, just don't," I interrupt, holding up one hand while

sliding my phone back into the front pouch of my hoodie with the other.

I stretch my neck to see over everyone's heads. Where the hell is she? We've been here twenty minutes and I still haven't seen her. Once I do, I'm hoping I can convince her to bounce. There are so many other places we can hang, especially tonight. Marcel would never even know I was here if that happens.

"Where's Bus and Nick?" I ask Quincy.

I immediately get an answer when I hear "You don't want this smoke, white boy!" shouted over the music.

Everyone around me turns toward the outburst. My stomach flips. Quincy and I exchange looks that both say *Oh no.*

It's Buster. We'd know his voice anywhere.

I lead Quincy through the crowd into the living room. The knot of people in the center of the room thins as we approach, revealing Buster and Nick, who are standing with their backs to us. Both are glaring in the same direction, at the group of dudes crammed onto the sofa I once accidentally spilled soda on, after which Marcel's mother criticized me for not having any decent home training.

Jared Lanford is the only person I recognize. We take English lit and physics together. He slowly stands up as Quincy and I step up beside Buster. Jared is one of them cocky *my daddy owns the world*–ass white boys. His entire crew of foot soldiers stands up too. They're just like him: white and entitled.

"Dude, what's your problem?" Jared says to Buster, his upper lip twisted by a sneer. "I already told you, we weren't sweating you. You're paranoid."

"Bus, why you popping off?" I ask, almost pleading.

The slightest thing will set Buster off. He'll take offense at how a person is breathing if he's in a bad mood. I knew bringing him here was a bad idea. Especially given how much he drank today.

Buster doesn't take his eyes off Jared. "I don't like the way dis punk-ass dude and his boys been eyeing me and Nick, texting each other and giggling like some bitches."

The music fades, so everyone clearly hears Buster say, "You betta get yo' li'l classmates, Amir. Let 'em know I ain't the nigga to fuck with."

I wince. A few people in the crowd gasp. I don't need this tonight. Not here. Not in front of these kids who already have me feeling like an outsider eight hours a day, Monday through Friday.

"Come on, Bus, chill," I say, softly pressing my hand on his chest. I feel his heart beating like a jackhammer.

"Listen to yo' boy," Jared says with a snide look.

Buster's nostrils flare. I look over and see that Nick's hands are balled into fists at his sides.

I shouldn't have come. *The things we do for girls.*

"Amir?"

The crowd to my right parts. Marcel steps out of the gap that's created, stopping between my crew and Jared's, a burly dude dressed in a black suit right behind him. He's one of the security guards who was checking for invitations at the front gate. We got in without one because he recognized me.

"What's the problem?" Marcel asks, looking at me.

"Nothing. Nothing, bruh," I say, irritated. "We got it under control. Right, Bus? It was just a little misunderstanding."

Buster smacks his lips, finally shifting his glare away from Jared and onto me. "Yeah, whatever. Not about to stunt this dude. Just keep him away from me."

"Gladly," Jared drawls, disappearing into the same gap Marcel and Security Dude emerged from. Jared's crew follows.

"What happened to the music?" Marcel yells, commanding the room's attention. "It's my *fucking* birthday! We're supposed to be turning up!"

The crowd cheers. A second later, the music kicks back on. Everyone quickly settles back into their pre-blowup configurations like nothing ever happened.

Everyone except us.

"Bro, I'm so glad you showed up," Marcel says after giving Security Dude a nod that sends him back to wherever he came from. "This is the best birthday present, for real."

Marcel lifts his arms and starts walking toward me. I take a step back, which makes him pause. His wide grin shrivels. Why would he ever think I'd let him hug me? I knew showing up would give him the wrong idea.

"How long have you been here . . . ," he says, the enthusiasm leaving his voice. His eyes dart to my right and left. ". . . with your friends?" he adds.

"*They* wanted to come through," I say.

It's a little gratifying to see the disappointment ripple across his beige complexion, which he shares with his mother, who is of Creole descent. The older he gets, the thicker his nose and lips become, features it's now obvious to my homeboys that I share with him. Marcel and his mother represent the life that was worth our dad cheating on my mother for. *They're* his real family and I'm just the *other* son.

"Wassup, Marcel? Happy birthday, dude," Quincy yells, stepping in front of me with his hand extended. "I'm your brother's best friend, DeQuincy, but everyone calls me Quincy—or just Q."

"*Half* brother," I mumble, but I'm sure none of them hear me over the music.

Quincy has this silly look on his face as he shakes Marcel's hand. It makes my jaw clench.

"Nice to meet you, bruh," Quincy says, dropping Marcel's hand. "I've heard a lot about you."

Marcel's eyes flick over to me. "Not sure how I should take that," he says with a nervous laugh.

Quincy takes a step back to check out what Marcel's wearing. "Liking the 'fit, dawg."

"Oh, thanks," Marcel replies, sliding a hand down the front of the emerald-green velvet blazer he's wearing with an unbuttoned white tuxedo shirt, black tailored pants, and designer loafers. Marcel's middle name should have been Always Doing the Most. The invitation said the dress code was "business casual." Most of the kids here showed up in something damn near formal, which has us standing out even more than we already do among the sea of white faces.

"I see now who got all the style in the family," Quincy tells him, looking back at me.

I look down at my jeans, which are frayed at the knees, and my limited-edition gold-and-black Jordans. I think back on the web addresses that popped up in Quincy's internet search history the other day while I was using his laptop. That has me wondering if him switching up on me tonight about this party is really about him wanting to meet Marcel for entirely different reasons than Buster and Nick.

" 'Sup, bruh. I'm Amir's other homeboy, Buster," Buster says, holding out his skinny hand.

Marcel briefly hesitates before shaking it, his eyes locked on me the entire time.

I know what he's thinking. He's questioning why I'm still hanging out with the person who got me into the trouble that prompted my mother to twist our dad's arm into paying for me to attend Truman. My mom can't stand Buster. She thinks he's "never gonna amount to anything" and will bring me down with him. She could be right. But he's still my boy.

After Nick introduces himself, Marcel points at my homeboys and says, "You all attended Douglas Egan High with Amir?"

They nod.

"We geekin' hard that our boy was raised in all *this,*" Buster says as we walk out of the living room into the foyer, where it's less crowded. "You been holding back on us, my G," he says, slapping me across the chest.

"For real," Nick chimes in.

"That's 'cause I didn't grow up here," I respond. "Only visited."

Until I stopped, I say to myself.

I look around again for the mane of blond hair that lured me here. The distraction I need from this conversation.

Marcel leans in. "Amir, can we talk?" he says to me. "I really wanna make things right between us. Life is too short, man."

He's just saying that last part because our grandmother died last year. *Whatever.* It's the same thing he's been spouting since I started going to Truman. Had he felt like this when we were younger, things wouldn't be like they are now.

"Y'all ain't got no liquor up in here?" I say, looking everywhere but at him.

Most of the ostentatious furniture his mother loves to brag about has been shifted around, or moved out of certain rooms, probably so Marcel's friends can have more space to dance and move around. The study, which sits to the right of the foyer, just before the staircase, has been flipped into a food area. Long tables dotted with silver chafing dishes line the walls. From where we are, I can see the large punch bowl in the center of one of the tables, a glistening ice sculpture in the shape of the number sixteen behind it. Green, gold, and purple balloons are scattered all over the floors in the living room, foyer, study, and dining room. A giant framed portrait of my dad's new family still hangs above the gold half-moon console table flush against the wall that separates the dining room from the study. But unlike the last time I was here, the picture of my dad, stepmother, and half brother is current, instead of the one that featured a ten-year-old Marcel.

"Try the punch," Marcel says after nudging my shoulder. "Paul and Danny spiked it with Tito's as soon as they got here."

He says their names like I know who the hell Paul and Danny are.

"Bet."

I turn on my heels and head for the study, leaving him with my homeboys. I hear Nick saying "Y'all's house is fire" as I'm maneuvering through people to get away from them. Not trying to watch my friends fawn over my half brother and this mansion, which could hold at least four shotgun-style homes like the one I live in with my mama.

My gaze travels up the stairs as I'm crossing the foyer. I wonder if the bedroom my dad used to say was reserved for me has been converted into something else. Marcel's mom was always talking about needing another closet. My dad no doubt let her turn my old room into one. He's a simp like that when it comes to her. Whatever Lily wants, she gets. Fuck everybody else—as in me.

Because I'm not looking at where I'm going, I slam into something.

"Uh, excuse you, Mr. I Wasn't Planning on Coming to This Party!"

Correction. Not some*thing.* Some*one.*

Chloe is standing in front of me, her pretty face distorted by a pursed look, one of her slim arms held midair, I'm assuming to keep the flute of spiked punch she's clutching in her hand from spilling onto her sexy dress. The tightness that's been squeezing my chest since I walked up to the front gate starts to ease at the sight of her. She's with a brown-haired girl I don't know, but I've seen Chloe hanging with her at school.

"I thought you'd look happier that I showed up," I say, putting some bass in my voice.

She drops her arm and gives me a flirty once-over with her ash-colored eyes. "I'm surprised you did. Figured you'd hold it against me that I'm friends with your brother."

"He's not a factor at all, trust me." I take a step closer. She smells like excitement mixed with regret. "You caught me off guard when you hit me up. You know, since the only dude I've ever seen you talking to, besides Marcel, is Trey."

"I'm not really talking to Trey anymore." She inches closer and starts tugging on the plastic beads I forgot are still dangling around my neck. "Looks like someone had a bountiful Fat Tuesday."

Nick, Buster, Quincy, and I have been together since six a.m., like we have been on the last day of the Mardi Gras season since the ninth grade. We went to the Zulu parade first, which was immediately followed by Rex. Then we bounced over the city all afternoon and into the evening, hitting up the various neighborhood block and house parties, sipping on the bottle of Hennessy one of Buster's uncles snuck us. We divided it up in cups from Popeye's so no one could tell what we were really drinking.

I freaking love Mardi Gras. There's this electric energy in the air. New Orleans comes to life more, and everyone wants everyone else to have a good time.

The flirtatious smile Chloe has on her face makes me look down at my feet and lick my lips. Keeping it all the way a buck, the girl is almost too freaking pretty.

"Outta the way! Outta the way!" someone shouts, tearing me from the inappropriate thoughts I was having.

Chloe, her friend, and I all turn just as two dudes come barreling toward us.

"Out of the way! Medical emergency coming through!" a dude shouts. He has one arm draped over the shoulder of a shorter guy who's bent over with both hands covering his nose. Panic is etched across the first guy's face. As soon as the shorter dude lifts his head and lowers one of his hands I see why. Blood is dripping from his nose so fast it's starting to spill into his mouth.

"Ewww," Chloe's friend yelps before stepping aside to clear a path through the doorway we're standing in front of.

The first dude and Chloe say something to each other as the two guys barrel past us—I don't know what, because the room starts to spin. I take a deep breath, grabbing the edge of the food table to my right.

Stop thinking about it, I repeat to myself, working hard to steady my breathing.

The *it* being all that blood.

"Are you okay?" I feel a squeeze around my bicep.

My vision is still a little hazy, but I can see the concern on Chloe's face. "Yeah, yeah, I'm good," I tell her, standing up straighter while I try to replace the bloody image in my mind by thinking about the pound cake I baked last week for Mama.

"Plot twist: the boy who loves to skulk through the halls at school every day gets weak at the sight of a little blood?" Chloe teases.

"That wasn't *a little,*" I say.

Pound cake. Pound cake. Pound cake.

"It wasn't a lot either," she replies.

"You got jokes," I say, tasting the shrimp po'boy I ate earlier in the back of my throat.

"Chloe, stop being a tease," her friend says, grabbing her hand and pulling her out of the study.

The friend says something about finding someone named Cameron as they leave. Chloe looks back and waves before they disappear around the staircase. Dude's bloody nose becomes an afterthought as I'm left behind, debating with myself whether Chloe Danvers was really worth showing up tonight after I promised myself I'd never set foot in this house again.

Not after I was accused of murder.

2

Marcel

My brother acts like he hates me, but he doesn't. Not really.

He's angry. Like, mad angry. But I'm going to make it right. I have to. He's my only sibling. I look up to him. I love him. Always have. That's hard for him to believe based on how I used to treat him during his weekend visits when we were little. Back then, my dismissiveness toward him was the behavior of an insecure boy who ignorantly believed our father didn't have enough love to share between the both of us. So I tried to make Amir feel like he didn't belong. Like he wasn't good enough. Things I wish I could take back. Pettiness that doubled down on how horrible my mother was to him. He hasn't said it to me, but I know our father is living with the same regret. Nana, our grandmother, used to say Amir and our father are so much alike. Both stubborn. Unwilling to do the work and meet each other halfway to fix their relationship.

That's where I come in. Nana said if anyone can bring our family together it's me. "You my little busybody," she said once.

"Just nosy and eager to be in charge, make everyone feel better. That's special. You're special." On her deathbed, she made me promise that I'd do what she never could. God rest her soul. I'm taking charge and bridging the divide in our family.

To do that, we all have to start dealing in truths and not the skewed versions of it we've allowed ourselves to believe. That includes Amir's mother. Amir's resentment toward us is twisted up in the lie she's perpetrated all these years. Something we'll need to confront down the road. First I have to own up to what I did four years ago. The thing that made Amir never want to come back here. That's where the healing will begin between us.

If only I could find him again to tell him that. I haven't seen him since he left with his friends forty-five minutes ago.

I've been caught up taking selfies with people who are posting them to their socials to wish me happy birthday, and trying to keep all these kids from tearing up our house. My parents threatened to take back the Tesla Model S and Gucci loafers they gave me for my birthday if they have to come out of pocket for any damages caused by my party. Them not being here is honestly the reason I haven't really been enjoying it. I'm stressing myself out trying to keep up with what everyone is doing—plus managing the small staff to tend to the food and clean up, and the security team my parents hired to ensure no one wanders in off the streets, given the open house vibes of the city during Mardi Gras.

I poke my head into the living room, scanning the makeshift dance floor, where a gaggle of girls (mostly white) are failing miserably at twerking to Big Freedia's "Azz Everywhere." Amir and his friends are nowhere in sight. I spin back around toward the foyer and slam into Nolan, who is the last person I wanna deal with right now.

"Wassup, baby?" he drawls, snaking his arms around my waist. He tries to kiss me, but I lean back, pushing my hands against his chest. "Come dip off in your bedroom for a bit. I got a birthday present for you."

I can practically taste his vodka-weed breath in the back of my throat. What did I ever see in him?

"Chill, boy, I'm looking for my brother," I say, failing in my attempt to wiggle free of his lecherous hands.

He pushes me up against the archway to the living room, rubbing his groin against mine. "Why is it okay for you to call me boy but you lost your shit when I said it to you the last time we hooked up?"

I latch hold of his wrists with both hands. "The fact that I have to explain that to you is why we'll never hook up again."

Nolan manages to slip his hands free and trap me by pressing them against the wall near my head. "You know I didn't mean it like *that,*" he says, pushing his face into my throat when I turn my head to avoid another kiss. His hot, wet breath crawls up the side of my neck. "Stop being so sensitive," he adds.

I wasn't being sensitive. But this Black boy doesn't want to hear *You like that, boy?* being moaned in his ear by a white boy. It wasn't just that either. Even before it happened, Nolan started making me feel like nothing but a fetish. Referring to my junk as a BBC (Big Black Cock) and making the offhanded comment that he usually isn't into Black guys but there was just *something about me* that turned him on. I should have blocked his number then, but he caught me at a weak drunk moment—okay, a *few* drunk moments. You live and you learn.

"Come on, Marcel." He takes one hand off the wall and tries to tease it through my thick curls.

Him removing his arm from the archway creates an opening I can use to get away from this god-awful sexual assault. "Find someone else to entertain you. I need to find my brother," I say to him.

Definitely blocking his number tonight. Ignoring him at school will be the challenge.

I take off toward the backyard, where a lot of the kids have migrated. On the way, my eyes wander toward the staircase and I pause. My parents forbade me to allow anyone upstairs. I threatened death to anyone who didn't stay on the first floor. But I wonder if Amir might be up there, visiting his old bedroom. The thought of him in there with his friends has my stomach doing somersaults. Mainly because of that dude Buster. Given the trouble he got Amir in and the altercation I had to break up between him and Jared tonight, I don't feel comfortable having him roam free all up and through here.

Amir's probably seeing if his old bedroom still looks the same. It doesn't. Last time he was here, the decor was geared toward the thirteen-year-old who slept in it two weekends a month. We upgraded the furniture last year—or rather, I did. My mother wanted to turn it into a second closet for herself. I had to get my father on my side to keep it for Amir.

I take the stairs two at a time.

"Yo, Marcel, where you going?" someone shouts as I'm nearing the top.

I pause and turn around. "Checking on something right quick," I say to Dustin Miller, who's standing near the entrance to our main dining room with a glass of the spiked punch clutched in one of his freckled hands.

"Hurry up, man," he says, his eyes dancing with excitement. "We just dared Aaron to eat the entire tray of sandwiches that's left. Gonna see if we can get it to go viral on TikTok."

Um, no thank you. "I'll be down in a minute," I lie.

There's a sliver of light shining through the cracks of the closed door to Amir's bedroom. I knew it. *Good, we can talk away from everyone,* I think as I walk down the hallway, the music downstairs fading into a mumbled melody.

I push open the door.

"Amir, can we chat right . . ." I stop in the doorway, my hand still on the knob. It's not my brother who's standing in the middle of the room.

I tilt my head, frowning at Chloe and Trey Winslow, who has the nerve to look offended that I entered without knocking in my own house. By the strained look on Chloe's face, I quickly realize I've walked into what must be fight number one thousand and three for them. I thought the saga of their relationship was over, as they supposedly broke up last week. My best-friend reflexes immediately kick in. I take a step inside.

Chloe is a fuckboy magnet. First it was Jared Lanford, and then Spencer "Trey" Winslow III, whose ego got inflated the day his father won that US congressional seat. Suddenly he expected us to treat him like Black royalty. That reminds me, I need to convince my dad not to donate to his father's upcoming re-election campaign.

The exasperated sigh Chloe lets out when our eyes meet stops me from taking another step toward them. Oh, that's right. I'm still mad at her for trying to ruin this party.

They're not your friends, she said to me during lunch period Friday. *They* being everyone here. I'm guessing since she and Trey imploded again she wants me all to herself. As if I don't already give her enough attention. Whatever. Tonight's supposed to be about me. I didn't want to hear anything she had to say. She knew how much I was stressing over the details, and she decided four days before my party to come out of left field with some story about how horrible everyone at our school is. The audacity of her showing her face tonight to be around the same people she *claimed* were "the fucking worst" is mad annoying.

"What are y'all doing up here?" I ask in a clipped tone.

"We'll be out in a second if you give us some privacy," Trey snaps.

Oh, this fool got the wrong one today. I step farther into the room, my mouth tight.

"Marcel, we're sorry." Chloe moves in front of him, a pained expression on her flushed face.

I want to believe she's apologizing for trying to ruin my party by telling me my friends are not my friends. Some of the tension in my shoulders lightens.

"Trey needed to talk about something important, you know, without all the eyes and ears that are downstairs," she continues.

Maybe he's getting the same speech she tried to give me at lunch. If so, I can understand why he's looking as irked as I was. But it's Trey. I don't like him, never did. So he gets no sympathy from me.

"You good?" I ask her, my eyes flicking over her shoulder at him. He turns his head like he's disgusted at the sight of me. *Feeling's totally mutual,* I think.

I never got a clear answer out of Chloe about why they broke up this time. She said they "grew apart." Whatever that means.

"Yeah, I'm good." Chloe nervously looks back at Trey, but her eyes go to the floor when she turns around again. "Please, just give us a minute. We'll be right down."

I linger for a second before I back out of the room. "Hurry up," I say. "I don't want anyone else to see y'all up here."

"Okay," Chloe replies, nodding repeatedly, her mouth a thin line.

I won't stay mad at her forever. As long as she *really* apologizes for whatever melodrama she tried to stir up.

A few seconds after I shut the door I hear Trey shout, "You tell anybody else?"

"No!" she mumbles on the other side of the door. "Your family is the *last* thing on my mind right now. Trust me!"

I can't shake the feeling that there's something different about whatever disagreement they're having from any other silly fights they've had before.

There's so much about Trey that rubs me the wrong way. His bullish obsession with his image topping the list. He's all about having a life that "looks good on paper." I stopped being a fan of his relationship with Chloe the first time he broke up with her—after a portion of the shopping mall and government complex her father's architecture firm designed collapsed during construction, killing two workers. Trey said the legal scandal that immediately followed "wasn't a good look." I begged her not to give him a second chance once the ordeal faded from the public's consciousness and he came sniffing around again, wanting her back.

His little sister, Tiffany, though, is nothing like him. That's why she and I get along so well. She's standing at the bottom of the stairs as I'm coming back down. Her dark, coiled hair pulled back from her oval face by two sparkling pink hair clips that match her puffy cocktail dress. Her eyes light up when she sees me.

"Hey, have you seen my brother?" she shouts over the music when I reach the bottom step.

"Upstairs, fighting with Chloe," I reply with a dramatic eye roll.

Tiffany rolls her eyes back. "I know she's your girl, but I wish he would just be done with her."

"I feel the same way about her with your brother."

We both laugh. No one else knows about me and Chloe's little tiff. I'd like to keep it that way. Even though commiserating about it with Tiffany right now is tempting.

Tiffany can be a little weird and awkward at times, but she's got all the personality in her family. Wish she'd give some of it to her brother.

"Chloe still being shady to you?" I ask.

When Chloe started dating Trey, her and Tiffany became inseparable. Chloe joked that Trey and Tiffany were a package deal. The only reason I'm thinking this breakup with Trey might actually stick is because Chloe has decided to cut Tiffany off too, which I told her was kind of messed up. She doesn't care. Chloe can be so self-absorbed—but I still love her. Despite how exhausting it is at times to be her friend.

"Now that she and Trey have fizzled out, she acts like it's inappropriate to be friends with me," Tiffany says. "That girl is just a bitch—sorry."

"Hey, have you by chance seen *my* brother?" I ask, wanting to change the subject.

"Yeah, he's out back with his friends," she says, nodding in that direction.

"Oh, let me holla at you later, then," I say, and I leave her standing at the bottom of the steps.

Amir and his friends are seated in some of the wicker chairs dotting our back porch. They've got four arranged in a semicircle around the matching table. The aroma from the weed they're smoking hits me as soon as I step out the french doors. About a dozen other people are scattered along the porch as well, with more people spread out across the modest courtyard that makes up the majority of our backyard.

The chill in the air must be coming from Amir. He's the only one who doesn't look up when I approach their huddle.

"Hey, Marcel, what's up?" Quincy says, sitting up straighter.

Amir's best friend is acting mad suspect. But I'm not trying to blow up his spot in case my brother doesn't know he's gay.

Had it not been for Amir, I'd definitely be entertaining the attention. Quincy has this infectious smile, and a slightly bowlegged walk that's hella sexy. Not trying to *go there* with him, though. That's all I need: Amir blaming me for turning one of his friends gay. He already blames me for enough.

I give Quincy a polite smile before turning to Amir. "Can we talk for a quick sec?"

He leans forward in his chair to hand off the half-smoked blunt to Nick, who's seated to his right. Amir doesn't bother to look at me when he dismissively replies, "For what?"

To understand why you bothered showing up tonight if all you were going to do is avoid me. I slowly exhale. "Amir, come on, bro. Just give me two minutes . . . alone."

He sits back, his gaze still pointed toward the courtyard, and releases a cloud of smoke that curls around my waist before floating toward my face. I start tapping my foot, waiting for him to say something. I can feel his friends staring, waiting to see how this little standoff will end. Really wish we didn't have an audience. This is between me and him.

"Please, Amir." I bend over, nudging the arm he has propped along the chair's armrest. "Just talk to me. It's only a conversation."

He finally makes eye contact with me. With his brow knitted and square jaw clenched, he looks exactly like our father when he's annoyed with me. Amir's dark features are a phantom of our father's youth.

"This is my family," he replies, waving his arm at his friends. "Anything you need to say to me, you can say in front of them."

They're *his family*? Something snaps inside of me.

"Then why'd you show up tonight?" I seethe. "So you could act all petty toward me in front of your friends—no, I mean *family*?"

Amir shoots up out of his chair, stepping in my face. I back up, already regretting that I lost my patience so quickly.

"Bruh, I know you ain't popping off at me," he says, eyes narrowed. "It's yo' birthday. I'm trying to be nice."

"This is you being nice?" I say. "Acting like you can't be bothered with your own brother?"

"What are you so pressed about?" Amir gives me an exasperated look. "You got it all, including my sperm donor's unconditional love and support after you came out, which apparently y'all couldn't wait to tell the rest of the world."

Why is he bringing up that article *Essence* published last week? No way he can be mad about it too. It was just a fluff piece, we—

My rib cage starts squeezing my heart.

It didn't mention Amir's existence. Something I'm betting my mother made sure of, like she's done so many times before. We're still treating him like he doesn't matter. Like he's invisible.

Fuck.

I put up my hands in surrender. "I'm not trying to start an argument with you. I only wanna make things better. I know you—"

"You don't know shit but whatever yo' mama tells you to think," he says, waving his hand in my face.

"Let's leave our moms out of this," I fire back. "You don't want to go there."

"What you trying to say?" he replies, the hardness returning to his face.

Quincy appears at his side and starts pulling on Amir's arm, trying to usher him back down into the chair. "Amir, chill, dawg. Everybody's watching."

I turn around. Sure enough, we have an even bigger audience now. Everyone in the courtyard has stopped to stare at us. That's when I realize that Jared Lanford and his band of yes-men are on the other side of the porch. Jared is holding up his phone in our direction. That's all I need—a video of Martin Trudeau's sons fighting to go viral.

"Scottie, yo' boy and Nolan's boy might rack y'all up some points tonight, depending on who wins," Jared says with a devilish smirk. "I'm betting on yours, Scottie."

I briefly lock eyes with Colin Perrier, the only one of Jared's friends who's remotely tolerable. He's looking the most disinterested in whatever Jared and Scottie Boseman are laughing at now. A blond blur moves in my right peripheral vision the second before Chloe steps in between me and Amir.

"Can y'all stop with the sibling rivalry? It's not sexy," she says. I watch, confused, as she seductively pets my brother's bicep. "Why aren't you being nicer to my friend?" she says to him. "It's his birthday."

"Chloe, please stay out of it," I say.

"Good advice," someone chimes in on my right.

Trey and Tiffany are standing in the open french doors. The way Trey is eyeing my brother has my heart knocking against my chest. If it was Chloe who initiated the breakup this time, Trey no doubt still sees her as his property. And if he tries to flex on my brother, this won't be good. Amir has never backed down from a fight.

"You want me to stay out of it?" Chloe turns and coos to Amir.

He's looking directly at me when he says, "Nah, since you're the only reason I even showed up."

What? When in the hell did Chloe and my brother start conversing? Amir hardly talks to anyone at school—including me.

"Is there something you want to tell me?" I ask Chloe.

"I sneaked your brother's number from your phone while we were singing happy birthday earlier and *encouraged* him to come to your party," she says with a guilty look.

Which she could totally do since she knows the passcode to unlock it, just like I know hers.

"How? By flirting with him?" I say, my reigniting irritation with her straining my voice.

First she tries to get me to disinvite everyone, and then she turns around and secretly invites my brother. This is a little too much, even for her.

"So wait. You wasn't really trying to hang tonight?" Amir says in a disappointed tone.

"No, she wasn't," Trey interjects from the sideline.

I really need him to shut up and stop glaring at my brother.

"I came out here to tell you that I'm leaving," she says to

Amir. "And since *certain people* think I can't get home safely by myself, I'm hoping you'll take a ride with me."

She was looking at Trey when she said *certain people.*

"He's not taking you anywhere," Trey says, inching closer to Chloe and Amir.

I move toward them too. So do Amir's friends. All of us for the same reason: to defend Amir. I quickly glance around, disappointed I can't find Kurt or any of the other hired security dudes.

"Slow yo' roll, Carlton Banks," Buster barks, rubbing his clenched fist with his other hand. "You don't want this heat."

Does this boy do nothing but get involved in altercations at parties he wasn't even invited to? I can see the headline now: *US Senator's Son Fatally Shot at Home of Famed Local Chef.* My mother would use it as further proof that Amir is some kind of bad seed that's going to smear the family's name. That's why my grandmother never cared for her. Nana hated the way my mother treated Amir. Said she didn't care how awful his mother was to my parents after she and my dad divorced, Amir had nothing to do with their drama. It took some growing up for me to finally see how right she was.

"Trey, let her go, dawg," Jared yells behind us. "She's had a *rough couple of days.*"

Jared laughs at his own statement, confusing the rest of us.

"Chill, dude," Colin pleads, eliciting a grimace from him.

Chloe turns her nose up at Jared and tugs on my brother's arm. "You gonna give me a ride home or what, handsome?" she says.

What is happening? Since when did she start crushing on Amir?

"I didn't drive," he responds with a nervous laugh.

"You can drive my car," she says, waving her keys at him. "Come on."

She's already dragging Amir past Trey and Tiffany before I can say anything. Amir's friends are the only people who follow me as I stumble behind the couple I never would have predicted.

"Hold up," I call out. But neither of them stops. "Chloe, what are you doing? Are you drunk?"

She looks back at me over her shoulder, giggling. "Not that drunk. Just having a little fun. I've been dying to get to know your brother."

The girl has literally never mentioned this before.

Amir gives me this cocky grin as they're walking through the foyer. I know what's on his mind. Why can't he have the same restraint and respect that I have when it comes to messing around with his friends?

"Y'all, hold up, for real!" I shout over the music as they're bouncing down the front steps.

They keep going, leaving me in the front doorway. Chloe dangling on my brother's arm, bent over laughing at something he whispers to her when they walk by Kurt, who's still posted at the front gate.

"Thanks for letting us crash, bruh," Buster says, slapping me on the shoulder as he, Nick, and Quincy brush past me out the door.

"Nice party," Nick mumbles.

Quincy gives me a lingering smile. "See you around . . . hopefully."

I don't even bother looking at him. His goofy attraction toward me needles the uneasiness I'm feeling as I watch my brother and Chloe stroll down St. Charles Avenue until they disappear into the restless night shadowing the city. Nothing about how she's been acting the past few days makes any sense to me.

3

Amir

Chloe hasn't said a word since she kicked off her heels and plopped down in the passenger seat of her BMW 440i, a car my mother would never let me drive even if she could afford it. Her quietly staring out the window doesn't create the opportunity I was hoping for to get to the truth about why she hit me up tonight out of the blue. I'm kind of thinking it had more to do with her meddling between me and Marcel and less to do with her really wanting to get to know me. She could have asked me to show up to make Trey jealous. Either way, I don't know how to feel about her.

The Hello Kitty charm dangling from her key chain keeps knocking against my knee as I cruise down Jackson Avenue toward South Claiborne Avenue. I don't know where she lives. I'm assuming it's in Lakeview, like a lot of the other white kids who go to Truman. Guess I'll be catching a Lyft home from there. Didn't think this one through.

"You good?" I ask while we wait at a red light.

Her shoulders twitch, which I take as a shrug.

What happened between Marcel's party and us getting to her car? She was talking up a storm, flirting her ass off ten minutes ago. That was most definitely her wanting to get under Trey's skin. And that's cool. Half the reason I agreed to this was to ruffle his feathers. That dude really deserves a beatdown.

I keep my head pointed forward and shift my gaze to the right to trace the irregular hem of the champagne-colored off-the-shoulder dress she's wearing. Her slender, exposed thighs spark a tingle between my legs.

"You gonna go, or what?" she says, jolting me from my thoughts.

The light is green. And Chloe has this impatient scowl on her face. The tingling sensation is now crawling up the back of my neck, warming my face. I'm betting she caught me checking her out.

"Sorry, I know I'm all over the place tonight," she says after I mash the accelerator.

"Yeah, what's up with that?"

She sighs. "I'm exhausted."

"Care to elaborate?"

There's a brief silence before she says, "Not really."

"A'ight. How 'bout you tell me where you live," I say.

"I don't wanna go home," she replies.

I take my eyes off the road for a second to see that she's staring out the window again, now with her hands folded in her lap.

"Then where we going?" I say after silence drags on one, two, three blocks.

"Take me someplace you think I've never been," she says.

That flirtatious glint she had back at the party is brightening her gray eyes again.

"Huh?" I respond with a nervous grin.

"Take me somewhere you think I've never been," she repeats, this time with more authority.

"How am I supposed to know that?" I say. "I don't really know you like that. Tonight is the most words we've ever spoken to one another."

She tucks a few strands of her fluffy blond hair behind her ear. "Marcel says you're pretty smart. I have faith you can surprise me."

I resist the urge to ask why my half brother would say that about me. "Yeah, *all over the place* is the perfect description for you."

"Shut up and drive."

"Yes, ma'am," I tease.

My phone buzzes in my pocket as I'm turning onto Martin Luther King Jr. Boulevard. I wait until we're stopped at another red light before I pull it out. It's a text from Buster.

Broooooooooo, you smashing 2nite? it says.

I start grinning. Then another text alert balloons across the top of the screen. It's from Marcel. What it says makes me frown.

Watch yourself with Chloe. She's nothing but drama.

* * *

"Are you trying to kill me?"

I shoot Chloe a *you can't be serious* look across the hood of her car. She has this stank look on her face as she glares across the street at the derelict church we're parked in front of.

"You said someplace you've never been," I remind her while rounding the car's front end to join her. "I know you've never been here before. No one has. This is my secret spot."

"I see why," she says, scrunching her nose.

We're on the 3300 block of Washington Avenue, not too far from where I live in Broadmoor. The street is dark and still. The abandoned Catholic church I've been claiming as my own is haloed in the glow from the two streetlights that flank it. The shadows the lights are casting across the church's peeling white paint have it looking even more ragged than it does during the day. Chloe keeps glancing up and down the street. As if she's afraid there's an ax murderer hiding somewhere in the darkness who's going to jump out and attack us at any second.

"Come on, it's safe a'ight." I grab her hand and start pulling her toward the church's chained front doors. "I come here all the time."

Her heels click on the concrete steps fronting the dilapidated building. "So this isn't, like, a drug den or a crack house?"

"No you didn't just stereotype my hood like that," I joke.

"Don't even; I'm not every other basic white girl we go to school with," she says. "That was a legitimate question, being that I don't really know you, remember?"

I let go of her hand once we reach the eight-foot-high double doors. "And yet, that didn't stop you from wanting me to take you home tonight."

"Well, that's because you're cute."

Still can't tell if she's playing with me or serious. I think about Marcel's text. Why would he say that about his friend?

"We're not going to get in trouble being here?" Chloe asks.

I feel her watching me as I kneel down and push my back against the left side of the chained door, using both hands to push the right side in the opposite direction. I've done this so many times that the crack it creates has grown easier for me to squeeze through. I motion for Chloe to go first while I hold the doors apart. After a hesitant scowl she pushes herself through the opening I've created. I follow her inside, the chain and padlock clanging together once I release the pressure.

"I can't see anything," she whines. "And it smells like ass in here."

"Chill," I say.

I pull out my phone, turning on the flashlight feature. I could navigate my way up to my usual spot without it, but I'm hoping being able to see a little better will calm her nerves, since the moonlight beaming in through the missing portions of the church's vaulted ceiling isn't enough for her. The hollow clack of the Mardi Gras beads still layered around my neck is amplified by the gloomy silence.

"Come on, follow me," I tell her before taking off toward the curved staircase to the right of the tattered lobby we're standing in.

I take my time, looking back every two steps to make sure she's right behind me as we climb up to the mezzanine level overlooking the old church's sprawling sanctuary of discombobulated pews and its weather-torn pulpit. Her breath catches once we reach the top and step out onto the partial floor that makes up the second level of the building.

She must understand now why I like coming here. From the mezzanine level we have a panoramic view of the Superdome and the Central Business District's twinkling skyline in the distance. That's made possible by the massive hole that was ripped out of the church's back walls by any one, or possibly several, of the hurricanes that have hit this city. The hole has been here since I started sneaking in a year ago. I discovered this place one bored afternoon while I was riding my bike through the neighborhood.

"Wow," Chloe sighs. "This isn't a bad view—if you like that whole *blown-out wall in a run-down church* vibe."

I smile. "I'll take that as me understanding the assignment."

"Definitely my first time here," she says.

I take hold of her hand again, guiding her to the gaping hole in the middle of the mezzanine's banister. We have to step around and on pieces of decaying wood, broken glass, and trash. I let go of her hand to sit down on the edge of the floor so that my legs can dangle off the mezzanine. The gap in the banister is probably wide enough to accommodate five people sitting within it. I shine my phone's flashlight on the spot next to me so that Chloe can see it's clean enough for her to sit down too.

"If I tear or get one stain on this dress, I will make you pay for it," she says while taking her time to drop down beside me. "This is Miu Miu."

I groan. "God, you sound like Marcel. It's all about, *look how much what I got costs.*"

"Don't make us seem so shallow," she says, playfully shoving my shoulder. "We like to look nice, that's all."

"Whatev," I mutter.

Chloe leans over a little to look down and starts swinging her legs like me. "Why do you hate your brother so much? He practically worships you."

"That dude does *not* worship me," I reply.

"Yes, he does," Chloe insists. "He talks about you a lot. It wasn't always like that. Started a few months before you began going to school with us. After his grandmother died. One of the things I love about Marcel is his ability to not give a fuck about anyone else liking him. But it's different with you. When it comes to you, he cares."

"Was he the reason you texted me tonight?" I ask. "You getting in the middle of our stuff?"

Her coy smile serves as my answer. "He's determined to make things better between you two."

"I wish he'd stop," I say.

"Why?"

Because I don't want to feel the rejection and the othering I had to endure when I was a kid. To be reminded of the life I could have had if my dad didn't leave us. Because my life is good now. Better without the other Trudeaus in it. It's me and my mama against the world. We all we got. I've settled on that being enough for me. My dad is never going to be the man I want him to be. He'll never see me the way he sees Marcel. I'll never be that perfect. That ambitious. That kind of Trudeau.

"It's complicated," I tell her.

"Uncomplicate it for me," she prods.

"I can't."

"Then why start attending the same school as him?" she asks.

Another question I'm not comfortable answering, although I'm surprised Marcel hasn't told her already. Or maybe he did and she wants to see if I'll tell her the truth.

Bump that. She's hot. And I'll smash if she down. But not if it'll take me revealing one little mistake that would turn into the hot gossip at our pretentious school. I can tell that a lot of kids there already see me as a thug who doesn't belong. I can give her a version of the truth, since Chloe isn't coming off as judgmental as some of them. There's something about her I'm kind of digging, despite Marcel's melodramatic warning.

"My mom wanted me to attend Truman," I say, admiring the glow of the CBD up ahead. "*It'll open a lot of doors for you,* she said. It's funny. She says she despises my dad and his *other* family, but sometimes it feels like her pushing me in certain directions is really her wanting to one-up them. Like she has to show my dad how great I turned out without him and his *new* money. Like who I am already isn't good enough."

Admitting that out loud loosened my chest some. I regret not saying it the day my mama told me she was pulling me out of my old school. I'm regretting having said it now. To Chloe Danvers, whose gaze is pressing into the side of my face.

Fuck. Please don't let her repeat this to Marcel.

"I hate the pedestal everyone loves to put our school on," she says.

Her disinterest in my unexpected truth moment is a relief. Her statement also makes me frown.

"You're one of the first people I've ever heard say anything negative about that school," I say.

"Truman is all smoke and mirrors, trust me," she says. "The administration loves a woke mission statement. If people only knew . . ."

She's looking down at her phone when I turn to see why she didn't finish her statement. The glow from the screen illuminates the creases in her forehead as she reacts to whatever she's reading.

I wait until she's done frantically typing to say, "Your ex?"

The swooshing sound as she hits send echoes in the hollow church. She tucks her phone back into a pocket I had no idea was in her dress.

"God, no," she says. "He's the worst."

"One thousand percent," I reply. "What's up between you and him? Y'all are usually so annoyingly lovey-dovey."

She stares out at the CBD view, but I can tell she's not really seeing it. She's envisioning something that's darkening her features. "He thinks I want to ruin his family."

"How?"

"Can't really unpack all that," she replies.

"Oh, but you was all up in my family's business a few minutes ago," I say, nudging my shoulder against hers.

I manage to get a ghost of a smile out of her.

There's a thud within the belly of darkness below. It's immediately followed by several energetic squeaks.

"Oh my God!" Chloe yelps, yanking her legs into her chest. "What the hell was that?"

I lean over, holding my side as I burst out laughing. "Calm down, yo. It's just rats."

"I'm gonna need a tetanus shot when I leave here," she says, slowly dropping her legs back over the mezzanine.

To distract her from the scavenging rodents, I ask what her favorite scary movie is. She tells me all the Paranormal Activity movies. Then she asks what mine are and I tell her *Get Out.*

"A movie that plays into a bunch of horrible things you probably already thought about white people," she says.

"Pretty much," I reply with a nod.

"Interesting," she mumbles.

The conversation bounces around from her asking what I plan to do after graduation (still haven't figured that out yet, but I lie and say I've applied to a few colleges) to me asking where she sees herself in ten years (pissing all the right people off, she says). There's talk of prom and the senior class trip, which I have no intention of going on, before she asks, "Can we get out of here?"

"Finally ready to go home?"

"Not really," she says with this faraway look. "I don't want to be alone tonight. My family is out of town visiting my grandmother, and I just . . ."

She doesn't bother to finish that sentence either. Anxiety

darkens her pretty face. I understand how she feels. I don't like being in an empty house either sometimes. Which happens a lot, since Mama is always working the night shift in the ER, like tonight.

"I can chill with you, keep you company for a few," I offer.

She raises an eyebrow at me.

"Nah, I ain't trying to smash," I say, reading her mind. "Unless you force yourself on me," I add with a smirk.

She tilts her head to the right while staring at me. "Marcel never mentioned your sense of humor in all his bragging."

I stand up, dusting off the seat of my jeans. "Because I'm not trying to be funny around him."

As she's standing up, I start toward the stairs.

"Never would have thought I'd be hanging with Trey Winslow's girl all night," I say. "Crazy where one little text can take a brother."

I don't hear her footsteps behind me. I pause at the top step and turn around. Chloe is kneeling near the spot she was sitting, bent over part of the exposed balcony like she's picking at something.

"You coming?" I ask.

She jumps. "Yeah, sorry," she says, straightening and dusting off her dress. "My dress got caught on something. Clean this place up if you're going to keep bringing girls here." She flashes me a quick smile before descending the steps ahead of me.

* * *

My stomach muscles are on fire, I've been laughing so much.

That's likely from all the weed we've smoked and the Hennessy I've sipped on since we got to Chloe's house.

She's not one of the Lakeview kids, like I thought. Chloe lives in the Garden District. Old money. In a two-story, Greek Revival home on Second Street. A neighborhood I used to daydream about living in—in the make-believe world where my dad stopped ignoring us and shared the wealth he earned after divorcing my mother, beyond whatever he pays her every month for child support. Chloe gave me a tour of the house when we first got here. The gourmet kitchen she said her father renovated last year looks like it belongs in one of my dad's restaurants. I could really throw down if I had that kind of space at our house. This place is filled with a lot of bougie stuff Marcel's mother probably likes. Apparently, she and Chloe's mother are good friends. Chloe mentioned something about them serving on a lot of charitable boards together.

"Okay, truth or dare?" Chloe says right after I take a drag off the third blunt I've rolled.

She changed out of the fancy dress she wore to Marcel's party into a pair of running shorts and an oversized sweatshirt that's cut around the neck so that it hangs off one shoulder. I narrow my eyes at her from the other end of the sofa we're sprawled on opposite ends of in their living room, our legs touching slightly in the middle.

"Hold up, when did we start playing this?" I say, then release the intoxicating smoke I was holding in my lungs.

I've been here at least two hours. Not that I'm complaining.

"The game starts now; my house, my decision." She sits up so she can grab the blunt I'm holding out to her. "Now pick. Truth or dare?"

I watch as she inhales. Learning that Chloe smokes surprised me a little. She comes off so prim and proper at school. I'm seeing a whole different side to her. Through our weed-laced convo I've learned that it was Trey, not Jared Lanford, who took her virginity. That shocked me since I also learned tonight that she and Jared became "boyfriend/girlfriend" in the second grade and didn't break up until the end of her sophomore year of high school. She watches a lot of Japanese anime, she hates seafood, and her parents are Obama-loving liberals, which sort of explains her attraction to Trey, given who his father is.

Truth or dare? I contemplate, eyeing the muted Taylor Swift music video playing on the flat-screen hanging above the fireplace mantel across the room.

"Truth," I say.

"Truth?" she repeats in this mocking tone. "You scared I was gonna dare you to take out your dick?"

I give her a seductive grin. "If you wanna see it, just ask."

Her eyes flick upward while she shakes her head. Still can't tell if she's really feeling me or just likes flirting.

Her face shifts to this serious look. "What's your biggest regret?" she asks.

"Oh, that's easy." I lean over to grab a potato chip from the bowl sitting on the coffee table. Chloe also put out some candy and leftover sandwiches from a party her mother hosted a few days ago for us to nibble on. "Letting my mother send me to Truman."

My response gets a soft nod from her. "You really hate it that much?"

"Just don't really vibe with anybody like I did at my old school."

"That's partially your fault, though," she says. After taking a quick puff and releasing the smoke she adds, "It's not like you make any real effort to get to know any of us, including your brother."

I swallow the second chip I just stuffed in my mouth before saying, "And I don't really want to. Not my crowd."

"Maybe you can help me convince your brother of that too," Chloe says.

"Huh?"

She tries to pass the blunt back to me, but I shake my head. It already feels like I'm floating. I need to slow down some.

"You interested in *reallllyyy* blowing things up at Truman?" She leans over to drop the blunt in the ashtray and then pops back on the sofa, placing one of its throw pillows across her lap. "Like, helping me do something that needs to be done?"

"Whatcha talking 'bout, girl?" I ask with an awkward grin.

She stares at me with a thoughtful look. Like she's contemplating whether she can trust me. Her phone chirps, stopping her from saying whatever's on her mind. She quickly picks it up and frowns at the notification. It's been blowing up periodically since we got here. She keeps looking vexed by it every time it does.

"Damn, Trey really in his feelings tonight," I tease.

The corner of her mouth curls. Her fingers dance across the screen before she drops the phone on top of the pillow. "I told you, that's not him."

"Oh, you got another dude on the line already?" I say. "Why you got me over here, then?"

"Wanted to get to know you," she says.

"You couldn't do that at school?"

Her head tilts to the right. "It was a time-sensitive type of thing—me making sure you're exactly the person I think you are."

"Who do you think I am?"

"The boy . . ." Her mouth slowly curls into a half grin. ". . . whose turn it is now to ask me the question."

So we're back to the game? Fine. I'm too high to keep up with whatever she's talking about anyway. But Marcel's text is starting to make some sense.

"Truth or dare?" I say.

"Dare," she eagerly replies.

She starts taunting me with this cocky smirk. Her way of teasing me about not accepting the dare option when she asked. She must be thinking I'll challenge her to do something uninspired, like get naked or kiss me. Too easy. Plus, I'd rather she does either one of those things because she's into me and wants to. I look down at her phone and an idea pops in my head.

"Let me DM someone from your Instagram account," I tell her.

Her mouth drops open. "Oh my God! *Who?*"

"Don't worry about that." I sit up and hold out my hand, palm up. "Give me yo' phone."

"You're so wrong for this," she squeals, handing it to me with her eyes closed.

As I'm opening the Instagram app, she scoots closer so she can watch what I'm doing. Her hair smells like rosemary. The fragrance tickles my nose. I run my index finger up and down the screen to scroll through her list of followers.

"Who are you going to message?" she asks.

"You asking too many questions," I tease.

I pause on a face I recognize from the party tonight. A skinny white boy who I think might be a junior. I click on his page. He looks nerdy enough. Someone who'd never stand a chance with her. Perfect. He'll probably tell all his friends he got a message from *the* Chloe Danvers.

"Oh God! Not Dustin Miller," she says as I'm clicking the Message button.

I type *U up?* with the horny devil emoji and hit the + button to send the message before she can protest further.

She rips the phone out of my hands while I bend over laughing.

"You are going to start so much shit with this," she says, putting her phone facedown on the sofa as if that'll make the message go away. "Payback is a bitch! Truth or dare?"

"Truth!" I reply, sticking out my tongue.

"Fine. Be a wimp." She squints, biting down on her bottom lip. "And I want the truth."

I lean back, spreading both arms across the edge of the sofa and crossing my legs at the ankles. Letting her know she won't rattle me.

"Why did you stop visiting your father?" she says.

The answer gets stuck in my thickening throat. My body is trying to keep the memory buried too.

Chloe sits back, folding her arms across her chest, watching as the enjoyment in my face gradually rearranges into dejection. She can tell I'm uncomfortable, and I think she likes that. Payback *is* a bitch.

"I want the truth," she repeats right when I open my mouth. Maybe she sensed I wasn't going to be honest.

I take a deep breath. Fuck it. It's time Marcel's friends knew the truth. Understood why I feel the way I do. I hear a car door slam outside it's so quiet.

"When I was thirteen and Marcel was eleven, I was staying at their house one weekend," I begin. "He and I were playing in the front yard. I was popping firecrackers 'cause it was Fourth of July. I think Marcel was tumbling in the front yard. I can't remember exactly. Anyway, his mom left her terrier, Sparkle, out there with us so the dog could do her business. His mom loved that dumb dog. Treated Sparkle like her child. I hated the thing. Marcel did too. He disliked it so much that he thought it would be funny to scare Sparkle by tying some firecrackers to her tail and lighting them. I tried to tell him not to, but he did it anyway. I also didn't fight too hard to stop him, which I easily could have. He scared her so bad that when the firecrackers started going off, Sparkle took off running across St. Charles. She ran right into traffic and got run over. My stepmother blamed me since I was the one playing with the firecrackers. And Marcel lied and said it was me and not him. The perfect son didn't want to lose his title."

Chloe covers her mouth with her hand, her eyes wide with disbelief.

I scratch my head, fighting the tears building behind my eyes. "My dad stood there and let her degrade me first before he started cursing me out. He told me he didn't want me at his house anymore if I couldn't respect his new family—if I was going to continue being *a problem.*"

"That's harsh," Chloe mumbles.

"*New family* is me paraphrasing, but that's basically what he meant," I say.

"That is so fucked up," Chloe says. "Marcel never admitted the truth?"

I pick up the blunt out of the ashtray. "Nope."

Chloe sits silently, watching me take a drag on the blunt, then release the smoke.

"And fuck my bitch-ass dad too," I say.

She takes the blunt when I offer it to her. "I couldn't agree with you more."

Her pinched mouth lets me know I'm not the only one in the room with beef toward their father.

4

Amir

"You killed her!"

"I didn't—"

"What's wrong with you, boy!"

Slam!

My eyes pop open. I'm panting.

It's not four years ago. I'm not in the front yard of my dad's house. And tears aren't building behind my eyes.

I'm sprawled across a sofa. Lil Nas X is silently sliding down a stripper pole into hell on the flat-screen that hangs above a fireplace mantel in a room I don't recognize. My head feels like it's detached from my body. My heart is jackhammering in my chest.

I scan my surroundings: the discarded ends of several blunts are cluttered together on the coffee table, along with half-eaten bowls of chips and candy. Bits and pieces of the night start to materialize within the fog clouding my thoughts.

Marcel's birthday party. Chloe. Us at "my spot." Me offering to keep her company. Truth or dare.

I sit up straighter. Where's Chloe? I dig in my pocket for my phone. It's 2:18 a.m.

Shit! I gotta get home before Mama gets off work!

I stand up. What time did I fall asleep? Chloe must have left me here on the sofa and gone upstairs to sleep in her bedroom. Last thing I remember is her saying she needed to give me something.

The memory of the incident that drove a bigger wedge between my dad and me gradually fades into the back of my mind as I lumber into the foyer. The creaking sound the hardwood floors make with each of my steps fills the haunting silence.

"Yo, Chloe!" I yell from the bottom of the winding staircase that extends through the center of their house.

Nothing. I wait a few more seconds, in case she has to crawl out of bed, before I start my way up. My head still feels weird, so I hold on to the wrought-iron railing to steady myself. Can't believe we've hung out all night. I wonder if that nerdy dude got that DM I sent from her account. The thought pulls a faint grin out of me when I make it to the top of the stairs. Was tonight just a one-off, or was it the first of many more with her? I'm hoping the latter.

I think her bedroom is the pitch-black one with the door open to my right.

"Chloe," I call out as I walk in.

The chill wafting through the house prickles my skin. I call out her name again as I blink my way through the darkness. I stumble over something on the floor and catch myself. I stop. This doesn't feel right. I don't recall anything being out of place in her bedroom when she gave me the tour earlier. It was as perfect and put-together as she always is.

I back up, extending my arms, wave my hands along the back wall. It takes a few seconds before I feel the light switch. The darkness solidifies into her recognizable form splayed across the bed right before I turn on the light.

"Chl—"

The rest of her name gets stuck in the back of my throat when I see all the crimson.

So much of it. All over the bed. Seeping from her lifeless body.

My stomach detaches and slides into my feet. I feel myself getting weak.

"Ch-Ch-Chloe," I stammer.

I need to look away. I have to look away. Because if I don't, I'm going to throw up. But I can't. I need her to not look so—

No, no, no . . .

She's lying on her stomach, her legs and arms spread out in wild positions. I can't see if she might be breathing, but I know she isn't. Her head is turned toward me. Her eyes open and vacant. The life that was in them two hours ago gone.

Oh fuck. Oh fuck. Oh. Fuck.

I start backing away from this violence I don't understand. The scene that looks nothing like the one I saw earlier. It looks like a tornado has been through here. Clothes are strewn across furniture, on the floor. Drawers are pulled out of the mirrored dresser, some tossed aside. Someone was looking for something. And when they didn't find it . . .

My head slowly loops back around to the bed.

. . . they killed her.

Oh no. Oh no. Oh. No.

Ice water is zipping through my veins. The room is spinning. The blood. So much that I can't think of anything else, and what it means that there's a lot of it. Who could have done this?

I begin to gag on my deep breaths. I'm going to be sick!

I whip around. Worried that whoever did this could still be here. Thankfully, the doorway is empty. I glance over my shoulder; Chloe is still dead in her bed. Her bloody bed.

All those chips and candy I ate earlier bubble up in the back of my throat. My body feels like wet noodles. I can't let that stop me. I use every ounce of strength I can muster to keep myself going forward. There's nothing I can do for Chloe. I can only save myself. So I run.

And I don't look back.

5

Marcel

My parents are seated across from each other at the small, round table in our breakfast nook when I enter the kitchen, dragging my feet. I rub the sleep from my eyes with a quiet yawn. All my limbs feel ten pounds heavier.

"Well, looka here, the birthday boy is finally gracing us with his presence," my mother says before sipping mimosa from one of the flutes my friends chugged spiked punch out of last night.

My father acknowledges me with an amused grin from behind the newspaper he's holding up to read in the sunlight beaming through the nook's bay window. He and my mom are wearing matching sweat suits, which they often do when traveling. It was a much shorter trip this time: the Ritz-Carlton on Canal Street, where they booked a room for the night while I had my birthday party. I start to think they must have checked out early until I glance down at my phone and realize it's almost noon.

"Daddy, you cooked?" I ask, pointing at the scrambled eggs and spinach, homemade french toast, boudin sausage, and diced fruit lined up in serving dishes across the island countertop. The greasy-sweet aroma wakes up my stomach.

"He was feeling generous today," my mother says.

"Consider it your *final* birthday present from me." My father flips the page of his newspaper without looking up. "Despite having given you more than enough already."

My father only cooks on special occasions, like holidays, if we're having certain guests over, or if he wants us to try out a new recipe. Any other time he puts our house staff in charge of feeding us. It suddenly dawns on me why things are so quiet and still this morning. They have the day off for Ash Wednesday, the sacred religious day that immediately follows the debauchery of Mardi Gras. I don't have school today since more than half of Truman's student body and staff is Catholic.

"Hush, Martin," my mother says, slapping his arm as I slip my phone into the pocket of my silk pajama pants and pick up the empty plate they left on the countertop for me. "A boy only turns sixteen once. He deserved the gifts."

"Uh-huh," my father grumbles.

My father considers cooking to be therapeutic. But he told a reporter once he doesn't do it as often as he used to due to the day-to-day demands of overseeing the operations at his three restaurants on top of everything else he has going on at any given moment, including TV appearances and now, recently, trying to launch his line of seasonings and signature sauces.

"How was the party?" my mother asks while I pile food on my plate. "I want all the details."

Her tone is chipper, her eyes dancing with excitement, which is good. Means she and my dad are satisfied with how the house looked when they arrived this morning. I stayed up past midnight making sure the hired help had everything spotless and back in its place—the way they'd found it. The party started breaking up shortly after Amir left with Chloe.

I was still feeling *a way* about her leaving with him. I almost texted her to tell her that but went straight to sleep once I made it upstairs to my bedroom. There will be a convo today for sure. I don't appreciate her going behind my back and manipulating Amir into showing up last night. Especially since it doesn't look like she's really interested in him the way it seems he is in her.

"It was straight, Mother," I say after scooping up all the spinach and eggs left in the serving bowl.

"Did everyone you invite show up?" she follows.

"Pretty much." I balance my full plate in my right hand while taking a bite of the boudin with my other as I'm walking to join them at the table. I plop down in the empty chair between them. "Oh, and Amir came too."

The newspaper crinkles as my father closes it and lays it across his lap. "He did?" he says to me, his thick brows raised.

My mother sighs after I nod.

"*Why* did he come?" she drawls.

I glare at her. "Because it was my birthday, and he's my brother. Duh."

I knew she wouldn't find my answer amusing; that's why I said it instead of the truth.

"Thought you said y'all don't talk much at school," my father says.

"We don't." I scoop a forkful of eggs into my mouth, quickly chew them, and then swallow. "Surprised me too, but in a good way."

"I can't believe he'd have the nerve to set foot in this house again after everything he put me through," my mother says as she refills her flute from the crystal pitcher of mimosa in the center of the table.

This would be the perfect time to do it. Tell her it was me who tied the firecrackers to Sparkle's tail and sent her to her death. Then what would she have to hold against Amir? Nothing except her contempt for his mother—which, if I'm being honest, isn't all that justified. But they just gave me the Tessie and I haven't driven it yet. I'll do it in a few days.

"Did he stay long?" my father asks.

His posture has perked up a bit. I can also tell he's straining to keep some of the excitement out of his voice. It's times like this I can empathize with my brother's frustration with our father. Amir is his son. His firstborn. He shouldn't care so much how his unconditional love for Amir makes my mother feel. It's one of the few things I ever heard Nana criticize him for. It also added to her dislike of my mother.

"No real woman with any kind of morals and the right upbringing would discourage a man—a Black one, at that—from being a father to his child," I heard her say to him once.

"He was here at least an hour," I tell my father.

Then left with one of my best friends, who's on the verge of becoming my ex-BFF.

I pull out my phone. Now that my b-day party is in the rearview, we can address this *your friends aren't really your friends* kick Chloe was on, along with why she's inserting herself into the drama with me and Amir. I'll text her and suggest we meet for coffee this afternoon. I stop myself from opening the Messages app because I notice an Instagram notification. It's alerting me that I have a new follower. Someone with the username ItsYoBoyQNOLA. I hiccup a chuckle once the person's page loads. It's Quincy.

My mother and father are discussing Amir, but whatever they're saying becomes mumbled background noise. I bite my bottom lip as my index finger hovers over the Follow Back button on Quincy's profile. Us following each other is innocent. I'm not gonna even Like his photos. Just browse and enjoy. A follow doesn't really have to mean anything. Amir and I follow each other, and it hasn't brought us any closer. I mean, there's a lot of deeper reasons why, but I don't need to think about them now. I press the button to follow his best friend too. *Payback for him leaving with Chloe,* I tell myself.

"Marcel, I know you hear me."

My mother's statement is followed by a sharp pain on my forearm as she pinches me.

"Ow!" I yelp, rubbing the spot. "What, woman?"

"Put down that phone and answer me," she says.

"Answer what?"

"I asked if your brother behaved himself last night," she says, fiddling with the emerald-cut diamond on her ring finger. "I know he's been hanging around a dangerous element lately. Did he come alone or with that friend he got in all that trouble with?"

I can feel my father staring at me too. If I tell them Amir brought that dude Buster here, they'll *both* throw a fit.

"He was by himself."

I quickly pop several cubes of cantaloupe into my mouth. As if the chewing will hide any obvious signs of my lying.

"Good." My mother picks up her flute. "Monica practically extorting your father to pay his tuition for Truman might actually do some good."

I swallow first and then say, "*Extort* is a strong word. Amir is his son, not some blackmailer looking for a come up."

"Your father already pays more than enough in child support for that boy," she says.

Apparently sipping his coffee and looking out the window is more important to my father than participating in this conversation.

"Does he, though?" I say. "Technically, Daddy wasn't making the kind of coins he does now when him and Monica divorced."

I don't know all the details, but Amir's mother tried to petition the court a few years ago, shortly after he stopped visiting us regularly, to increase our father's monthly child support payments for Amir. The judge did up the amount slightly, but nowhere near the level Monica wanted, according to my mother.

She said my father was only legally required to keep Amir in the lifestyle our father shared with his first wife, which was nowhere near how we're living now.

"*I'm* telling you it's more than enough," my mother asserts, pressing her hand to her chest.

My father has picked up the newspaper again and is back to reading. Part of me wants to call him out on it, but I'm not trying to get on his bad side. Again, the Tessie.

"How was the party y'all attended last night?" I reach for the pitcher of mimosa. I need something to wash down the food that's starting to feel like sand sliding down my throat.

My mother's face lights up. "Oh, Marcel, you should have seen some of the god-awful gowns those women wore. You'd think the ball's theme was Gaudy Trash and Make It Sparkly."

As I'm pouring mimosa into my flute, I say, "Who was worst dressed? Do I know them?"

She doesn't respond, so I look up. Her mouth is dropped open, her eyes wide.

"Oh my Lord," she blurts. "Is that Chloe?"

My head whips around in the direction of her fixed gaze. She's staring at the muted flat-screen that hangs beneath the cabinets near the stove. I didn't realize it was on until now.

Chloe's yearbook photo from last year fills the right side of the small screen. On the left is a reporter who looks like he's standing outside Chloe's house. A knot twists in my stomach.

"Lily, where's the remote?" my father says, dropping the newspaper and turning around in his chair.

I hear my mother pick it up. My eyes never leave the television.

". . . has been identified as sixteen-year-old Chloe Danvers, the daughter of prominent architect Aubrey Danvers." The serious-faced male reporter's voice echoes loudly throughout our kitchen. "Police tell us the girl's body—"

Body?

"—was discovered in her bedroom around nine-thirty a.m. by her family when they returned home from an overnight trip."

"Wait. What does he mean *body*?" I say, setting the pitcher of mimosa back down on the table.

I stand up and slowly make my way toward the TV, the knot in my stomach inching into my chest.

"A spokesman with NOPD just informed me that the victim was fatally stabbed multiple times in the middle of the night after attending a friend's birthday party," the reporter says.

My mother gasps. "What in the world?" She's behind me to my right, my father now on my left. I didn't even hear them get up.

Chloe's picture blinks off the screen, exposing the reporter's entire background. Police are scurrying in and out of Chloe's house. Yellow crime scene tape hangs from the front of the wrought-iron fence surrounding their manicured yard.

"This can't be real," my mother says, squeezing my arm.

The knot is now a tennis ball in the back of my throat.

"Police are asking for the public's help in identifying a young man who was caught fleeing this house shortly before two-thirty a.m. on the smart doorbell camera of the neighbor who lives directly across the street," the reporter says right before the screen fills with grainy footage of a guy barreling out the front door to the fence and then running down the street. "Because he's wearing a hoodie, the camera didn't capture a clear image of this person's face. This footage was recorded within the window of time police think the girl was murdered."

A deafening ringing explodes in my ears. The reporter is right. You can't see the guy's face because the dark hoodie is covering it in shadow. But something else the person is wearing tells me all I need to know: limited-edition black-and-gold Jordans. The same ones I, along with everyone else at my party, saw Amir wearing last night.

6

Amir

My nana taught me how to cook. She didn't see the kitchen as a woman's place. She said my grandfather, who died before I was born, enjoyed being in the kitchen more than she did. They both passed on their knowledge and recipes to my dad. "I wasn't raising a man who expected women to slave all day in the kitchen for him," she said more than once. Nana started teaching me how to cook when I was old enough to see over the kitchen countertop of her Creole cottage home in Tremé, the neighborhood where my parents met and became childhood sweethearts. Cutting up vegetables led to her letting me stir sauces and batters. By the time I was thirteen, I could bake homemade cakes and cook gumbo without her supervision.

Cooking became an emotional outlet. When I'm happy, I bake dessert. Feeling sad or disappointed, I'm in the kitchen whipping up comfort food like soups and stews. If I'm angry, I'll deep-fry some meat in a skillet.

Then there are the times I use cooking as a distraction. A

way to forget the outside world exists. Like my problems aren't there still waiting for me. Since I started at seven this morning, I've cooked shrimp and grits with mustard seed chowchow, candied bacon, and vegetable scrambled eggs. Then I put on a pot of red beans and sausage with a side of white rice. Twenty minutes ago, I started the seafood gumbo I'm stirring now. Its thick brown roux bubbling as hard as my stomach is.

If I stay in the kitchen and keep on cooking, then I don't have to worry about somebody recognizing me from that clip every news outlet in the city has aired and posted on their websites. The only thing that could remotely link back to me are my limited-edition Js. The kids I go to school with barely pay attention to me. I doubt they remember I had them on at Marcel's party. Just to be on the safe side, I threw them away, along with the rest of the stuff I was wearing last night.

No sneakers, no case! I kept telling myself.

I couldn't fall asleep once I made it home. Every time I *tried* to close my eyes, I kept seeing all the blood and Chloe's lifeless body. Threw up three times because of it. Heard Mama come in from work around four-thirty in the morning. I waited forty-five minutes until I was sure she was asleep to sneak out of the house with the garbage bag I packed my clothes and Js in. I tossed it in the dumpster of the convenience store two blocks from our house. If the cops show up, I'll lie and say I don't own any shoes like the ones that person had on. I got so many kicks, Mama won't remember them. Even though I didn't see any blood on my jeans or hoodie, tossed them too—just in case.

I start stirring the gumbo harder.

But what about all the people at Marcel's party who saw me leave with Chloe? Makes it a little harder to lie that I wasn't at her house last night. She and I entered her place through the back door, which opens onto their driveway. That must be why no footage has surfaced yet of us entering the house together.

Damn, fool! Why did you run out the front *door!* I scold myself.

I wasn't thinking clearly, obviously. Just wanted to get the hell out of Dodge.

I'm stirring so hard the spoon is scratching the bottom of the pot. I don't stop.

Somewhere outside a car door slams. My heart starts beating so fast it hurts.

That's them, I think. *The police are about to roll up in here and arrest me for something I didn't do!*

I pause to listen for the hollow echo of their footsteps on our porch. The gumbo stock's gurgling and popping, the only thing filling the silence. After minutes go by and there isn't a knock on the door, I start stirring again.

No one is going to recognize you; stop tripping, I tell myself.

There is a good chance someone will, though. Maybe I should have kept the clothes. It'll make me look guilty if I don't have them, right? They probably could have done forensic testing on them to see that I didn't stab her. Crap.

Who could have stabbed her like that? How did they get in? How the fuck did I sleep through her getting murdered? And why didn't whoever did it kill me too? How did we go from truth or dare and smoking weed to her being stabbed to death and me becoming the suspect the police don't know they're looking for? Only guilty men run, the police will say. Nah, Black dudes who wake up in a white girl's house and find her dead run. And we run 'cause we don't get the benefit of the doubt. Everyone sees us as a threat. We can't go to the store, jog through a neighborhood, drive nice cars, or sell DVDs outside a corner store without being pegged a nuisance or dangerous. Emmett Till was abducted, brutally beaten, and lynched just for being *accused* of flirting with a white woman. Not much has changed since then. A dead white girl linked to a Black boy still means presumed guilt. *That's* why I threw away my Js and clothes!

The spoon is scraping the bottom of the pot again.

This isn't working. Cooking. It's not blocking out the rest of the world like it usually does.

I gotta calm myself down. Nothing has happened yet. And if the police come knocking on our door, asking where I went last night after leaving Marcel's party, I'll say I dropped Chloe off and then came straight home. No one saw us together after the party. They won't know I'm lying. I'll say, "Go check my closet. I don't own any clothes like the ones that person in that video had on." As long as nothing else surfaces that can prove I was there, I'm good . . . right?

"Boy, you got it smelling *good* up in here!"

I jump, knocking the spoon out my hand. A few droplets from the boiling stock sting as they splash across my forearm.

Mama is posted up in the doorway that leads to the rest of our shotgun-style house. Her shoulder-length hair pulled back in a messy ponytail. Her oversized T-shirt and pajama pants just as wrinkled as the frown lines across her forehead.

"What's wrong with you?" she says. "You about jumped out of your skin."

Act cool, bro. Normal, I say to myself. *This woman has that special sixth sense God gives all mothers.*

"I was in my thoughts, that's all," I say with a half smile, wiping my forearm with the dishrag I left on the countertop to the left of the stove. "You snuck up on a brother."

She saunters over to me. I lean in for the kiss she places on my cheek. "Why were you up so early cooking today?" she asks, peering over my shoulder into the pot. "Is something wrong?"

"Noooooo," I reply with a nervous laugh. "Got up to do something nice and make you breakfast and didn't feel like stopping. Made us some dinner for the rest of the week too."

She lifts the lid on the pot of red beans. "This *and* gumbo? You doing it up, huh?"

"Always for my number one girl," I say.

She starts smiling hard, like she always does when I say that.

Everything is normal. It's just another day. Like any other day in this house. Not the day I'll get accused of stabbing a girl to death.

"The Trudeau nose and lips were enough." My mama opens the upper cabinet to the left of the stove and pulls out a plate. "You had to inherit the culinary skills too?"

She says that almost every time I cook.

"Well, it ain't from *him,*" I say. "This is all Nana."

Things got strained between Nana and my mama during the divorce. I think Nana was disappointed Mama tried to discourage my dad from sticking with his dreams. And in turn, Mama got a little jaded that Nana wasn't as upset as she was about her son cheating on his first wife and then marrying his mistress because of it. But they were always respectful to each other. What my dad lacked in love and compassion, Nana made up for double. I always called her my *other* number one girl.

"*Chiiille,* that ER got its money out of yo' mama last night," she says while scooping some of the shrimp and grits onto her plate.

Guess we're shifting from her first least favorite topic to her second one.

I'm back to stirring the gumbo. "They did?"

"Did they," she replies with a sigh. "Seven gunshot wounds. Folks losing their damn minds at the parades. You and Quincy weren't running the streets all night, were you?"

"Nah, we came home early," I lie.

"Amir, so many Black boys your age come through there almost bleeding to death from gun violence." I hear her open the refrigerator behind me, probably to get some orange juice. "A lot of 'em fell in with the wrong people. So glad you ain't running all over town with Buster anymore."

The truth needles the back of my throat.

"Any day now I expect him to come through either shot up or dead too," she says.

I turn around. "Ma, chill. That was kind of dark. Bus ain't that bad."

She settles onto one of the barstools at the island in the center of our cramped kitchen. "'Ain't that bad'? After all the trouble he got you in?"

The mistake that, in a way, has led to something far worse. Had Buster not got me caught up in my first run-in with the law, Mama wouldn't have pulled me out of public school and sent me to Truman. Then I wouldn't have met Chloe and be scared for my life right now.

Stop it, Amir. No one will recognize you.

Please don't let anyone recognize me.

"You not eating with me?" she says, waving at the empty barstool beside her.

"I ate already," I say.

The lies are rolling off my tongue this morning.

"Come sit down and talk to me anyway." She takes a bite of the candied bacon. "I been working so much, and you busy with schoolwork, that I haven't had any good one-on-one time with my baby."

Her dark eyes are lit up by her warm smile. God, I'ma miss that smile if—

Stop it, Amir. No one has come looking for you yet.

I lower the temperature on the burner cooking the gumbo before plodding over to the island and hoisting myself onto the barstool.

"You haven't been complaining as much about Truman," she says after swallowing the bacon she was chewing. "Does that mean you starting to like it?"

I look down at my hands in my lap, trying to figure out how

I want to answer the question. They're covered in crimson. I gasp. It takes me blinking several times to make the blood go away.

There's no blood on my hands. I didn't kill her.

"It's cool. I—"

Bam, bam, bam, bam, bam!

There they are. The knocks I've been waiting on all morning. They're urgent and hard. Pushed my heart into the back of my throat.

Mama stands up before I have a chance to react.

"Why is somebody knocking on my door like the po-po?" she says while passing through the living room.

Because it is, I think.

I stand up from the stool, my eyes fixed on Mama as she opens the door. My racing heart is pinching my chest again.

"Martin?" she scoffs. "Why you beating on my door like you don't have any sense?"

"Where's Amir?"

My dad steps around her into our house.

We immediately lock eyes. His are wide and he's breathing hard. When Mama steps to the side I see Marcel in the doorway too. His face distorted with alarm.

"What did you do?" My dad rushes through the living room into the kitchen. He grabs me by the arms with both hands. "What happened to that girl?"

"I didn't do it! I didn't do it!" I cry.

My mama appears beside my dad. "What the hell is going on?"

"WHAT DID YOU DO?" my dad shouts.

"Nothing, man," I scream. "I didn't touch her!"

"Martin, let him go!" Mama yells, tugging on my dad's arms.

I see Marcel over their shoulders. Standing in the middle of the living room, watching this all unfold.

"I didn't do it, bruh," I say to him, the words getting caught in the back of my throat. "I found her like that."

I can't tell if he's frowning because he doesn't believe me or because he believes me but realizes the same thing that I do: I'm fucked!

"Martin, do *not* come up in my house accusing my son of anything." She yanks as hard as she can on my dad's arm, but he doesn't ease his grip on me. "Let. Him. Go!"

"Monica, you got any idea how much trouble this boy has gotten himself into now?" my dad shouts, veins protruding from his neck. He starts shaking me and says, "Tell me what happened. *Now!*"

"I don't know, man," I sob. "I told you, she was dead when I woke up."

"Who's dead?" my mother yelps.

"Then why'd you run?" my dad barks.

"Stop yelling at him, Martin," Mama retorts.

"Y'all, stop!"

The three of us pause and turn toward Marcel.

His eyes flick to the right, and that's when we see them. Two NOPD officers framed in the front doorway. Their eyes on me. My father finally lets me go.

"Amir Trudeau, we need you to come with us," the tall white one says as he enters the house, walking past Marcel and into the kitchen, where I stand with my parents.

"What is going on?" Mama asks the cop.

"Monica, hush," my dad says to her before turning to me to add, "You don't open your mouth and say one word until I call my lawyer."

"Will somebody tell me what's going on?" Mama shouts, her eyes glistening with tears.

It becomes difficult to breathe when the officer starts unlatching the handcuffs from his duty belt. "Amir Trudeau, you're under arrest . . ."

Everything he says after that gets drowned out by Mama's screams.

7

Marcel

There really hasn't been time for me to mourn the murder of the girl who knew all my secrets, insecurities, and fears. My thoughts have been consumed with Amir, who's been in jail since Wednesday. Booked for first-degree murder six hours after those two police officers walked him out of his house in handcuffs, in front of all the neighbors who were standing outside their homes watching him get escorted into the back seat of a police car. He was forced to remain in jail until the court could hold a bail hearing, which only happens three days a week: Mondays, Wednesdays, and Fridays. So here we are, two days later, praying that this judge will let him go home today.

How did we get here?

For the first two hours after his arrest, most of our information about Chloe's murder and what the police *think* Amir did came from the media. The lawyer my father hired has told Monica and my father more, like what Amir said when the police questioned him, but none of that has been shared with me yet. All I know, based on what I've seen and read in the news, is that the police think Chloe was stabbed in her sleep since there were no defensive wounds on her body. Her killer likely used one of the Danverses' steak knives, which is missing from their home and *still* hasn't been found. There was no forced entry or signs of a break-in. Amir was the only person there. And the only one seen running away—thanks to that security doorbell footage the news has been playing on a loop any time they've reported on this story.

Two days of wall-to-wall media reports have already decided Amir's guilt.

Two days of countless texts from kids at school who care more about whether *I* think Amir really did it than how I'm feeling about one of my best friends being dead.

Two days of my mother claiming she knew Amir was a troubled boy after what he did to Sparkle. Two days of me still not being man enough to tell her the truth. Two days of my father yelling at Amir's lawyer over the phone, demanding that he do everything he can to clear Amir's name.

My father is seated next to me now. His right leg bouncing so hard it has the stiff wood bench we're sitting on trembling. During our drive to the courtroom this morning I told him not to believe the police or the media, that Amir didn't kill Chloe.

"But it looks—"

"I don't care how it looks, Daddy," I argued. "Amir would never stab anyone. He can't handle the sight of blood."

"Still?" my father replied.

"Yes!"

You'd know that if you made more of an effort to stay in his life, I say to myself, since it isn't the right time or place to say it to him.

I did say it to the detective who showed up at our house yesterday to interview me about Amir's hemophobia. He didn't seem convinced that it was enough to prove Amir isn't guilty. My father started nodding when I reminded him in the car.

"That's good to know," he said in a somber tone.

Monica is seated next to my father. Her eyes are puffy and red. I can only imagine what these last two days have been like for her. She actually looked relieved when she saw my father and me enter the courthouse. She was sitting alone on a bench with Amir's lawyer. It has to be lonely being in that house with no one to talk to while the city is accusing your son of murder.

We're not the only ones in this drab courtroom. The family members of other arrested individuals are scattered about, sitting in clusters along the rows of hard wooden benches. There's also a gaggle of reporters crowded in the back corner. They're only here for Amir. Eager to get the next morsel of breaking news. My mother claimed they were the reason she was staying home. She didn't want cameras in her face, she said last night.

"That's probably best," my father replied. His mouth tight and eyes exasperated.

He tried to discourage me from coming today—he's concerned I might fall behind in my schoolwork.

"I'm going to be there, even if I have to drive myself," I told him.

I know he wanted to object. My parents already let me skip yesterday when the police called and said they wanted to speak with me. Instead, he backed out of my bedroom and quietly closed the door. Too exhausted to have an argument he knew he'd never win.

We've been here for over an hour, waiting for the bailiff to usher Amir through the gray door to the right of the judge's bench, like he has with the six people who've already had their bail hearing since we got here.

I put my hand on my father's knee and squeeze it. His leg immediately stops bouncing.

He's giving me a strained smile when I look up. I try to return it with a reassuring one, but I can't muster the strength. I'm worried about Amir. Especially after what his lawyer told us right before walking us into the courtroom.

"The judge could deny bail," Mr. Dillard said, which made Monica gasp. "If he does, stay calm. All is not lost. But it will take finding out who really killed that girl to get him released."

Amir's lawyer is named Cedrick Dillard. He's supposed to be one of the top criminal defense attorneys in the city. He works at the law firm that handles various facets of my father's businesses and branding. I looked up his profile on the firm's website. Most of the cases that were highlighted on his page were ones he won defending affluent white men. Given that he's Black, and around my father's age, I guess one way to prove to potential clients that you're the best is showing that rich white men trust you with their defense. He's someone I wouldn't mind having as a mentor.

I used to joke with Chloe that I'd become the male Annalise Keating, but without all the murder cover-ups.

"Bailiff, you can bring in the next defendant."

My eyes immediately whip toward the gray door. My heart is pounding as Amir appears in the doorway, escorted by the same stone-faced bailiff who's led everyone else out. He looks like he smells of tobacco and Old Spice cologne. Amir is wearing the same orange jumpsuit and matching sliders the other defendants had on, his hands cuffed in front of him like theirs have been.

Mr. Dillard rises and steps through the thigh-high partition that divides the courtroom into two halves. He plops his leather briefcase on the empty wooden table on our side of the courtroom, where the bailiff is taking Amir. Monica scoots up to the edge of the bench on the other side of my father, her hand covering her mouth. Her eyes glassy with tears as Amir comes closer but still feels so far away from us. He briefly makes eye contact with me before quickly shifting his glum gaze past our father. His eyes land on his mother. It's fleeting, but I swear I notice his bottom lip tremble before his eyes drop to the floor as the bailiff tells him to take a seat in the chair next to the one Mr. Dillard is standing in front of.

The chill in the courtroom enters my bones.

"Case number 5657745923, Amir Trudeau," the female clerk seated below the judge reads from the white sheet of paper taped to the manila folder she plucked from the stack on her desk.

"Will both counsel representatives identify themselves for

the record," the angry-mouthed judge says without looking up from whatever he's reading.

"Your Honor, Cedrick Dillard, attorney for Amir Trudeau," Mr. Dillard says with his shoulders back and head held high.

"Traci Jackson, city prosecutor, Your Honor," announces a white lady who I didn't notice at the table on the opposite side of the courtroom. She's got dry, damaged dirty-blond hair and she's wearing an ill-fitting business suit. She looks like a person who holds on to her purse a little tighter if she sees a Black man walking alongside her on the street. That might be an exaggeration—I don't know this woman. Still, I can already tell I'm not going to like her. When she glances over at us, I realize I've seen her before. She was one of the serious-faced individuals flanking the district attorney during the televised press conference the night of Amir's arrest. The wide-nosed district attorney claimed his office would put its full force behind getting justice for Chloe's family, regardless of who Amir's father was. I turned off the TV right after he said it.

"Mr. Trudeau, will you please stand," the judge says, looking at Amir over the rim of his reading glasses.

Amir does what he says. It annoys me that he referred to Amir as "Mister." Amir isn't an adult. He's seventeen. A kid. A person who has his entire life before him.

"Mr. Trudeau, I'm not here to determine whether you're guilty or innocent," the judge says in a monotone voice. He's probably said this so many times he has it memorized. I can't help but wonder how many other Black boys he's said it to who were also falsely accused of a crime. "I'm only here to set your bail based on what information I have in front of me. Do you understand that?"

Amir nods.

I wish I could see his face. It must be as pained as my father's is as he watches this unfold. His right leg has started bouncing again.

"Under the United States legal system, you are innocent until proven guilty," the judge continues. "So do not say anything about the facts of your case. Don't discuss the facts of your case with anyone but your attorney. Anything you say to me can be used against you; do you understand?"

"Yes, Your Honor," Amir replies, his voice hoarse and rough.

The pounding of my heart is starting to echo in my ears. My brother is really standing before a judge. My father ready to pay anything to see that he's released.

And above all, Chloe is dead. I'll never see her again. We'll never get to say our "I'm sorrys" for the tiff we had right before my birthday.

But I can't think about that right now. Amir is the priority.

"Mr. Trudeau . . ."

He's a kid, not a mister! I want to scream at this judge.

"You are being accused of first-degree murder for the death of Chloe Danvers," the judge says, his eyes on Amir. "If convicted, you could face the death penalty or life in prison without the benefit of parole, probation, or the suspension of the sentence."

Monica's gasp reverberates through the courtroom.

My father drapes his arm over her shoulders. She rests her head on his chest, biting down on her clenched fist. The reporters in the back of the courtroom feverishly scribble that detail in their notebooks. I want desperately to go over and rip them out of their hands. Thank God the judge wouldn't allow any cameras in here. Though we'll still have to face them on our way out, just like we did coming in.

"Keep your head down and don't say a word," my father told me as we were walking up the courthouse steps.

"You are accused of fatally stabbing the victim, Chloe Danvers, three times in her bedroom early the morning of February fourteenth, sometime between one and two a.m.," the judge reads from the paper he's holding. "Investigators arrived at this conclusion based on footage captured on the smart doorbell camera of a neighbor who lives directly across the street from the victim's family. That footage showed a young man fleeing the scene wearing the same clothes you had on the night in question, which investigators proved through pictures posted on social media that had you in the background of a party you and the victim attended earlier that night. Several witnesses at that party also identified you as the person in that footage."

I learned on the news that investigators searched Amir's house looking for those clothes but didn't find them. On that same report, Mr. Dillard refused to provide an explanation as to why but told the reporter that Amir was cooperating with the investigation as best he could. I'm thinking he threw them away. Which, okay, looks a little suspect. There has to be some logical reason he got rid of them. Like, maybe some of Chloe's blood got on him and he didn't want the exact thing that has happened to happen if police came knocking on his door asking questions. If it wasn't for that doorbell camera, I wonder if he'd even be a suspect.

"Based on a previous incident involving a home invasion and robbery that landed you in the New Orleans Police Department's crosshairs, prosecutors are confident they can build a case around why you murdered the victim," the judge continues. "Do you understand this?"

It takes a few seconds before Amir says, "Yes, Your Honor."

Monica starts quietly sobbing in my father's chest.

"Based on the facts as they are presented now, I'm setting your bail at one million dollars," the judge announces.

My heart drops. Monica's head pops up.

"It's all right, I got it," my father whispers to her.

"If you're able to post bail, you are to remain on good behavior while you're out awaiting your trial if you are indicted on these charges," the judge says. "If you're brought back to jail for any additional charge your bail may be revoked. The court will be in touch with your attorney for an arraignment, but that's not a trial date."

"Your Honor," Traci Jackson says. "The DA's office is asking that the defendant also be placed on house arrest as a condition of his bail."

"I don't see why that's necessary," Mr. Dillard retorts.

"Your Honor, the boy is the son of a prominent member of this community," Ms. Jackson argues. "A man with considerable resources, making his son a flight risk."

"That's absurd," my father blurts out.

Mr. Dillard spins around, his eyes wide. *Martin, no,* he mouths.

"I know emotions are high right now, but I demand folks refrain from outbursts," the judge says, eyeing my father.

"Your Honor, our apologies," Mr. Dillard says. "This family is not accustomed to these proceedings. It has been an emotional few days for them."

"And I understand that, but make sure it doesn't happen again," the judge says.

"Yes, Your Honor," Mr. Dillard replies.

"As I was saying," Ms. Jackson continues in an irritated tone. "The boy could be a flight risk. And given the circumstances of the crime, he could be a danger to the community. House arrest would give us the opportunity to keep tabs on his whereabouts."

"Your Honor, that is really not necessary," Mr. Dillard asserts. "My client has never been accused of a violent crime, and up until two days ago was a normal teenager attending one of the most elite schools in this city."

"He's a young man who also isn't a stranger to criminal activity, let's not forget," the judge says. "I'll grant the prosecution's request for house arrest. Mr. Trudeau will be allowed to attend school and freely roam until a given nightly curfew. I think that's reasonable."

This is crazy! House arrest? Does that mean he'll be wearing an ankle monitor from now on?

My head starts spinning as the judge rattles off more

stipulations of Amir's house arrest and next steps once he's released on bail. I don't realize he's been escorted out of the courtroom and the judge has moved on to the next person until my father yanks on my arm and tells me it's time to go.

We walk out of the courtroom with Mr. Dillard. We're followed by the reporters, who approach my father and Monica as soon as we enter the hallway.

"Don't come near them, they have nothing to say," Mr. Dillard barks before any of them can ask a question. He then ushers us into a small conference room across the hall.

As soon as he shuts the door Monica says, "Didn't the state legislature adopt that Raise the Age Act, or whatever, to stop kids like Amir from being tried as adults—it sounds a lot like that's what they're doing, treating him like he's a grown man. The death penalty?"

"That law was geared toward keeping seventeen-year-olds arrested for *nonviolent* offenses out of the adult prison system," Mr. Dillard beats me to explaining.

This room is so cramped that the small round table and three chairs in here give us very little room to spread out. It's drenched in the horrid fluorescent overhead lighting that's illuminating the anxiety imprinted on our faces. I latch on to the back of the chair I'm standing by. Trying to steady myself as the world I know seems to spin out of control.

"What are we supposed to do now, Martin?" Monica snaps at my father. "They're gonna make an example out of my baby, all because of *you*."

"This has nothing to do with me," he replies.

Monica huffs. "Have you *seen* what they've been saying online?"

"*They* who?"

"Monica, Martin, please," Mr. Dillard says, holding up his hands.

Amir's mother rolls her eyes, turning her back to my father to face Mr. Dillard. My father briefly looks at me before he pinches the bridge of his nose.

"I pulled y'all in here to talk about what happens next," Mr. Dillard says.

"I bring my baby home, that's what," Monica snaps.

"*After* that," Mr. Dillard says in a clipped tone. "Normally, we'd have up to one hundred and fifty days before the DA's office might present a case involving a felony to the grand jury, which basically determines whether there is probable cause for a person accused of a crime to stand trial."

Monica's and my father's brows are both wrinkled as they listen to Mr. Dillard explain something I learned in my mock trial class last semester.

"I found out from a source I have in the DA's office that they intend to expedite this case," Mr. Dillard says. "This has become high profile, given the familial connections of both kids involved—"

"One of them being a dead white girl, at that," Monica interjects then purses her lips.

"I'm hearing the DA intends to present this case the next

time the grand jury is scheduled to convene, which is in thirteen days."

I gasp.

"What does that mean?" my father asks.

"That the police are already certain they have their guy, so for them, the investigation is over." Mr. Dillard takes a deep breath. "If Amir is indicted for this girl's murder, things change and it's time for me to start building his defense for trial."

"And in the meantime?" Monica says.

"Pray that in the next two weeks, I can get to the bottom of what really happened in that house while your son was asleep," Mr. Dillard replies.

8

Amir

This ankle monitor feels like a ball and chain on my leg. My daily reminder of the hellish prison I'm facing because, somehow, I wasn't murdered that night too. I heard on a podcast once that Black men are seven times more likely to get wrongfully convicted of murder than white people. Not just white *men*—white people as a whole. Every day going forward is a countdown to my conviction for stabbing a girl I barely knew.

The same nagging weight pinching my ankle is also squeezing my heart.

Why did someone kill her and not me?

I quietly enter our house behind my mama. We haven't said much to each other since she pulled me into the tightest hug ever after they escorted me out of the holding cell at the courthouse. I'm wearing the same clothes I had on the day I was arrested. The dank smell of the city jail emanating from the sleeveless T-shirt and sweatpants. I immediately head toward the back of the house. I haven't had a shower since Wednesday morning.

"Uh-uh, come sit yo' behind down in here," Mama says as I enter the kitchen. "We need to talk."

She's standing in the center of the living room. She slides her purse off her shoulder, dropping it on the coffee table. She points down at the sofa. I knew this was coming. The two phone calls I got to make to her while I was in jail were filled with concern for my well-being and her prayers to get me back home. Now that I'm here, she wants answers. Wants to understand how I've gotten myself into trouble again, and this time possibly facing the death penalty because of it. She's looking for answers I can't give her.

A knot begins to tighten in my chest as I drag my feet back into the living room and plop down on the sofa. Through the window behind Mama the sun has started to dip below the roof of Mrs. Lee's house next door. Our living room is shaded in its tangerine glow. I feel my mother's eyes on me. I can't stop staring at my hands, which I've got folded in my lap. If I look up at her, I'll cry. She's not just disappointed in me this time. I know she must also be scared and angry. Three emotions I've never had to handle combined before.

The silence is suffocating. I think she's waiting for me to speak first, but I don't know what to say. I don't know if there's anything I could say to ease all the things she has to be feeling.

"What were you doing at that girl's house so late?" she asks.

I open my mouth to answer, but before I can, she adds, "You were hanging around with Buster that night?"

I knew he'd be at the top of her Blame List. Especially after the DA's office used our run-in with the law last summer to build their argument that I killed Chloe so that I could rob her. Speculation, Mr. Dillard said, they based on her ransacked bedroom. It didn't matter that none of the expensive stuff in that house was missing—not counting the steak knife that was probably used to kill her.

I never stole anything out of the house Buster broke into either. I didn't even know what he was doing. He told me to wait outside a house we drove to in the Bywater while he "took care of something right quick." That "something" turned out to be him climbing through the bedroom window of his ex-girlfriend to take back all the stuff he'd bought for their daughter 'cause he was salty his ex was dating a dude he didn't like. She pulled up with her parents as Buster was coming from around the back with a trash bag full of toys and clothes. Things got heated. The cops were called. Him and I were detained since her parents wanted to press charges. I didn't end up getting arrested because Buster took full responsibility for what happened. He told the cops the truth, that I had no idea what was going on.

None of that mattered to Mama, though. Her getting called off her job to come down to the police station was enough. The next morning, she was on the phone with my dad. By the end of the week, I was told I wouldn't be attending Douglas Egan with my friends for my senior year.

"Boy, if you don't look me in my face when I'm talking to you," she barks, snatching me back into the present.

My bottom lip starts to tremble as I lift my head. "Mama . . ."

"Mama what?" she snaps.

"He ain't have nothing to do with what happened," I say, my voice strained.

Who did is the thing we should be focused on. Did they spare me just to frame me? If that's the case, why didn't the person plant the knife on me while I was sleeping?

"I told you I didn't want you hanging around that boy anymore," Mama seethes. "You said you weren't, but you lied. Just like you lied about not going to your brother's birthday party. Didn't you tell me you never wanted to set foot in yo' father's house again after they accused you of killing that heffa's dog? What changed, Amir?"

Chloe Danvers texted me.

I can't tell her that. She wouldn't understand. This conversation will go even more left than it already has.

"You have any idea the hell you've put me through these past two days?" she says, clearly not interested in anything I have to say. "I thought sending you to Truman would expose you to kids who were trying to make something of themselves. Give you some direction you lack. Keep you out of trouble."

She walks over to the love seat and drops down on it, rubbing her temples and taking labored breaths.

"Mama, I didn't kill her," I say after a few seconds of silence.

Her head pops up, her brow knitted. "You think I don't know that? I know my son. I know you're not capable of what was done to that girl."

Mama's words sit on my chest, crushing my heart with their weight. Someone else *was* capable of getting in that house somehow and stabbing her to death. Someone who left me sleeping in the living room. Who could have hated her that much?

"Amir, I'm scared the truth isn't gonna matter since people, *white* people for sure, have already made up their minds," Mama says, interrupting my train of thought.

Our doorbell rings. We sit in silence for a beat, looking at each other in confusion. Mama finally stands up. She inches toward the door with a groan. Her shoulders tighten the second she swings it open.

"H-h-hey, thought I'd stop by and check on Amir," I hear Marcel say.

Wonderful. Now I gotta deal with him *too.*

He and my dad were waiting outside the jail with Mama when I was released. My dad pulled me into the most awkward hug ever after Mama let go of me. I stood there, motionless, as he squeezed me and said, "Be strong, son. We're gonna get through this."

I could tell by the way Mama was side-eyeing him that something must have went down between them that day. Betting my dad tried to blame her for what happened.

Given how much money he had to pay for my bail, plus my lawyer's retainer, I forced myself to give him a weak wave goodbye as him and Marcel were climbing into his truck to go home.

Mama steps aside, revealing Marcel in the doorway biting his lip.

"Good, get in here," she says to him, pointing at nowhere in particular behind her. "I wanna know exactly what went down at that party between Amir and that girl."

He enters the house, rubbing the back of his neck. His eyes bounce around the living room and then shift back and forth between me and Mama after she roughly shuts the front door. Seeing Marcel's patronizing face in the courtroom was enough. Now he's here, in our house. For what? To make sure our dad isn't squandering his college tuition to keep me out of jail for killing his best friend?

"Sit down," Mama says to him, pointing at the spot on the love seat she just got up from.

Marcel does, rubbing his hands down his jeans. I scrutinize him. Itching to call him out if he does or says anything that comes off as pity or judgment about where we live. But he keeps glancing up at Mama and then looking away. Making me realize this might be the first time him and Mama have really interacted, without either of his parents around.

"Why did you let him go home with that girl?" Mama demands, looking down at Marcel with her hands propped on her hips.

"I tried to stop him but—"

"Why didn't you try harder?" she interrupts.

Marcel is already looking like a deer caught in headlights. He opens his mouth to answer her.

"Every time my son goes to y'all's house he gets caught up in some mess," she fumes. "And it always involves you."

"Monica, that's a little unfair," he says. "I didn't even know Amir was coming to my party."

I sit up straighter, remembering something I now want an explanation for. "Why did you send me that text?"

Marcel tilts his head slightly, his brow furrowed, like he doesn't know what I'm talking about.

"The *watch yourself . . . she's nothing but drama* text," I remind him. "Who did she piss off so bad they'd want to kill her?"

He shrugs. "That's what I wanna know. I sent that thinking she was meddling in our stuff. Not 'cause I thought someone wanted to murder her."

"See, this is why I told you don't be messing around with them white girls," Mama says, pointing at me. "It's always some bullshit between them and our Black men."

Marcel casts a perplexed look down at the floor. When she's said this to me before, I've told her she's trippin'. That she doesn't have to worry about that with me. If only today's me could go back to one of those times and tell myself why I should listen to her.

"What happened at that party?" Mama asks Marcel.

"Nothing." He breaks eye contact with her to lock eyes with me. "I barely even saw Amir. After I broke up a little argument his friends got into with some boys from our school, I didn't see him again until he left with Chloe."

"And after that?" she follows.

"That's the same thing I'm wondering," he replies with a shrug.

Mama turns to me, brows raised.

"Talk," she hisses, folding her arms across her chest.

So I do. I tell them that Chloe asked me to take her someplace she's never been, so we went to the church on Washington

Avenue. Marcel perks up with interest as I tell them about me offering to go home with Chloe because I could sense she didn't want to be alone that night. Which now has me wondering, did she know her life was in danger? Something was definitely off with her.

"Then what did y'all do?" Mama asks.

"The same thing I told Mr. Dillard," I say.

"Tell me," she says through clenched teeth.

I sigh. "We smoked some weed, vegged out, and played truth or dare."

"That's it?" Mama quizzes.

I nod. "Then I woke up; it was two-eighteen in the morning. I know 'cause first thing I did was check my phone, and then I found her . . . you know. That's when I ran."

"You didn't see or hear anything?" Marcel asks.

I shake my head.

"What was that girl into?" Mama says, and turns to Marcel. "Wasn't she yo' friend? Who hated her? Who would do that to her? 'Cause it wasn't Amir."

I sit up straighter, needing the answers to these questions myself.

"That's what I wanna know, Monica," Marcel replies.

"Well, you need to find out fast!" Mama snaps. "Before Amir . . ."

Ends up on death row, I mentally finish for her.

We sit silently in the quiet that swells between us. None of us making eye contact.

"Shit! I need to get ready for work," Mama says, eyeing the

digital clock that hangs beside our flat-screen TV. "I already missed two days and it's too late to get the shift covered."

She eyes my ankle monitor; then her frustrated gaze travels up to my face. "Guess I'll at least have some peace of mind you can't go anywhere."

The judge set my curfew for six p.m. I can't go out until seven a.m. every day. If I ever need an extension, for whatever reason, I must have it approved. I was told by the jail officer who put the monitor on that it has a GPS tracker in it and that I'll need to charge it every night while I'm sleeping with the charger they gave me. If the battery dies, it'll trigger the alarm and a law enforcement officer will come out and arrest me.

"All the food you cooked Wednesday is still in the fridge if you're hungry," Mama says before taking off into the kitchen and on to her bedroom at the back of the house.

I stare straight ahead out the window. The sun has completely dropped behind Mrs. Lee's roof, the sky outside now a combination of tangerine and purple.

"Daddy said—"

I cut Marcel off. "I don't really care what he said."

"Come on, bro. He's worried and scared just like all of us."

"Does he think I did it?" I ask, intensely holding Marcel's gaze.

"What kind of question is that?" he says.

I turn back toward the window. "So yeah."

"No," Marcel cries. "Amir, no. He believes me."

"Yeah, *you,*" I point out.

"I didn't mean it like that." Marcel turns his body toward me while still seated. "I reminded him that you get queasy at the sight of blood."

"You remember that?" I say, some of the tightness in my chest softening.

With a quick shrug he says, "Yeah, you're my brother."

"That ain't what you came in here saying two days ago." I look back over at him, my mouth pinched as I remember that day. "You was looking like you thought I did it. Or like you wasn't sure."

"Everything was happening so fast, that's all," he says. "I wanted to understand what went down, that's all."

I smack my lips. "Cap."

"Amir, bro. I'm here, supporting you. Believing you. Trying to help."

"Ain't shit you can do for me," I snap. "I'm gonna go down for this. My life is over, and you'll get to continue living in yo' mansion with our punk-ass dad. Y'all can do what you been doing, acting like I don't exist."

That would be easier, and he knows it.

"That's not true," he mumbles.

"Bruh, just leave," I say, my voice cracking. I feel the tears coming, and I'm *not* about to let this fool see me cry.

When he doesn't move, I glare at him. He looks back at me with what I think is regret clouding his eyes.

"Brothers don't let each other wander in the dark alone," he says in this somber tone.

"Negro, what?"

"It's something Nana told me right before she died," he explains, a faint smile stretching his lips. "She acted like it was something profound she made up, but I think she read it somewhere."

A grin pulls at the right corner of my mouth but quickly dissolves. I didn't get to see her right before the end. She started living with my dad once the liver disease got so bad that she needed around-the-clock medical care. She'd probably still be with us if she wasn't like so many older Black people who neglect annual checkups due to their distrust of doctors and the medical industry. Had she been the one who wrapped me in her thick arms when I was released from jail and told me *We're gonna get through this,* I might feel a little more optimistic. She had that kind of power. And I don't know why.

Her funeral was the first time I saw Marcel in person after the dog drama. Before that I'd take quick glances of the framed pictures of him Nana kept around her house. I'm sure he did the same thing with me. We barely said anything to each other that day.

"She said that to me when she made me promise to fix things between us," Marcel tells me. "I'm going to keep that promise to her. She'd want me here right now. Sticking beside you, bro."

The tears are pricking my eyes.

"Just leave me alone, man," I say, my throat tightening. "Please. I'm tired. I haven't really slept in two days. I wanna be alone."

He waits a few seconds before he finally stands. I'm staring straight ahead when he pauses at the front door and looks back over his shoulder. Maybe he wants to say something else, but I'm relieved when he doesn't and quietly leaves instead.

As soon as the door closes, I grab one of the throw pillows on the sofa and press my face into it. I don't want Mama to hear me sob.

9

Marcel

"We will show empathy, be polite and remorseful. And under *no* circumstance will we let these people think we're here to proclaim your brother's innocence. Got it?"

My mother doesn't catch me shaking my head at what she said. She's walking a few steps ahead of me, her eyes pointed at the walnut door up ahead. The same one Amir darted out of after finding Chloe dead in her bedroom. The narrow cobblestone path leading up to the front porch of the Danverses' Garden District home amplifies our determined steps. The white balloons attached to the plastic strings we're each clutching in our hands bouncing in unison to our rhythmic gaits. White was Chloe's favorite color.

Not knowing how we'll be received inside has got me feeling a little dizzy.

Even though the NOPD appears to have already closed the case, if Mr. Dillard's sources are correct, the police department still hasn't released Chloe's body to her family. The latest report that aired on the evening news last night claimed the coroner's office is still trying to scrub any viable DNA evidence off it, likely to build the DA's case against Amir. But friends of the family and kids from school are gathering at Chloe's house today to hold an intimate balloon release to honor her memory. Which we found out about during last night's news segment as well. It ticked me off since Chloe was one of *my* best friends and no one from school reached out to let me know. I had to stalk some of my classmates' social media pages to suss out the details, which also led me down the rabbit hole of the public opinion surrounding Chloe's murder and Amir's arrest. Didn't improve my mood, not one bit.

My father tried to talk us out of showing up today.

"Don't you think her family might be a little . . . put off by y'all being there?" he said last night after my mother and I said we were coming.

"Daddy, she was my best friend and I've barely gotten the chance to mourn her with everything happening so fast with Amir," I argued. "I have every right to be there to say my goodbyes to her."

My mother added that Chloe's mother was one of her good friends as well and that us *not* showing up after such a tragedy would be disrespectful. "We didn't cause this," she told my father as he poured himself a shot of bourbon in our living room. "Your son . . ."

My father looked up at her then with the meanest stare I've ever seen, and she didn't finish her sentence.

If my father has read any of the stuff I read online last night,

I can understand why he doesn't want to be around people. Black Twitter especially was dragging him pretty hard. Saying they didn't even know he had another son, that he must have been ashamed of Amir for some reason. A lot of Black women blamed it on colorism, accusing my father of casting Amir and his mother aside after he became successful and married my mother, who is light-skinned with "good hair." And then there were the Dr. Umar Johnson followers who claimed they would no longer support a man who put me, his gay son, on a pedestal and ignored Amir, the straight one, who could actually "carry on his legacy." But given that Amir had "gotten caught up with a white girl," the same people turned their time lines into think pieces criticizing my father's parenting and calling him a sellout.

"Mother, I'm not letting these people talk shit about Amir," I say as we reach the door.

She pauses as she's about to ring the doorbell and turns toward me, her face blanched. "Excuse me?"

"I'm not *not* going to defend Amir if somebody says something out of line," I say, poking out my chest. "He is innocent. I'm not going to pretend he's not."

"You don't know that for certain."

"I do," I insist. "So does Daddy. Maybe he'll stop shading you if you start to believe that too."

I reach out and press the doorbell before she can respond. She huffs and starts brushing imaginary lint from the black vintage Roberto Cavalli dress she's wearing. Her hair is pulled back in a tight bun. She fixes her face with a plastic smile the second the door swings open, revealing Mattie Bordelon.

Mattie flinches at the sight of us. She and Chloe were barely acquaintances. But I know, through my social media stalking last night, that she is the self-appointed organizer of this ceremony. Why she's chosen to insert her pointed-nose, busybody, last-season's-Gucci-loafers-wearing ass in *my* best friend's murder is beyond me.

"Marcel, um, *hey*," she says, her beady eyes ticking back and forth between my mother and me. "Didn't realize you were invited."

I have to press my lips together and deeply exhale to stop myself from going off on her.

"My son is here to pay his respects," my mother says, brushing past Mattie into the house. "Chloe meant a lot to him."

I enter behind her, sneering at Mattie as I cross the threshold. Her coppery hair is pulled up in a high ponytail that reveals freckles dusting her pale, thin neck as well as her cheeks.

"I just didn't think you'd have the nerve to actually show your face here," she says as she's closing the door.

I turn around. "Is that why you didn't tell me about this? I was Chloe's best friend. If anyone should have been organizing this, it's me, not you."

Mattie pauses, looking me up and down. "That may be true. But I don't think anyone would object to my being here, since, like, my brother didn't kill her."

She stalks around me. I spin on my heels, my mouth fixed to call her the first thing that comes to mind (it rhymes with *witch*). But I'm met with several questioning glares from the few people gathered in the foyer. I quickly relax my face and straighten my shoulders. That's all I need, people calling me *aggressive* because of how I responded to disrespect from a white girl. I came here, against my father's probably better judgment, to pay my respects and mourn the death of my friend. I have every right to be here. *She* would want me here—if for no other reason than to ruffle a few feathers. Chloe loved that type of drama.

Beyond the foyer, near the winding staircase, my mother is beckoning me with her eyes. Her upper lip twists with a sneer as Mattie walks past her toward the back of the house. Chloe would get a kick out of this. "No one throws shade better than you and Lily," she used to say.

I glance into the living room as I'm heading toward my mother. Amir said he fell asleep in there. If that's true (and I'm not saying it isn't), how did the person who *really* killed Chloe not see him sprawled out on the sofa? The living room sits immediately to the left of their front door. Obviously they had to have gotten in some other way. It doesn't make sense that the person killed Chloe but not him. Amir could have woken up at any time, heard what was going on, and caught the killer in the act. Why would her killer risk leaving him alive downstairs while they were upstairs stabbing her to death?

"What did she say to you?" my mother asks in a hushed tone once I get to her.

"I'll tell you later," I reply dismissively, my anger toward Mattie supplanted by my questions about what went down in here that night.

We move through the house in silence, giving tight-lipped

smiles to the disapproving stares and gaping mouths our presence garners. I've never felt so out of place among people I've shared a social circle with. Mattie has already disappeared into the kitchen by the time my mother and I pass the staircase. The console table flush against the wall of the hallway that leads to the kitchen usually holds only a vase of fresh flowers in the center. Today it's crowded with candles and framed pictures of Chloe throughout the years. I know most of the pictures well—I should be in some of them with her. I stop, my stomach clenching when I realize my presence has been removed by someone who strategically placed other photos over me.

I'm starting to regret not listening to my father. Too late to turn back now, though. Leaving, especially after what Mattie said to me, might make Amir look even guiltier. Not being here would look mad suspect. Like we couldn't face a family we've shared countless dinners with because there's truth to what the police have *accused* my brother of doing.

There are a few people I don't recognize milling about in the kitchen. Serving platters piled with food are scattered everywhere. We continue through the house, toward the backyard. Through the window on the back door we can see that most of the people here are gathered outside. There's a man posted in front of a table topped with a helium tank and a small pile of deflated white balloons to our left as soon as we step out onto the back porch. He politely nods at us. It's the only pleasant reaction we receive.

The hum of conversation comes to an abrupt stop as we step

outside and everyone sees us. My mother slips her free hand into mine. We weave our fingers together and maintain composed looks as we face the crowded backyard. We descend the steps in silence. My head feels as if it's detached from my body and might float away with this balloon if I let it.

My mother lightly squeezes my hand. "Act normal and keep your emotions in check," she whispers.

I have to keep telling myself, *You deserve to be here; she was your best friend.* It doesn't make this feel any less awkward, though.

Gradually everyone returns to their conversations, but I can still feel eyes on us. My mother is maintaining a stoic demeanor—she can fake it better than me—but I can't hold anyone's stare too long. I'm afraid to read their faces. I don't need to. Their disapproval has me feeling ten degrees hotter around my neck and ears.

"Let's find Aubrey and Savannah and express our condolences," my mother says.

I let her lead me by the hand, assuming she's already spotted Chloe's parents among the swaying white dots of balloons. As she's weaving through the clusters of people, my eyes momentarily linger on a woman—her lip curled, she lightly taps the arm of the man standing next to her. I'm about to look away until that man lifts his head and I realize it's our principal, Mr. Braswell. He acknowledges me with a curt nod and a smile so tight it makes his lips disappear. There's a handsome older Black man standing beside him. I've only briefly seen his picture once in Mr. Braswell's office, but I'm certain the guy is his husband.

"Remember what I said," my mother tells me over her shoulder.

A second later the crowd opens up and I see Chloe's parents. They're standing near the cherub fountain in the center of their backyard with her little brother, Justin, who seems confused. I want to lift him up into a hug—he loved his big sister so much, even though he enjoyed annoying her too—but the look on her father's face the second he sees us approaching stops me from doing it.

"Savannah, our hearts are just breaking for y'all," my mother says, leaning into a stiff hug with Chloe's mother. "These kinds of losses, no parent should ever have to endure."

Mrs. Danvers smiles politely, her eyes bloodshot and puffy. "Th-thank you. That means a lot," she replies, but only after glancing at her husband, who looks like he can't stand the sight of us.

"If you need anything, *anything,* you let us know," my mother says to Mrs. Danvers. I'm grateful she's talking. Everything I thought I wanted to say is lodged in the back of my throat. "Marcel loved Chloe so much. We all did," she adds.

"And your stepson, how did he feel about her?" Mr. Danvers scoffs. "Guess he loved her to death."

I turn to him, anger rising in my chest. My mother squeezes my hand so hard her nails dig into my skin and I suck in a breath from the sharp pain. I get it. *Don't say a word!*

But I want to. When that building collapsed and the public branded Mr. Danvers a murderer, we didn't turn our backs on him or treat him differently. We still showed up for dinners, supported him even though it was entirely his fault. I know Chloe's gone. I'm hurting over that too. It doesn't give him the right to treat us like we killed her, though. If he ever really trusted us and valued my parents' friendship, he could give us the benefit of the doubt and not assume that Amir is the person who took Chloe away.

A blur steps between us and the Danverses. It's Victoria, Chloe's cousin who was more like an older sister. Victoria basically looks like an older version of Chloe, except with shorter hair and a sharper nose. Her jaw clenches when she looks at me.

"Uncle Aubrey, the pastor is here," she says, lightly tugging on Mr. Danvers's arm. "Why don't we go ahead and get started."

Mr. Danvers nods and she slips away again without a word to me. Victoria and I were always cool. Guess that's changed now too.

"We'll let y'all get things underway—again, our deepest sympathy, Savannah. Really," my mother says before pulling me off to the side with her to stand near part of the brick fence. "And before you even start," she says to me, "I didn't stop you from saying something to Aubrey just now because I didn't want you defending your brother. This isn't the time or place for that. Those poor people have lost their daughter in the most unspeakable way. If it had been you, if the roles were reversed, the truth wouldn't matter to me either. Not when everything is still fresh. They want justice. They're angry. And right now, your brother is the only answer they've got. Don't hate them for wanting to latch on to that, okay?"

My eyes lower toward the ground, but I nod in agreement. What she said actually makes sense. It also hurts.

An older, bearded white man emerges from the crowd and shares compassionate hugs with each of Chloe's parents. Then he steps up onto the ledge of the fountain so that he can see over the crowd. This must be the pastor Victoria mentioned.

"We're all gathered here today for an occasion no parent ever wants to endure: having to mourn the loss of their child," the man says, eliciting a wave of agreeable nods from the crowd.

Mrs. Danvers wraps her arm tighter around Justin. The nine-year-old nuzzles up to his mother, resting his head on her forearm.

"Let us begin by saying a prayer," the pastor continues. "Bow your heads."

When he starts praying, I'm reminded of something I either read or heard on a podcast. That sometimes, killers like to attend the memorial services of their victims. Like, they get some sick satisfaction out of seeing the havoc they caused. Now that the attention is off us, I scan the crowd, wondering in the back of my mind if that's true and Chloe's killer is here.

Colin Perrier is looking about as uncomfortable as I'm feeling. He's standing on the other side of the fountain, facing us. His hands stuffed in the front pockets of his pants. Chloe knew him as long as she knew Jared, but they became somewhat estranged after she broke up with him. Jared is here as well, standing over by Colin. Nolan too. He texted me shortly after Amir's arrest was announced on the news. *Dude, is this true about what your brother did to Chloe?* it said. I finally did what I should have done a long time ago: blocked his number.

I spot a few teachers and some of the girls who were on the volleyball team with Chloe. Then I see Senator Spencer Winslow II standing stoically beside his resting-bitch-face wife. Trey and Tiffany are flanking their parents. I recognize several members of our school's board of directors mingled within the collection of classmates and their parents.

"Chloe's father would like to say a few words before we release the balloons," the pastor says, pulling my gaze back to him. "Aubrey, speak from your heart."

Mr. Danvers steps forward, his shoulders drooped but his chin lifted.

"Let me first thank Mattie and all of Chloe's friends who put this together," Mr. Danvers begins. "You guys loved her as much as we did, which makes this such a senseless tragedy. Chloe was our fighter. She wanted to change the world. I regret any time I ever discouraged her from doing so."

That's weird. I can't remember a time Chloe ever said he did. Protesting was considered quality time in her family. Whether it was police reform, equal rights, or environmental justice, the Danverses showed up with their kids. And never shied away from pulling out their checkbooks to fund progressive movements.

Mr. Danvers's head drops. The pastor gently pats his back while Mrs. Danvers sobs into a crumpled tissue she's got clutched in her hand.

"We have some comfort today knowing that the person who took our little girl away from us will not get away with what he did," Mr. Danvers says. "Justice is already on its way to being served."

My mother is digging her nails into my hand again.

Don't look up. Don't look up. Don't. Look. Up! I repeat to myself.

"We won't ever have peace without her, but knowing her killer won't walk free will give us solace," Mr. Danvers says, his voice choking up. "Pray for us. Pray for my wife, who will never understand why this happened. Our little girl will live on, we'll make sure of that. Chloe, we love you, baby."

Mr. Danvers dissolves into guttural sobs. It's hard to watch.

"At this time, let us release these balloons as symbols of Chloe's soul lifting toward the heavens, where it belongs," the pastor says.

I let mine go and look up as it joins dozens of others—white orbs float toward each other and are carried away by the wind. I wish I could float away with them. Be anywhere but here, forced to listen to Mr. Danvers continue to sob. In addition to the pastor and Victoria, someone else steps up and starts rubbing his back. When I realize who it is, I gasp.

Mr. Danvers can't stand to look at us because he thinks my brother killed his daughter, fine. But there he is allowing Jared Lanford's father to console him. After what Jared did to Chloe, how he could ever forgive that man, who acted like his son being physically abusive to his then fifteen-year-old girlfriend was "nothing to get up in arms about"?

The hypocrisy is too much.

"I need to use the bathroom," I say to my mom before wiggling my hand out of hers.

I don't even wait for her to respond. I take off, making a beeline for the house, keeping my head down as I weave in and out of people toward the back door. I stop when someone steps in my path.

"You okay?"

It's Tiffany. Her girly face shadowed with concern. It melts some of the tension in my neck. She's the first person to ask me how this is all affecting me.

"No. I want to scream, but I can't," I say. "But thanks for the concern. Haven't been getting a lot of that lately."

"Yeah, I saw some stuff online." Tiffany presses her thin pink lips together. "Figured I'd ask, since I know how much you care about your brother, you know, even though . . ."

He acts like he doesn't care about me, I know she wants to say, but doesn't.

"What is he saying, about what happened?" she asks.

"That he didn't do it."

She nods. "Yeah, of course."

I can't tell if she really believes him or is just saying that because she knows it'll make me feel better. I don't care. I'll take it.

"Tiff, come on." Trey steps between us, his back to me, one arm hooked around his sister. "Dad's asking for us."

Their father is watching from across the yard, his brow knitted, when I look over at him. I sharply suck in a breath through my teeth.

"Bump this," I mumble.

I stomp around Trey and Tiffany, leaving them behind as I retreat to the house. There are a few people shuffling around in the kitchen when I enter through the back door. They're filling their plates with food, so they don't pay attention to me. I need to be alone. As I'm squeezing between two women, my eyes stop on the wood knife block on the countertop near the sink. By the handles I can tell all but one of the slots are filled. Which means that slot must have held the knife that was supposedly used to kill Chloe. The one that's missing.

Why do they still have that in here?

I feel like I might throw up.

I go straight to the bathroom, which I know is the first door past the threshold of the kitchen, and yank on the knob. It's locked.

"Someone's in there, sweetie," a lady calls from the kitchen.

Yeah, I can see that now.

"There's another bathroom on the second floor," she adds.

"I know."

I take off for the winding staircase up ahead. As I'm doing so, I hear, "Isn't he the brother of the boy that killed her?" from the same woman.

I take the stairs two at a time to keep myself from spinning around and popping off at her. Unlike downstairs, the second floor is quiet. I pause and realize that I've stopped right at Chloe's bedroom. The door is partially open, and I'm drawn to it. The floorboards crack under the weight of my footsteps. As I enter, I glance over my shoulder to make sure no one is behind me before shutting the door. There's enough sun pouring in through the windows that I don't need to turn on the lights.

My heart is suddenly ten pounds heavier. I'm in Chloe's bedroom. Likely for the last time ever. It's immaculate. Just the way I remember it. Nothing out of place. No signs that a gruesome murder took place in here three nights ago. It's weird.

It's hard to picture the scene Amir described to me and his mother: blood splatter on the wall, the room looking as if a tornado had torn through it. How do you go from that to this so quickly? To a scene that's devoid of the heinousness that has changed our lives, maybe forever?

I start grinning as I stare at her bed. Chloe and I spent who knows how many nights sprawled across it, talking about boys. Which ones we hated, which ones we wanted to hook up with. It was on that bed, Halloween night our freshman year, that I confirmed her suspicions about my sexuality. That night was the first time she invited me over and up to her bedroom, and I mistakenly assumed she was trying to shoot her shot with me.

"Of course you are," she'd responded matter-of-factly. We were dressed up as Antony and Cleopatra. "You're too freaking fabulous to *not* be gay."

I laughed so hard that I cried. A weight had been lifted off my shoulders. This girl I was beginning to love as a friend would know the true me. After that moment, we moved on like it wasn't the big deal I had made it out to be in my head. That's what I'll miss most. Her bluntness.

Knowing this is likely my last time in here, I wander around the room, mentally cataloging everything I want to commit to memory. Brushing my fingers across the antique mirrored dresser where she spent hours filming makeup tutorials that she kept for herself. I idly flip through some of the fashion magazines stacked on the corner, thinking about all the times she'd send me selfies she had taken in front of the full-length mirror tucked in the corner on the other side of the room, for an outfit critique. I pick up a few bottles of perfume arranged on the mirrored tray next to the magazines. One of them I gifted to her this past Christmas. As I replace the diamond-shaped bottle, I realize I'm wearing the sterling silver bangle bracelet she gave me.

There's nothing on her nightstand but the see-through glass lamp. The nightstand is where she always put her cell phone, which I'm sure the police have. I open the top drawer out of some morbid curiosity. It's mostly filled with what I first assume is random junk. As I'm about to shut the drawer I pause, though, and pick up the small blue Tiffany & Co. box that's slightly hidden under some slips of paper. Inside is a diamond tennis bracelet, along with a handwritten note that says *Please forgive me.*

I huff, rolling my eyes. *Trey,* I think. He's the only person I'd assume would be buying presents to get back in Chloe's good graces. I close the box to sift through the rest of the contents of the drawer, suddenly intrigued. There's also a black velvet jewelry box. I open it to discover a heart-shaped diamond pendant. A smaller square box underneath holds a pair of ladybug-shaped diamond earrings, with another handwritten note in the same crooked script. It says *You'll always be my ladybug.*

That's a nickname I've never heard him use before. I'm

betting the amount of jewelry I've found aligns with how many times they broke up over the course of their on-again, off-again relationship. I'm guessing I never saw Choe wearing any of this stuff because the second time she took him back after saying she was done, I told her I didn't want to hear about anything else involving them. They were exhausting. I let her know that as often as possible.

I hear a creak behind me. Like the sound the floorboards made when I snuck in here.

My heart drops.

I spin around. Through the crack along the bottom of the bedroom door I see a shadow grow larger. Then the knob twists to the right.

Shit! Somebody's coming.

I quietly drop the jewelry boxes back into the drawer before quietly closing it with my leg. I look around the room for somewhere to hide and slip into Chloe's closet, managing to silently shut the door just as her bedroom door opens.

My heart is beating in the back of my throat.

I stand perfectly still in the confined darkness. Cocooned in my dead friend's hanging clothes. Measuring my breathing. Realizing how bad this looks if someone catches me. Why I'm hiding in my friend's closet, the friend my brother is suspected of murdering, will be hard to explain.

There's the hollow thud of drawers opening and shutting hard. I press my ear to the closet door, straining to hear what's going on over my racing heart. After a few seconds of silence, I think the person may have left, until I hear another thud and a yelp. Sounds like the person knocked their knee or foot or something against a hard surface.

I quietly twist the doorknob and crack open the door. I make out the back of a black blazer first. The person, who appears to be a male, is bent over, rummaging through one of the bottom drawers of Chloe's mirrored dresser. I push the door open just a little wider. The person jolts upright, their reflection popping up in the mirror.

It's Trey.

I jump back into the darkness when I see in the mirror that his eyes are about to shift in the direction of the closet.

He didn't see me. He didn't see me. Please don't come over here.

I'm holding my breath. I let it out once I hear him rummaging through another drawer. Still nowhere near me. What is he looking for? Maybe all that jewelry he gave her.

I silently watch him go from one drawer to the next. Tossing around their contents in a frantic state. Once he has looked through all six drawers he stands up, rubs his hand across his low taper fade haircut, and mumbles, "Where the fuck is it?"

He said *it.* Okay, so not the gifts, apparently.

Trey's eyes wildly bounce around the room and then stop on the closet.

I shrink back again, thinking he may have seen me. Or worse, that he's about to make the closet his next target for whatever scavenger hunt he's on.

His steps toward me make my heart thump louder and louder in my ears. This is going to go left quick. It always does with Trey.

"What are you doing in here?"

The question isn't aimed at me, though. I'm still safely within the embrace of darkness.

"Um, I wanted to—to—" I hear Trey stammer.

"You shouldn't be in here," the other person, a female, hisses.

I realign an eye with the crack in the door, but I can only see part of Trey. He has this deer-in-headlights look on his face. I have to lean farther to the side to see who he's looking at. It's Victoria.

"I was only paying my respects," Trey tells her. "Wanted to do it privately, up here where we spent a lot of time together."

Liar!

"Oh, *now* you want to respect her?" Victoria fires back. "After you gave her so much shit and dumped her because you didn't like the mirror she was putting up to you?"

"You don't know anything about our relationship," Trey says.

"I know enough to know you shouldn't be in here," Victoria replies, her tone laced with venom. "I never liked you. I never trusted you. You couldn't even set your own shit aside while she was going through stuff with her dad. You're as snaky as your father."

"Whatever, dude," Trey says. "Chloe and I knew what we meant to each other. Find someone who wants to tolerate you and maybe you'll understand."

"Get out, before I have my uncle throw you out," Victoria orders.

I wait until they've both left the room before I emerge, my head spinning.

What the hell did I just overhear?

Something scratches against the floor as I take a step toward the bedroom door. I look down and yank off the slip of crumpled paper that's stuck to the bottom of my shoe. Must have been on the closet floor. The engraved words at the top of the wrinkled sheet say *THE BELMONT HOTEL.* The number *2709* is scribbled on it in Chloe's handwriting. I think that's the hotel her family frequents for Sunday brunch. *Must have fallen out of the pocket of something hanging in her closet,* I say to myself. I ball it up and toss it in the small trash can on the other side of the door as I sneak out of the room.

My mother is downstairs, looking tortured as I descend the steps. Her face lights up at the sight of me, and she meets me at the bottom of the stairs.

"You ready to go?" she asks. "We've done about all we can do here."

Guess the harsh glances and whispers are finally too much for her. I don't see Trey or Victoria among the people moving around.

"I've been ready to go since we got here," I tell my mother.

She starts toward the front door, and I follow but stop, surprised, when she disappears behind the staircase. I look back in the direction of the kitchen, then slowly turn toward the staircase. Chloe's killer couldn't have used the front door. For that to be true, the neighbor's doorbell camera would have recorded whoever was entering just like it caught Amir leaving. Amir said he and Chloe entered through the back door, not the front. The killer must have done the same.

"You coming?" my mother asks impatiently from the foyer.

"Sorry, yeah."

As we're passing the living room, I continue my train of thought. Realizing that if someone did come in through the back door and go straight upstairs to Chloe's bedroom that night, they wouldn't have seen Amir sleeping downstairs. That means they might not have known he was in the house.

10

Amir

Truman Academy takes up the entire corner where Freret Street intersects with Nashville Avenue, the campus stretching all the way back to Loyola Avenue. The three metal-and-glass buildings that make up the school starkly contrast with the historic charm of the surrounding neighborhood. I thought it looked more like a vo-tech school than a high school the first time I saw it. A place young adults who didn't go to college attended to learn the skills required for decent-paying, blue-collar jobs. But in fact, Truman is far from that. The school's mission statement is engraved on the brick sign that centers the school's manicured front lawn.

We foster an environment for our students to grow and learn, encouraging them to embrace new ways of thinking within a background of traditional learning built on a solid foundation of diversity and inclusion.

That last part is a joke, given there are so few kids of color here.

Walking the halls today is even more uncomfortable than it normally is. The stares I'm getting as I make my way to my locker scream *You shouldn't be here! How could you show your face after what you did to her?* and *I knew he was nothing but a thug.* I sagged my uniform pants some today (which is explicitly forbidden in the student handbook), hoping it would completely conceal this albatross around my right ankle.

To say I've felt "othered" since I started attending Truman would be an understatement. Even before I was falsely accused of murder, this place made me hyperaware of the space I take up. These hallways are a sort of echo chamber of how noticeably I'm Black. Even among the other Black kids I don't fit in. I'm a novelty, the thing that doesn't quite belong, even though my dark gray uniform slacks are properly tailored like all other dudes'. I always make sure my white button-down shirt, which we're required to wear under a navy blazer with the school crest sewn on the upper left side, is crisp and my standard hunter-green-and-navy-plaid tie is neatly knotted, because I want to blend in as much as possible.

I knew coming in that people here would have preconceived notions about me since I don't share the privilege they do. So for eight hours, five days a week, for the past six months, my thoughts have been consumed with how the kids and faculty see me, and intently modifying my behavior to make all these white people feel comfortable with my presence in this space.

I've never been able to shake the feeling that there's some

inside joke circulating here that I'll never be part of. I've never shared this with anyone, not even my mama.

Today, everything I've ever felt is multiplied by, like, a thousand.

Mama is down bad for forcing me to show up.

"We're spending too much money for you to be missing class," she said this morning as she barged into my room.

I swallowed the flippant response that popped into my head. She was giving me that *don't try me, boy* look as I slowly got out of bed. It wasn't the time to be snarky and remind her that it's actually my dad who's "spending too much money" on my tuition.

We learned on the news last night that the police found the clothes and shoes I threw away. A numbing chill coursed through my veins as we watched the two-minute segment. The reporter walked us through how investigators had tracked the route of the garbage truck that emptied the dumpster I told police I had tossed them in, and how they then spent three days raking through the trash in a certain area of the city's landfill. In his on-camera interview with the reporter, the spokesman for the police department expressed disappointment that they haven't found the steak knife they believe was used to kill Chloe. It probably has DNA evidence on it that could clear me. Probably why the person didn't plant it on me while I was sleeping.

"What's the probability of the murder weapon being out here?" the reporter asked the police department's spokesman, the landfill framed behind him.

"No way of knowing," the spokesman said. "We'll keep looking, don't worry."

Mr. Dillard called shortly after the story aired, telling us not to be alarmed.

"There are all kinds of chain-of-custody issues I can use to discredit any argument they use to make those clothes or shoes support their case," he said. Mama had the call on speaker so I could hear him too. "They've been exposed to the weather and mixed with trash for at least four days. And most importantly, Amir didn't kill Chloe, so there won't be anything on them that will dispute that . . . *right?*"

I pictured him raising his brows.

"Yes, sir," I replied. "I threw them away 'cause I panicked. Like I told them."

"Then we're good," Mr. Dillard said. "You continue living your life while I work to make sure you can do that out of prison."

Guess Mama interpreted that as me continuing to go to school even though it's clear everyone here thinks I'm a murderer.

Some of the tightness in my chest loosens when I see Marcel standing by my locker waiting for me. His locker is three halls down, with the other juniors'. His face immediately brightens once we make eye contact. If this were any other day, I'd be annoyed. He used to try to strike up conversations with me when I first started here. He got the hint that I wasn't interested after I ignored him enough. But today he's a lifeline I can latch on to. Another example of how one night has changed my day-to-day.

"Glad you showed up. Was getting ready to text you," he says, straightening his posture.

" 'Sup?" I say, twisting the dial of my combination lock.

"Didn't you say Chloe's bedroom was ransacked when you found her?"

I sigh. He wants to talk about that here? Within earshot of everyone. The first time I've ever *wanted* to engage with him at school and I'm already regretting it.

"Hello?" he prods when I don't respond.

"Yeah, man, why?" I mumble, looking around to make sure no one's listening.

Marcel adjusts his backpack on his shoulder. "Saturday, when I was at the balloon release at Chloe's house, I caught Trey rummaging through her bedroom, looking for something."

"So?"

I take my American history textbook out of my backpack and place it in my locker, then grab my physics book.

"Bruh, he was seriously looking. Like, *desperately.*" Marcel leans in closer, his jaw set. "It got me thinking. The police said there was no forced entry into her house. That could be because Chloe let someone in, like Trey, while you were asleep."

I drop my physics book into my backpack. Where's he going with this?

"The night of my birthday party, I walked in on them arguing in your bedroom," he says.

My bedroom? So they kept it? Even though I stopped visiting? I try to keep the surprise out of my face.

"You thinking what I'm thinking?" he continues.

I frown. "Nah."

He rolls his eyes with an exasperated sigh. "Bruh, what if Trey went there that night because he was still angry about her leaving my party with you?"

"Hol' up. If you caught him, why didn't you just ask what he was looking for?" I quiz.

"I couldn't," he replies, awkwardly lowering his eyes. When I give him a side-eye, he adds, "He didn't know I was in the room. I was hiding . . . in the closet."

I pause in the middle of grabbing a binder out of my locker. "Bruh, what was you doing in the closet?"

"Long story; not important." Marcel takes a deep breath as I'm stuffing the binder behind my physics textbook. "The point is: Trey was a jealous boyfriend she recently dumped. He could have killed her in a crime-of-passion-type scenario and left you alive to frame 'cause he thought you were smashing his girl."

"You been watching the ID channel too much," I say, zipping my backpack.

"No, I'm serious," he insists. "Just can't figure out yet what he could have been looking for in her bedroom. Maybe something that would directly link him to her murder."

Marcel was staring at me but not really seeing me when he said that last part. Like he was talking more to himself than to me.

I slam my locker shut. "Not about to get my hopes up. My life ain't like yours. Shit don't be that easy for me."

"This ain't gonna be easy," Marcel says. "But I thought about it all last night. Got an idea how I *might* be able to prove I'm right."

"Okay, Sherlock Holmes."

I take off to my right. There's only a minute left before my first class.

"Wait!" he shouts. "Why you being like this? Don't you wanna know what really happened? You gotta be just as sick as I am of everyone believing you killed her."

His statement draws sideways glances from people nearby.

"Would have been great if you'd felt like that the day your mom's dog got run over," I say.

I leave him standing at my locker, a pained expression on his face.

Ironically, waiting for me when I enter physics class is the same word his mother screamed at me the day Sparkle died. It's scribbled in red lipstick across my desk.

Murderer!

11

Marcel

Not about to let my brother's stank attitude derail me from my mission. Not with all the guilt-by-association shade I've had to deal with my first day back at school after Chloe's murder.

It started this morning in the student parking lot. As I was leaning in to grab my messenger bag out the trunk, Emily Addaway rushed up in my face with some other sophomore girls and said, "Hey, I want you to know that you have all our support. I can't imagine what you must be going through. Your brother killing one of your best friends like that."

"He didn't do it; they arrested the wrong person," I quickly responded.

Her downturned mouth completely shifted the empathy that had just been in her long face. She said nothing in response. She and her friends just backed away silently. Once I made it to my locker, I started to think Emily must have been a test I didn't pass. Because I didn't say what they wanted, which I think was for me to believe in Amir's guilt, no one has really spoken to me all day. When Mr. Braswell led a moment of silence during homeroom announcements, nearly everyone in class gave me the same wounded look. Like *I* was responsible for the unexpected tragedy that now haunts our school.

This has to end. I can only imagine it's ten times worse for Amir. Making his dismissive attitude toward my theory about Trey annoying AF. Doesn't he see that I'm trying to help him? Helping him helps all of *us* get out from under this cloud of hostility that hangs over our family. The only way this ends for us is by proving that Amir is innocent.

I know something no one else at this school does: Trey is hiding something. Something that has to do with Chloe. I have no idea what he was looking for in her bedroom, but it has to be connected to her murder.

I can see a scenario where Trey is her killer.

He's the type of person who would think Amir was a downgrade compared to him. His ego couldn't handle that. If he couldn't have her, he damn sure wasn't gonna let Amir. And after the way my brother and his friends checked him at my party, Trey likely viewed framing Amir as a way to really take him down a peg—if I'm wrong about her killer *not knowing* that Amir was asleep downstairs.

I know Trey would never tell me the truth if I straight-up asked what he was looking for in Chloe's bedroom, but I can at least test my *he might be the killer* theory. I came up with how to do it last night, and now is the time to put my plan in motion.

Worst-case scenario: Trey doesn't react the way I expect him to, which will throw the entire thing into flux.

Lunchtime is really my only opportunity.

There isn't much intermingling of the grade levels. The school's main building is sectioned off, with freshman and sophomore classes mostly held on the first floor and classes for juniors and seniors on the second floor. The grade levels are further divided into wings on each floor, with juniors and freshmen on the west wing and seniors and sophomores on the east. The only time we juniors mix with the seniors (besides when we sneak off into the other wing, which Chloe did a lot while dating Trey) is at lunch period. Upperclassmen have lunch together, followed by the lower classmen.

I enter the cafeteria, instantly setting eyes on Trey. He's seated at one of the back tables like he always is with some of the student council and some members of our school's Young Democrats. The boy lives for politics, just like his dad. That's why I don't trust him as far as I can throw him, and he's at least twenty pounds heavier than me, so that ain't far. The bottle of cranberry juice I just purchased from the vending machine outside dangles from my right hand. I loosen the top as I make my way through the noisy room toward Trey's table. His back is to me, so he can't see me approaching.

Good.

On a normal day I'd be bouncing around from table to table, getting all the tea. But no one is saying *Marcel, come here right quick. Guess what happened last night!* or *Yo, Marcel, come holla at us* as I maneuver through tables. Just like all day, no one makes eye contact with me, but I feel their eyes on my back as I pass them. Ain't no telling what they're saying about me or my brother.

Amir is usually brooding by himself. I glance around the cafeteria when I don't see him. Wonder if he said fuck it and left for the day. I know he already felt out of place here; today must have been a fresh kind of hell for him. Chloe was popular, though clearly not everyone loved her. Still, nothing brings people together like a villain everyone can hate.

I'm a few steps away and Trey's back is still facing me. I take the cap off my bottle of cranberry juice.

Time to give the performance of my brother's life.

I purposely trip over my own foot and then jerk the bottle of juice with enough force to send some of its wine-colored contents flying directly at Trey.

"What the fuck!" he shouts as it splashes across his back and droplets run down his uniform pants.

My heart is racing when he shoots up and turns around. I immediately adopt an apologetic expression.

"Oh my God, man, I'm sorry," I say, holding up my hands.

His eyes flick toward the bottle of cranberry juice I'm still clutching in my right hand. Everyone sitting at the table with him watches with curiosity.

"What the hell is wrong with you?" he fumes, looking over his shoulder to see the damage I've done. He's wearing the hunter-green V-neck sweater the school allows us to wear in place of our blazers. Which is perfect, since the cranberry juice stain is more glaring on it than it would be on navy. He'll be more inclined to do what I need him to do.

"I'm sorry, I'm sorry," I say pitifully. "I tripped. Wasn't watching where I was going."

"Bruh, just move!" he orders, pushing me out of the way as he storms toward one of the exits. Likely heading to the bathroom to dry off his sweater. Leaving behind exactly what I came in here for.

I reach over and grab a handful of the napkins someone has stacked near their plate on the table behind me.

"I'm such a klutz," I say to the people still sitting at Trey's table as I drop down and start wiping up the spots of cranberry juice that spilled on the floor near Trey's book bag.

"At least you didn't stab his ex to death," Sonya Gilliott says in a mocking tone.

She was sitting next to Trey. She's Black and a senior, like him. Her father is a lobbyist for the oil and gas industry. I can't stand her, haven't since way before that little dig just now. She's been crushing on Trey forever and is always trying to get between him and Chloe one way or the other. Maybe she killed Chloe to finally get what she wanted.

I give her a sour look, and she and the rest of the table return to whatever conversation I purposely interrupted, ignoring me.

Good.

Makes it easier for me to slip my hand into the front pocket of Trey's book bag and get what I need—his car keys. I pride myself on being a person who pays attention to the little things.

Like seeing Trey always drop his keys into the front pouch of his book bag whenever he gives me and Chloe a ride to or from school.

I shoot up, stuffing the keys in my back pocket as smoothly as I can.

"You didn't wipe up all the juice," one of the kids at the table says as I'm dashing off.

I keep walking, never acknowledging whoever said it.

Step one is complete. On to step two.

I'm practically running out of the cafeteria, working up a sweat as I dash through the covered breezeway to the main building. I should have enough time; lunch period isn't over for another twenty minutes. Trey won't need his keys until the end of the day, when school's out. I'll lie and say I found them in the hall when I give them back to him.

I dart up the steps two at a time to get to Mr. Fairweather's classroom. I need him to be eating his lunch alone in there, like most days. The next part of my plan comes to a screeching halt if he's not.

My footsteps sound like thunder echoing through the quiet hall. I slide to a stop in front of Mr. Fairweather's classroom. Through the narrow window in the door I see him hunched over his desk, stuffing a sandwich into his mouth as he reads a thick magazine that's probably one of the scientific journals he's always quoting in class.

There's a determined smile on my face in my reflection in

the window. This should be the easy part. Mr. Fairweather's eyes light up whenever anyone shows the slightest interest in something he's taught in chem class. I never thought his lessons on how law enforcement agencies use science to solve crimes would be something I'd need.

I pound on the door. I'm bopping around like a little kid who has to use the restroom as I watch him casually look up and frown before dropping his sandwich and slowly walking to the door.

"Marcel, shouldn't you be at lunch?" he says, sliding his thick glasses higher on his nose.

I push past him into the classroom, my excitement causing his brow to furrow. "Mr. Fairweather, I need a huge favor. I couldn't wait until class tomorrow to ask."

"Okay." He slowly shuts the door. "What's got you so worked up?"

"Can I borrow your black light, and do you have any more of that luminol you used for that lesson on forensic science a few weeks ago?"

He stuffs his hands into the pockets of the white lab coat he wears over his clothes every day, for who knows what reason—this is a high school classroom, not some chemical lab doing bioresearch. "Yes, but what's this about?"

"Didn't you say black lights can be used to pick up traces of things like urine, semen, and blood?" I ask, even though I already know the answer.

"Yeeessss," he drawls, still eyeing me cautiously.

"Don't tell anyone, please; my father would kill me," I plead.

"But I want to prove to him how lazy the waitstaff is at one of his restaurants. Let's just say I think a lot of them have been hooking up in the storage room, and I'm hoping that showing him proof of that will make him a little more supportive of the money he's spending on my tuition here."

Mr. Fairweather still looks unsure.

"I thought about your lesson and figured you'd let me borrow your portable black light and that stuff you spray to pick up the fluorescent molecules in body fluids. Help a brother score some points with his dad," I say with an enthusiastic smile.

"Gotta say, this is the last thing I'd expect your family to be thinking about, given what's going on, but I can understand needing the distraction." He starts toward the supply closet. "Plus, I'm glad you were paying attention and are applying what you're learning in the real world."

My insides are vibrating. I knew he would bite.

"I'd be inclined to give you some extra-credit points if you tell me your findings," he yells to me while he's rummaging in the closet. "Maybe film your use of these. Write up a little report. And I'll see what I can do for some bonus points."

He emerges with the portable black light in one hand and the spray bottle of luminol in the other. "Deal?"

"Deal."

With fifteen minutes left, I run out to the student parking lot. We're not supposed to be out here except during arrival and dismissal, so I crouch down and weave through the cars so no one can see me. Trey's black Camaro ZL1 sits in the center of the lot, three rows in front of my Tesla.

My stomach twitches as I near his car.

Don't let all this have been for nothing.

If Chloe was bleeding as much as Amir said she was when he found her body, there's a good chance some of her blood splattered onto the person who stabbed her. If I'm right and it was Trey, he has to have had blood on him. And some of that blood would likely have gotten on the interior of his car, especially his steering wheel—unless he showered or washed his hands at Chloe's before he managed to sneak out. Highly unlikely, given the time line we're working with.

I mash the Unlock button on his key fob.

Even if he had his car cleaned, which he likely did, the black light should still pick up traces and smudges of the blood or cleaning agent—at least, that's what Mr. Fairweather told us.

I open his car door and kneel down with the portable black light and the spray bottle.

Please let this work. This could change everything.

Trey's car isn't messy, but there are loose papers stuffed in compartments and cup holders. A pair of sneakers and a gym bag are strewn across the back seat.

With ten minutes left before my lunch break ends, I start dousing the driver's seat with the luminol. Hopefully the sun will have dried it by the time school lets out. I hit the steering wheel too, and the floorboard, in case he stepped in any blood.

After setting the spray bottle on the concrete, I turn on the black light.

Beneath the light's ultraviolet rays, blood gives off a bluish glow. It did when Mr. Fairweather showed us examples in class.

My pounding heart slows as I run the black light across the driver's seat. Nothing. Not even a speck. My ribs squeeze my lungs when the same thing happens with the steering wheel. More disappointment on the floorboard.

Noooooo!

I turn off the black light and drop it on the driver's seat, defeated.

Yeah, *CSI: Truman Academy* was a long shot. But it was a logical plan.

I lean inside Trey's car and search, desperate for something, anything that will prove I'm not thinking about this all wrong. I prop my knee on the driver's seat and reach into the back to look through his gym bag. Periodically I glance over my shoulder to peer out the front window and make sure no one's coming. If I get caught, there's no telling what the consequences will be. I don't want to face anyone unless I have evidence that will clear Amir.

All I find are stinky gym clothes, a jump rope, and workout gloves. No bloody garments, which he probably wouldn't still be driving around with anyway. I check the bottom of the sneakers in case he wore them that night. I spray the soles of each. The black light reveals nothing. I frantically look around the interior: less than five minutes before the bell rings. I'm going to be late for class. And for nothing.

As I'm backing out of the car, my wandering gaze stops on a folded piece of paper jammed in the cup holder between the driver's and passenger's seats. It's familiar. I've gotten enough parking tickets in this city to know one when I see one.

I pull it out and unfold it, and my heart picks up again. It wouldn't be out of the ordinary for Trey to have a ticket, except for the date and time scribbled at the top.

I stand up, knocking my head on the roof of the car, and study the flimsy piece of paper more closely.

Trey Winslow was illegally parked on Washington Avenue at 1:45 a.m. the night Chloe was murdered.

Two things about that make me stand a little taller: he was illegally parked somewhere more than two miles from where he lives and just three blocks from Chloe's house, within the time frame police believe she was murdered.

Trey was in Chloe's neighborhood the night she was killed.

That was all I could think about in political science, which I was tardy for even though I ran all the way from the student parking lot. Finding bloodstains would definitely have given the police another likely suspect other than Amir. But that parking ticket is useful. I can't wait to see how Trey tries to explain what he was doing on Washington Avenue in the middle of the night.

I'm about to jump out of my skin, waiting outside Mrs. Ackerman's class for the bell to ring so I can catch him as soon as he emerges. I know he takes English lit right now because I came over with Chloe a few times to meet him. One of those times was when I discovered that Amir was in the class too, and when he first rebuffed my friendliness. It was embarrassing for it to happen in front of everyone, especially Trey and Chloe.

The bell rings and the hall floods with noisy seniors. I have to wait a few seconds before Trey walks out. I see him as he's tossing his book bag over his shoulder, midconversation with Patrick Rawlings, one of his good friends.

"Yo, Trey, these yours?" I call out, holding up his keys.

His face relaxes when he sees what's dangling from my hand, and he heads my way.

"I found them in the caf," I say, dropping them in the palm he's holding out to me. "Must have fell out of your bag."

"Yeah, good looking out," he says, and turns to rejoin Patrick.

"Hey, where did you go after my party?" I ask, my heart racing.

He pauses and shoots me a confused look. I can't tell if it's real or an act.

"You know, the night Chloe was . . . ," I say, not wanting to finish the sentence.

He tilts his head. "Bruh, what's up with you questioning me?" he says. "I was at home. Asleep."

Got him!

"Really?" I reply with dramatic flair, and pull the parking ticket from my back pocket. "Then who illegally parked your car on Washington Avenue around twelve-forty-five that night?"

His eyes stretch wider than I've ever seen them.

"What were you doing so close to her house that time of night?" I say. "And why did you just lie about it?"

"Did you steal my keys?" he yells, ripping the ticket out my hand. "What's with you Trudeaus? Your brother is a murderer and you're doing auto break-ins now?"

We're starting to attract an audience.

"Don't bother getting rid of that," I say, pointing at the ticket he crumpled in his hand. "I took a photo of it—you know, so I can have the cops pull the number."

Trey's face goes dark. "Oh, is that it? You trying to accuse me of killing her so your trash-ass brother doesn't go to jail?"

Overlapping remarks buzz all around me.

"I *did* witness that argument y'all had the night of my party," I say, holding my ground. "It looked intense. Like maybe you were still in yo' feelings about y'all's breakup. You being in the area that night coupled with you sneaking into her bedroom during her memorial looking for who knows what . . ."

His eyes narrow. "How do you know about— You fucking following me?"

I give him a smug grin, crossing my arms behind my back.

"Trey, bro, wassup?" Patrick says, appearing beside us.

The tension in Trey's face relaxes. "Nothing, dude. Let's go."

"Make sure you answer your phone!" I yell after them. "The police will want to talk to you after I—"

Before I can blink, Trey whips back around, yells, "You faggot-ass!" He snatches hold of my blazer with both hands and lifts me up on my toes, demanding, "What are you trying to do to me?"

A blur sweeps up beside us to my left. And then I hear, "Hold up, hold up. Calm down, man. Let him go."

It's Amir. He's gently patting Trey's right arm, only Trey doesn't let go. He's looking at me like he wants to kill me.

"Trey, Trey, come on, let go," Amir pleads.

Just as quickly as he hemmed me up, Trey takes his right hand and shoves Amir in the face. "Don't fucking touch me!"

"Hey, *get off my brother*!" Amir barks, rushing back up and shoving Trey so hard he releases my blazer and goes flying backward, crashing into the lockers on the other side of the hall.

The crowd explodes with excitement.

Amir looks at me. "You good?"

I'm about to nod when Mr. Horace, who teaches calculus, snatches Amir by the collar. "Trudeau, let's take this to Mr. Braswell's office," he says, dragging Amir away.

Trey has already quietly disappeared into the crowd as I'm left standing in the hall, watching Amir grow smaller and smaller in the distance, my mind swirling over how quickly things went left. A warm feeling swells in my chest. Amid all the confusion with Trey, something happened that has never happened before: Amir didn't refer to me as *half* just now.

He called me his brother.

12

Amir

The way Mama's lips are pinched when Mr. Braswell escorts her into his office makes me slouch lower in the chair. I've been sitting here for at least an hour, alone, staring at his neatly arranged desk. He ordered me to stay put after Mr. Horace dropped me off, then left me to go hear Mr. Horace's version of what went down between me and Trey. I didn't realize he'd left me in here because he was also waiting on my mother to arrive.

She starts rubbing her forehead with her fingertips after she drops into the empty chair next to me.

I know what she must be thinking: *Not again.* First a murder charge. Now I'm getting into fights at school. She's eyeing me, probably searching for some understanding. I can only stare at my feet. Him calling her here ain't good.

Could this day get any worse?

I've gotten evil looks all day, even from some of my teachers. I have no idea who wrote *Murderer!* on my desk this morning.

My teacher claimed he didn't see anyone do it, and he didn't seem to want to investigate—just gave me some paper towels to clean it off and started the class. The rubbernecking and sly comments continued as the day dragged on. I skipped lunch and grabbed some chips out the vending machine to avoid the cafeteria. Ate them by myself on the aluminum bleachers out by the soccer field. Maybe feeling like an outsider was all in my head before, but it's not anymore. No one wants me here. And I wish I didn't care so much that they don't.

"Amir!"

I jump in my seat. Mama's glaring at me with her lips pursed.

"You not going to answer the man?" she says, nodding in Mr. Braswell's direction.

He's got his hands clasped on top of his desk. Mr. Braswell wears a three-piece suit every day. The man's beard and hair are always trimmed to perfection. A picture of him and his Black husband vacationing on a yacht, in a place where the water is so blue it looks fake, is centered on the credenza behind his desk. The husband looks at least fifteen years older. I've never got the feeling this dude likes me. Even before I got arrested.

"Sorry, didn't hear ya," I say.

"Sit up straight," Mama commands, slapping the armrest on my chair. "And watch your tone," she adds as I adjust myself.

That means *Don't use a lot of slang when you talking to this white man; talk like you belong here.* I never had to code-switch at my old school.

"I asked if you would like to tell your mother why you attacked Trey Winslow this afternoon," Mr. Braswell says.

I lean forward. "I didn't attack him. He pushed up on—"

"Tone!" Mama interjects.

I close my eyes, taking a breath. "Trey was physically assaulting Marcel. I tried to calmly squash what was going on. Then *Trey* shoved me in the face, and I defended myself."

"My son isn't an aggressor, Mr. Braswell," my mother adds.

Mr. Braswell looks at me, his face blank. Given what everyone thinks I've done, I'm betting that statement isn't landing like Mama meant it to.

"Trey says you and your brother confronted him in the hall, accusing him of killing Chloe Danvers," Mr. Braswell says.

"What? I didn't do that, he's lying," I protest.

About me, at least. That was all Marcel. Guess he was spinning up the same theories he was spouting at my locker this morning.

"Patrick Rawlings and a few other students who witnessed what happened confirmed this to be true," Mr. Braswell says.

Funny. They could confirm that, but not Trey snatching Marcel up.

It was a knee-jerk reaction, me intervening between Marcel and Trey. Since we were little, I've always looked out for my half brother, even though I never felt he deserved protection. Back when I still visited my dad, Nana would threaten to beat me with a switch if I didn't protect Marcel. "You're the big brother, that's your job, you hear me?" she'd say. Black boys aren't allowed to be sensitive, well-groomed, soft spoken . . . *different.* If we don't subscribe to the toxic masculinity ideals programmed into our heads at an early age, we get bullied. Didn't matter how much I disliked him, I still didn't want to see him get beat up and taunted like other dudes. If anyone was going to tease him, give him a hard time about anything, it would be me. And not because I had a feeling he was gay—I couldn't give a shit. My issues with him run much deeper than that.

"Ms. Trudeau, I won't drag this out any more than I must," Mr. Braswell says, turning toward Mama. "In light of recent events, it might be best if Amir stays at home and shifts to a virtual learning model until things settle down."

"'Settle down'?" Mama repeats. "What does that mean?"

Means he doesn't want me on campus anymore. Not until I'm cleared of murder. Which likely won't happen.

"Tensions are so high here right now. . . . Chloe was loved by everyone," Mr. Braswell says, ignoring my mother's question. "Kids are angry."

"And they should be, but not at my son," Mama argues. "He's innocent. Does innocent until *proven* guilty not mean anything here?"

Mr. Braswell gently lays both palms on his desk. "I'll make sure Amir gets all his assignments so he doesn't fall behind."

"I don't want that. He needs to be at school," Mama says.

"This isn't a choice," Mr. Braswell replies. "The school board is supporting my decision. They feel Amir staying at home will remove a lot of the commotion that Chloe's murder has stirred up."

My mother tilts her head. "And how long is he supposed to do this?"

The look on Mr. Braswell's face says *Until he's no longer accused of murdering a classmate.*

His office door swings open. My dad comes barreling in, looking frantic. I can't believe this man called him too.

"What's going on?" he says to Mr. Braswell, who looks a bit taken aback. My dad looks over at me and adds, "Amir, what have you done now?"

And there it is again: His disappointment. His blame. Again, he's having to stop his life for the son who's been nothing but an inconvenience.

Mama stands up. "They're basically kicking our son out of this school. He's become a distraction, they say."

"Who's *they*?" my dad snaps.

"Him and his board," Mama replies, looking down her nose at Mr. Braswell.

My dad steps up to the desk with his index finger pointed at Mr. Braswell. "I paid this school a whole lot of money to get Amir admitted. I'll be damned if I let you treat him like—"

"Mr. Trudeau, you can take this up with the board, but as I've already told your ex-wife, they fully support my decision," Mr. Braswell says. "Amir will get his assignments. And this arrangement will allow him to focus on other things, like the legal troubles he's about to face."

His condescending tone twists my gut. First I'm accused of

murder, and now I'm exiled from school. *What have I done to deserve this?*

It dawns on me who called my father when we storm out of Mr. Braswell's office. Marcel is waiting in the main office.

"What happened?" he asks.

Mama and I push past him. Neither of us saying anything.

Nana would probably roll over in her grave to hear it, but right now, I'm regretting not letting Trey beat Marcel's ass.

13

Marcel

Mr. Braswell basically kicking Amir out of school is bullshit! Trey was the aggressor. He snapped, clearly because he didn't like the questions I was asking. But nothing happened to him. When I brought that up to Mr. Braswell after Monica and Amir left his office, I was advised to "move on," or else I'd be facing the same disciplinary action as Amir since *I* "technically inflamed" the situation between Trey and my brother.

Amir probably thinks I did too. I know he's gonna find some way to blame me for what happened, ignoring the significance of what I discovered today and how that might help prove he didn't kill Choe. Getting more proof could help me smooth things over, especially if it keeps him from getting indicted in ten days, should the DA's office present the case to the grand jury when Mr. Dillard said they would.

I step out of my car onto Washington Avenue. I managed to find a parking spot about a block away from the renowned Commander's Palace restaurant on the corner of Washington and

Coliseum Street. As I peel off my school uniform blazer, I glance up and down the street. It's mostly a residential thoroughfare, canopied by the sprawling limbs of trees, with a few businesses dotted on the corners where it intersects with other streets. The Lafayette Cemetery takes up the block between Coliseum and Prytania. I can't imagine any reason Trey would be parked out here that late at night other than to sneak to Chloe's house undetected. All the businesses on this street would have been closed that time of night.

He illegally parked within blocks from her house with the intent to hurt her. I can find out exactly why later. Right now, I'm on the hunt for further proof that he was here. I pull out my phone, making sure I have enough battery power. I'm going to need at least two hours to do what I came to do.

A neighbor's doorbell camera implicated Amir. I'm hoping some other security footage might do the same to Trey. He obviously didn't use the same route Amir did, otherwise he would have been seen on the same footage that captured Amir. But if he parked three blocks down from Chloe's house and used an alternate route, maybe there are other homes with similar cameras in the area that recorded him.

Instead of doing homework this afternoon, I mapped out a three-block radius around Chloe's house to walk. I'm going to record the addresses of any homes I see with one of those doorbell camera systems and any businesses that might have surveillance security cameras. I'll give the list to Mr. Dillard, who I'm certain could get a court order to secure any footage they might still have from that night. If need be, I'll help comb through it all to find proof of Trey not only coming and going but, fingers crossed, getting rid of the knife too.

If there is a God, make this happen. Amen, I say to myself as I'm turning the corner onto Magazine Street toward Second Street, where Chloe lives.

It takes about forty-five minutes for me to walk both sides of Magazine, and up and down a few blocks of Fourth and Third Streets, in case he used one of them to take a back way to get to Chloe's. I've keyed more than a dozen addresses with doorbell cams I could see from the sidewalk into my Notes app. I skip Chloe's street and turn down First, walking deeper into the Garden District before taking a left on Coliseum, which will lead me back to Washington Avenue. I make a left from Coliseum onto Washington, by Commander's Palace. I'm approaching Chestnut when I see something that brings me to an abrupt stop.

It's the Belmont. A chic, Renaissance-style mansion on the corner of Chestnut and Washington that has been renovated into a boutique hotel. Something about the emblem in the center of the awning over the front entrance intrigues me. I've seen it before. Somewhere recently.

And then the memory clicks into place.

It was on the letterhead of that piece of paper that was stuck to the bottom of my shoe in Chloe's bedroom. There was a number scribbled on it in her handwriting too. What was it?

Oh, that's right. 2709.

Wonder what that means. The question pulls me across the street, and as I get closer, I can see through the hotel's panoramic first-floor windows that there's a bar and restaurant to the right of the double-door entrance. I have to walk around a BMW parked along the curb, waiting for valet service and a doorman, I presume.

I stand on the sidewalk out front, staring at this place. Am I reading too much into this? Is it really so strange that she scribbled a number on a sheet of paper that had obviously been torn from a notepad somewhere inside this building? I shake my head, feeling a little silly.

This is not why I came out here. She could have written that number down who knows how long ago. Proving Trey killed Chloe, that's my focus. Not this.

"What's up, pretty boy. You stalking me?"

I turn around to see Amir's friend Quincy approaching me. He's wearing black slacks and a white T-shirt and has what looks like a red polo slung over his left shoulder. His enthusiastic smile lights up his dark eyes.

"It's more like *you* must be stalking *me,*" I say with a playful grin. "What are *you* doing in *this* neighborhood?"

"*Wooow,* so you saying I don't look like I could afford to live around here?"

I wince. "No, no, that's not what I meant—"

He bends over with laughter. "Chill, bruh. Just messing with you."

He licks his lips. I feel myself blushing and try to hide it by holding my fist in front of my mouth.

Keep it in yo' pants, Marcel. He's Amir's best friend.

"I work here," he says, nodding at the hotel.

That's when it dawns on me the red shirt that's dangling on

his shoulder matches the one on the valet behind the podium near the entrance.

"You work *and* go to school?"

"We can't all live in mansions, attend expensive private schools, and receive brand-new Teslas for our birthday. But it's nice to know some of us is winning, like your family is."

I wouldn't necessarily call what we're going through winning, but he might see my family's current situation as more of an Amir problem than ours. That's why I shrug and say nothing.

"I work here part-time after school," he continues. "To help my moms out. You know, so she won't have to worry about buying me stuff and can focus on getting whatever my little brother and sister need."

He's all about family and working hard. His lean, muscular arms are also looking good in his T-shirt. I'm picturing a tight little six-pack underneath.

"You meeting someone?" he asks, pointing at the Belmont.

"Nah, I was in the neighborhood to . . . well, trying to help Amir," I decide to admit.

Seriousness enters Quincy's face.

"How's he holding up?" Quincy asks. "We hit his cell the day he was released on bail, you know, to let him know the police talked to us too."

"What'd they ask y'all?"

"They were trying to see if maybe it was a setup," Quincy says. "Like, Amir let us in to rob that girl's crib and then what happened, happened. Once they realized our alibis checked out, they were through with us. Wasn't even interested when we tried to tell them Amir ain't the type of dude to kill somebod."

"Same when I talked to them," I interject.

"He hasn't really responded to any of our texts or phone calls," Quincy says. "I dropped by the house Saturday, but no one answered, even though I know his ass was home on house arrest."

"He could have been sleeping," I offer as an excuse.

"That's what he'll say, but I know him," Quincy says with a shrug. "This is what he does. Ghosts us whenever shit gets tough and he doesn't wanna really deal. He did it when y'all's grandmother got sick and died. And for a little while when he stopped attending Douglas Egan with us to go to Truman with you. He closes himself off and then will resurface acting like nothing happened."

But he called them his family. Should make me feel better he treats his friends just as foul as he treats me, but it doesn't.

"I'm out here hoping to prove that he's innocent," I say, rubbing the back of my neck.

"How?"

I tell Quincy about Chloe's balloon release, seeing Trey go through her room, finding that parking ticket, and our confrontation at school today.

"See, I knew I didn't like that Carlton Banks knockoff," he says when I'm done.

"I stopped here because when I was in her room, I found a piece of paper with this hotel's letterhead on it and— Hey," I say, shifting my weight from one foot to the other. "Is the number 2709 related to anything here? It was written in Chloe's handwriting on that paper."

Quincy frowns. "Probably a room number. They're all four digits."

Why on earth would she need to scribble down a room number here?

"Could you do me a favor?" I say to Quincy.

It won't hurt to have him do a little side detective work for me while I continue to focus on Trey, who coincidentally *was* parked on the same street as this hotel the night of Chloe's murder.

"Anything," he replies, licking his plump lips again.

You cannot hook up with him. You cannot hook up with him. You. Cannot. Hook up. With. Him.

"Could you check around and see if that room number could somehow be linked to her—Chloe?" I say. "Just for the hell of it, see if there was someone staying there the night she was murdered."

He nods. "Anything to help my boy out. What you think going on?"

"I really have no idea," I say, more to myself than to him.

"Yo, Q, come on, man!" the valet at the stand yells. "I ready to clock out dis bitch!"

"I think you better go before you get fired," I tease.

"Check it. If I find something out, how am I going to reach you?" he asks. "Since you don't answer your DMs on the Gram."

I look down at my phone and unlock it. "You DM'd me?"

He nods.

I haven't really been on social media since Amir's arrest. It took seeing a few comments from strangers saying he deserved the electric chair to force my break from it.

"How 'bout this." Quincy yanks my phone out my hand. He starts typing and says, "Here's my number. I just called myself so I can have yours."

He hands it back to me when his starts to ring in his pocket. After saving my number he says, "Now maybe it'll be harder for you to ignore me, pretty boy."

I'm starting to blush again.

"I better go." I begin walking off. "But hit me up if you find out anything, okay?"

"Most definitely."

I still feel his eyes on me when I'm a block away. I look back over my shoulder and Quincy is standing in the same spot on the sidewalk watching me as I continue down Washington Avenue.

Jesus, be a cold shower.

14

Amir

I'm gliding up to my abandoned church on my bike when my phone starts vibrating in my pocket. I wait until I've propped my bike against the side of the ratty building, like I always do, before I check it. It's texts from Marcel.

> Need to ask you something important.
> I'm in the area.
> Can I swing by?

I groan but ping him my location anyway. I've got some things I need to get off my chest. Before I drop my phone back into my pocket, I check the time. My curfew starts in an hour and a half. Mama should be leaving for work by then. I needed to get out of the house for a bit. It's suffocating having her there too. Her disappointment is filling the house stronger than the scent of the shrimp in the gumbo I made on Wednesday.

I squeeze through the chained doors. This is my first time back since the night I brought Chloe here. As I'm walking up the winding staircase to the mezzanine level, I'm going over in my mind what could possibly be so important that Marcel needs to see me. I reach the top and stop abruptly.

Someone is kneeling near the torn-out space along the banister where I usually sit, feeling around on the floor. I can't tell who it is. All I can make out is that they're wearing a black hoodie with an elaborately embroidered face of a cartoon bear on the back, and they're white.

"Yo, what you doing in here?" I ask, and the person shoots to their feet, startled. They whip their head around but stop before I can see their face.

"Fuck!" the person yells, then squats and leaps off the mezzanine through the gap in the banister.

I suck in a sharp breath. "Oh damn!" I yell as I watch dude go falling toward the first floor.

I know it's a guy because of his sneakers and the bass that was in his voice. I hear him hit the floor below, crashing down on God knows what.

He's struggling to stand up when I peer over the rail. His hoodie managed to stay on during the fall, so I still can't make out who it is. He pulls himself to his feet and I'm shocked to see him start hopping toward the chained doors. Why aren't his legs broke?

"Hold up, man!" I shout, scrambling toward the staircase. I need to know who it is and what he was doing up here.

I trip as I'm rushing down the stairs. I grab hold of the wall to catch myself. When I finally make it down, the person's already managed to squeeze out the door. I contort my body and cram myself through the chained double doors as quickly as I can, spilling out onto a quiet street. My instinct is to go right, but there's no movement that way. I spin around—if not right, he had to go left—but that side of the street is just as still. Dude vanished into thin air like some kind of ghost.

Behind me I hear a door open and turn to see Marcel getting out of his car. He looks around and spots me in front of the church and heads my way. He's still wearing his school uniform—minus the blazer. I took mine off when I got home today, feeling some type of way because there's a good chance I might never put it on again.

"Bruh, did you see who that was running away from here?" I ask, pointing back at my run-down church. "White dude with a cartoon bear stitched on the back of a black hoodie. He had to be limping a little."

Marcel scratches his bush of black curls with a frown. "Uh, no. Kinda wasn't paying attention either. What is this place?"

"My spot," I reply, looking past him up the street before casting a confused look over my shoulder to make sure I still don't see whoever that was.

How did he vanish so quickly?

Today is the first time there has ever been anyone here besides me. Why did dude take off so fast when I showed up? If he happened to stumble upon this place like I did, wouldn't he have stuck around and asked questions?

"Is this where you brought Chloe?" Marcel asks, taking in the derelict church with the same scrutiny she did that night.

"Yeah."

The mystery of my unexpected guest starts to fade into the back of my mind, replaced by my aggravation with Marcel, now that he's here.

"Speaking of, did she mention anything to you about the Belmont Hotel?" he says, face serious.

I shake my head.

"Cool. May be nothing, may not be." He stuffs his hands into his pockets. "You good? I mean, I know you're not, after what went down at school. That's the other thing I wanted to talk to you about. I'm sorry how—"

"Nah," I cut him off. "I need to get this off my chest first. Did you accuse Trey of killing her? Is that why he was about to stomp yo' ass?"

Marcel yanks his hands from his pockets and throws them out, exasperated. "He was in Chloe's neighborhood around the time she was killed," he says, voice rising. "I stole his car keys, to do something that ended up being a dead end, but I found a parking ticket he got near her house around the time she was murdered."

"So let me get this straight," I say. "You stole dude's keys and snuck into his car, but *I'm* the one that got in trouble."

His shoulders crumple. "I'm sorry about that."

"Bruh, stop!"

"Stop what?" he replies, his brow furrowed. "Trying to keep you from getting indicted?"

Something snaps inside me.

"Why is it that every time *you* do something stupid, it's me who suffers the consequences?" I yell.

He takes a deep, pained breath while closing his eyes. He has to know I'm talking about his mother's dog too.

"You making shit worse, not better," I rant. "That's all you ever do. Mess up *my* life while you come out smelling like roses."

"I'd hardly call my friends not talking to me anymore *smelling like roses,*" he replies.

"Awww, poor you," I say mockingly. "He's mad 'cause his shallow friends won't talk to him anymore. Boo-*fucking*-hoo! I'm dealing with real life! My life! Which is pretty much over."

"Only if you give up, and I'm not giving up. If we—"

"If we nothing!" I shout. "There is no *we.* Never has been. There's only me. And niggas like me don't get out from under the shit I'm facing."

"You can't if you sit back and just let it happen," he rails.

I smack my lips. "You'll never understand where I'm coming from. You ain't really Black like me."

He flinches. "What's *that* supposed to mean?"

My frustration with him, his entire being, has flared into resentment so strong it's burning up the back of my neck and snaking its way behind my ears.

"You're privileged, Marcel!" I shout. "Privileged to live in your bougie bubble where you don't have to think about race or worry about anyone thinking less of you. You have the money. The status. They've accepted you."

"They *who*?"

"White people! Your friends. This world, *them,* they don't see you the way they see me," I say, stabbing myself in the chest with my finger.

"So what are you saying?" he says. "That because I haven't struggled, I'm not Black enough? Why does everything about the Black experience in this country have to be about struggling?"

"Because for most of us, it is."

He huffs at my response.

"What's the first thing that comes to yo' mind when the cops pull you over?" I press.

"That I hope I don't get a ticket."

"Mine is that I hope I won't die," I say through clenched teeth. "That's what I'm talking about. You don't move through the world like I do. The rest of us don't get out of situations like the one I'm in. We get sucked into the system. Then our lives become all about survival. And that's what I need to be focusing on right now, surviving."

"I'm not about to apologize for who I am; not to you, not to anyone," Marcel snaps. "I'm also not about to let you cast me like I'm some out-of-touch wannabe who could never understand where you're coming from. I'm glad that I get to move in the circles I do. It's taught me how not to give up. How to fight for what I want and the people I love. How to be smart enough to play the game just as hard, and win. That's what I'm trying to do for you. I'm here, Amir. Fighting. For you. Even though you treat me like shit."

"'Cause all you do is fuck up *my* life, as if you haven't taken enough already," I reply.

"What have I taken from you?"

"The life I was supposed to have!" I scream, letting years of frustration pour out of me. "You got it all. Even our father. You were born, and I became the *other* son. He didn't want me anymore. Didn't even really try to stay in my life. Just let my mother have me and said fuck it. What's there to fight for when your own dad barely acknowledges you after he falls out of love with your mother? You have any idea what that does to a person, to know your own parent who brought you into this world was ready to toss you aside after he created a new family?"

He can only stare back at me, a pained look twisting his face.

"Why wasn't I enough?" I ask, tears pooling in my eyes. *"Why wasn't I enough?"* I shout, startling him.

He takes a few seconds to breathe deeply. "Amir, I want to be a better brother. Show you that you don't have to sit back and let this happen to you. We can fight this. We can get to the truth."

I don't want a pep talk from him. There's more I have to get off my chest. Things I've always wanted to say to him. And there's no time like the present.

"You know what the truth is, bruh?" I begin, my voice low and measured. "I wouldn't have to stand here and be dealing with this, with you, had our father not been a simp and fallen for a woman who had no problem being a sidepiece, wrecking a happy home, then acting like she's so above it all after she got pregnant to secure a ring. Doubt your gold-digging-ass mama would have married him if he hadn't finally become a success after leaving us."

Marcel swallows hard and then bites down on his bottom lip. "Let me burst your bubble right quick, *brother*," he says, and takes a step forward. "Yeah, my mom slept with a married man, and I'm not saying that like it's something to be proud of, but she wasn't a home-wrecker. That house was already falling apart. Monica opened the door when she stopped believing in our father when he was struggling and they could barely make ends meet. I doubt Daddy would have even entertained an affair had Monica not given him an ultimatum: her or the restaurant."

"Bruh, you really standing here trying to justify his cheating?" I say through clenched teeth.

Marcel takes another step toward me, his mouth tight. "And another thing: I know your mother *told* you our father turned his back on you after he left her, but that was a lie. He fought for you. He was going to challenge Monica for joint custody of you in the divorce."

"That's a cap and you know it," I snap.

"It's the *truth,*" he says. "The only reason he dropped it was because of Nana. She told him that he had already hurt your mother enough by starting the affair with mine, that it would be cruel to also fight her in court for you. So he took her advice and settled for the weekend visits Nana talked your mother into. I know that's not the version of the story she told you. *Both* of our parents did fucked-up stuff."

This dude will say anything to win an argument. To save face after I called *his* mother out. I'm glad we got to do this. Maybe this will end his dumb crusade to honor the dead woman we both loved.

"Don't believe me, ask Monica," he continues.

"Keep my mother's name out yo' mouth." I swipe away a tear, closing more of the distance between us by stepping forward. "Or I'll finish what Trey started."

He doesn't look fazed by my threat.

"I'm thinking she's been lying to you out of jealousy," he says. "Or she was hurt. Probably both. Making sure you hated our father as much as she did was the only way she knew how to deal with the unfortunate truth that if she had held on a little bit longer and our dad not cheated on her, he would've still been married to her when everything turned around for him."

That turnaround moment happened two years after Hurricane Katrina, when I was approaching my first birthday. An actor who was overseeing a recovery effort project in the city rolled into my dad's first restaurant, Tru, one afternoon and ate food so good, it was all he talked about in interviews after that. The actor hired my dad as a private chef for some of the fundraising events he hosted, and things just snowballed from there. Made him into the man he is today.

"There are a lot of people you have a right to be mad at, bro," he says. "And your mother isn't exempt from that."

And then, before I can open my mouth to respond, he turns and walks off, leaving me with something I refuse to believe.

Mama drags in from another night shift in the ER as I'm turning off the burner under the skillet I made breakfast pizzas in.

"You got it smelling good in here again," she says, dropping her purse and duffel bag on the love seat.

It's the nicest thing she's said to me since we got home yesterday. She's looking like she always does after work: her hair slightly disheveled, her shoulders slumped, and her face etched with worry lines.

Even though I didn't have to wake up for school this morning, my eyes still opened at six-thirty. I didn't really get much sleep last night. The stress that has become my life has my mind wired. Needing to think about anything except prison, I started cooking.

"You hungry?" I ask as I scoop two breakfast pizzas onto a plate for her.

"You don't even need to ask that, boy, you know I am."

She smiles at me. Haven't seen her do that since I was bailed out of jail.

I set the plate down in front of one of the stools at the island. While I'm fixing a plate for myself, she walks over to the refrigerator and pours us each a glass of orange juice, then sits.

It feels like any other school morning. Her coming home from work and us eating breakfast together. Of course, I won't be rushing off today. I got an email yesterday evening with my log-in credentials and instructions on when and how I'll need to sign in to Truman's student portal later this afternoon for my assignments.

"They got their money outta me last night," my mother says as I'm carrying my plate over to the island.

She says that almost every time she gets home from work.

"What was the wildest thing that happened?" I ask, plopping down on the stool across from her.

"Chile, this group of drunk frat boys come stumbling in around three a.m. with a boy who jumped off the roof of their fraternity house and almost cracked open his head," she says. "Oh! This freaky couple rolled up too. I'll spare you the details. I'll just say, something that should never be inserted in someone's body got stuck someplace it shouldn't be, and it wasn't the woman's body."

I chuckle, shaking my head. "Your job is wild."

We eat in silence a few minutes. I look up at her, my mouth stuffed with pizza, when I feel her eyes on me. Her forehead is wrinkled with lines of concern.

"How you doing over there, kiddo?" she says.

I sit up straighter and shrug. "I'm good. Maintaining." I swallow my bite and add, "You know how I do."

My reassuring grin doesn't relax the tension in her face.

"Yeah, I know how you do. That's what I don't want you doing, feeling defeated," she says, breaking off a piece of her pizza with her hand. "We're gonna get you through this. I don't know how yet. Just know I'm not letting them take you away from me."

I push my plate aside, even though I haven't finished. I know she thinks it's her job to always be positive. Keep me encouraged. But she can't really believe that. Not about what I'm facing. I'd rather be sitting here talking about how we'll get through me going to jail. Who's gonna look after the yard, the house. But I also don't want her to worry. Nana used to say, *That's what mothers do . . . worry. Ain't no stopping it.* It still makes me feel sick to see Mama like this, though.

"You heard from Mr. Dillard?" she asks. "He making any progress keeping this indictment from happening?"

I shake my head, my eyes focused on the plate of food I no longer have an appetite for.

"I'ma call you father today and see what he's paying all this money for if getting you out from under this isn't that man's top priority," she says, stuffing the piece of pizza she broke off into her mouth and chewing it aggressively.

"That grand jury thing ain't happening for another nine days, Mama," I remind her.

"You act like that's a long time; be here before you know it," she says, her voice rising. "This man is supposed to be the best. I want results."

I take a sip of orange juice. "Don't worry, he ain't the only one working on the case."

Mama's eyebrows shoot up. "Really? Who else is?"

"Marcel."

Her head jerks back. "What's he supposed to do?"

"Calls himself investigating, I guess." I sigh. "That's why I got into it with Senator Winslow's son yesterday. Marcel was confronting Trey about something he found in his car. Long story short, he thinks Trey could have killed Chloe. He was her ex."

"Really?" Mama leans forward, her eyes widening. "It usually *is* the boyfriend. Might need to be a little nicer to the li'l spoiled brat if he's finally being selfless—unlike his mama."

"Don't be," I huff, thinking of our argument yesterday. "You know he called you a liar?"

"Who did?" Mama replies, surprised.

"Marcel."

"What could he possibly say *I* lied about?" she says, her eyes flicking upward as she breaks off another bite of pizza.

Some of the anger I felt yesterday simmers in my chest.

"He tried to say that the Man Who's Name I'm Not About to Say in This House wanted joint custody of me, and that the only reason he didn't pursue it was because Nana asked him not to," I tell her. "Lying 'cause he was mad I called his mama a THOT who threw herself at a happily married man. You right about them. They don't want to see us happy. It's a trip how they hate on us after they did all the foul sh—*stuff*."

I'm expecting her to laugh with me. Maybe curse in agreement. But the silence that follows hardens my stomach. Her downturned mouth is answer enough. I start to feel light-headed.

"Mama, that's crazy, right?" I prod, trying to give her a lifeline. Force her to deny it. "He made that up, *right*? You said that man gladly gave you sole custody since he had another son on the way."

She slowly clenches her fists. "Amir . . ."

"Amir nothing," I snap, shooting up off the stool. "All I want to hear you say is that he was lying."

"Watch yo' tone," she warns.

I slam my fist down on the island countertop. "Watch nothing! Is that true?"

"It doesn't change everything your father put you through," she argues.

"But it *does* change how you look in all this," I reply. "So was

Marcel right about why you've been lying to me all these years too? You were jealous that Dad got rich after he left you."

"I believed in him," she shouts. "It was me who was paying all the damn bills and working my ass off in that restaurant when it was nothing but a money pit. I was the one stressed with being a new mother and trying to build up a man who was flailing. I could only do and take so much. That restaurant was an albatross. Did he once thank me for all I had to sacrifice? No, he cheated on me!"

"And then you lie and say he didn't want me either," I yell. "What else did you do to come between us?"

She stands and darts around the island to get up in my face. "Don't you dare go there with me, boy! I sacrificed everything to make sure you still had love, a good life. I ain't ballin' outta control like your father, but I ain't some welfare queen either."

"But you lied to me about him—about the part you played in what happened between us." I'm holding back tears.

It looks like she's about to cry too, but I don't care.

"I'm out, man. Both of y'all ain't shit," I say, storming to my bedroom.

"Amir!" she calls after me, but I keep walking.

"None of that changes how much I love you," she yells. "I did the best I could!"

She says other stuff, but I don't hear any of it. As soon as I slam my bedroom door, I put on my noise-canceling headphones and drown in Lil Baby lyrics and my blinding rage.

15

Marcel

I'm straightening the knot of my uniform bow tie when my phone chimes. I adjust the navy V-neck I chose to wear today instead of my uniform blazer and I grab my phone off my nightstand. There's a text from Quincy. Seeing his name pop up in my notifications is rejuvenating.

Can you talk? he asks.

Yeah, I reply.

My ringtone immediately sounds and I hit accept. "Hello," I answer.

"You happen to have any dreams about me last night?" he says, his voice sounding even sexier over the phone.

"Boy, I need to eat breakfast so I'm not late for school," I say, but for some reason I sit down on the edge of my unmade bed instead of grabbing my messenger bag off my desk and heading downstairs like I need to.

"I know. I know." I hear a door close in the background. "I'ma miss my bus if I don't stop playing around. But wanted to drop some intel I got on that number you gave me yesterday."

That conversation feels like it took place last month instead of sixteen hours ago. I had forgotten it even occurred until just now. After my blowup with Amir yesterday, I said I was done. With him and with trying to keep him from getting indicted. A person can only take so much, and him basically calling my mother a side ho was my breaking point. I had intended to find an easier way to break the news that his mother lied about our father giving her sole custody because he didn't want anything to do with her or Amir after the divorce. Blurting it out in anger was the only comeback I could think of after what he said about my mother. Yes, my parents' affair was indefensible, but they're still my parents. My mother didn't even know my father was married at first. She only found out later. My father was supposed to just be a "one-night type of thing" after a bad breakup, something my mother was forced to explain to me after I overheard Monica call her a home-wrecking ho during a heated exchange when Monica was dropping Amir off for a visit when we were younger.

As for all the custody drama, I learned the truth from Nana, who told me before she died how Amir had repeated some of his mother's lies to her over the years. She could never bring herself to correct him, Nana claimed. Even though she felt it was wrong, she forever empathized with Amir's mother.

"Cheating is a hard thing for any woman to ever really get over," she said. "But your brother needs to know—not that I think it will change how he feels about yo' daddy," Nana also said to me. "We'll never heal until we start dealing in truth. I just don't have the strength to fight anymore."

Now I don't know if I do either.

If Amir wants to wallow in pity and resentment, maybe I should let him. I'm sick of his attitude, especially toward me. He has a lawyer; let Mr. Dillard worry about keeping him out of prison. However, I *am* still curious why Chloe scribbled down that room number.

"Does it have anything to do with Chloe?" I ask Quincy.

"Nah, not her; yo' boy," he replies.

"Who?"

"That dude Trey. Carlton Banks two point oh."

"How?" I ask, immediately intrigued.

"Check it, folks at the hotel were tight-lipped when I started asking questions," Quincy says, speaking louder as a car zooms by in the background of wherever he is. "It wasn't until I talked to Mrs. Ruba, who works in housekeeping, that I got some tea on this. She likes me. Says I remind her of her grandson. It also helped that I told her whatever she knew might help Amir. She doesn't like how they're painting him in the news. Told me all the ladies on her church's usher board are praying for him."

I frantically nod, forgetting that Quincy can't see my impatience through the phone. "Quincy, focus. The number," I say.

"Yeah, right. Sorry. Apparently, that's the number of the room Winslow books every time he meets up with this white lady he's been smashing for a hot minute."

"Wait. So Trey was cheating on Chloe with some older

woman?" Saying it out loud doesn't sound believable. But it doesn't feel natural either. Doesn't feel like it fits into a narrative that I've built around why he would've killed Chloe.

"Nah, bruh. Not him, his father," Quincy says. "*Senator* Winslow."

A heavy feeling fills my gut.

"And the woman he's been meeting up with ain't his wife," Quincy adds.

"No shit, his wife is Black." I stand up. "You know who she is? The white woman?"

"Vivian Crane, or Crosby, or Cody—shit, I can't remember what Mrs. Ruba said," Quincy says. "The white woman is the one who reserves the room, I guess to keep yo' boy's father's name off the reservation books."

Vivian Crane. That name sounds more familiar than the other ones Quincy said. I just can't connect why in my mind.

"Does this help Amir?" Quincy asks.

"Maybe. I'm not really sure yet."

Quincy doesn't need to know about our fight, or that I've decided to disengage myself from Amir's legal defense.

"Cool. Well, my bus is pulling up." In the background I hear the *soosh* of air brakes. "You owe me now."

"For what?"

"This! My detective skills," he says.

I can tell from the sound of his voice he probably has a flirtatious smile on his face.

My heart is doing that flutter-kicking thing. "What do you want as repayment?"

"I'll let you know. Have a good day, pretty boy."

This tingling feeling in my chest might have lasted longer after Quincy hung up if I weren't reeling from everything he just told me.

The Belmont Hotel is where Trey's father has been meeting up with his sneaky link on the regular. In room 2709. Which Chloe wrote down on a piece of paper from a notepad with the hotel's letterhead.

I open the Google app on my phone. Who is this Vivian Crane woman? It only takes a second for the search results to come up, and I know immediately why her name sounds so familiar. She's the executive director of Christian Families First, an alt-right conservative group that prides itself on being on the wrong side of nearly every debate. Things like abortion, critical race theory, book banning, transgender rights—you name it. Chloe showed me a clip once of this woman using the great replacement theory to defend the organization's stance against our country's immigration policies.

A clip that went viral of Trey's father berating her organization during a congressional meeting over their efforts to ban the mention of slavery in school textbooks is included in the search results too. What Senator Winslow said in that clip sparked chatter among political commentators about his possible run for a higher office, like governor, or in a few years, president.

Senator Winslow is cheating on his wife with Vivian Crane?

If his constituents, the Black ones especially, knew this, he could forget getting reelected this year. He's basically sleeping with the enemy. Cheating on his *Black* wife with a woman who doesn't think white kids should have to learn about slavery in school because they shouldn't be made to feel guilty.

I might be thinking about this all wrong. What was it that I overheard Trey shout to Chloe at my party? I rack my brain, pacing around my bedroom. Their tension looks completely different when I add the love notes and expensive gifts in the closet to the equation. Was Trey trying to buy her silence?

You tell anybody else? is what I remember Trey saying after I shut the door. And I *think* Chloe said something about his family being the last thing on her mind. If Trey didn't believe she was telling the truth, one fail-safe way to make sure no one else found out what his father was up to was to make sure that person couldn't. I'm guessing Chloe found out about the affair first, then told Trey, who no doubt wouldn't want the story getting out. But knowing Chloe, she'd want the world to know the senator isn't the man he presents himself to be, given how much she used to build him up. Trey had to be worried she'd say something to someone. Maybe to me. Maybe to her parents, who like mine were also big donors to Senator Winslow's campaign. The media would have a field day.

There's a motive to kill that feels more like Trey.

I only have twenty minutes to eat breakfast and get to school. I grab my messenger bag and haul ass downstairs.

As I'm descending the staircase, I can hear my father's voice from inside his office. I slow down, quieting my steps. He sounds frustrated. I tiptoe across the foyer, edging up against the wall next to the doorway. My father is standing in the middle of the room with his back to me, his phone pressed to his ear.

"This is absurd. We were ready to go into production next month," he complains. "This deal was worth millions."

After a brief pause he says, "They shouldn't be allowed to back out this late in the game. I can't supplement the amount of capital it's going to take to keep the current timetable."

He must be referring to his seasonings and sauces line. His sole focus for the past year.

"Is there anything we can do to stop them from pulling out?" my father asks in a defeated tone. The silent ten seconds that follow feel like ten minutes. "I'm not doing that, Paul," I finally hear him say. "He's my son. I need to stand by him. I got to stand by him.

"Don't see how you're so *caught off guard* by that," he says. "He is my son."

After another brief silence my father hisses, "He's innocent. He says he didn't do it. And if you want to keep your job, I better not hear you question that, or my parenting of him, again!"

Someone's watching me. I look up and see my mother directly across the foyer, standing near the doorway to the kitchen. One of her perfectly arched eyebrows lifts before she beckons me with the curl of her index finger.

"What's going on?" I ask, entering the kitchen.

Our house manager, Mrs. Young, looks up from the iPad she's cradling in her hands on the other side of the island, no doubt making her daily checklist of things she'll either need to do herself around here today or make sure the part-time staff does it. She's worked for us since I was seven. I jokingly call her Auntie. Plastic wrap covers a plate of eggs, sausage, and two waffles on the island countertop. I'm guessing she cooked that for me. But I don't seem to have an appetite anymore.

"The investors for your father's seasonings line have pretty much pulled their financial backing," my mother says, stopping in front of the steaming mug of coffee beside a copy of this morning's newspaper on the other end of the island. "They don't like all the *negative press* his brand has become entangled with."

"You can't be serious," I say.

My mother folds her arms across her chest and leans her hip against the island before crossing one ankle over the other. "And the hits keep coming. All this negative press is hurting the restaurants too. Folks have been canceling reservations at Truffles since Friday. It's practically been a ghost town there and at Trudeau's the last four days. Things at Tru aren't as bad, so there's that."

Truffles is my father's fine dining offering, while Trudeau's is the elevated sports bar down the street from it. Trudeau's usually draws a mixed crowd that heavily leans white, while Truffles has a more affluent customer base that is predominantly whiter. Tru, his first restaurant, in Tremé, remains the popular haunt for the Black community, which is fitting since it's in one of this country's oldest Black neighborhoods.

"The city is sending a clear message," my mother says.

"And what's that?" I say. "Disown your son for killing a white girl and then we'll eat your food again, signed White People?"

"Maybe he should," she says. "Your father has worked too hard for his reputation, his brand, to get damaged beyond repair."

Watching her casually sip her coffee after she says that

stiffens my jaw. Nana's biggest issue with my mother was this. The way my mother did more to divide my father and Amir than bring them closer.

"What kind of woman discourages a man—a Black man, at that—from being a father to his child?" I heard her say to a friend once when she thought I wasn't listening. "I tell you what kind: 'I ain't sayin' she a gold digger, but she ain't'—you know the rest."

This is for you, Nana. You too, Amir, I say to myself with a tug on the strap of my messenger bag.

"Mother, don't go there," I warn, brow furrowed.

"Marcel, stop it," she says, holding up a hand at me. "I know you want to have some great relationship with that boy, but he's troubled. He doesn't make good choices. And we have no idea what all he's into. This looks—"

"I know how it looks," I blurt. "Doesn't mean he's guilty."

"Need I remind you what he did to Sparkle?"

This is it. The moment I do what I should have done a long time ago. Be the brother I should be.

I lean forward, my face serious. "News flash: He didn't kill Sparkle. I did."

My mother's eyes flick over to Mrs. Young, whose mouth has dropped open.

"Angela, can you give us a minute alone, please," she says to Mrs. Young, her face tight.

"Yes, ma'am," she says as she leaves the room.

The same panic that immediately came over me after I ignored Amir and set off those firecrackers on Sparkle's tail tingles in my chest right now. I've taken from her the thing she used to build up her contempt toward my brother. Does all of that now get directed at me?

My mother waits until Mrs. Young is gone before saying, "Rewriting history isn't gonna make your case, so don't."

"I'm not rewriting anything, I'm finally telling the truth," I say.

I don't let the disappointment in her eyes stop me from purging the guilt that's attached itself to me, needling every self-righteous emotion I've had up until this moment.

"Amir didn't tie the firecrackers to Sparkle's tail," I continue. "He actually told me *not* to. But I did it anyway. Not with malicious intent. I just did it to do it. 'Cause I thought it would be funny. And her running in the street and getting hit by the car wasn't even the worst of it. After it happened, I stood there and let Amir take the fall, knowing deep down you'd believe he did it. You wanted any reason to hate him just because you couldn't stand his mother, who, let's be honest, had every right to despise you. That's why Amir hates me. *I* hate me. I let what I did come even further between him and Daddy."

My mother presses her hand to her chest, shaking her head at me. "That's not true. Marcel, that's not true. Tell me it's not."

"It is, and I'm sorry," I say. I already feel lighter now that this secret is out in the world. "Do you think *I'm* troubled now? Is it possible I could kill someone after what I did?"

"Of course not, Marcel. You and that boy were raised differently," she counters.

A dam breaks inside me. She'll never understand all the ways we've collectively let Amir down unless I tell her. What better time than now, in this moment when I've already cracked the foundation of the delusions she built around our family? The only truly innocent person among us is Amir. It's time she heard that. From someone she won't be able to compartmentalize her feelings for so easily.

"Mother, let this be the last day you act like an evil Disney stepmother to my brother," I say, pointing at her. "Amir is so hurt by everything *we've* done to him. Could it be that these *bad choices* he's made in life are directly tied to feeling rejected by his father, his stepmother, and his brother? Whatever beef you have with Monica, leave it between y'all. He needs our support right now, even though he acts like he doesn't want it. He needs it. And I swear to God, if you don't give it to him, you're going to lose my love and my respect. I'm serious."

I spin around just as the tears are about to fall.

My father is framed in the doorway behind me.

"You did what?" he barks at me, with the same deep frown he had the day he told Amir to never set foot in this house again.

16

Marcel

I shift my mental energy to Trey, his father's affair, and whether it's the link to Chloe's murder. The rage and disappointment my father hurled at me after overhearing my confession about what really happened to Sparkle will have to wait. If I can prove that Amir is innocent, and repair my father's brand in the process, maybe it'll lessen the blame Amir's put on me for damaging his relationship with our dad. My parents didn't even want to look me in the eye after my father dismissed me. They didn't want to hear anything else. As if I'm solely to blame for Amir's contempt toward our father.

I'm shocked I made it to school on time. There are still five minutes left before classes begin. The first thing I spot when I enter the commons area, where everyone gathers in the morning, is the framed enlargement of Chloe's school portrait that's mounted on a wood easel in the center of the vast indoor space, encircled by a white funeral wreath. I'm able to read the engraved inscription on the frame once I'm up close.

Gone but never forgotten.

I can feel everyone watching me as I stare at her image, struggling to hold in my emotions. We were still supposed to have so much time together. Had made plans for our lives. Convinced ourselves we would remain friends well into adulthood. Her children would call me Uncle. And all of it's been ripped away. Possibly by the person who's seated on a bench across from me. Surrounded by his friends and sister.

Everyone's eyes follow me as I march over to Trey.

I have more information now. I may not know how it all fits together yet, but I can use what I do know to trick him into filling in the gaps for me.

Trey worships his father. Spends hours after school and on weekends working on his father's reelection campaign. If Chloe had information that could derail that, was that motive enough for Trey to kill her? Could be. What doesn't make sense yet is what Trey was looking for in her bedroom. Maybe Chloe had more damaging proof of the affair. That slip of paper from the Belmont Hotel with the number scribbled on it doesn't prove anything without context.

As soon as I step into his sight line, he stops talking.

"Hey, Trey, hoping we could pick up on our little convo from yesterday," I say.

"Oh shit," someone behind us shouts. "We got Trudeau versus Winslow, part two!"

"Bruh, you need to fall back with this," he says, dismissively waving his hand at me.

"I don't think I can," I say. "Not after what I've found out about room 2709 at the Belmont."

Trey's eyebrows drop and his nose crinkles. Tiffany is giving me a panicked look. She steps in front of her brother. "Marcel, please don't do this, not here."

The desperation in her voice tightens my chest.

"Pause, Tiff, I got this," Trey says, pulling his sister behind him. Forever the protector when it comes to his family. "Is that the plan?" he says, his voice lower and nostrils flared. "Bring down another Black man to take the heat off yo' brother?"

"Is that something you heard Vivian Crane say?" I ask with a cocky grin.

"I have no idea what you're talking about," he says. He flashes me a smile, but it doesn't match the panic in his eyes.

"What happened, Trey?" I tuck my hands in my pockets, speaking louder to keep the attention on us. "Chloe threaten to expose what your dad has been up to? Nah, she wouldn't do that to you. She actually cared about you. Was it that you just didn't like that she knew? Were you paranoid that maybe on Mad Day she would say something and then it would all come out anyway? Did she even have proof? I bet she did, didn't she. 'Cause there's no way you would have believed her without it, right?"

"Trudeau, I advise you to shut up," he fumes.

"Or what? Do I have a target on my back now because I know?" I retort. "I damn sure won't keep this to myself if it'll keep my brother from being indicted."

The first-period bell goes off like an explosion in my ears.

Trey and I remain still, eyes locked.

"Come on, let's go, Trey," Tiffany says, pulling on her brother's arm. "Please, Trey. Not here. Not in front of everyone."

Trey huffs at me before letting his sister pull him away. Leaving me with the same questions I had when I approached him.

17

Amir

My legs feel like they're on fire by the time I roll up to Trudeau's on my bike. My dad opened what he calls an elevated sports bar two years after he launched Truffles, his fine dining restaurant. Both are located on North Peters Street, two blocks apart, between Iberville and St. Louis Streets. Keeping up with his business affairs through the press has been my form of emotional cutting. New reasons to deepen my bitterness toward him.

I learned an hour ago that my teachers apparently "didn't have the bandwidth" to upload my assignments to the portal for me today, so instead, Mr. Braswell gave the materials I need to Marcel, who texted me five minutes after I got the email.

> Got yo' stuff. Come get them at Trudeau's . . . or not.
> That's where I'll be till 4:30 p.m.

Had we not got into it yesterday, I know he would have stopped by my house to drop everything to me. He's still in his feelings. Cool. So am I. I ain't gotta be in here long. Grab my assignments from him and bounce. Easy peasy.

I leave my bike propped against the wall next to the open-door entrance to this place. There are hardly any people here, I assume 'cause it's three in the afternoon. It takes a few seconds for my eyes to adjust to the dim lighting after being in the sun for so long. The air smells like deep-fried meats and beer. The decor is all dark leather and polished wood, mounted TVs and walls cluttered with paraphernalia that leans heavily toward the Saints and New Orleans culture. On first sight, I'm not understanding what's so "elevated" about this place. It's giving typical sports bar to me.

Someone calls my name and I turn to find Marcel seated in one of the circular booths lining the wall to my right. He's not alone. Our dad is eyeing me too, along with Mr. Dillard. The sight of them all together, waiting for me, can't be good. I should have known this was some kind of setup when Marcel said to meet him here. I roughly tug on the straps of my backpack as I approach the booth. Mr. Dillard slides closer to my dad to make room for me. There's a basket of buffalo wings in the center of the table that looks untouched. They all have drinks in front of them. And they're all only half-full.

Marcel is seated directly across from me. We don't make eye contact as I'm settling in for whatever is about to go down.

Does this have something to do with my clothes and shoes they found? Or maybe they finally recovered the steak knife.

None of which I should be nervous about. I know I didn't

kill her. That fact doesn't settle the queasiness in my stomach, though.

"You holding up okay, son?" my dad asks.

I can't help but notice the bags underneath his eyes.

"I'm good," I say with a nonchalant shrug. "Just here for my assignments."

"Before we get to that, I wanted to update you on some things," Mr. Dillard says, folding his hands on top of the table.

Here we fucking go. What now?

"I'll get a bit of bad news out of the way first," Mr. Dillard begins. "The DA's office thinks they have enough evidence to present to the grand jury to get an indictment, so that's definitely happening next week."

What could be the good news? I wonder, swallowing the bile I taste in the back of my throat.

"We got some *goodish* news," Mr. Dillard says. "There wasn't any blood or blood residue found on your clothes, which helps in your defense should this thing go to trial. I'm sure they'll attempt to argue you could have washed them before you tossed them or had not been wearing them because you and the girl had sex before you murdered her—we'll get the coroner's report showing no signs of sexual activity to shoot that theory down."

Good to hear, but it still doesn't sound like enough to keep me from going to prison.

"And your brother might have come through with another suspect we can use to establish reasonable doubt ahead of a possible trial," Mr. Dillard says.

"I'm paying you to *stop* this from ever getting that far," my dad interjects.

"Martin, even if he's indicted a trial won't happen for some time," Mr. Dillard says.

"I want this over ASAP," my dad rails, stabbing the table with his index finger. "This is affecting our entire family."

I've seen what people have been saying about him online. I'd feel happier about them calling him out for being a shitty father if my life and freedom weren't on the line because of it.

Mr. Dillard waits a beat to finish his thought. "Marcel has given me some circumstantial evidence I could use to throw suspicion on this girl's ex-boyfriend, that senator's son, in the media," he says. "Sparking reasonable-doubt debates in the public discourse can help in cases like this."

I look over at Marcel, whose eyes are on Mr. Dillard. Whatever he's found out about Trey has to be legit for Mr. Dillard to think it's usable. Won't let that soften my feelings toward him.

"I don't like this," my dad says. "I don't want us potentially tearing down another prominent Black family if we don't have to. The evidence needs to be solid that his son could have done this."

"Daddy, what about them tearing us down if Trey really killed her?" Marcel argues. "He's letting Amir take the fall, and look what's happening to us."

"Marcel, I'm not going back and forth with you about this," my dad replies, his voice getting louder. "I'm not with that crabs in a barrel bullshit we can do to one another. No one should have to deal with what this is doing to us."

Him not wanting to tear down another Black family to win back the public's favorability proves he can be unselfish . . . when he wants to. Where was this man seventeen years ago?

"Fine, we won't call him out in the media yet," Mr. Dillard says. "There may be another option. While my investigator was checking out some of those addresses you gave me, Marcel, he was able to get ahold of some surveillance footage from a convenience store in the neighborhood. Apparently, y'all's principal was in the area too around the time of the murder."

"Mr. Braswell?" Marcel asks, eyebrows shooting up.

Mr. Dillard nods. "I wouldn't think much of it if we didn't also learn that he lives in Algiers."

That's nearly six miles away, on the other side of the Mississippi River. Dude may have stopped in that store that late on his way home from a Mardi Gras party. But unless said hypothetical party was in the Garden District, wouldn't he have stopped at a store across the river in Algiers instead?

Marcel and I briefly exchange perplexed looks.

Even though I can't picture our principal being the person who somehow got inside that house and stabbed Choe to death while I was asleep downstairs, the petty side of me would love it if we found out it was him. The perfect karma for him kicking me out of school.

"He doesn't have a reason to kill her, though," Marcel says.

"None that we know of yet," Mr. Dillard replies. "I'll have my team do a little digging, see if he's someone we should be focusing on for answers."

"You hear that, Marcel?" my dad says with a knitted brow.

"*His team* can handle it. As much as I appreciate what you've done for your brother, which you more than owed him, you running around town like a detective ends today. This ain't no game or one of your mock trial cases for school. This is serious. Whoever did kill your friend is walking around free, and I don't want you getting caught in their crosshairs. I can't be worrying about both of y'all more than I already do."

Did he say he's been worrying about me? Can't be.

"Listen to your dad," Mr. Dillard says to Marcel. "But I appreciate the effort and the leads you put together. Your dad might be right about you becoming a better attorney than me someday."

That has Marcel beaming.

After telling me to keep my head down and not lose hope, Mr. Dillard promises to be in touch soon. I slide out of the booth so he can leave, and my dad slides out as well, to walk Mr. Dillard to his car. There must be something he wants to ask without me hearing it.

The air thickens once it's just me and Marcel. I can't look him directly in the eye. It irks the hell outta me that he was right about Mama. He doesn't deserve to be able to check me about my life.

"You got my assignments?" I ask, looking everywhere but at him.

He leans down to pick up the textbooks I didn't notice there beside him. He drops them on the table so hard it shakes. I slide off my backpack and quietly place the books into it one by one. I feel him staring at me the entire time.

"Thanks, Marcel. Good looking out for me, despite how foul I treat you," he says in a condescending tone. I'm stuffing the last textbook in my bag when he adds, "Marcel, my bad for calling yo' mama a ho. That was messed up, uncalled-for, especially given everything you've been doing to keep me outta prison. I don't deserve a brother like you."

This dude, always with the dramatics.

I smack my lips. "You feel better now that you got that outta yo' system?"

"Really?" he says, sliding out of the booth. "That's all you got to say to me?"

"Man, I ain't got time for the drama, I got real shit I'm going through," I reply, slipping my backpack on.

"We're going through it too," he says with conviction.

He can't possibly think he's suffering more than I am. Yeah, I know Chloe was his friend and he's mourning, but I'm about to lose my life. A life that was already shit. He's mad because his friends won't talk to him anymore. We are not the same.

I swallow the guilt that's inching its way into the back of my throat.

"I'm out," I say, walking off before he has a chance to say anything else.

My dad walks in just as I'm nearing the entrance.

"Amir, can we talk for a minute?" he asks as I squeeze past him out the door.

"I need to get home before curfew," I mumble without looking at him.

It definitely won't take me that long to get back home before six, but it's all I can come up with to avoid whatever conversation this man wants. I have to assume Marcel told him about our blowup yesterday. Hope he doesn't think me learning the truth changes anything. Doesn't change the fact that he cheated on my mother *and then* acted like he couldn't be bothered with me when I used to visit. He'd hand me off to his new wife to babysit. And all she did was treat me like I was a burden.

He still trash. Period.

The sun stings my eyes once I step out onto the cobbled sidewalk. My bike is waiting exactly where I left it. I let what looks like a group of tourists walk by before I reach for it.

"I know the truth now, son," he says as I'm pulling my bike off the wall.

I turn with a frown. "About what?"

"Sparkle." He approaches me slowly, as if he's scared I'll hop on this bike and dash off if he makes any sudden movements. "Marcel told his mother what really happened this morning. Why didn't you tell me the truth when it happened?"

I bite down on my lip, shaking my head. "Why were you so quick to believe that I did it? Same way you immediately thought I killed Chloe too."

He takes a pained breath, closing his eyes.

Marcel and Mama were the only two people who knew from jump. Knew I could never be capable of doing what was done to Chloe. Marcel even going so far as to try to prove it. He's right,

I've been treating him like shit when it's really the man in front of me I'm most upset with. I'm tired of holding it back from him.

"Do you also know about me and Marcel's fight yesterday?" I ask.

My father nods. "That's why I wanted to talk. Your mother really made things difficult after our divorce. After I hurt her. She wanted to turn you against me."

"Oh, so it's all her fault that you weren't man enough to be a father?" I say, jaw clenched. "I'm glad Nana talked you out of fighting her for joint custody of me. You never had time for me anyway. I came over and you were *never* around. You let Lily treat me like I didn't mean anything to you. And now what? You think you can just apologize and shit gonna be okay between us 'cause I'm mad with my mama right now too?"

I'm talking so loud people walking by are slowing down and staring, making my father uncomfortable. I keep going like they aren't there.

"You never stopped once to think how I would be affected by everything that was happening," I rail. "You had a responsibility to be a man, to be a father to the child *you* brought in this world! What did I do that was so wrong that you've always thought the worst of me? Was it because of my mother? How much you hate her? And by proxy, you hate me too?"

"Amir, of course not," he says. "Would I be doing everything I am now to keep you out of prison if that was true?"

"Man, you can keep everything you doing. It probably won't do any good anyway," I retort. "I almost want to go to prison if it would haunt you for the rest of your life. Make you feel like the piece of shit you've made me feel like all my life. But that probably wouldn't happen. We both know you've never loved me enough to really care how I turn out."

I hop on my bike, swiping away the tears so I can see as I take off.

I pedal as hard and as fast as I can. Finally getting that off my chest didn't feel as good as I thought it would. It's the opposite, actually. I wish I'd never been born at all.

18

Marcel

But how did dude get in the house?

The "dude" Quincy is referring to in his text is Trey. We've been chatting all day. Started this morning as I was getting ready for school, and we've continued sporadically throughout the day between classes. His tone alternating between flirty and inquisitive about Chloe's murder and the possibility that Trey could have killed her, though he was asking about Amir when he first hit me up. My brother is still ghosting his friends.

I'm about to text back *Chloe had to let him in* but I pause, frowning at Quincy's text as a thought pops into my mind. It's obvious Chloe's killer, who quite possibly is Trey, used the back door to get in that night, just like her and my brother did. Chloe could have let Trey in while Amir was asleep. But all the news outlets reported that the coroner's office said Chloe was stabbed in her sleep since there weren't signs of a struggle. That would mean she'd have to have let Trey in, taken him up to her bedroom, and fallen asleep, and *then* Trey went downstairs, grabbed the knife out of the kitchen, and went back up to kill her and ransack her room, looking for whatever he feared would expose his father's affair with Vivian Crane. That would take a good bit of time. And all with Amir asleep downstairs.

I sit up straighter in my desk, tuning out whatever Mrs. Graceson is saying as I remember why Chloe always used the back door to enter and exit her house. Which would explain how Trey could have snuck in without her or my brother knowing.

I think I know! I finally reply to Quincy, my heart racing. *He used her key.*

I'm sure the three rippling dots that follow are Quincy typing something like *Huh?* Or *How?*

I start grinning, knowing how I'll respond.

"Mr. Trudeau, either put the phone away or I'll take it from you."

Mrs. Graceson is glaring at me when I look up. My Mock Trial II classmates are all staring blankly at me too.

"Sorry, Mrs. Graceson," I say, tucking my phone in my pocket and slouching in my desk. My phone vibrates against my seat with Quincy's response.

"Cut him some slack, Mrs. Graceson. His brother did get arrested for murdering someone," Jared Lanford says, eliciting some gasps.

Mrs. Graceson rips off her reading glasses. "Mr. Lanford, no sir. We're not going to make light of tragedy. And you will not disrespect your classmates. Is that understood?"

Our Mock Trial II teacher was the first Black woman to

make partner at one of this city's most prestigious law firms. She's semiretired now. Semi because she teaches here three times a week. Mrs. Graceson commands any room she's in. You can just tell she wasn't no joke in the courtroom. Like now, all it took was a raised voice and a stern look to get Jared to shrink in his seat. Something few faculty and students here can achieve.

"Now that I have *everyone's* attention, here are the assigned roles for the case we'll be tackling over the next month," she says, reaching around to grab a sheet of paper off the desk she's perched on.

This is one of my favorite classes. It serves as both an elective and an extracurricular activity, since the class annually competes in a nationwide mock trial competition. Truman has won several years in a row under her leadership. I've been gunning for an attorney spot this semester, but it slipped my mind lately with everything going on with Amir. I even forgot today was the day we were gonna find out what roles we'd be taking with this first practice case.

The fictional legal issue we're tackling involves the prosecution of a high school security officer who shot, allegedly in self-defense, a suspected gang member after a football game. The excitement I initially felt about the case has waned, given the real-life legal drama I'm involved in right now. But I try to push all that aside. Having something else to focus on could be what I need at the moment. However, all the questions regarding Trey's possible guilt keep humming in the back of my mind as Mrs. Graceson reads off names.

She begins with witnesses for the prosecution and the defense, then announces that Jared will be the security officer, who has been indicted on one count of attempted second-degree murder and one count of first-degree assault.

"I'm innocent, I swear," Jared blurts out with a goofy grin, getting a few laughs and an irritated look from our teacher.

"Marcel and Tiffany, you will serve as his defense lawyers," Mrs. Graceson says.

I don't hear what two students are serving as our opposing counsel. Everything becomes mumbled background noise as Tiffany and me lock eyes across the room. The sneer she's giving me causes the back of my throat to ache. A week ago, being paired with her would have been no problem. I like her. And Tiffany is smart. But everything has changed. I've accused her brother of killing my best friend. How are we supposed to work together now?

I break eye contact with her and catch Jared glaring at me too. He sits two rows to the left of Tiffany, and he's turned around completely in his desk with a devious grin splitting his face in half.

"Okay, I'd like you all to break into your respective groups for the remainder of class," Mrs. Graceson says. "The witnesses for the prosecution over here. Defense witnesses over there. And both my attorney teams there and over there; Jared, you obviously in a huddle with Marcel and Tiffany."

My stomach is in knots as I gather my things and make my way to the three desks in the back corner of the room that Mrs. Graceson designated for us. Tiffany and I don't look at each other as we're pulling our desks closer to the one Jared plopped down in.

"Is this gonna be a problem?" he asks, his eyes ping-ponging between us. There's zero concern in his voice. Just a morbid amusement lighting up his hazel eyes. When he doesn't get an answer from either of us, he says, "I mean, it would definitely be a problem for me if my co-counsel was coming at my brother for murder."

I sigh, opening the binder with the case materials. "I think we should start by outlining a probable defense. I'd like to win this thing."

"Hoping to gain a few pointers to help your brother out, I presume," Tiffany says, her voice laced with venom. "Here's one suggestion: keep Trey's name out of it."

Yeah, I don't know how this is gonna work. She's angry. And I get it. I'm feeling the same way, but on a much larger scale.

"Tiff, it's nothing personal—"

"Nothing personal?" she parrots, her voice rising. "Trying to make my brother look guilty because everyone thinks yours is—I take that *very* personal."

I ignore Jared, who's sitting up straighter in his desk, enjoying the tension he created.

"Amir is innocent," I say.

"So is Trey," she retorts.

"It doesn't look that way," I reply before I can catch myself.

I don't want to do this with her. Not here. Not like this. Tiffany doesn't deserve this. But neither do I.

"What do you think you know?" she says.

"Tiff, come on, not now. We don't need to go there."

"But you had no problem *going there* in front of everyone in the commons area yesterday," Jared interjects.

Why couldn't someone have stabbed *him* to death? I don't think anyone at this school would miss him.

"We can talk about this one-on-one—not around *everyone,*" I say, cutting my eyes at Jared.

"I want you to take back the accusation." Tiffany's eyes are intense, her mouth tight. "My brother doesn't deserve that. He's a saint."

"That's debatable," I reply.

"Take it back," she says, her voice growing louder. "Amir doesn't even like you. Why are you fighting so hard for him?"

"Same reason you're riding hard for Trey," I say. "He's my brother."

"You don't know a damn thing," she fires back.

"I know your brother was in the neighborhood around the time of Chloe's death," I reply.

"He was confronting our father about . . ." Her eyes shift to Jared, remembering we have an audience who would find pleasure in telling everyone about her father's affair with Vivian Crane. ". . . you know . . . *defending* our family," she continues. "He wasn't concerned about that girl."

"Hold up, what was your dad doing in the Garden District that late?" Jared interjects.

"Then why doesn't he come out and say that?" I reply smugly, as if I didn't hear Jared's messy question.

"Just leave us alone!" she shouts.

The entire room goes silent. Everyone is staring at us.

"What is the problem back there?" Mrs. Graceson asks from her desk.

"I think I'm gonna need new lawyers," Jared says, smirking.

"Not happening." Mrs. Graceson stands up, her heels clicking across the floor as she marches to the back of class where we are. "Ms. Winslow, Mr. Trudeau. Is this going to be a problem?"

My heart is racing, my breathing labored as I stare at Tiffany, who has her arms folded on top of her desk, her mouth pinched. Nothing about this feels good. What my father said about not wanting to tear down another prominent Black family echoes in my thoughts.

"Not that I care," Mrs. Graceson continues. "I suggest you settle this little tiff y'all are having and get this assignment done. I'll be expecting opening arguments from each of you by next week."

And with that, Mrs. Graceson turns and glides back to her desk.

For the last fifteen minutes of class Tiffany and I carry on a stilted conversation as we try to work through the particulars of the case, with Jared hardly contributing anything. I've never been so happy to hear the bell ring.

I ignore the urge to shoot out of my desk and escape into the hallway. I hang back, and as soon as Jared and the rest of our classmates are out of earshot I lean into Tiffany and say, "Tiff, I don't want to fight with you."

"Whatever," she mumbles, following everyone else toward the door.

"I'm serious," I say, grabbing hold of her wrist. "I don't want to hurt you."

She spins around, ripping her arm away from me. "You know why Trey was out there so late?" She yanks her phone out her pocket, fumbling as she uses one hand to unlock it. "He was getting *this*!"

Tiffany holds her phone out to me. The class is nearly empty when I grab it. A dark image of two people on a street fills the screen. Upon taking a closer look I realize it's her father and Vivian Crane; they're coming out of the Belmont Hotel. I look up at Tiffany, a little confused about why she's sharing it with me.

"Check the time stamp," she says with a raised brow.

The photo was taken at 1:25 a.m. the night of Chloe's murder. Twenty minutes *before* Trey got that parking ticket I found in his car.

"Our father denied it when Trey first approached him after Chloe told my brother about the affair," Tiffany says, jerking her phone out my hand. "Trey camped out there that night to see for himself, get concrete proof that it was happening. He got that parking ticket because after taking this pic, he followed my father to his car and confronted him, saying he would show our mother and leak it to the press if he didn't end things with that woman." As she's stuffing her phone back into the pocket of her skirt, she adds, "It would be impossible for Trey to be in two places at once."

My insides are tied in a knot. She's right. Amir said he was woken up around 2:18 a.m. by a door slamming, which we can logically assume was her killer leaving out the back door.

"Mr. Trudeau and Ms. Winslow, everything okay?"

Mrs. Graceson is eyeing us from her desk.

"Yes, ma'am. We're *talking things through,*" I say. I wait until our teacher has looked back down, then say to Tiffany, "I only thought what I thought because I caught him searching her bedroom at the balloon release."

She sighs. "It wasn't as nefarious as you think. He was looking for the love notes Chloe wrote to him. He gave them all back to her in the mason jar he had collected them in out of anger when she broke up with him this last time."

Shame needles my chest. Exchanging love notes at school was their thing.

"Y'all can't just text each other like normal people?" I teased once.

Chloe had convinced herself that it somehow meant more to have a boy write down his feelings by hand.

"After she was . . ." Tiffany shifts her weight from one foot to the other, seeming to not want to finish the sentence. "Now that she's *gone,* well, they mean more to him."

That's something I can definitely understand. After Nana died, the little things tied to her identity took on a greater meaning for me: the spoon she always used to stir cake batter, the birthday cards she'd signed, her favorite shawl. I have them all stored in a keepsake box in my closet as a way to keep her memory alive. I've been so focused on seeing Trey as her killer I never considered his actions could be tied to his grief.

"Why didn't he ask her parents for them?" I ask.

"He tried, but her father said no," Tiffany replies. "He was in his feelings over Trey giving them back to hurt Chloe. Trey thought he could just steal 'em since they were technically for him."

"Did you know about it—your father's affair?" I say, steering things back to the secret that fueled my suspicions around her brother.

Her chin trembles. "I found out the same morning your brother was arrested. I . . . At . . ." She looks away, maybe because she's ashamed of whatever she's about to say to me. "At first I thought the same thing you did. I heard Trey sneak back in late that night, so when I saw the news the next morning . . ."

She thought her brother had killed his ex-girlfriend.

". . . I confronted him, and that's when he showed me the picture," she says quietly.

"Tiff, I really am sorry," I say, meaning it.

The anger returns to her face. "Just keep my family's name out of this mess. Okay?"

Before I can respond, she storms out of the classroom. I follow less energetically. By the time I make it to my locker, my body feels like it's been chewed up in a grinder. I toss the case binder in with the rest of my books. Why is life so fucked up right now? There's no outcome that will make everything go back to the way it was before my birthday. Maybe if I'd never had that party none of this would have happened. Chloe would still be alive. Amir wouldn't be accused of her murder. I wouldn't feel so alone at school anymore.

Jared and his gang are gathered in front of the lockers across from me when I turn around. My eyes stop on Colin Perrier as I'm sliding my messenger bag onto my shoulder. He's putting on a black hoodie over the V-neck sweater he's wearing. My lips part when I see what's on the back of it: a cartoon bear. Everything around me seems to slow down as I think back to what Amir said when we met at that dilapidated church. And when Colin and the others start down the hall together, I notice something else.

He's walking with a slight limp.

19

Amir

Marcel and I have already said enough to each other this week, so I decline his call the second his name pops up on my phone. I'm sitting in bed, trying not to fall asleep, finishing an English lit assignment that's due today. My guess is he's calling about me going off on our dad yesterday. And in that case, I *really* don't have anything I want to discuss with him.

Dude really meddles too freaking much.

My phone chimes with a text notification, and I glance down to see that he's sent me a photo.

I open it. The pic causes me to sit up straighter and set my textbook aside. It's a picture of the black hoodie with the face of the cartoon bear. The same one the dude who ran away from my church on Monday had on. I'm typing a reply as Marcel calls again.

"Yo, that's the hoodie the dude I saw was wearing," I answer, my irritation with Marcel superseded by my curiosity.

"You sure?" Marcel asks.

There's a lot of background noise on his end. Sounds like he's still at school. I realize I'd be going to my last class of the day now if I was there too. My sense of time has gotten messed up being at home all day.

"Yep, that's the one; dude has the same build too," I tell him. "Who is that?"

"Colin. Colin Perrier, you know, who hangs with Jared Lanford."

Once he says Jared's name I can vaguely picture who Colin might be. "You mean that skinny dude, the one with the shaggy brown Justin Bieber haircut?" I ask.

"Yeah, him."

"That's . . . weird" is all I can say.

"Right?" Marcel follows. "Colin lives in Lakeview. Why would he be at an old run-down church in Broadmoor?"

"You tell me."

"*And* he was walking with a li'l limp today," Marcel says. "Didn't you say that day the person you were running after was limping?"

I scoot off the bed and start pacing in front of my dresser. "Yeah. That jump off the mezzanine was pretty high. He landed hard."

"What kind of coincidence is that?"

A knot forms in my chest. *I have no idea.*

"Oh, and yeah, I was wrong about Trey," he adds.

I pause. My confusion flipping from wondering why Colin was at my old church to wondering what changed his mind about Trey.

"But I think I know how someone could have snuck into the house that night. . . ."

Guess he's not going to tell me why he's scratched Trey off the list.

"Me and Quincy are thinking about—"

"Hold up," I interrupt. "Quincy? *My* Quincy?"

After a silent beat, Marcel says, "Hey, gotta run. Walking into class."

He ends the call before I can get another word in.

I drop down on the edge of my bed.

He's been chatting it up with my *homeboy?* I toss my phone onto the bed. Why is Marcel inserting himself into every part of my damn life? Did he reach out to Q, or was it the other way around? I bet the latter—I've been ghosting everyone since I was bailed out of jail. I know Q. He gets in his feelings about everything. It's not enough that he can't even be honest with me about who he is. Now he's going behind my back and linking up with my half brother?

I throw myself back on the bed, arms sprawled over my head.

Q and Marcel doing whatever it is they're doing ain't what I need to be focusing on. Getting some extra time to finish this boring-ass reading assignment is. I sit up, sliding my laptop from underneath my English lit textbook. If I want an extension, I'll need to log in to our school's instant messaging program to ask for it. During the pandemic, before I attended Truman and everything was virtual, teachers and students primarily communicated with one another through the school portal. Now that things have returned to in-person, the portal is primarily used by students only to communicate during school hours since we're *technically* not supposed to have our phones out during class. Since I don't socialize with anyone at school, I've rarely logged in to the portal, which is why it takes me a few tries to remember my password.

The note from Mr. Braswell that was included in the packet of assignments Marcel gave me said my teachers will begin routinely checking their inboxes in case I need to communicate with them. I have more than fifty unread messages waiting for me, likely the automated alerts the school sends out for various announcements. The preview line for the first message in my in-box sends a chill down my spine.

> From: Chloe Danvers
> Subject: PLEASE READ!!!

* * *

I pull out my phone after squeezing through the chained doors of my church. The cryptic message from a dead girl still filling the screen after I unlock it. It's time-stamped 9:00 a.m., almost eight hours after Chloe was murdered.

> Amir,
>
> There's a reason I got you to go home with me. It's the same reason I didn't wake you up to leave after you fell asleep. I was afraid of being alone tonight. There are people at our school who'd rather see

me dead than have what I know about them made public. You reading this means they got what they wanted. But the fuckers underestimated me. I lied about my dress getting snagged in that church. I was hiding something for you. When you find it, look in the folder labeled "The Game." PLEASE show it to your brother. He'll know what to do and where to start. I tried going to him first, but he didn't want to hear what I had to say. He'll listen to you. Your family is different. I know their silence can't be bought like it was with mine. Remember what I said about smoke and mirrors. Don't trust anyone at school—especially if they're white!

Chloe

My hands are shaking. Chloe was afraid for her life. She wasn't being flirty 'cause she liked me, she wanted me around that night so she'd feel safer. And in case I wasn't enough (which apparently I wasn't), she made sure whatever secret she knew didn't die along with her by sending me this cryptic-ass message right before her fear became my nightmarish reality. I've been a pawn this whole fucking time?

I take the stairs to the mezzanine two at a time, my heart pounding to break free of my chest. I need to understand what this is all about. Hoping whatever she hid here can clear my name. Pieces from that night flash through my mind: Me and Chloe here. Her texting someone, claiming it wasn't Trey. The vague comments she kept making about Truman. Her emotions were all over the place. Now I know why. She knew something about people at our school that they were willing to kill her for knowing. What in the White People Nonsense is going on?

I immediately go to the spot where she was sitting, which is a few feet away from where I caught that dude (Colin, maybe?) looking around the other day. I drop to my knees. Was he looking for whatever Chloe left for me to find? If it's not here, guess that means he beat me to it.

I reach over the edge of the mezzanine, where some of the floorboards are broken and curling upward because the wood is so rotted. As I begin to feel around, I realize there are holes and crevices where the boards are peeling away from the base. Carefully, I lean forward so that I can see into some of those dark spaces. I reach my hand into one of them. It's cold, damp. My fingertips graze the edge of something smooth and hard. With some effort I manage to securely lock whatever it is between my index and middle fingers and pull my hand out.

A tingling sensation walks up the back of my neck as I look down at the hot-pink USB flash drive in the palm of my hand. How does it fit into her death?

20

Marcel

"If you believe ol' girl about her brother, why you still wanted to come here?"

Quincy is talking about Tiffany and Trey. I gave him a rundown of our blowup today on our way to the Garden District after I scooped him up from school. I'm parked two houses away from Chloe's, and we've been watching her house.

I turn in the driver's seat so that I'm facing Quincy. "I thought we went over this already when we were texting earlier."

"We did; what I mean is"—he sighs—"if you don't think ol' boy used the spare key her family keeps in some fake rock in their backyard to sneak inside and kill her, I'm not fully understanding what we doing here now."

I remembered the fake rock in the Danverses' backyard when Quincy and I were speculating on how the killer could have gotten in that night since there were no signs of forced entry. Last summer, I used that spare key once a week, for a month, to check on their house and bring their mail inside while

Chloe and her family were on vacation in Europe. Trey knew about it too. He used it a few times to sneak into Chloe's house late at night, while her parents were asleep. Chloe said it spiced up their hookups. It would perfectly explain how he got in—*if* it had been him.

"Trey obviously didn't use it, but I can, to sneak in and look around her bedroom some more," I explain to Quincy again. "There has to be something in there that can help me figure out who killed her. I don't know what else to do."

"Bet," he replies, slouching back in the passenger seat. "You sure this woman leaving soon?"

I nod. "Her mom picks up her brother from his after-school baseball practice every Monday, Wednesday, and Friday. Once she leaves, we should have a good window of time to grab that spare key, get inside, and look around."

I was going to do this alone, but Quincy insisted on coming. I'm not gonna lie, I'm glad. I like how effortless it is being around him.

"What about her ol' man? He's not gonna roll up on us, is he?"

His apprehensive look is cute. I have to stop myself from leaning over and pecking his kissable lips. He looks like a slow, passionate kisser.

Focus, Marcel!

"Nah, he usually doesn't get home until way past six," I reply.

Goose bumps are starting to ripple across my skin as we continue to wait. It's been over thirty minutes.

"How's my boy holding up?" Quincy asks.

"Still angry at the world," I say, my gaze locked on Chloe's house.

"What about you?" Quincy's thick eyebrows are drawn together when I turn back toward him. "How's you and your family doing?" he adds.

It hasn't felt right to talk about how everything that's happening to Amir is also affecting us. *He's* the one facing prison, and possibly a death sentence. He's the one everyone thinks killed someone. He stands to lose a lot more than we do. But in this bubble with Quincy, someone I barely know, it finally feels okay to say out loud the other thing that's driving me to do what I'm doing.

"It's been *a lot,*" I say, relaxing my shoulders and pillowing my head on the seat's headrest. "My dad's businesses have taken a hit. His investors on a new venture even pulled out—said there's too much drama going on around his brand right now. Like, these folks really want him to distance himself from Amir. I'm sure you've seen how Black Twitter has been coming for my dad too, saying it's all his fault what happened. Like, had he been more of a father, Amir wouldn't have gotten in trouble. Crazy shit."

"Yeah, I saw some of that," Quincy says. "But did you see, last night, Orlando Houston posted that message in his Instagram story basically calling them fools out for turning on yo' old man so quickly. A whole bunch of blogs reposted it."

"For real?" I sit up straighter.

Orlando Houston is a big reason my father has the career

he has. Him eating at Tru while he was doing recovery work at Hurricane Katrina, then bragging about it in interviews and to his other celebrity friends, turned my father into a household name, sort of overnight.

Quincy pulls out his phone, opening the Twitter app.

"Just scroll down," he says, handing it over to me. "He even got a hashtag going. I Stand With Amir."

There are endless tweets in the thread. Strangers all voicing their support for my brother. Posting situations where white people who looked guilty of homicide were granted a lot more leniency from law enforcement and the media, often in cases where they turned out to be the killers. People who talk like they have law degrees making a case for Amir's innocence. Some even go so far as to tag the New Orleans Police Department and the district attorney in their online rants, calling both out for wanting to close the case quickly just because a rich white girl is the victim.

Warmth explodes in my chest after I read the tweets about my father. One says *The YTs couldn't wait to find something to bring Martin Trudeau down. And y'all on Martin Luther King's internet just singing along.* The term *YTs* meaning white people and *y'all* being Black people. Someone else posted *It's really feeling like folks want this dude's son to be guilty just to make the argument that having a lot of money won't help you beat the system if you black.* And another person wrote *Why is the media so quick to tear us down when they see a black person level up? #IStandWithAmir*

I keep scrolling. Eventually coming across the post that started all this. It's the screenshot of the message Orlando Houston posted on his Instagram story late last night.

> I know Martin Trudeau. Know his heart. Him and his family deserve our prayers and support right now, not our judgment. My deepest sympathy to this girl's family. But this country has wrongfully convicted too many black men for us not to be questioning how this was handled. Still too many unanswered questions. #IStandWithAmir

Had I not stopped checking social media, I would have seen some of this. Now that I've seen it, I have to show it to my dad. He needs to see there are people who want him to win. And Amir should know I'm not the only person who believes him.

"Is that her?" Quincy says, ripping me back into the present.

Chloe's mom is getting into her car when I look up. I hand Quincy back his phone. "Told you she'd be leaving soon," I say.

We watch in silence, my heart racing, as Mrs. Danvers slowly backs out the driveway and cruises past us. I duck down a little in my seat, wanting to ensure she can't see me, which is probably pointless since my windows are tinted.

"Okay, let's do this," I say, reaching for the door handle.

"Hold up, pretty boy," Quincy says, snatching my arm. "We can't just be lurking around these white people's house in the middle of the day."

"It's cool," I say with a shrug. "I've been to Chloe's house so many times. They know my face around here."

"Which is precisely why we can't just walk up and swipe that key when they aren't home." Quincy reaches into the back seat to grab the book bag he brought with him. "Things have changed. Your brother is suspected of murdering the girl who used to live here. We are two young Black men in a rich, predominantly white neighborhood. We can't move like they do."

I shrink a little in the driver's seat. My argument with Amir two days ago resurfacing in my thoughts. How I don't see and experience the world the same as they do.

"How are we supposed to do this if we don't get out of this car?" I say, a little annoyed.

Quincy reaches into his book bag and pulls out a cream shirt that's folded in a square. "That's why I brought these."

He hands the shirt to me, and I unfold it to get a better look. It's a button-down that has *City of New Orleans* stitched on the upper left side of the chest and a patch on the other side that has the name *Tyrone* stitched in the center.

"What is this?" I ask with a frown.

Quincy has an identical shirt splayed across his lap. He digs into his book bag and pulls out two matching navy-blue snap-back caps. "My cousin works in the city's department of public works. I got him to let us borrow these for the afternoon. We put them on and the neighbors will think we work for the city and are at the house reading the water meter or something. Perfect disguise, right?"

His goofy smile makes me laugh. "Is this really necessary?"

"Yes. That way no one knows Amir Trudeau's brother was here," Quincy says. He's already pulling off the T-shirt he's wearing. I look away, the sight of his washboard abs and the thin trail of hair disappearing into the waistband of his underwear making me think about us doing something I know we shouldn't. "And if anyone approaches these folks later and says they saw two Black guys who work for the city around their house, your name won't pop up at all."

I nod. The logic is there. I just wish I didn't have to put on this ill-fitting polyester shirt. I peel off my blazer and start loosening my tie. "Is this your ploy to see me undress?"

We can flirt. Flirting is harmless.

Quincy is already buttoning his shirt. "I'll look away. Don't want you thinking I'm some fuckboy."

He winks at me, and my insides melt.

He does what he says, glancing out the passenger window while I take off my white uniform shirt and put on his cousin's. I wait until I've tucked my curls into the baseball cap that also has *City of New Orleans* stitched across the front to ask, "How do I look?"

"Cute. Like, I'd tap that," he says, opening the passenger-side door. "Come on, let's do this."

Quincy is holding a clipboard in his right hand when he rounds the front of my car.

"What's that for?" I ask, pointing at it as I shut the driver's-side door.

"To complete the look." He nestles it up to his chest.

I tuck his cousin's shirt into my school uniform pants because

I can't stand how it billows around my waist. "When you commit to an idea, you really commit, huh?"

"You should take note of that," he says, winking at me.

We start making our way across the street to Chloe's house.

"Does my brother know about you?" I say, needing something else to think about now that Quincy has planted the seed of how getting caught could look. I don't want what we're doing to have unintended consequences for Amir. "You know, that you're gay? Please don't tell me you on the low."

He chuckles. "I'm figuring it out. I've dated chicks. Had some dealings with a couple dudes, no full-on sex yet. But I've *experimented*—if that's what you asking."

"I'm just an experiment?" I ask, a little offended.

"No, it's not like that." There's sincerity in his eyes. "I'm very curious about you. More than *sexually* curious. Kinda interested in seeing if it can be something more . . . meaningful."

His wistful smile gets me blushing. "So, no, Amir doesn't know all this," I say.

"Nah," Quincy replies, shaking his head.

"Not ready to have that convo with him yet?" I ask.

"It's not that," Quincy says, his expression growing serious. "I need to figure things out before I can tell him what's what. You might complicate that."

Good. Glad I'm not the only one concerned about how Amir will take whatever is happening between me and his best friend.

"When all this is over, when he's out of trouble, I'll do it," Quincy says as we reach the sidewalk. "Hopefully you'll be in love with me by then."

I roll my eyes, but with a grin pulling on the corner of my mouth.

We both get quiet as we near the side gate to the wrought-iron fence bordering the front of Chloe's house. I wait a few seconds before I open it, glancing quickly to ensure no one is watching us. My heart is trying to break free of my rib cage. Quincy's reassuring smile serves as the nudge I need to push the gate open and walk in.

Their backyard seems bigger than it did Saturday when it was crowded with people. Quincy can't maintain a steady gaze on anything as we round the back corner of the house and the full backyard comes into view. He's no doubt impressed by what he's seeing. I, on the other hand, peer straight down at the rock garden flanking the back door and bordering the back of their house. Quincy remains close on my heels as I walk toward the one slightly discolored rock among the bunch. My pulse is racing as I pick it up. I feel Quincy's breath on my neck as he stands behind me and watches me flip it over and use my thumb to slide back a panel and expose its hollow inside.

The bottom falls out of my stomach. The rock is empty!

"What the fuck?" I say. "It's gone."

"Maybe one of them lost their key and is using it," Quincy says over my shoulder.

I keep staring into the empty casing, as if doing so will somehow make the purple-and-gold key materialize. Now how am I supposed to get inside? I slide the panel closed and set the rock back down.

"What you wanna do now?" Quincy asks as I'm climbing the steps to their back door.

I tug on the doorknob, which of course is locked. "That key is always in that rock."

"Can you just visit them and then sneak into her bedroom?" Quincy asks from the bottom of the steps.

"No. Things aren't great right now between our families."

"Yeah. Right," he says, defeated.

I peer through the door's four-paned window, cupping the sides of my face with my hands so I can see clearly into the kitchen. My gaze is drawn toward the knife block on the counter to the right of the door. One slot still empty. In the window, something dark and quick hops up on my shoulder. I yelp, whipping my body around. Quincy does too when he sees my startled expression. A black cat meows at us from atop the brick fence enclosing the backyard.

"Not this cat rolling up on us stealthlike," Quincy teases with a laugh. "Where did it come from? A neighbor?"

His question pulls me down the steps and in the feline's direction. *Where did it come from?* is a good question. One that makes me realize how easy it would be for a person to jump that wall.

"Where you going?" Quincy asks, still standing near the stairs to the back door.

"To see something," I say as I'm passing the cherub water fountain in the center of the yard.

The cat scurries off as I get closer. Leaping down to wherever it came from before it scared me half to death. The Danverses' back wall is shrouded with Virginia creeper. The five-leaflet plants tickle my hands and exposed arms as I jump up and grab hold of the ledge, pulling myself up just enough to see down below. I catch the cat's black tail just as it's disappearing around the right corner of the wall, which I realize faces Coliseum Street. Something else occurs to me while I'm up here: there's enough space in back between the Danverses' wall and the neighbors' fenced yard for someone to walk through from Coliseum Street. That could explain how someone snuck onto their property without that across-the-street neighbor's camera catching them.

"I might know how someone got in." I jump down, slapping my hands together to clean off the residue from the plants and the fence's sun-drenched bricks. I eye that fake rock. "What if Trey and I weren't the only ones who knew about that spare key?"

"You know someone else who did?" Quincy asks.

I shake my head, looking over my shoulder at the spot where the black cat was perched. I might be thinking about this all wrong. Maybe Chloe didn't know her killer, but her killer knew her. Had studied her routine. Knew her habits. Had seen me, Trey, or one of the Danverses use that spare key, knew it was there. Knew the layout of their backyard. That's how they got in undetected. A possibility that has my heart beating quicker.

"What's wrong?" Quincy asks with a frown. "Why you looking like you about to cry?"

"Because I don't know what to do next," I tell him.

21

Amir

This feels off. Me impatiently waiting for Marcel to show up at my house.

He finally responded to the text I sent after finding the flash drive. It took him an hour. I would have told him to meet me at the old church if he'd responded right away, but I had to come home so I wouldn't miss my curfew. Mama is at work, so there's no chance of them running into each other. Ain't no telling what she'll say to him next time she sees him.

The second I hear the doorbell I spring up off the bed, throwing down the remote. I was considering catching up on *Rap Sh!t.* Figured the melodrama would be a good distraction while I waited for him to get here. I leave the jump drive sitting on the corner of the TV stand. I haven't gone through it yet. I wanted to wait for him.

"Bruh, what took you so long?" I say as I'm swinging the door open.

Marcel has on his school uniform pants with the top three

buttons of his white shirt unfastened and half of it spilling out of the waist. I've never seen him so messy.

"I went to Chloe's to scope the place out, see how someone could have got in without y'all knowing," he says, rushing into the house. When I shut the door and turn around he says, "I remembered the Danverses have one of those key rocks by their back door. I was going to use it today to sneak in and look around in Chloe's bedroom for more clues, but it's gone—the key, not the rock. I think the person who killed her jumped their back fence. You can access it from Coliseum, that's why that doorbell camera didn't catch them."

I'm nodding as he talks, waiting for an opportunity to tell him about *my* discovery.

"That spare key being missing doesn't feel right," he continues.

"Who else knew about the key rock besides you?" I ask, intrigued by his train of thought.

"Just Trey—that I know of. But it couldn't have been him. He has a solid alibi." Marcel's brow knits. "What is it you want to show me?"

"Right," I say, taking a breath. "After we got off the phone earlier, I logged in to the school portal to shoot a note to my English lit teacher. Bruh, guess what was in my inbox. . . ."

He shrugs, brows raised.

"A message from Chloe, sent *after* she was killed."

Marcel's head snaps back. "What?"

"Come on," I say, and gesture for him to follow me. There's

this look of wonderment married with confusion when he enters my bedroom. It dawns on me that he's never been in here before. I stand silently for a few seconds and watch him take it in. He scans the clutter on my dresser, his eyes raking over the bottles of cologne, books, Mardi Gras beads, sunglasses, hats, and framed pictures of me goofing around with my homeboys or Mama. Then he glances at the Miles Morales Spider-Man poster hanging above the headboard of my unmade bed. The tower of clear containers where I keep my sneaker collection gets a once-over before he looks down at the television screen, his lips parting after he reads the list of shows I've recorded and saved to my DVR.

It's too late, I know he's already seen them, but I snatch the remote off my bed anyway to turn off the television.

"Here it is," I say, picking up my laptop and handing it to him. Chloe's note is already pulled up on-screen.

Marcel drops onto the edge of my bed, his lips moving as he reads silently. I stand impatiently to the side, my arms folded across my chest and a lump thickening in the back of my throat as I wait for his reaction. The seconds drag on. His blank look never changing.

"Bruh!"

He jumps. "Sorry. I . . . This is . . . It sounds like she knew there was a chance she would die that night."

"I know. Creepy as fuck. But how could she have sent that after she died?"

"That I can explain." He turns the laptop around so I can see the screen. “You see this little symbol next to the time stamp?” he says, pointing at the small stopwatch icon next to the time. “It means Chloe set this as the time she wanted you to receive it.”

“Oohhhhh,” I drawl, my jaw dropped.

If I used the portal more, I would know that.

“It also means she could have unsent it if you hadn’t read it by that time.” Marcel turns my laptop back toward him. “So she wrote this *before* she was killed. What did she want you to find?”

I pick up the flash drive off the TV stand and hold it out to him.

His eyes go wide. “That’s hers!” He snatches it out my hand. “What’s on it?” he asks, studying it with new curiosity.

“I don’t know yet,” I say with a shrug. “I was waiting on you to look through it with me. Apparently that’s what she wanted. What was she trying to tell you before she died?”

Marcel frantically sticks the flash drive into one of the USB ports on the side of my laptop. “Chloe stored everything on this—pictures, schoolwork, those makeup videos she used to shoot in her bedroom . . .”

Okay, guess he’s not answering my question, ’cause I know he heard me.

“She became kind of paranoid about using Cloud services after her father got sued.”

“Why?”

“These cyberbullies hacked into her father’s business and personal accounts, trying to expose conversations he’d had about that complex he designed," he says. "They really wanted to smear his name and his business. She used this to store anything personal. Like, she would download the contents of her phone at least once a week, if not more often, then delete everything off the phone."

"That's one way to stop those annoying notifications you don't have enough storage space on your phone," I joke.

"For real," Marcel says with an agreeable grin.

I drop down next to him on my bed to see what he's looking at. He's right: I mostly see what appear to be folders for each of her classes, containing school assignments, photos, videos, and various other documents. Nothing worth hiding, on the surface.

Marcel clicks on the search box. "What folder did she say to look in?"

"The Game," I say, my heartbeat quickening.

He hits enter and the hundreds of blue folders disappear, leaving only one.

"Slave trade game?" we both read out loud.

The folder is filled with jpeg images, the first dated February 2. Marcel clicks on it, bringing forth a grainy photo that I can tell at a glance is a screenshot of a thread from SnapMessages, a social media app.

"*Nigger Sale*?" I blurt out, reading the bold title at the top of the screen. The words are followed by two dark-skinned farmer men emojis. "What the fuck is this?"

Marcel mashes the + key to zoom in on the image and make the words easier to read.

TODAY

theotherNEGAN CHANGED THE GROUP NAME TO MONKEY FARM 🐒🐒

theotherNEGAN CHANGED THE GROUP NAME TO MONKEY AUCTION 🐒🐒

theotherNEGAN CHANGED THE GROUP NAME TO THE SLAVE TRADE 👨🏿👩🏿

I_AM_IRONMAN:

Why we changing shit up?

theotherNEGAN:

Was brainstorming. I like Slave Trade. What y'all think?

TheotherNEGAN's question got twelve thumbs-ups. My ears start burning.

"Bruh? What the fuck is this?" I fume.

"I'm just as lost as you are," Marcel replies, rubbing his temple with his thumb.

"Why is the image so grainy?" I say. "Did she take it with a first-generation iPhone or something?"

"It looks like a picture somebody's phone took of the screen of another phone," Marcel says.

"Why didn't they just screenshot it from whatever Proud Boys group posted this bullshit?" I ask.

"Because SnapMessages would tell everyone in the group

that she did," Marcel says. "That's why folks use the app—they want to send messages back and forth that they don't want captured as screenshots. Plus, the messages disappear after a person reads them. DL boys love it. They can send pics and not get outed. No cyber receipts. The bigger question is, why would Chloe have these?"

I lean closer to read the user names. "You recognize any of the handles?"

"Nah," Marcel replies.

He clicks on the next image, also dated February 2.

THE SLAVE TRADE 👨🏿👩🏿

TODAY

suckmyYeezys:

100 bucks for Sonya. That booty was sitting today!

GoingProB*tch_25:

Back off. She's mine. Ain't ready to sell. Still a good bed wench.

suckmyYeezys:

Pass that chocolate around. Lol. She bent over in the hall today, almost 💦

theotherNEGAN:

We pass the nigger 😽 around.

suckmyYeezys:

She'd make some pretty mulatto babies with me.

First.Class.Diva1:

Ew. Gross.

suckmyYeezys:

Calm down **@First.Class.Diva1**. You'd still be wifey. Black 🐱 just hits different. :P

What I've read has me breathing hard.

"Oh shit!" Marcel says.

"What?"

"I think these are kids who go to school with us," he says. "Sonya, big booty . . . They're talking about Sonya Gilliott."

Marcel is looking at me like he expects me to know who he's talking about. Seeing how confused I am, he adds, "She's really pretty. Hangs around Trey a lot. Part of the Young Democrats."

My mouth drops open. Now I know who he's talking about. We don't have any classes together, but I've seen her in the halls, acting like her shit don't stank. Not the kind of chick I'd ever want to deal with. I always got the vibe she was crushing on Trey.

"Wait. Does that mean these are kids at our school being racist as fuck?" I say, pointing at the computer screen.

Marcel opens another screenshot. This one dated two days later than the previous one.

THE SLAVE TRADE 👨🏿👩🏿

TODAY

whos_on_top69:

Got me a good breeder! Marcel's got the biggest 🍆!! I should get at least $1,000 bonus points for tackling it.

I_AM_IRONMAN:

| We all know how you know that, cocksucker! LOL!

whos_on_top69:

| Proud of it :P

I_AM_IRONMAN:

| Meet me after class;)

First.Class.Diva1:

| GAAAAAYYYYY!!!!!!!

I_AM_IRONMAN:

| A mouth is a mouth!

BaddieAF$07:

| **@whos_on_top69** just likes nigger dick **@I_AM_IRONMAN**

theotherNEGAN:

| **@whos_on_top69** Doesn't count. Marcel ain't breeding no women!

whos_on_top69:

| Fuck you! This is a game. He'll do what I want. I'll whip his ass like Django! Hahahahaaa

GoingProB*itch_25:

| LOLZ

suckmyYeezys:

| LOLOLOLLOLLL

theotherNEGAN:

| Fine cocksucker. You get $1,000 for yo BBC boy toy!

What little color Marcel has is drained from his face when I look up from the screen. His hands are trembling over the keyboard. I don't have to try hard to imagine what he must be thinking and feeling right now. My fists are clenched tightly after reading all that.

"That snake-ass . . . ," Marcel mumbles, biting his bottom lip. His eyes filled with rage.

"Who? You know who said this about you?" I say, standing up from the bed.

"Nolan Branston, for one," Marcel says. "His SnapMessages username is whos_on_top69. And we smashed the night before this convo."

Whoever Nolan is could get an ass whipping right now, along with everyone else on that thread. I start pacing around my bed while Marcel clicks through the screenshots in the folder.

"Oh shit, Amir, they're talking about you too," he says.

I snatch hold of the laptop and spin it around so I can see the screen. The photo he has open is dated February 6.

TODAY

BaddieAF$07:

> I'm ready to sell Amir. His hair was so nappy today! Plummeting my stock! **@NOLAWarlock** You want him? Yo plantation looking dry as hell right now.

First.Class.Diva1:

> Cut him some slack. He don't have money like his brother.

BaddieAF$07:

> He definitely deserve to be in the fields. Hopefully he gets a haircut soon.

First.Class.Diva1:

> Wonder if he packing like his brother 👀

"You all right?" Marcel says, his expression cautious.

I close my eyes and take a deep breath. Everything in me wants to hurl this laptop at the wall.

"No the fuck I'm not all right!" I drop the laptop and start pacing again, slamming my fist into my open palm. "Bruh, I'm ready to go back to that school and stomp the mess outta . . ."

Marcel shakes his head at the screen. "These are all screenshots of bits and pieces of this thread. And they mention nearly every Black kid or minority student who goes to our school. TheotherNEGAN called Trey a house nigger, and whoever *owns* him apparently has the most points because Trey's not problematic like some of us."

"Are you freaking serious?" I hiss.

"There are dozens of these screenshots. Why did Chloe have this?"

I spin around. "Because clearly she was one of the Karens and Kevins talking shit about us."

"Amir," he says, "I knew her. She would never be a part of something like this. That's not how she was raised. She was quick to tear into anyone who tried to *all lives matter* anything."

"That right there makes me glad I didn't bother getting to know anybody at that damn school," I say, pointing at my laptop.

Marcel's mouth drops open right before he says, "This BaddieAF person called Chelsea Griffin a pickaninny because of her wide mouth."

I start pacing again. Don't know who Chelsea is, but that doesn't stop me from being mad for her.

"On February seventh there's a back-and-forth about Trey's sister, Tiffany," Marcel continues. "GoingProB*tch wanted to sell her after she tripped and dropped her plate in the cafeteria that day. *Can't stand a clumsy colored, lol.*"

I need to punch something. Hard. Correction: make that some*one.* Preferably someone white who attends Truman. This entire time, it wasn't just in my head. Us Black kids are nothing but a joke to those privileged brats. And a lot of them, Marcel included, were running around smiling in their faces and calling them friends while they were making fun of us behind our backs! This feels like a violation of a whole other magnitude.

"I can't understand exactly what this is," Marcel says, still squinting at the screen. He needs to stop reading that mess. "It's like they're pretending to own us and then they build up points somehow, or money, and they sell and trade us based on stuff we do," he says.

"I don't need to understand anything about this—except for who's responsible," I say.

"On February eighth, whoever *owned* Darrius Gunner gifted

himself with a hundred dollars because Darrius was named the district's top student this year," Marcel says. "*Got me a smart one,* he messaged."

"Bruh, please stop reading before I tear this fucking room apart," I say, slamming my fist down on my TV stand.

"It doesn't make sense that Chloe could be linked to this," Marcel says, his voice quavering.

"How much proof you need? It's right there!" I shout, waving my arms at my laptop, which he's still balancing on his thighs. "Maybe she had a change of heart and turned on them after they started that bullshit."

"This has to be why she stole my phone, got your number, and texted you that night about coming to my party," he says, his gaze pointed at my TV stand. "She needed you to help her do something I didn't give her a chance to."

"Man, whatcha talking 'bout?" I say, my upper lip curled.

"Chloe and I had an argument a couple days before my party," he says. "She was in my ear about canceling it, claiming the kids at school weren't my friends. That was her trying to put me on to *this.* I was too caught up in party planning to listen. She got frustrated, accused me of me being blind to the world around me, and I told her she didn't have to come since she was acting like she didn't want to be there. I was shocked when she showed up anyway. Now I know why," he adds, looking up at me.

"But why at my party?" he continues. "She could have given you the flash drive and explained everything to you at school."

What he says causes me to reflect on something similar I told her while we were talking on her sofa.

It was a time-sensitive type of thing, I remember her saying.

"She was afraid to be alone," I remind him. "That night, when she said something about wanting to get to know me, I asked why she didn't wait till we were at school. She made it seem like she didn't have that long."

"She couldn't wait a day or two?" Marcel says, more to himself than to me.

"Someone, or some *people,* must have threatened her the day of your party," I say. "She said people at school *would rather see her dead.* And a lot of people from school was at yo' party, bruh."

"That flash drive must be what her killer tore through her room looking for," Marcel beats me to saying.

"What now?" I ask. "She said you would know what to do."

Marcel's face is serious. "Well, I know Nolan is one of the people in this thread. But there's someone else we know, someone who also goes to school with us and who might be the person you caught fleeing that church—the same church where Chloe hid this flash drive."

I stand up straighter. "The Colin dude."

Marcel nods. "How much you wanna bet he was looking for this?"

I don't gamble, but I'd be willing to bet my life on it.

22

Marcel

It took more than an hour for Amir to calm down last night. Can't really blame him. Anger was sizzling through my blood as well; it still is. Today being the first day I've walked onto this campus feeling stupid for ever thinking I belonged here. For assuming these kids I've socialized with, invited into my home, gone on dates with, partied with, shared secrets with, saw past my race. Considered me an equal. This world where I thought being Black didn't really matter when you could keep up with the Joneses was all a lie. At the end of the day, I'm a joke to some of them. And the one friend who tried to show me the truth is dead because I didn't want to listen to her.

I'm here today to right that wrong.

I stand up as soon as Colin Perrier enters the cafeteria, flicking his dumb-looking head to the side to sling his shaggy brown hair out of his face, no doubt looking for his friends. Jared and the rest of their crew are huddled around one of the tables near the back. I make a beeline for Colin at the same time he spots them, leaving my food behind.

Kids are still throwing shade at me following Amir's arrest. Today I welcome it, since I don't know who's part of the slave game. I'm taking Chloe's advice: *Don't trust anyone at school—especially if they're white!*

"Colin, we need to talk," I say, stepping in his path.

He tugs on the strap of his book bag, his blue eyes darting nervously around the room.

Right now, he's the only possible link we have to Chloe's flash drive. It can't be a coincidence, him having the same hoodie as the person who was in Amir's church. If I'm being honest, Colin has always given off a serial killer vibe. He's the kind of white boy people tell reporters was "such a quiet young man" after he's committed a mass shooting. He must have been looking for that flash drive. Which means he's connected to that fucked-up game.

Colin has known Chloe since kindergarten. The social politics of this school, and her breakup with Jared, caused them to slowly drift apart. Chloe became popular and Colin sort of faded into the background. After she dumped Jared, she and Colin hardly talked anymore. Jared forced him to pick a side and he picked Jared's, deepening the divide between him and Chloe. Could he have known about the Danverses' spare key? Maybe.

"What's up, Marcel," he says, raking a hand through his hair.

"Funny thing," I say, shifting my weight from one foot to the other. "I was in the Broadmoor area the other day, and I could have sworn I saw you running out of this old run-down church."

I study him, waiting for a reaction. Some tic to tell me he knows I'm on to his secret.

There is none. Colin's acne-dotted face remains blank.

"It struck me as odd, because why would you be over there?" I continue.

"Sorry, dawg, must have been my doppelgänger," he responds casually before stepping around me.

I turn and follow him. "Oh, so you weren't looking for that pink flash drive my brother found?"

That stops Colin dead in his tracks.

I grin as he slowly makes an about-face. The alarming expression I was expecting a few seconds ago is there now.

"So it *was* you that Amir walked in on," I say. "Interesting little, um, *game* we found on that drive," I add, my expression hardening.

Colin closes the space between us. He's suddenly so close I can smell the peanut M&M's he must have eaten on the way here. "Drop this shit, Marcel," he says, his voice low. "Don't get involved, please. You don't understand."

"I understand that you and way too many other kids here have been calling me a nigger behind my back," I stress.

"That wasn't me, it wasn't like that," he pleads.

"Then tell me, what was it like?"

There's a tightness around his eyes as he rapidly blinks at me. "I can't. Look, man, let this go. I mean it," he says while backing up.

"Did you kill Chloe because *she* wouldn't let it go?" I say.

Colin swallows hard. "Fuck no. But you're gonna end up like her if you don't."

And with that, he walks away.

My suspicions about Colin's connection to Chloe's murder sink in my gut as I watch him join his friends. There was fear in his eyes when he said that last part about me ending up like Chloe. Did he hurry off because he didn't want the person who killed her to see him talking to me?

"Bae, why you been avoiding me?" someone says as an arm drapes over my shoulders while I'm still processing what just happened.

It's Nolan.

I step away from him, spin on my heels, and punch him in the stomach.

He doubles over, clutching his midsection. "What the fuck, man?"

Everyone around us is watching as he gasps for air and I walk off.

Sucker punching him hardly feels like enough after what I read last night.

23

Amir

I put down the spoon I'm stirring with the second I hear Marcel's knock at the door.

I've been waiting all day to hear what went down with Colin. I quickly lower the burner under the pot of crab and shrimp étouffée I started thirty minutes ago.

Scurrying from the kitchen to the living room, I rub my damp hands along the inseam of the sweatpants that, along with a white tank, have become my new school uniform.

Marcel has a folder of class assignments for me tucked underneath his arm when I open the door.

" 'Sup, man. Come in," I say to him.

He loosens his uniform tie and unfastens the top two buttons of his shirt as he holds the folder out to me. "Damn, it smells good in here," he says as he enters.

"Thanks."

I shut the door and head back into the kitchen. The étouffée should be ready in a few minutes. I'm starving.

"Wait, you know how to cook?" he asks. He's standing at the island, eyeing the pot of étouffée with raised brows. I already know what he's thinking when our eyes meet. *Just like our dad.* I don't want to go there with him.

"What happened with ol' boy today?" I say, changing the subject. "Who all is in on that slave trade bullshit?"

His shoulders drop. "I have no idea. Colin clammed up on me."

"Thought you said you were going to let him have it?" I say.

"Didn't get a chance to, really." Marcel slides onto one of the barstools at the island as I go back to tending to my pot of étouffée. "He had no reaction when I mentioned him being at that church, though that changed the second I mentioned Chloe's jump drive."

The étouffée needs just a few more minutes to simmer, so I put down the spoon and turn to face Marcel. I lean against the counter next to the stove, cross my legs at the ankles, and fold my arms across my chest. "And then?"

"When I brought up the screenshots, it's like the fear of God entered his face. He told me to drop it or I'd end up dead like her."

"It's gotta be him, then, right?" I say.

I'm hoping we can avoid an *Oh, so now you believe me that Chloe didn't have anything to do with that game?* convo. I know Marcel knew her better than I did, but *knowing* a white person and being friends with one doesn't mean they can't still be racist or participate in racism on some level. But I don't think he's ready to acknowledge that. He's spent his whole life thinking he belonged. That he was just like them, only a little darker. That's the conversation I wouldn't mind having with him.

"I don't know, man," he says, shaking his head. "Colin's voice was trembling. He was scared. Like he was trying to warn me, not threaten me."

And there he goes! Letting this white boy play him. Did he not read what his friend Chloe said? We can't trust any of the white kids at school!

"Colin was in my church looking for the flash drive," I say. "He's a part of it for sure. Chloe said there were *multiple* people who wanted to keep that game under wraps."

"Yeah, but how did Colin even know where to look?" he retorts.

"Good point."

"I'm thinking there must be someone else involved who has more to lose if it gets out, like the person who started it."

"Any idea who that is?"

"Not yet." He pulls out his phone, unlocks it, and pauses to read whatever is on his screen. "You know what else has been bugging me about Chloe's message . . . ?"

Other than the part about me receiving it after she was murdered? I ask myself.

"This part she wrote about our family not being bought like hers," he says. "Who could have bought her silence?"

"Yeah, 'cause ain't her family already rich?" I say.

"When I was at her balloon release, I overheard her cousin telling Trey that Chloe was *going through stuff* with her dad," he says. "Wonder if there's a connection."

That could explain the tension I picked up on when I was telling her why I stopped visiting my dad.

I turn off the burner on the étouffée and open the cabinet to grab two dinner plates. "Can you ask her—the cousin?"

"I'm trying. DM'd her last night, but she left me on read," he says.

I'm betting that has to do with me, and her family still thinking I killed Chloe.

"We need to suss out who all is involved in that thread. I think I know how we might be able to do that," Marcel says.

He's still looking down at his phone when I look back over my shoulder. "How?"

"I made a burner account in SnapMessages," he says. "I'm gonna ask to join the group."

"You want something to eat?" I ask.

"Yeah, sure," he replies.

"But what if the administrator's bitch-ass asks who you are, wants a pic or something?" I say as I'm piling white rice on his plate. "This don't seem like the kind of group they'll be letting just anyone in if they willing to kill somebody to keep it a secret."

"I'll cross that bridge when I get to it," he says. "Just requested to join. We'll see what they say."

I pour two ladlefuls of étouffée over the rice and then give the plate to Marcel. I fix myself a plate too, grabbing us silverware and two Cokes out the refrigerator before joining him at the island. We both take our first bites around the same time.

"Oh my God, bruh, this is so good," Marcel moans.

A little pride swells in my chest. "Thanks," I say after swallowing.

"Does Daddy know you can cook like this?"

I pause. "No, and don't you say shit either."

"Amir . . ."

"Don't start, bruh, okay? We were doing good. Just let it be."

We eat in silence for the next few minutes. Then he asks if I read the comments from the #IStandWithAmir thread that he texted me this morning.

"Yeah, I looked at it," I say.

"And?"

"It's cool."

After a beat he says, "That's all. Cool?"

"Yeah," I say with a shrug.

It's weird seeing strangers commenting and making declarations about my life as if they know me, know what I'm thinking and feeling. I'm also not liking how divisive my situation has become online, primarily with Black people. The more I've read, the more it's starting to feel like a lot of people are only supporting me because it's the "woke" thing to do, or because they want to jump on the Orlando Houston bandwagon. It's not that they actually believe in my innocence. I've become yet another example to them of how the criminal justice system doesn't treat young Black men the same as it would treat white people. And yeah, that's no doubt true, but I'm innocent. It would be nice if their arguments were centered on *that* and not just my skin color.

I *do* understand why Marcel sent it. He's trying to make me feel better about my situation. Give me some hope. Can't hate him for that.

"Say, bruh." I push some of the étouffée around on my plate. "My bad . . . you know . . . for what I said the other day about yo' moms. It was messed up . . . on my part."

His mouth slacks, almost curling into a faint smile. "Look, I know what I told you out of anger won't change how you feel about Daddy, and I understand why, really, I do. That's between you and him. Still, I felt you should know the truth. Only wanted it to come out in a better way."

I swallow hard, hesitant to be vulnerable with him. But it feels okay, given everything he's done for me in spite of how I've treated him. "My life is so fucking messed up, bruh."

"Did you talk to your mom about it?" he asks.

"Not really," I admit. "Once I realized you weren't lying, wasn't really in the mood to hear nothing else she had to say."

He gives me a blank look.

"What?" I ask with a shrug.

"Why do you avoid the tough conversations?" he says, putting down his fork. "You're doing it with your friends, now your mother."

I bet Q told him that.

"Man, you don't know what you're talking about," I say, annoyed.

"I don't?" he says. "Amir, if anything you should talk to your mother, try to understand where she's coming from."

"What is there to understand? She lied. And for what?"

"If you'd talk to her, maybe she could help you understand. People operate a lot more in the grays than just black and white."

I smack my lips, dismissively waving off his comment.

"It's like you enjoy wallowing in the anger and the hurt instead of confronting it or, in the case of your friends, allowing people to be there to support you when you need it most," he says. "Yeah, it was messed up that Monica lied, but she's your mother, man. The only one you got. Why ice her out when she's stressing over what might happen to you?"

"Bruh, eat your food," I respond.

I need to shut this down. This convo is about to go left if it continues, and I don't want that. Not when we might have stumbled onto something that could actually get me out of the bullshit that has ironically brought us the closest we've ever been. We've talked and been around each other more this past week than all last semester when I started going to Truman.

His body crumples into itself once he realizes I'm not about to go there with him. He forks more étouffée into his mouth, chewing it hard. The silence that has settled over us feels suffocating. I know he's right about my mother, and about how I've been icing out my homeboys. Which annoys me even more. He'll never understand why I'm so hurt by Mama's lie.

She was supposed to be the good one. The one I could always count on, no matter what. My shero. To learn that she tried to manipulate me onto her side of a feud I didn't want to be part of is something I don't know how to get past.

Marcel's phone chimes, cutting through our silence. He quickly picks it up.

"I got a message from theotherNEGAN," he says.

I hop off my stool and rush to his side to look over his shoulder.

"Who dis?" Marcel reads aloud.

He gives me a deer-in-headlights look.

"Bruh, I told you he might do this," I say. "You should have thought this through."

"Fuck it," he says, looking back down at his phone.

He types *This is Erik Pennington.*

I have no idea who that is. I'm hoping it's a white boy who goes to school with us. Marcel needs whoever this is to think that he must have somehow heard about this thread and wants in. If this is by invite only, we're done. Then we've tipped them off that someone who shouldn't know does, if that Colin dude hasn't told them already.

What theotherNEGAN types back makes my heart beat faster.

> You're lying.

Marcel casts a worried look back at me before replying, *For real, dude. Trying to get in on this fun. Heard this group is a safe space to put niggers in their place.*

"Bruh, really?" I sigh.

"Too much? I want to sound convincing," Marcel says.

TheotherNEGAN's reply makes Marcel's breath hitch.

> Nice try, Marcel. Suck on a dick!

The message is immediately followed by an app alert that says theotherNEGAN has blocked Marcel's burner account from contacting him.

"What the . . ."

When Marcel tries to search for the slave trade group again, nothing comes up.

"That bastard completely blocked me."

I walk back over to my stool, my heartbeat slowing to a dull thud. "Bruh, it's gotta be Colin who's behind it, then. He's the only one that knew you knew about it. Or he told whoever that Negan person is."

"But you weren't there today," Marcel argues. "He looked scared, Amir. Like whoever created this thread is the one who went after Chloe."

"He was playing you," I reply. "Your friend said it herself, them white kids at school are snakes. Can't be trusted."

"Not all of them. Not Chloe," he retorts. There's a sadness in his voice that cools some of the anger bubbling in my chest.

I'm about to admit he's right when the front door opens. Mama comes wobbling in with grocery bags dangling from both hands. Her face twists into a grimace the second she sees Marcel sitting with me in the kitchen.

"Can you help me with these bags, Amir?" she asks.

I groan, sliding off the stool. She tries to give me a smile as I meet her in the middle of the living room to take the bags she's holding, but I avoid eye contact.

"Had to make a grocery run since you've been at home all day cooking everything in sight," she says after retrieving the bags she left on the porch. "You got the folks on the night shift hankering for more, boy."

I put the bags on the counter next to the refrigerator. I feel Marcel watching me. The silence between us is even thicker now than it was a few minutes ago.

"Hey, I need to get started on this work," I tell him, nodding at the folder he brought me, which is in the middle of the island countertop. "I'll holla at you later," I add, reaching over and picking up his plate of unfinished étouffée.

I don't give him a chance to protest. I dump it in the garbage can. My mother is setting bags on the counter behind me, and I walk around her, dropping Marcel's empty plate into the sink before turning to grab my plate and dump it too.

"Uh, yeah. Okay, Amir. We'll talk later," Marcel says, awkwardly sliding off the barstool. "See you later, Monica," he mumbles, then quietly walks out the front door, casting a look back at me and my mother.

"Has he been dropping by here a lot?" my mother says as soon as the door shuts.

"Yeah," I respond dismissively, then leave her in the kitchen and retreat to my bedroom.

Forget what Marcel said. Not dealing has become my coping mechanism.

24

Marcel

I'm about to press the door release handle on the Tessie when I hear "You couldn't *wait* to come between me and my son, could you?"

Monica is standing on the front porch when I turn around. A hand propped on one hip, her face stern and her mouth tight. I had a feeling this moment would come. What I didn't expect was that she'd try to frame this as me wanting to create a wedge between her and Amir.

Oh no, that's not happening on my *watch!*

"Excuse me?" I respond, inching my way back to the bottom of the stairs that lead to their porch.

"First you don't tell the truth when you should, to get Amir's father to turn on him," she says. "And now you go running your mouth again so Amir will turn on me. Is that all you and your shallow mama good for, ruining our lives?"

I've always been a little afraid of Monica. She's rough around the edges. Has an authoritative tone that always feels like yelling.

My father has called her a pit bull (and a lot of other not-so-nice things). Her no-nonsense approach to life is something he said she's always had. It was what initially attracted him to her when they met as kids growing up in Tremé. And then the thing he once loved became the very thing that drove him away. I guess bullish, realistic viewpoints are great until they're coming at you.

Given the venom her and my mother have spewed at each other, I get why she may never like Mama. But me, I've never done anything to Monica. Guess my very existence is enough.

I take a deep breath. "Monica, no disrespect, but *you're* the only one coming between you and Amir, not me."

"Amir got too much scary, life-changing real stuff he's dealing with right now to have you bringing up old shit!" she yells.

"Yeah, and *I've* been here every day to get him through that," I reply, stabbing myself in the chest with my index finger. I need to stay calm, think straight. I've been waiting to say this for a long time, and I want it to land exactly how I intend. "He talks down to me, rarely shows me any kindness, and yet I'm still showing up, doing whatever it takes to make sure he doesn't get indicted. Trying to keep him out of prison for *you*—for us!"

"Y'all don't care about nothing but yourselves," she says with an intense stare.

"Stop it. Stop it!" I yell.

"Stop what?"

"Doing *this,*" I reply through clenched teeth. "Painting me as a villain. Look, your beef with my mother is legit, but that ain't got nothing to do with me and Amir. And I'm not going to let you come between us anymore. Not you. Not my mother. Nobody."

She opens her mouth to speak, but I cut her off with "Amir and I didn't ask to be here. Caught in the middle of the adult crap you got going on. You need to get over your hurt. That was seventeen years ago. You want to fix the damage you've done with your son, tell him it's okay for him to forgive our father. No matter what he says, I know Amir wants a relationship with him. But I think part of the reason he's scared to have it is you. He doesn't want you to feel alone. To feel that he picked a side. That he's choosing us over you—and you know it's true. That's why you lied about the custody stuff."

Monica looks down at her feet.

"Amir is hurting, but he doesn't have to be," I say. "He's scared, but he doesn't have to be alone. He needs you, our father, *and* me to get through this. I'm not going anywhere, Monica. No matter how much you try to push me away. So you better get used to it. Get used to me. Once this is behind us, I'm not letting you or him push me out of your lives. I made mistakes too, I know that. I wasn't always the best brother. This is me wanting to change that. I'm gonna show you how much I love Amir. Prove it by doing everything in my power to keep him out of prison. I promise you that."

"Don't make promises you can't keep," she says.

"Watch me."

She's still on the porch, glaring at me, when I'm in my car. And she's in the same spot when I look in the rearview mirror as I'm driving away.

25

Amir

My emotions are ping-ponging between anger and angst. Marcel and I are sitting on a concrete bench near the McDonogh Oak in City Park, waiting for Colin to join the group of dudes, and a girl, who are crowded around a picnic table across the way from us, beneath one of the sprawling trees that create the Southern-Gothic-postcard aesthetic people love so much about this park's Historic Oak Grove. On the ride here, Marcel kept repeating to me all the things we could say to force a confession out of Colin. He's the only link we have to the slave trade game and Chloe's murder at this point.

I don't think it'll be as easy as Marcel makes it sound. The world doesn't work like that for me. My life is Mercury in constant retrograde. Marcel seems sure, though. This has become so personal for him. Like he's trying to win something I don't know about. Cool. If whatever it is keeps me from going to prison, I don't care what his angle is. I just want this to be over.

If he thinks Colin is our direct path to making that happen, I'll put faith in this working out for us.

Just gotta keep reminding myself not to knock dude's head off over all the things he and his friends have been saying about us in that thread.

"You sure he coming?" I say, leaning forward to prop my elbows on my knees as I watch the group.

"Yes, I know for a fact Friday afternoon is when he comes out here to play Dungeons and Dragons with his group," Marcel says, his eyes hidden behind a pair of sunglasses I'm sure cost more than the flat-screen TV in my room. "Chloe teased him about it once. I checked their Facebook group this morning, and this is the day they meet."

Traffic hums behind us down City Park Avenue.

My right leg starts to shake. "We been here almost thirty minutes and he still hasn't showed up."

"He must be running late." Marcel checks the time on his phone. "I don't think he ever misses this."

I bet Colin is theotherNEGAN. He's the only person in that group who knew Marcel found out about it. Marcel isn't one hundred percent convinced I'm right. He keeps bringing up how scared Colin looked when he warned him. I told Marcel if we don't get anything out of this fool, we take what we know already to the cops, or at least give it to Mr. Dillard. Maybe he can intimidate dude to talk through some legal means. Chloe's message to me has to work in my favor somehow, I said to him.

"Yeah, I'll think about it" was Marcel's response on the way here.

Ain't no thinking about it. I'm not sitting on everything we've learned in the past forty-eight hours much longer.

"There he is," Marcel says, pointing ahead.

In the distance, Colin's lanky frame is speed walking toward the picnic table we've been watching, the black hooded robe he's wearing over his uniform pants, shirt, and tie blowing in the wind like all the Spanish moss bearding the trees out here. He kinda looks like an extra for a Harry Potter movie.

"Hold on," Marcel says, holding out his arm just as I'm about to stand up. "Let him sit down first, get a little comfortable. Then we'll go over and ambush him."

This dude, always with the dramatics, I think as the side of my mouth curls.

I wait on Marcel. My leg still jumping like crazy.

After a minute that feels like an eternity, Marcel says, "Let's go."

We shoot up off the bench, darting toward the picnic table in unison.

My heart is tapping against my chest: *Get him. Get him.* Colin is seated with his back to us. He doesn't see us approaching. But some dude wearing a pointy wizard cap does. He's already glaring at us, his shaggy eyebrows squished together. But he's not alerting anyone else at the table to our presence.

"Colin," Marcel barks.

Everyone quickly looks up, but Colin takes his time twisting his upper body around to face us. He sighs, muttering "Fuck me" under his breath the second his eyes land on Marcel. His chin dips into his chest and his shoulders sag at the sight of me. Marcel figured my presence would intimidate Colin. Make him feel guilt being face to face with the person he's framing—if he's really the one who killed Chloe. I do my best to look like I'm two seconds from giving him a beatdown, which isn't that hard. I already told myself not to lose control, no matter what this dude says or doesn't say. Assaulting him would feed right into the prejudices he has against us. Probably wouldn't help my defense either, if I do end up on trial.

"Sorry to interrupt y'all, but we need to have a serious chat with Colin right quick," Marcel says. "About *another* game he likes to play."

Colin swallows hard, not taking his eyes off us.

"Dude, you were already late. We have to jump on this quest, and I need my wizard to do that," says a thick white guy, who looks a little too old to be in high school, with an annoyed look aimed at the back of Colin's head.

Is that why Colin has a robe on? Because he's a make-believe wizard? *Hold up.* That must mean Colin is the NOLAWarlock person BaddieAF$07 was trying to "sell" me to. Going upside dude's head would feel so gratifying right now.

"This will only take a minute," Colin says, standing up with his mouth set in a determined line.

"Or not," I huff, looking Colin up and down as he nears us.

"I don't have anything to tell you," he says in a hushed whisper, more to Marcel than to me.

"In that case, I guess my brother and I can assume *you're* the one behind that Make America Great Again thread and that you killed Chloe, what, because she was going to tell everyone about it?" Marcel says with his chest poked out.

Everyone from Colin's Dungeons and Dragons group is watching us with blank stares.

"I did *not* do that to her," Colin seethes.

"But you know who did, right?" Marcel says. "That's why you told me to drop this at school yesterday?"

"Leave me alone, please," Colin says, his eyes desperate.

I'm starting to understand what Marcel was talking about. He's lacking the brashness theotherNEGAN had when he blocked Marcel. I couldn't see this dude busting a grape, let alone killing someone.

"What's it gonna be, Colin?" Marcel demands in an impatient tone. "Talk to us or take the fall for that thread?" Marcel looks past Colin at the table full of people still watching us. One of them is Black, and the girl is Asian. I immediately know what Marcel is about to say when I see him look back at Colin. "Want your friends here to learn what you like to pretend to buy and sell—"

"All right, *all right*! I'll talk."

Marcel gives me a proud look.

"I'll be right back, guys," Colin says over his shoulder to his Dungeons and Dragons friends. "Need to clear some things up."

We lead him back to the concrete bench near the McDonogh Oak. The oldest tree in this park seems like the ideal backdrop for hashing out how one of this country's oldest sins became a game that led to a girl's murder.

“Sit down,” I tell him, pointing to the bench.

He hesitates a few seconds, giving me this annoyed look. I raise an eyebrow and return a *don’t even try it* frown at him before he drops down, combing his hand through his floppy hair.

“If you didn’t kill Chloe, tell us who did,” Marcel says.

Okay, guess we’re jumping right into the deep end. I fold my arms across my chest.

“First I want a verbal agreement that you’ll hand over the screenshots if I tell you,” he says.

Hold up. Does dude really know who killed her? I wonder.

“Why would we do that?” I say, to establish he’s in no position to be demanding shit from us.

“I want this game behind me, what happened to Chloe off my conscience,” he says. “And those won’t matter anymore if what I say helps clear your brother’s name, right?”

Marcel looks at me nervously. I don’t take my eyes off Colin.

Nah, bro, that ain’t happening. Those screenshots are the only proof we have of the game. I want my name cleared *and* what they’ve been doing exposed. I gotta believe Marcel wants the same thing.

“We’re not giving you the flash drive or those screenshots.” I lean over so that I’m eye level with him. “If you don’t like that, how about you call me a nappy-headed nigger to my face, like you and your friends did in that thread.”

“I didn’t say that; I don’t think like that, man,” Colin whines. “I never said *anything* about any of y’all in that group. I promise.”

Marcel tugs on my forearm, pulling me upright.

“Then why be a part of it at all?” Marcel asks.

“’Cause I didn’t want Jared giving me shit for dipping out,” Colin says.

Marcel and I exchange knowing glances. He’s realizing the same thing I am: four months ago, Jared Lanford came to school dressed as Negan from *The Walking Dead* for Halloween. Everything about that dude screams *everyone is beneath me, especially Black people.* Now I’m regretting not letting Buster stomp him at Marcel’s party.

“Plus, if I had left the group, I wouldn’t have been able to help Chloe,” Colin says, refocusing our attention on him. There’s a sadness clouding his face.

“What do you mean you helped her?” I ask.

“Chloe wanted to expose the thread too—expose Jared, really. He’s the administrator—the ‘master,’ ” Colin says, making air quotes when he says “master.”

“Was she in on the group too?” Marcel says, taking off his sunglasses.

Colin shakes his head.

“Then how did she find out about it?” he presses. “When and how did it start?”

Colin huffs. “Unofficially, at Jared’s house, during his family’s annual Christmas party over break. Jared and a few kids from school whose parents are friends with the Lanfords were being crass, spinning dumb hypotheticals about what they would do had they lived back during slavery. Somehow that morphed into them talking about some of the Black kids at school and joking about which ones would have done good on the slave market.

Jared and Patrick Rawlings had just watched that movie *Antebellum,* I think that's what prompted it all."

The urge to hit something, hard, is coming back. I hug my clenched fists tighter to my chest.

"Jared has been saying dark, inappropriate stuff about Black people ever since Chloe started dating Trey," Colin says. "They were talking about Trey when Chloe found out about the game."

"Which started . . . ?" Marcel prods.

"When we came back to school after winter break," Colin replies. "The night before our first day of class, I received a notification that Jared had added me to the group. The other people were everyone who was at his family's Christmas party. I was uncomfortable the second Jared started listing the rules of his new game."

"So uncomfortable that you didn't say anything to them about it," I say, rolling my eyes.

I don't care how tortured this dude is looking while he's telling us this. Being *uncomfortable* around racism and not actively participating in it doesn't make him any better than the people who did participate. Some things are never okay to turn a blind eye to.

"What were the rules?" Marcel says.

Colin rakes his hand through his hair, his eyes nervously shifting between us. "Again, I wasn't involved, *like that,* in this."

"Taaaaaalk!" I bark.

He takes another deep breath. "Jared assigned each of us a

minority classmate. Some got more than one, since there were only ten of us initially. We each got a certain amount of points, and from there we could amass more based on how our sla—student acted day-to-day. It was dumb. So dumb. Points if they did things like made good grades, achieved some positive recognition, looked good. And deductions if they got in trouble, made bad grades, or had jacked-up appearances. People in the group would try to accrue more points by influencing their assigned student to do things that would shed a good light on them. Help them study for an upcoming test, sway them to do certain things, date certain people—stuff like that."

I want so badly to know who made the comment about me not having a haircut. But there are more important things we need to get out of him while we can. Like who he thinks killed Chloe.

"If you had enough points, enough to buy someone else's *person,* you could trade or buy them from someone else," Colin continues. "And things went on from there."

"And this was entertainment to y'all," I say.

"To *them,* not me," he claims.

"How did Chloe get involved? You said something about Trey," Marcel quizzes.

Colin waits until a lady walking her dog behind him down City Park Avenue is out of earshot before he answers. As if she was some kind of spy. Dude is too paranoid.

"I was in the library and had opened my SnapMessages to erase that day's thread—you know, since it vanishes after you check the messages," he says. "That's when she saw. I don't remember what they were saying about Trey that day, and I didn't realize she had walked up behind me and was reading over my shoulder. Before I could exit the app, she snatched the phone out my hand and saw what was going on. And you know how Chloe was about stuff like this," he says to Marcel. "She was livid. Started going off on me. She knew Jared was behind it after seeing his username in the thread. She gave me so much shit for not saying anything to anyone about what was going on. Said I was no better than anyone in that group if I didn't do something to stop the game."

Marcel was right about her. Good to know at least one white person at school had our backs when we couldn't be around to defend ourselves.

"She guilted me into exposing the thread," Colin says. "Said it was the only way I could make things right, not be branded a racist like the rest of them. I agreed to help her. I wanted it to end. I did. I swear. And she wanted to take Jared down. Knew he'd be canceled so hard his head would spin if that game got out. He could forget his Ivy League college, even with his legacy status. He'd get kicked out of Truman. This was a stain she wanted to follow him forever. Marcel, you know yourself how much she hated him after they broke up."

"Why are you so scared of dude?" I ask, referring to Jared.

"Our fathers do business together, or rather, Mr. Lanford's foundation bankrolls a lot of my dad's business endeavors," Colin says to me. "You meet Jared's father, you understand why Jared thinks he can do whatever he wants. Our friendship isn't organic. It's an extension of our parents' business relations. What happens between us affects their bottom lines. Piss off the wrong friend, deals suddenly go sour."

Marcel's sidelong glances have me thinking he understands what Colin is talking about. Why is nothing ever simple in their world? It all comes back to money somehow. Who has it, who's getting the most, and who doesn't deserve respect because they don't have it.

"Then what?" Marcel says to Colin. "How was Chloe planning to expose the game?"

Colin rakes his hand through his hair again. "Since you can't screenshot the app without everyone else knowing, and messages vanish after they're read, we would meet up at certain times during the day at school. I would open the thread, and she would take a picture of the messages with her phone and save them on that flash drive." His eyes shift to Marcel and he says, "The week before yo' party, she said she was going to Mr. Braswell with them."

"What did he say?" Marcel asks, leaning forward.

Colin shrugs. "I have no idea. When nothing happened after a few days, I inquired. She copped mad attitude when I did. Said she didn't want to talk about it. And we didn't—not until the night of your party, when Jared confronted *both* of us." He takes a labored breath. "Somehow, he found out what we were up to," he continues, his voice trembling. "He straight-up told Chloe that night that he would *end* her if she said anything about the game. He mentioned something about it being in her family's best interests that she didn't. He looked like the freaking devil when he said it."

"But how did he find out that she knew?" Marcel asks.

"I. Don't. Know," Colin insists. "I asked her the same thing, but she wouldn't give me a straight answer."

"You're lying," Marcel barks. "You told him, didn't you?"

"I didn't," Colin whines. "I swear."

"Pause," I say, holding up my hand. "Are you telling us that Jared killed her?"

Colin's chin starts trembling. "He said he would end her. Chloe acted like she was unfazed; the next morning, she turns up dead."

Her response to Jared's threat was obviously a front. If she was really unbothered by what he said, she wouldn't have wanted my company the rest of the night.

"You have proof Jared killed her?" Marcel asks.

Colin shakes his head.

"Then how can you be certain, bruh?" I say out of frustration.

"Didn't you hear what I just said?" Colin says, cocking his head. "He threatened to end her, and she was murdered the same night."

"And yet that hasn't stopped you from hanging around with him at school," Marcel fires back.

Colin hangs his head. "What else am I supposed to do? Jared is untouchable. The kid gets away with everything."

"You could go to the police!" Marcel shouts. "Tell them what you know. She was your friend too! If you think he—"

"I don't have any proof, Marcel," Colin rails. "It would be my word against *theirs.* After he threatened Chloe, Jared said he'd get everyone to turn against me and say that *I* started that group if I didn't get those screenshots back. I . . . I just want . . . I didn't know . . ."

Colin looks like he's on the verge of tears. So does Marcel, but for entirely different reasons. As emotional as this is for them, there are still questions I need answers to. And this dude is the only person who can give them to me. I don't think he has it in him to commit a murder, but now I'm thinking he's weak enough to get forced into being complicit in one.

"You were in my church, looking for her flash drive," I say, pulling their attention to me. "Why? How did you even know she hid it there?"

After raking a hand through his hair again, he says, "Chloe said she had to find *another way* to expose the game."

His stare lingers on me.

"It didn't make sense what she meant until I saw her leave the party with you," he continues, pointing at me. "I started texting her, telling her it wasn't worth it anymore. That she needed to leave Jared alone because he was becoming unhinged. I suggested we get rid of the screenshots. She said she wouldn't. I told her I wouldn't help her anymore. That I was done. Was stupid enough to threaten to take the flash drive from her just to get Jared off my back. She texted me *good luck,* said she hid it someplace I'd never find it."

My hands fall to my sides as more memories from that night flood my mind. Her having that attitude when we first got in her car. Her constantly texting someone. It wasn't Trey, like I thought. It was this dude.

"How would you have known where to look?" Marcel says, beating me to the next question that popped into my mind.

He holds his head down, shielding part of his face with his stringy hair. "Chloe and I have been sharing our locations with each other since middle school. We never stopped, even though we didn't hang as much anymore." He briefly pauses, then says, "After she left with Amir, I tracked her all night. Saw that she was stopped somewhere on Washington Avenue when she sent that text about hiding the flash drive. The app lets you zero in on a person's exact location. That run-down church ended up being the rectangular-shaped thing her phone was pinging from. When I heard the news stories about her bedroom being tore through, figured Jared had done that looking for the flash drive. With her dead, it was the only proof left of the game. The day after her balloon release, I drove there. The first night I started searching, it got dark so I had to leave. I went back that day after school to find it. That's when you caught me," he says, looking up at me.

"You were looking for it to do what?" Marcel yells. "Give it back to Jared, then go on with your life like nothing was happening to my brother? Didn't care he might go to prison for something you think *your* friend did? You were just going to sit on all this information? What about Chloe?"

Colin buries his face in his hands, his shoulders hunched. "I don't want anyone else to get hurt." He lifts his head, his eyes glistening with tears. "I just want all this to be over. It got so out of hand so fast."

"Did you tell him we have the flash drive?" I ask.

If dude would kill once to keep his game a secret, what's stopping him from doing it again?

It takes a few seconds before Colin nods in response to my question, unable to make eye contact with either one of us.

"You're going to help us prove that he killed her," Marcel says. "You owe it to us, to Chloe."

"I already told you what you wanted to know," he yelps, standing up. "I don't want any part of this. I'm out!"

"But Jared—"

"Is untouchable," Colin interjects. Then he looks at me and says, "I'm sorry. I am. I don't know what else to do. I'm not racist. I never said anything bad about anyone in that group. I just got caught up in a fucked-up situation—"

"Your silence is compliance," Marcel says.

"It's not happening anymore, I promise," Colin pleads.

"I have to save my brother!" Marcel shouts.

His outburst catches me off guard. The raw emotion vibrating in his voice opening my chest up, giving me more room to breathe. Something I haven't felt in days.

Colin's eyes nervously shift to me. I get hopeful that Marcel's passion will convince him to change his mind and help us—help me. But the light in his eyes dims as they return to Marcel. I know his answer before he says it. The breath of fresh air deflating from my chest.

"I'm sorry," he mumbles.

And with that he storms off, back to the picnic table and his make-believe world of dragons and magic. Back to his life, like nothing happened.

Marcel has already taken off toward his car when I turn to him. I have to jog to catch up. I call his name repeatedly, but it only seems to make him walk faster.

"You a'ight?" I ask once we're inside the quiet of his car.

"No, I'm not all right," he snaps, making me jump in my seat. "You and Chloe were right! These kids are *not* my friends. They never were."

A tear dribbles down his cheek. I wish I knew what to say. Everything I'm thinking would only upset him more.

He turns to me. "But you were wrong too."

"About what?"

"Them accepting me," he says as more tears spill from his eyes. "Clearly they don't. I'm a joke. We're a joke to them. Our lives are a joke. These people I've invited into my home, broken bread with, don't give a fuck about me. At the end of the day, Colin chose someone he believes is capable of murder over me, and I've only ever been kind to him. What did I do to them to deserve this?"

"Fuck Colin, for real," I say.

Marcel starts pounding his fist against his steering wheel. I've never seen him this angry.

"Chloe tried to tell me, but I didn't listen. And now she's dead." He wipes his cheeks with the back of his hand. "If I had just listened to her, maybe she'd still be alive."

He covers his eyes with his hands and continues to cry.

"Bruh, stop this," I say, reaching over to softly grab the back of his neck and shake him. "Don't let them determine your worth. You know who you are. You know what Chloe told me that night? That one of the things she loved about you is your ability to not give a fuck about being liked. On some level, I think she understood why you didn't want to hear her out, and that's why she came to me."

But it's different with you, she said about Marcel that night in the church. *When it comes to you, he cares.*

"She knew she needed a different messenger," I tell him.

He tilts his head back, sniffing. "And that our family couldn't be bought like hers."

I pull my hand back, a little confused by the sudden determination in his tearstained face.

Marcel mashes the button that starts his car. "Finding out why she said that might be the way we figure out whether Colin is right about Jared."

"How we supposed to do that?" I ask as he hits the gas.

"By talking to the only person who knew her better than me," he replies.

26

Marcel

It's starting to feel like I skipped my morning classes today for nothing. I have yet to see Chloe's cousin Victoria enter or exit Richardson Memorial Hall on Tulane's campus. I've visited the university's school of architecture once, with Chloe. It was another Monday morning when she talked me into skipping first period with her to meet up with Victoria beneath the same tree I'm sitting under now. Chloe was doing a surprise "wellness check" after Victoria's breakup with a longtime boyfriend.

I recall Chloe calling her cousin an old lady because Victoria preferred early-morning classes. I check my phone. It's almost nine a.m. I've been here since eight-thirty, looking as out of place as I feel in my school uniform. Ambushing Victoria on her way to or from class is the only option I've got, since she didn't respond to any of the DMs I sent her over the weekend, begging her to talk. She would know what Chloe meant about their family being "bought." She's also the only Danvers I could likely get to talk to me about it. Before Chloe's murder, Victoria and I were cool. She's hung out with me and Chloe quite a few times. I'm hoping the message her cousin sent my brother will convince her to trust me.

"Marcel? Really!" I hear as I'm watching all the students milling around in the quad unaffected by the murder of a friend.

Victoria is standing a few feet to my right, one hand propped on her hip, her eyes narrowed at me.

I stand up, my heart starting to knock against my chest. "H-h-hey. Forgive me for showing up out of the blue like this, but you wouldn't respond to my DMs."

"And somehow that wasn't a strong enough indication that I have nothing to say to you?"

She takes off toward the entrance to Richardson Hall. I have to sidestep a trio of girls heading in the opposite direction to follow her, the sun warming the back of my head.

"Victoria, wait. *Please.*"

She keeps going. Her bobbed blond hair bouncing with every deliberate step.

"My brother didn't kill her!" I shout, eliciting looks from the students loitering in front of the beige brick building. "Chloe sent him a message that night, fearing for her life and asking for his help."

That stops her. I pause too, waiting for her to turn around. Her brow is furrowed when she does.

"What are you talking about?" she says.

I hold my phone out to her after I've pulled up the screenshot of Chloe's message to Amir. Victoria purses her lips at me before yanking it from my hand. I wait silently as people shuffle around us, watching intently as she reads her cousin's last words. Some of the color has drained from her face once she looks up.

"She sent that through our school's instant messaging program," I explain. "Amir didn't see it until a few days ago. But the time stamp shows that Chloe set it to drop in his inbox the morning after she was killed. I think she wrote it that night while my brother was sleeping downstairs."

"Why?"

"She was trying to rope him into exposing something messed up that's been going on at our school," I tell her. I'm purposely not mentioning the slave trade game to see if she already knows about it. It appears she doesn't, given her dumbfounded expression. "All we know so far is that Jared has something to do with it."

As soon as I mention his name, Victoria rolls her eyes. "What was she talking about?" she says, handing me back my phone. "What did she want him to find?"

"We're still trying to figure that out," I lie. "But I don't understand the part where Chloe said she wanted my brother's help because my family couldn't be bought like y'all's. Why would she say that?"

Victoria adjusts the strap of her book bag on her shoulder. She bites her bottom lip and shifts her eyes away from my stare. She definitely knows what Chloe was talking about, but she isn't sure she wants to tell me.

"Come on, Victoria," I plead. "You know me. You know how much I loved her. I would never defend my brother like this if I really thought he'd killed my best friend. And why would she be DM'ing him asking for help if she didn't think she could trust him?"

She sighs. "If Jared is involved with whatever she's referring to, then she's talking about those new construction projects Uncle Aubrey's firm recently landed."

"You mean the design work y'all are doing on that new concert hall and those residential complexes?"

Victoria works part-time at her uncle's architecture firm while she's in school.

She nods. "You know for yourself my uncle was in danger of closing that firm after the lawsuit over that collapsed government building. No one in this city wanted to hire him to even design a doghouse after the fallout."

"What does that have to do with Jared and what Chloe said?" I ask.

"Those projects are economic development endeavors being funded by Deacon Lanford's foundation," she says. "Jared's father basically *gifted* them to my uncle as a lifeline."

Suddenly, it's tougher to breathe.

"Wait, when did they announce those projects?" I ask, the time line already shifting into place in my head.

"On February eighth," she says. "I know because it was my mother's birthday."

That was five days before my party, and the day after Chloe tried to tell me about the game.

"I walked in on an argument she and Uncle Aubrey were having about the whole thing when I showed up to do laundry one afternoon," Victoria says. "My uncle was fuming about her reaching out to some journalist, and Chloe was screaming about him being the worst. I tried to ask her about it, but she didn't want to talk to me, said I was *part of the establishment* that didn't want her to expose the truth about the world—whatever that meant. I knew she would be pissed about her father getting in bed with the Lanfords, given what Jared had already put her through, and I totally supported her in that. But I also knew how much my uncle's business was suffering. He needed those projects to restore his reputation, his firm. Things got so bad between Chloe and Uncle Aubrey that he threatened to ground her and take her car if she didn't give him what he needed to close the deal with Deacon Lanford. He gave her till the morning we came back from visiting my grandmother to do it."

That would have been the day after my birthday party.

"What's with the shocked face?" Victoria says to me. "You know what my uncle wanted from her?"

I do. Now it makes sense why Chloe hid the flash drive that night. She didn't want her father to have it and potentially destroy the only evidence she had of the game to secure his deal with Mr. Lanford. I'm betting that had she not been murdered, Chloe was going to lie to her father, claim she'd lost the flash drive, to buy herself a little more time, 'cause he'd think she was telling the truth when he searched her room and personal belongings and didn't find it. Then she could have unsent that message to Amir and probably made a second attempt to tell me what Jared and the others had been doing, *or* maybe meet with whatever journalist she had reached out to, which she had to have done about the game, given the time line.

And in case Jared followed through with his threat, she spent her last night on earth leaving enough bread crumbs for me and my brother that we could pick up where she left off.

Chloe, I fucking love you!

The only thing I really know about Jared's family is that they're part of the New Orleans old-money brigade. Wealth tied to plantations that grew sugarcane, tobacco, and cotton, with a family tree boasting decorated war veterans and political leaders. What I've learned the past few hours while Googling between classes is that Jared's father is the chief executive officer and president of the Crescent City Foundation, a decades-old nonprofit organization that functions sort of like a brokerage for philanthropic endeavors.

Tax records posted online show that the foundation has an annual operating budget of more than seven million dollars, and that it funneled more than six hundred million dollars in donations to various civic initiatives, scholarship funds, and economic development projects last year. I found pictures of Deacon Lanford, Jared's father, posing with nearly every notable leader and prominent official at the city, state, and national levels.

Google has also given me clarity about Mr. Lanford's business dealings with Colin's father. Nearly all the projects Deacon

Lanford's foundation supports are thoroughly vetted and analyzed by Colin's father's consulting firm. The relationship has been *very* financially beneficial to Colin's family. Chloe's father's architecture firm will earn more than two million dollars to design the two projects Victoria said Jared's father *gifted* to her uncle, according to a news article announcing the deal.

What I still can't figure out is how Jared tipped his father off to stop Chloe from exposing that fucked-up game. It seems like the Lanfords interfered before she could go to Mr. Braswell with it. Must be why she didn't want to talk to Colin about what happened.

"Look, bruh, I don't think you need to be confronting him alone," Amir tells me over the phone between classes. "I ain't there to stop dude if he gets reckless. You saw how shook he has Colin."

He's worried about me. I knew he cared.

"I got this, okay? I ain't scared of him," I say, weaving between the sluggish kids in front of me. "He ain't gonna stab me in front of everyone."

"Yeah, but he might sneak into yo' house and gut you like her," Amir interjects.

"Look, I might get a confession outta him, or get him to slip up and say something we can use to prove that Colin is right."

Is Jared capable of murder? I wouldn't put it past him. The whole reason Chloe dumped him was because of how crazy possessive he got with her toward the end of their relationship. The breaking point being when he accused her of flirting with some guy at an end-of-the-year party they went to her sophomore year. He slapped her and started choking her while they argued about it that night.

Now that I think about it, it wouldn't surprise me if Jared knew the Danverses kept a spare key to their house in that fake rock. Jared and Chloe dated a long time.

"I don't like you confronting him by yourself," Amir says.

"It's cool, all right? I got this," I say. "We're running out of time, Amir. The grand jury meets on Thursday—in *three* days."

"More reason to let my lawyer in on all this," he says.

"Look, I gotta go. I see him up ahead," I say, and hit end.

I don't need the lawyer's help. I can do this myself . . . for Chloe. I owe it to her.

I turn on the voice-recording feature on my phone and slip it into the inner breast pocket of my uniform blazer. If he does trip up and confess to something, I want the receipts to prove it. The fluttering feeling in my chest grows stronger as I approach his locker.

"Jared, didn't realize you'd be taking your mock trial assignment as a murderer quite so seriously," I say, leaning against the locker next to his.

"Da fuck you talking about, Trudeau?" he says, his mouth twisted.

"Don't play dumb. I know your little lackey, Colin, has already told you what we know."

Had Colin been willing to help us take Jared down and end this, I wouldn't have thrown him under the bus so easily.

"He also tell you that he thinks you killed her?" I say, leaning closer to Jared so that my phone can pick up his voice over all the noise buzzing through the hallway.

"That's unfortunate," Jared responds calmly. "Here I thought you were stopping by my locker 'cause you wanted to help Nolan score a few more points by being a good breeder for me—oh wait, I'd definitely be a top. Sooooo, my bed wench?"

I lurch at him, itching to pound his smug face as hard as my heart is pounding behind my rib cage. But Jared's quicker. He's able to press his hand into my chest before I make contact. This fucker has zero shame. Doesn't give a damn about how his game makes us feel.

"Now, now, Trudeau," he coos. "Let's keep our hands to ourselves. . . . You saw what happened to your brother."

I get up in his face. "I'm gonna take you down. For Chloe, for my brother, for every Black kid y'all joked about in that thread," I fume. "I doubt you'll have that cocky grin once the inmates get ahold of you in prison."

"I would never hurt Chloe," he says. "She was my first love, my ladybug. You never forget your first love. No matter how hard she tries to—"

"Wait. What did you just call her?"

Jared gives me a blank look.

I don't really need him to repeat himself. I heard him loud and clear. He referred to her as his *ladybug,* reminding me of those earrings I found in Chloe's nightstand. Along with all those other gifts I assumed were from Trey.

You'll always be my ladybug.

"Oh my God," I whisper.

"What now?" Jared responds, his upper lip curled.

"All those gifts—the jewelry—they were from you." I shake my head in disbelief. "You were trying to get Chloe back. Wow, that *reeeaaaaaly* gives you more motivation to kill her."

Tension enters Jared's chiseled jawline, and he glares at me.

"Your ex-girlfriend, the girl you yourself just called your *first love,* didn't want anything to do with you," I continue. "Then you somehow find out the girl you were spending all this money on to win back was actively trying to expose you for the racist piece of shit you are. You're so angry she won't leave her *Black* boyfriend for you that you start a slave trade game with your friends. That she finds out about. And when your father can't bribe hers to keep your *ladybug* quiet, you threaten her yourself. Even though you know that won't work either, 'cause Chloe is a shit starter. It was bad enough she had those screenshots. You didn't want to take a chance on her running her mouth about the game either. So you made sure it couldn't happen. That about cover it?"

"You skating on thin ice now, Trudeau," Jared says in the coldest tone.

"It *was* you; it had to be. I'm going to prove it too."

He steps forward, so close to me that his breath tickles the hair in my nostrils. "We'll see about that," he whispers, then slowly leans back and air-kisses me before walking off.

* * *

I barge into Mr. Braswell's office, bypassing his secretary's plea for me to sign in and wait. My heart is about to explode out of my chest after my confrontation with Jared.

"Mr. Braswell, we have to stop him," I blurt, catching my breath.

"Who?" he replies with a frown.

"Jared—all of them. They've been pretending to sell us Black kids like slaves. I have proof!"

Mr. Braswell quickly stands up and heads toward the door. His secretary is about to enter, chasing me in here, but he shoos her away before softly closing the door in her face. As he returns to his desk, he keeps clenching and unclenching his fists.

"Okay, Mr. Trudeau, take a deep breath," he says after sitting down. "What's going on?"

I roll my eyes and repeat what I said. The lack of outrage and shock I was expecting from him causes my ribs to squeeze, my lungs tightening and constricting my breathing.

"You gonna do something about it?" I snap when he doesn't say anything in response.

"Mr. Trudeau, this is a wild accusation."

"It's not an accusation." I lean forward and press my hands on his desk. "We have proof! The same proof Chloe had. This is why someone killed her, Mr. Braswell. I think it was Jared. He didn't want her blowing up his spot."

"Mr. Trudeau, the Lanfords are a powerful family." Mr. Braswell rocks back in his chair, steepling his hands. "You're really in no position to be making such inflammatory statements about another student. First Trey Winslow, now Jared?"

He can't be serious!

"This is different, Mr. Braswell," I say, smacking my lips. "Trust me. You have a duty to protect the mental well-being of *all* your students. You won't be doing that if you let Jared and his friends get away with what they've been doing for weeks, during school hours. Someone has to stand up for us. You're in the position to do that."

"Marcel, listen to me," he says. "You don't want . . ."

Whatever he says after that I don't hear. My attention drifts past him, landing on a framed picture on his credenza that answers for me how Jared and his father found out Chloe knew about the slave trade game.

"He got to you too," I say to Mr. Braswell.

"Excuse me?" he says.

"Jared's father," I reply, pointing at the photo behind him.

In the picture, Mr. Braswell is shaking Deacon Lanford's hand as they smile. It looks like they're at one of the annual fundraising galas Truman hosts. The picture reminds me of another important title Deacon Lanford holds: chairman of the school's board of directors.

"You tipped the Lanfords off about the game after Chloe came to you with those screenshots, didn't you?" I hiss.

"I *demanded* Jared stop the game," Mr. Braswell responds.

"And did nothing to him!" I shout. "Why? Because Mr. Lanford threatened your job? You report directly to the school's board of directors. They have the power to fire you, don't they?"

Mr. Braswell slowly rises from his chair. "Mr. Trudeau,

choose your words wisely. Or else you'll be facing the same fate as your brother."

The troubling thing is I'm not sure if he means I'll be forced off campus or framed for a crime. Chloe's message said there were multiple people at school who wanted to silence her. I remember now what Mr. Dillard told us about Mr. Braswell's whereabouts Mardi Gras night. Making sure Chloe stayed quiet served as job security for him.

"Why were you in Chloe's neighborhood the night she was murdered?" I ask. "And don't deny it. There's surveillance footage of you stopping at a convenience store in the middle of the night."

The color drains from his face.

"You live in Algiers," I continue. "What were you doing on that side of town that late?"

"Mr. Trudeau . . ."

"Wanted to make sure your job was safe, knowing Chloe was the type of person who wouldn't be easily derailed from what she was doing?"

"Get out of my office . . . *now*!" he shrieks.

I leave his office exactly the way I entered it, bypassing the secretary and punching through the double doors to the suite of administrative offices. I speed walk through the hall. My blood coursing through my veins. Chloe probably felt like this too: Frustrated, alone. Betrayed by the adults she thought would be on her side. Unsure of what her next move should be.

Tears are building in my eyes as I whip around a corner. I slam into two blurs walking in the opposite direction.

"My bad," I apologize, my chest throbbing in the spot where it collided with someone's shoulder.

"You already late for class; no need to hurry now, Marcel," a familiar voice says as I'm wiping the tears out of my eyes.

Once my vision clears, I find Tiffany Winslow and Dustin Miller standing before me with blank looks. And they're holding hands. An unexpected development that on any other day would be something I'd playfully tease her about before inquiring when and how they started dating. But today, seeing her hand in hand with this white boy intensifies my already seething anger.

"Be careful," I say to her, leering at Dustin.

His distant gaze matches Tiffany's.

"Careful of what?" she asks.

"Them," I say, pointing at Dustin. "Jared and some of the other kids here have been playing a racist game, trading us like we're slaves. *Their* slaves. You and your brother included. Saying all kinds of fucked-up shit behind our backs."

"Whooooa, I don't know what he's talking about," Dustin says, holding his hands up in surrender as Tiffany side-eyes him.

Tiffany tilts her head at me inquisitively. "Marcel, what are you talking about?"

"My brother found proof of it," I say. "On Chloe's flash drive, with screenshots of the game thread she collected on it."

"He did?" Tiffany says, her expression transforming as what I've said sinks in. "What all was on it?"

"How some of them really feel about us," I tell her. "I don't know who we can trust, not even the faculty."

Dustin takes a step toward me but pauses when I narrow my

eyes at him. "Bro, seriously, I'm not a part of something like that. I have no idea what you're talking about," he says.

"Like I said, watch your back," I say to Tiffany.

I stalk off before either of them can respond. I'm done with Truman. Done with everyone here. It's time to burn it all to the ground.

27

Amir

This might have been a mistake!

I curse at myself to pedal faster. The wind slapping me in the face as I zoom down South Broad Street, holding the handles with one hand 'cause I'm using the other to hold the white plastic bag containing my fried catfish po'boy from Broadmoor Deli. My craving for it being the reason I only have seven minutes left to get home before curfew. I should have just eaten some of the leftovers I cooked this week, then I wouldn't be sweating this hard to be home in time. This is what I get for choosing to run out and buy something to eat as a way to avoid being in the house with Mama. She was waking up after another night shift as I was leaving. I think she's off from work today. Guess that means I'll be spending most of the night locked in my room, still avoiding her.

I whip my bike onto our street with five minutes left before my curfew kicks in. I can make it. Had I not been forced to wait for them to fry a new batch of catfish, I would have had more than enough time to make it back.

Our house is completely dark when I approach, which is kinda odd since Mama's car is parked out front. Maybe she was so tired from her shift that she went back to sleep. Wouldn't be the first time that's happened.

I make it across our threshold with three minutes to spare. I drop my keys and my po'boy on the island countertop before flipping on the lights. The hallway leading to our bedrooms is pitch-black, so Mama must be asleep. I'd see at least some light under her bedroom door if she wasn't.

I begin to take off my hoodie and make my way toward my bedroom, flipping the lights on in the hallway as I go, and my heart drops.

Mama is sprawled out on the floor on her stomach. Not moving.

I call out to her, dropping to my knees. That's when I see the blood and my head starts spinning.

28

Amir

Good news: Mama isn't dead.

Bad news: Chloe's flash drive is gone.

The ten minutes I couldn't wake Mama up after calling 911 were the scariest of my life. Even scarier than when I turned on the lights and found Chloe dead in her bed. The thought of losing Mama had me sobbing, and screaming for her lifeless body to move. Terrified that the deep gash across her forehead had been a fatal blow. The weakness that usually comes over me at the sight of blood suppressed by the fear of possibly losing her.

She finally started moving about a minute or so before the ambulance arrived, followed five minutes later by two NOPD officers and then Marcel and his parents. He was the next frantic call I'd made after 911. I kept screaming to him that Mama was dead. He stayed on the phone with me until the ambulance arrived. In the background I could hear my dad and Lily arguing over the quickest route he should take to get to our house. I think they were supposed to be going to some charity banquet Marcel mentioned.

It wasn't until after they got here and Mama was being attended to by the EMTs that I realized the flash drive was gone. My bedroom had been ransacked, just like Chloe's. The flash drive was in the top right drawer of my dresser. I haven't told Marcel yet. Making sure Mama was okay was first priority. I know it isn't a coincidence that the flash drive was stolen after Marcel confronted Jared yesterday. It had to be Jared or punk-ass Colin who swiped it. If Mama had *really* been hurt, or worse, I would now have two *legit* murder charges added to my pending case. They might have finally gotten their hands on that flash drive, but what they don't know is that I downloaded the screenshots and emailed them to Marcel this morning. He's trying to link up with some reporter to break the story about the game.

The adrenaline that's been coursing through my blood since I found Mama unconscious is finally subsiding as the EMTs pack up to leave and the officers gather us in the living room now that she's strong enough to talk.

I can already guess what happened. But I want to hear her say it first.

She's seated in our recliner, me standing to the side. The two officers are in the center of the room, their backs to the kitchen. Marcel is with his mother on the sofa, and my dad is standing to the side of them, near the front door. Mama's eyes flared a little when she saw Lily enter behind my dad earlier. Lily barely looked at me. Guess she's feeling guilty after learning I wasn't the one responsible for her dog's death.

"Mrs. Trudeau . . ."

"Yes," she and Lily respond at the same time.

This super-awkward silence fills the room. We men cast annoyed looks at one another. The white officer, who introduced himself as Officer Boykin, seems slightly amused by this intersection between my dad's past and present.

"Sorry," Lily says with a strained smile.

Mama's eyes flick toward the ceiling. I think some small part of her likes that it bothers my stepmother that Mama still uses my father's last name.

"*Ms.* Trudeau, can you tell us what happened?" Officer Boykin says. "Judging by your son's bedroom, it appears there was some sort of break-in."

Jared, or maybe Colin, got in through my bedroom window. I forgot to shut and lock it after cracking it open last night to feel the cool air. The officers took a picture of a partial muddy shoe print on my floor. I took a picture of it too with my phone. Plan to scroll through social media tonight to see if the print matches up to any kicks Jared or Colin are wearing in photos they've posted online.

I can feel Marcel's gaze burning a hole in the side of my face, but I don't take my eyes off Mama, who draws a deep breath.

"I woke up around five-thirty to find something to eat, a little while after I heard my son leave," she says. "I don't know who, but someone jumped out of Amir's room as I was coming down the hall and attacked me."

"Did you happen to see a face?" asks Officer Copeland, who's Black.

My mother shakes her head. "He was wearing a ski mask and dark clothes. I barely got a look at him before he overpowered me and slammed my head into the wall. That's when I blacked out."

Lily sighs. "Oh my God."

"What did he steal?" my dad asks the officers.

"We can't tell yet, sir," Officer Boykin replies.

I step forward. "He stole a flash drive."

"What?" Marcel yelps, scooting to the edge of the sofa.

I lock eyes with Officer Boykin. "It's the only thing missing from my room."

"What was on it?" Officer Copeland says.

The room is silent. Everyone waiting for my answer. The truth sits in my throat. Wanting to come out, but not to them. Jared has finally gotten what he's already killed for. He might have killed Mama too, had he not found it. Pointing the finger at Jared will only come off as a wild accusation from a suspected murderer wanting to get the heat off himself.

"Amir," Mama says, grabbing my hand.

I blink out of my thoughts. "Just some school assignments," I lie to the officers.

"You're telling us someone broke into your house to steal a flash drive with nothing but some homework on it?" Officer Copeland says, skepticism clear on his face.

"Yes, sir," I say in a convincing tone. "It's the only thing that's missing."

After raising a brow at Officer Copeland, Officer Boykin scribbles in his notebook. "We're going to finish processing the scene and we'll get out of y'all's hair. You've had an eventful night."

"Ma, you need something? Aspirin?" I ask when she starts rubbing the back of her head.

"Yeah, baby, two Tylenols would be great," she replies.

I scramble into the kitchen, where we keep a bottle, while the officers disappear down the hall to my bedroom. They stay another fifteen minutes, and as soon as they walk out the front door, the energy in the living room shifts.

"What the hell is going on, boys?" my dad says. "I caught how the two of you were looking at each other. Amir? Talk. *Now.*"

Mama looks up at me from the recliner, her lips pursed. I throw a look at Marcel, stretching my eyes to say *They need to know what's up.* Time to do what I've been itching to do since we found those screenshots.

"It wasn't Amir's flash drive, it was Chloe's," Marcel announces.

"Hers?" Mama says. "Why would you have that?"

I tell them about Chloe's message, which triggers gasps from Mama and Lily and a concerned look from our dad.

"She left her flash drive for me to find," I explain. "She hid it in that abandoned church I go to sometimes on Washington Avenue," I add for Mama. "You know, where I took her that night."

"What was on it?" Lily asks, more to Marcel than to me.

"Screenshots of a thread from this app called SnapMessages," Marcel explains. "A group of white kids who go to school with us started this messed-up game called the slave trade, where they would pretend to own Black kids, then sell and trade us like a slave auction."

Mama sits up straighter, spinning around in the recliner to face me.

"They were saying mad racist stuff about us," I add.

My dad's mouth falls open and his brows pull together. "What kind of *stuff*?" he huffs.

Marcel mentions what they said about my hair.

"You better be lying to me," Mama hisses, clenching her fists.

"I want names, *right now*!" my dad roars.

Lily snatches his hand, taking a few deep breaths. "Do y'all know who was behind it?" she asks.

Marcel nods. "Jared Lanford."

It takes a few seconds, but my dad's expression rearranges itself when he makes the connection. "Wait a damn minute. Does any of this have anything to do with why his father's office reached out to me today?"

Marcel and I exchange looks. It's happening again.

"What did he say, Daddy?" Marcel asks.

"Nothing yet," my dad replies. "It was his secretary, wanting to set up a meeting this week. She implied that Deacon knew I was having trouble getting financing for my seasonings line. . . ."

His gaze nervously shifts in my direction.

"It's been a tough couple of weeks," he continues, his voice somber. "There were a lot of party cancellations at Truffles after Amir's arrest. Business at Trudeau hasn't been the best either. A lot of people we thought were friends just haven't been all that friendly lately."

Hearing that causes the back of my throat to ache.

"Mr. Lanford did the same to Chloe's father after she told our principal about the game," I say. "Mr. Lanford lined Mr. Danvers's pockets by picking his architecture firm to design two big developments the Crescent City Foundation is overseeing."

"I wondered how Aubrey was able to land those projects after that lawsuit," Lily says.

"But Chloe wasn't going to drop it," Marcel says. "Jared threatened her about it at my birthday party. That's why she reached out to Amir."

"To do what?" Mama says.

"To expose the game," I say. "She knew I hated Truman. Knew how I would react to what was going on. Knew I could get Marcel on board too. She figured there was nothing Mr. Lanford could do to stop us the way he blocked her from outing Jared and his friends. At the time, he had nothing to use as leverage with my parents like he'd done with Chloe."

"And Mr. Braswell too, obviously," Marcel adds. "Mr. Lanford is chairman of the school's board of directors, remember."

"He threatened his job," Lily correctly assumes.

My dad starts pacing the room. "Lily, when I see that man . . ." He bites his bottom lip.

"How do y'all know this?" Mama asks.

"We forced Colin Perrier to tell us how the game started," I say. "After we found that flash drive."

"Chloe twisted his arm to make him help her expose the game," Marcel follows, then explains how I caught Colin at the church trying to look for Chloe's flash drive last week, and how we connected the rest.

"Why didn't y'all tell this to the cops just now?" Lily says.

"As if they would have believed us," I say. "Colin refuses to help us. Jared's father has Mr. Braswell and Mr. Danvers on a leash."

"Wait, back up," Mama says. "Are y'all saying you think this Jared boy killed that girl?"

Marcel and I look at each other before nodding.

"Oh my Lord," Lily says, covering her mouth with her hand.

"How could you keep this from me?" Mama says, glaring at me.

Can't answer that truthfully. Not with Lily and my dad here.

"This is dangerous," she says to me before turning to Marcel. "Is this what you meant with your promise?"

"Dillard told y'all to stay out of this?" my dad says, anger darkening his features.

"He's moving too slow," Marcel argues. "The grand jury meets Thursday. He's more focused on a trial, more billable hours, than on stopping this from getting to that point. I don't want Amir to get indicted for something he didn't do. His situation is affecting all of us. I'm not about to apologize."

"But you could have gotten Monica killed," Lily says.

"This ends *now*!" my father shouts, pointing at me and Marcel. "Do you hear me? This is dangerous. A girl is already dead. Your mother is hurt. This is all bigger than y'all. This is an adult problem. Y'all should have come to us."

"Your father is right," Mama says, standing up and grabbing my arm. "What does this mean? That there's no way to prove that this Jared boy killed her without that flash drive?"

"Pretty much," Marcel mumbles. "He has it now. He wins."

"Dude, no he doesn't," I say, pulling everyone's attention to me. "Bro, don't you remember? I emailed all the screenshots to you! We still have those."

Marcel's eyes light up. "That's right!" He turns to his mother and says, "I reached out to this reporter with the *Times-Pic* but haven't heard back yet."

"You should have come to *me,*" his mother says. "You can't do everything by yourself."

"But I wanted to do it for Chloe," Marcel replies, tears building in his eyes. "To make it right for not listening to her when she tried to tell me."

His mother jerks him into a tight hug on the sofa.

"Let me call Dillard," my father says, taking out his phone. "He needs to get over here. There has to be some legal trick he can do to put some heat on this boy." He walks outside to make the call.

"Monica, I'm sorry," Marcel says, lifting his head from his mother's chest. "I didn't mean for you to get hurt."

"I know, Marcel, I know," Mama says with a warm smile.

"But your father is right," Lily follows. "It's time for us adults to step in. We are Trudeaus, and you know what that means."

"What?" Mama says with a frown.

"They've messed with the wrong family," Lily replies.

A chill shoots through my body: Lily and Mama just had an exchange that didn't end in shouting.

Hell has frozen over.

"Ma, you good?"

I find Mama sitting up in bed, watching an episode of *Golden Girls,* the cup of tea I made for her sitting on her nightstand.

Marcel, my dad, and Lily have been gone for over an hour. Before they left, my dad arranged for a security guy on his payroll to camp outside our house tonight, "just in case." I recognized him when he knocked on the door to introduce himself. It's one of the guys who worked Marcel's birthday party. Lily also put in a call to a TV reporter she said owes her a "big favor" from her days working in public relations, before she became a full-time housewife. Apparently, this person is someone she trusts to properly report on the slave game. She and my father already have an interview set up with her tomorrow morning. Mr. Dillard will be there too.

We're about to accomplish the very thing that cost Chloe her life. We're hoping outing the game to the public will be the first step in connecting her murder to Jared. With the grand jury set to meet in two days, Mr. Dillard asked us to temper our expectations. But he thinks Chloe's note and the screenshots will work in my favor.

"If I had known it would take getting clocked over the head to get you to finally pay attention to me again, I would have done it to myself," Mama teases while I'm leaning through her bedroom doorway.

Had I lost her tonight, I wouldn't want to live anymore. She's my whole world. One lie shouldn't have changed that. Not when she's worked so hard to make sure so much other stuff in my life is good.

"Come here," she says, patting the side of her bed. She must sense what I'm thinking. "I wanna tell you something."

It's time we do this; I want to do this. She mutes the TV as I sit on the edge of the bed, facing her. I open my mouth to tell her I'm sorry but stop when she grabs my hand.

"I don't think it's healthy how you shut down, close yourself off, whenever you're feeling things you don't know how to deal with," she says. "You didn't start out like that. As a baby, oh God. You were an affectionate, lively, handsome little thing. Whenever I dragged myself home from the hospital my first year in the ER, seeing you look up with your toothless grin while in your nana's arms would melt all that exhaustion away. Made me feel less guilty about not being home with you more."

Some of the lightness in her face fades. "You were the only thing I had worth holding on to after your father left me for another woman. I was hurt by what he did; it made me selfish. I did not want to share you. Not with him and *her.* You were mine. Your brother is right, though. About everything. Your nana talked Martin out of challenging me for custody as long as I'd let you visit regularly. I agreed, but that wasn't enough."

I scoot closer to her as she continues to tell me about this part of my childhood, which she's never shared with me before.

"It was hard," she says, her mouth downturned, "having your father choose his dreams over me, and then accomplishing them so quickly after he left me. I became even more bitter once he moved up tax brackets. So much so, it became part of who I was."

I squeeze her hand, hoping I can provide some comfort. I don't want her to stop. I need to understand what she got out of lying to me.

"Turning you against him was my form of revenge," she continues. "I knew how much he loved you. And having you hate him, making him think you hated him because of what he'd done to me, was how I coped with our divorce. And that was wrong."

"Ma—"

"No, Amir, let me finish," she interrupts. "Martin was a piece of you-know-what for cheating instead of being a real man and ending his marriage first because he wasn't happy anymore. But despite that, he was a good father. My anger with him should have been separate from your relationship with him. You have every right to be mad and disappointed with me. I purposely came between y'all. Made it as hard as I possibly could for Martin to *want* to be in your life, even though I know how desperately you want him to be. And don't *you* lie and say you don't. I know you recorded that entire season of *Top Chef* that he judged on. I saw it in your DVR."

I drop my head, grinning at myself. Marcel noticed that too, the day he was in my bedroom.

"You love to cook, just like him, and you're good at it," she says. "I'm ashamed of letting my pettiness and my vindictiveness hurt you like that. Of making you think you weren't good enough. Making you think your life didn't matter to him."

I'm blinking hard, fighting back tears.

Mama tenderly caresses the back of my head, and I look up at her. "It's okay to be mad at him and still want him in your life. I want you to know that I'm stepping aside and encouraging you to do whatever *you're* comfortable with, with regard to your father. Not saying you have to forgive him. But know that he loves you, Amir, as much as I do. Anything I've ever asked of him for you, he came through. Wanted to do more, but I wouldn't let him.

"Right now, we're both scared out of our damn minds," she says as a tear dribbles out of her eye. "Sick to our stomachs that all the hurt we've let fester between us has somehow contributed to the mess you're in. Do something for me: Don't be like me. Learn how to forgive. Me. Your father."

"A'ight, Ma," I say, folding my hand over hers and holding it up to my chest, pressing it so she can feel my heartbeat. "You need to know something: you'll always be my number one girl, no matter what."

"I better be," she says, playfully rolling her neck.

We lean into each other, laughing. She pauses to kiss me on the forehead as I'm pulling back.

"Ma, I'm scared," I admit. "What if—"

"Don't talk like that," she says, wiping away the tear falling down my cheek. "We gonna pray. We gonna have hope. You heard Ms. My Shit Don't Stank. We're Trudeaus. They're messing with the wrong family."

There's a playful smile on her face, easing some of the tension in my body.

"That boy is really crazy about you, Amir," she says.

I frown.

"Your brother," she clarifies. "It's actually cute. He was so concerned about your safety."

I chuckle. Marcel twisted my arm into sharing our locations with each other—at least until all this is over. If it's ever over. "I'm not trying to spy, it's just a way to keep tabs in case anything else happens," he argued. I gave in; it seemed easier than arguing.

"Who knew that woman could raise a human that's actually pretty decent?" Mama adds.

"Y'all was kinda getting along tonight," I say. "I mean, you weren't threatening to drag her like you've done before."

"That was me being nice," she says, rolling her eyes. But I can tell she really isn't that annoyed. There isn't an edge to her voice. "It was weird, huh? Having all us together in the room like that."

"For real."

"To the casual observer, we probably looked like—"

"A family," I finish.

29

Marcel

Amir and his mother are both giving me apprehensive looks when I open our front door—for very different reasons, I imagine.

As Monica is crossing the threshold, I realize this might be the first time she's ever been *in* our house. I don't remember her ever making it as far as the circular driveway when she used to drop Amir off every other weekend, before he stopped visiting. Her eyes are bouncing all over the place, taking everything in. I'm praying that seeing how we live doesn't stir up anything negative for her. It felt good having her and my mother in the same room last night, without it escalating into something bad. That had to have taken a lot, given the history between them.

"Didn't have any trouble getting the extension on your curfew?" I ask, looking down at Amir's ankle monitor.

"Nah, they were cool about it," Amir says to me as he walks in behind her. "You know, since I told them I was going to be here."

He pulls back the hood on his navy-blue sweatshirt as we do one of those one-handed-handshake hugs. I know he's hoping the news segment they've come here to watch with us will be enough to stop the grand jury from formally indicting him with Chloe's murder tomorrow. Like him, I want this nightmare to end tonight.

"Come on, we're in the den," I say, gesturing for them to follow me.

"How did it go today?" Amir asks as we walk, our footsteps echoing through the foyer.

"What all did they say to that reporter?" his mother adds, referring to my parents.

It was decided last night, on the advice of Mr. Dillard, that my parents would do the on-camera interview with the reporter my mother had reached out to. Mr. Dillard felt that our father's involvement, him speaking out for the first time since Amir's arrest, would get attention—even though Daddy wouldn't specifically be talking about Amir's arrest and proclaimed innocence. Mr. Dillard also advised us against talking about Chloe's message.

"This is about swaying public opinion, teeing things up," he told us last night. "Let's first foster outrage over the game and the lack of disciplinary action upon its discovery. I'm not sure that calling out Chloe's father for a possible role in his daughter's death will go over well."

Mr. Dillard is meeting with the DA's office right now about all of it, though, including how Chloe reached out to Amir and what she implied in her message.

"They told her everything we went over last night," I tell Amir and his mother as we pass the staircase and enter the narrow hallway that opens to our den. "She interviewed me too. I couldn't name Jared specifically, but the reporter had a way to imply his involvement."

"For real?" Amir says, his voice high.

I nod.

Our on-camera interviews with Patrice Daily, who I learned today studied journalism at Dillard University with my mother, happened around noon in our backyard. I didn't go to school today, and according to my father, I might never go again. He made it known in the interview that he intends to pull his sons and his money out of Truman, whether they fire Mr. Braswell and expel the kids who were involved in the slave trade game or not.

"That damn school did nothing to protect my sons or any of the other Black kids!" he yelled on the car ride home from Amir's house last night. "No telling what those white kids have been getting away with. I don't like it, Lily. I never did! I only sent Marcel there because *you* thought it would be an *enriching experience.* He would have been fine in public school. I turned out fine."

She didn't defend her stance last night. I was a little surprised by her silence. She of course wants the best for me, but not if it means me being subjected to the very bigotry she thought our elevated social status would shield me from. She didn't have to say it. The longer he ranted, the more she winced.

"I can't wait to see how Mr. Braswell and the school's board of directors try to get out of this," I say to Amir and Monica.

"Did the reporter talk to Jared?" Monica asks as we're stepping down into the den, where my parents are still on the love seat with the TV muted, like they were when I left them to answer the door.

"Don't know, but Deacon Lanford was blowing up my phone all day," my father says as he stands up. He meets us in the middle of the room, sharing an awkward handshake with Amir and an even awkward-er hug with Monica. "I didn't even bother talking to him."

"Hey," my mother timidly says to Amir, who gives her an apprehensive wave before she turns to his mother. "Monica," she says, her voice strained.

"Lily," Monica responds with a tight smile.

Amir and I share amused looks. Our moms are clearly playing nice for us. How far we've come, and how far we still have to go.

This is so new. Us all being together. I like it. I want more of it. Just under better circumstances. A part of me does worry that we'll settle back into old patterns if we're able to clear Amir's name. I want to believe that we wouldn't. But I know there's still so much, mostly between Amir and our father, that needs to be worked out.

"Monica, Amir, like anything to drink?" my mother asks as one of the maids working today enters the den with the glass of wine and tumbler of whiskey my parents asked for right before Amir and his mother arrived.

"We've got liquor, water, soda, whatever y'all want," I say with an awkward smile, hoping to divert Monica's attention from the maid and toward me. As if that'll distract her from how different our lives are compared to theirs.

"Water," Monica mumbles.

"Yeah, me too," Amir follows.

The maid doesn't leave quick enough for me after giving my parents their respective drinks.

"A few kids were blowing up my phone today," I say, motioning for Amir and his mother to take a seat. Amir drops down on the other end of the sofa and I sit next to him. His mother plops into the recliner on the other side of him. "They started rolling in after they saw the news van parked on campus, filming."

Among the flurry of texts one was from Tiffany, who first reminded me that she and I were supposed to be presenting the draft of our opening statement for the mock trial today, which I'd totally forgotten about. After telling me Mrs. Graceson is giving us an extension, Tiffany asked, *Is the news here about that game you said was on Chloe's flash drive?*

Yeah, I replied.

What did you tell them? The news? she wrote.

Watch the six o'clock segment tonight and find out, I wrote. *Spoiler: I'm not letting them get away with this shit!*

Scorch the Earth, she replied with fire and Earth emojis.

"Every parent of a minority student needs to be pulling their kids outta that school," Monica says. "I regret sending you there, Amir. Private don't always mean better."

"For what it's worth, I thought the same," my mother follows. She reaches over and places a hand on my knee. "I'm sorry too, sweetie."

I squeeze her hand and give her a sad smile. She and Monica probably blame themselves. For sending us to the microaggressive hotbed that is our school. For what's going on with Amir on some level too. None of it would have happened if neither one of us had set foot on that campus. I'm still feeling stupid for thinking our wealth and social status meant I wouldn't have to deal with this level of discrimination.

"It's starting!" my father announces, snatching the remote off the armrest of the love seat to unmute the TV.

After the graphics for WWL-TV roll across the wide-screen, Patrice Daily's perfectly made-up face appears.

"Tonight, shocking details of a racist game targeting minority students at one of the city's most prestigious private schools," she says with the Truman Academy campus framed in the background.

The maid quietly enters with Amir's and Monica's bottles of water as the scene cuts to a reporter outside city hall giving a quick takeaway of whatever story he spent the day on, followed by another teasing the top sports story of the day.

Our doorbell rings.

"I'll get that." My father tosses the remote down on the love seat. "It must be Dillard," he says while leaving the room.

If my prayers are answered, Amir's lawyer will walk in here and say that what we've uncovered so far about Chloe's murder is enough to stop Amir from being indicted. And then this news story we're about to watch will be the final nail in the coffin for Mr. Braswell and the rest of the kids involved with the game.

"Patrice is the best," my mother says, never taking her eyes off the TV. "She got some computer expert to verify the identities of some of the kids through a public records database of some kind—you know, because they were dumb enough to use their cell phone numbers to register their accounts through that app."

"For real?" Monica replies in astonishment. "Let's get the names out there. Black Twitter will handle the rest."

"Black what?" my mother replies, confused.

"Twitter," Monica repeats, giving my mother a look that screams *How do you not know what I'm talking about?* "Gurl, you can't be *that* bougie you never heard the term Black Twitter."

"How is it different from regular Twitter?" my mother replies.

Monica's dumbfounded expression makes Amir and me giggle.

"I'll break it down for you later, Mother," I say when she tosses a bewildered look at me.

My father returns with Mr. Dillard just as the anchors are turning over the broadcast to Patrice Daily.

"Here we go," my mother announces, an unnerving giddiness in her voice.

"Doug and Lauren, thank you," Patrice Daily says, our school campus still framed in the background of her live shot. "Truman Academy is one of the most prestigious schools in the city, but tonight, we learned that some of its students—white students—have allegedly been involved in a secret thread called the slave trade game, in which they pretend to sell and trade this school's Black and other minority students. Those messages, posted through the app SnapMessages, then disappear. The messages are charged with racial bigotry."

The scene cuts to my parents, seated beside one another in two of the wrought-iron chairs on our veranda. She's in the Dior dress she settled on after spending all morning debating with me whether it made her look fat. My father is wearing a complimentary beige pin-striped blazer and button-up shirt she picked out for him.

"*Disgusted* doesn't even begin to describe how we feel," he says to Patrice, who's sitting off camera.

"Disappointed," my mother chimes in, her tone low and even. "Disappointed that things like this are still going on."

In the voice-over, Patrice says, "Celebrity chef and restaurateur Martin Trudeau and his wife, Lily, learned about the game this week from Martin's two sons, both of whom attend Truman Academy and were subjects in several screenshots from the thread, which the Trudeaus shared with WWL-TV."

The screen switches to rotating graphics of the screenshots we found on Chloe's flash drive. Any real names blurred out, along with all the explicit language. Patrice reads out some of the messages, skipping over derogatory words and instead referencing named individuals in the thread as simply "girl/boy" or "a Black student."

My face fills the screen next. I scoot up to the edge of the sofa to hear what I already know I said.

"I thought these kids were my friends, but clearly not if they could say the things they did about me and all the other Black kids who go here," I say.

"Martin's younger son is questioning his friendships while he and his family grapple with the uncertain future of his half brother, who was arrested in connection with the murder of Chloe Danvers, the sixteen-year-old Truman junior who was found stabbed to death in her home two weeks ago. Marcel Trudeau says Danvers was in possession of the screenshots from the thread. He thinks she may have been trying to expose the game before she was murdered."

"How do you know that?" Patrice Daily asks me off camera.

"Ask our principal," I respond.

"*Brruuuuuhhh,* you called him out like *that*?" Amir says to me with an amused smile.

I respond with a shrug and mischievous smirk.

"The school's principal, Cyrus Braswell, did not return multiple calls today for comment on this story," Patrice Daily says over footage of her attempting to enter the school's administrative offices but being stopped by one of the school resource officers. "When our cameras showed up at school today, we were ordered off campus. Thirty minutes later, I received this prepared statement from the school's board of directors. . . ."

A graphic of that response pops up on-screen.

"*'We do not take allegations like this lightly,'*" Patrice reads in her voice-over. "*'We intend to launch a full investigation into whether there is any truth in these outrageous and hurtful claims. Truman Academy remains an institution that prides itself on inclusion and diversity and would never tolerate such behavior from its students.'*"

"But y'all did!" Monica yells at the TV.

The shot of Patrice on campus fills the screen again. "I reached out to a computer expert today, who was able to trace the identities of some of the usernames that appear in the thread. Most notably the individual who identified himself as theotherNEGAN, who appears to be the self-proclaimed master in the thread."

My heart is racing. This is it. Jared is done for.

The expert Patrice mentioned appears on-screen, explaining how he was able to deduce theotherNEGAN's identity through the cell phone number registered to the account.

"The telephone associated with theotherNEGAN's account belongs to Jared Lanford, a senior at Truman Academy and son of prominent businessman Deacon Lanford, chief executive officer and president of the Crescent City Foundation," Patrice Daily says. "When I reached out to Mr. Lanford for comment on this development, he hung up after saying, quote, 'I have nothing to say; don't know anything about all that,' end quote. Back to you, Doug and Lauren."

My father is already grabbing the remote to mute the TV as the scene shifts back to the anchors in studio.

"They didn't link it to her murder, though," Monica says. "I thought all that was to point the finger at him for killing that girl."

My father opens his mouth to respond, his face strained.

"Monica, we couldn't come out and link that boy to the murder publicly," Mr. Dillard says, prompting my father to close his mouth. "The reporter subtly implied all we could say at this point to avoid legal ramifications." He sets down the briefcase he's holding and loosens his tie. "If nothing else, at least that story will stir up things at the school. I'm sure there will be blowback. The kids who participated in that thread will start turning on each other. One of them may say something that more directly links the Lanford kid to the murder."

"Did you meet with the investigators and your contact at the DA's office?" my father follows, sitting down next to my mother on the love seat. "What did they say about that message she sent my son?"

Mr. Dillard slips his left hand into his pocket. "You want the good news or the bad news first?"

"Bad news?" Monica barks, verbalizing my shock.

What bad news could there be? Tonight's news story, everything we learned about Jared threatening Chloe to cover it up, her reaching out to Amir, this was all supposed to be the game changer that flipped everything in our favor.

"The bad news is it's an election year and this is a high-profile murder. The DA wants to win public favor to keep his job. That means his office is still presenting the case against Amir to the grand jury tomorrow." Mr. Dillard points an apologetic look at my brother, who has lowered his head. "Everything we got so far is circumstantial. Nothing indicating actual guilt toward Jared. The DA's office is arguing that Amir could have sent that note to himself from Chloe's account after he killed her."

"Are you serious?" I explode. "Why would Amir say the things she said in that message?"

"The DA will now likely spin the narrative that your brother killed her because he somehow found out about the game and believed Chloe was part of it," Mr. Dillard says. "And that Amir said all that stuff in her message to him to throw suspicion off himself after that doorbell camera footage surfaced."

"That's absurd!" my father barks.

"Nothing points at actual guilt toward my son either, just him being at the wrong place at the wrong time," Monica says, prompting nods of agreement from my parents.

"True," Mr. Dillard replies with a loaded sigh that says so much more. That Black boys aren't afforded the same grace in the criminal justice system as privileged white boys.

"So all of this was for nothing," my father says, irritated. He isn't the only one.

The disappointment in Mr. Dillard's face relaxes. "Not really. The police department said they will be looking into the possible connection between the slave game and Jared's guilt. Although I'm not entirely confident it'll be top priority for them. They're working on getting a warrant to search his closet and see if any shoes he owns match the muddy footprints found in Amir's bedroom last night."

"And this is supposed to be the good news?" Monica says, crossing her arms over her chest.

I've never loved her smart mouth more than in this moment.

"Also, I had someone on my team talk to Chloe's parents." Mr. Dillard turns to me and says, "Their spare key is missing. But they didn't know that it was. My associate said they looked pretty shaken up by it, by everything y'all discovered the last few days."

"Do they still think my son killed her?" my father beats me to asking.

"I can't say," Mr. Dillard replies. "But I think if we keep at 'em, the father in particular, we might be able to get him to crack. We've planted some seeds of doubt. Those *could* sprout in our favor."

The more he talks, the more my heart shrivels.

"Listen, my focus is shifting from trying to stop Amir from getting indicted to preventing him from going to prison. That means building a case of reasonable doubt, which we're on the right track for," Mr. Dillard says. "We got Trey Winslow, who had motive. We have this Jared kid too. *And* I think we can build a case around the principal as well."

"Trey's out," I say, forgetting that I never followed up with him after talking to Tiffany. "It wasn't him. I'm certain of it."

"Okay. Well, my team will widen our search for surveillance footage in the area, based on the list you gave us, Marcel, and we got footage of the principal going into that corner store a few blocks from her house late that night," he says. "We could establish he had motive to silence her too."

True.

"We just need to show a jury that there are many other suspects the police didn't look into," Mr. Dillard continues. "NOPD doesn't have the best reputation."

"But Jared did it," I argue. "It's not enough that he gets exposed for that game. He needs to go to jail for killing her."

"Marcel, we're gonna work that angle, we'll have time," Mr. Dillard says. "But as of right now, nothing, and I mean nothing, places Jared in the area during the window of time Chloe was killed. Not to mention we'll be up against his father and the money and connections he has."

"I don't want my son going through a trial, Cedrick," my father says to Mr. Dillard. "He's only seventeen. He's supposed to be planning his future, picking colleges, figuring out his life. Not worried he may end up on death row."

"I know that, Martin, but at this point, we may not be able to avoid it—unless there's some picture out there of this Jared boy holding the murder weapon and coming out of her house," Mr. Dillard says. "I know y'all are stressed, but don't lose hope yet. If he was in that area, if there's something that connects him, it may turn up. Everyone makes mistakes. Some of the toughest cases were cracked because criminals slipped up on a minute detail."

"That's not good enough," I say, becoming angry again as I reflect on Jared's cocky attitude the day I confronted him at his locker.

This has become way more personal. He killed my best friend, is framing my brother for it, and thinks my existence is inferior to his. He doesn't get to blow up my life and get away with it. He thinks he's untouchable. I'm about to show him how wrong he is.

30

Amir

I woke up today with one thought: I'll probably be indicted for first-degree murder. That thought metastasized into a gnawing sensation touching every part of my body. At any moment, my phone will ring and it'll be Mr. Dillard. Calling to inform me of the next series of events that will take place leading up to the trial for Chloe's murder.

Mama had to work an early shift at the hospital this morning after taking a day off yesterday as a precaution after her head injury. She didn't have to say it, but I could tell she wasn't mad about picking up the shift today. She needed the distraction, I'm thinking. Its slow torture being forced to sit and wait alone, like I'm doing. I only lasted an hour before I called Marcel and asked him to come over and keep me company. Figured he'd say yes since he didn't go to school today. But he claimed he had something else important to get done and promised he'd be in touch later. Quincy and the rest of my crew are at school (although they'd probably talk mad shit if I called them, given how much I've been ghosting them).

By one o'clock I jumped on my bike and went to the dilapidated church. Only lasted twenty minutes there before I was on my bike again and pedaling into Tremé. Cruising past Nana's old house, then the street where Mama grew up. Stopping outside the building sitting on the corner of Governor Nicholls and Henriette Delille Streets. I sit on my bike a moment, staring at this place I've never set foot in because I never saw it as just a restaurant. It has always been the thing I blamed for taking my dad away from me. Its existence a constant reminder that I could never compete with what it brought to his life.

I enter Tru, my heart heavy. It's time to rip this Band-Aid off.

I'm greeted at the hostess stand by a girl not much older than me. She's getting ready to say whatever she says when she greets customers but pauses the second she sees me. She tilts her head, recognition stretching her eyes.

"Oh. Hey," she says. "How are you?"

Scared as shit. I know she doesn't want the truth. She's just saying the first thing that popped into her mind in this awkward situation. She clearly knows who I am, even though I've never been in here—at least, not in *years.* I'm sure she has all kinds of ideas about why I stopped by today.

"I'm—uuhhhh, I'm," I stammer, not able to settle on how to respond.

"Your dad's in the kitchen, I'll go get him," she says, then scurries off.

I saw his truck parked outside, so I knew he was here.

Tru doesn't appear to be suffering from the backlash his other restaurants are. Nearly every table is full. I look around, soaking up the casual decor and laid-back vibe. There's a small stage tucked in the back corner where I suppose live bands play for the Live After Five cocktail hour that's advertised on the glowing black writing board near the hostess stand. Young wait-staff dressed in red T-shirts with the Tru logo on the top left of their chests move through the spacious diner with easygoing smiles. Sun lights the dining area through the panel of windows that gives a panoramic view of Governor Nicholls Street. Wood ceiling fans, spinning in unison, help spread the smells of fried seafood, savory sauces, and mouthwatering sides.

"Amir? Hey, son," my dad says, walking up to me. He's wearing a black-and-white version of the waitstaff's T-shirt and jeans, and a white apron, the top half of which he has folded down at his hips. "This is an unexpected but welcome surprise." He wipes his hands on his apron. "Wait, did you hear something from Cedrick?" he asks, worry clouding his face.

"Nah, nah, I . . ." I scratch the back of my head. "Real talk: I didn't want to be alone. I was going stir-crazy."

He curtly nods at my honesty. "Come over here, sit down. Been wanting to talk to you for a minute."

My stomach feels empty as I follow him to one of the few tables where no one is seated. It's off to the side of the room, near the double swinging doors to the kitchen. The girl who greeted me at the hostess stand emerges through them, quickly acknowledging us with a smirk as she stalks past to return to her post.

"Doesn't look like business is hurting much in here because of me," I say after dropping down in the chair across from him.

My attempt at a joke to ease the tension manages to pull a faint smile from him.

"Things will pick back up," he says. "Once it's all over. That's the least of my concerns . . . me; my businesses. I have some investments to tide me over until . . ."

"Until what? I get sentenced to prison and then people forget about your *bad* son?"

I wince; the words just spilled out of my mouth.

"Amir, you are not my 'bad son.'" He straightens his shoulders and sits back in his chair. "Your mother told me about y'all's talk after we left the other night."

I can't believe she did that without telling me. *Learn how to forgive. Me. Your father,* she said to me. If there's one thing I've learned this week about the adults in my life, it's that nothing I did or said influenced their behavior.

"I wanna start off by saying I'm sorry for what I did to your mother." He folds his arms on the table, intensely staring me in the eye. "No matter how bad our marriage had become toward the end, it didn't give me the right to do what I did. I'm apologizing to you for that because I know me hurting her so bad is why things got so toxic. This is my fault. All of it.

"I could have been more present after I gave up the custody fight, but I wasn't. I was too focused on work. I wasn't there like

I should have been to check Lily on how she treated you. In reality, I took the easy way out of a mess *I* created. I hope you can forgive me, son."

Seeing the hurt reflected in his words softens me. I've been so convinced *I* had done something, that I wasn't good enough, that he no longer loved me because he had a new, *better* life.

"I should have fought harder for you," he says, leaning forward. "That might have showed you how much I loved you. Amir, you are part of my heart. I thought I was doing the right thing, letting your mother have what was the best part of our marriage. Knowing that seeing me succeed without her had to be a hard pill to swallow."

My gaze falls to my lap.

"This last week, all I could think is that what's happening to you is my fault," he says. "That if I had showed you how much I loved you, you wouldn't have made decisions based on thinking I didn't give a damn about you. That's the furthest thing from the truth, son."

"This ain't yo' fault, Dad," I say, my voice cracking. "I was in the wrong place at the wrong time."

"If you go to prison for this, a part of me will die," he says. "I'll forever regret not fighting for you. For not sticking up for you against Lily. It's funny, I think she's starting to realize the same thing your mother has. That Marcel won't give up on the promise he made to yo' nana. And honestly, I'm glad he won't."

I'm stuck. Not knowing what to say. Remembering what Mama said about my relationship with him being different from hers. I hate how he hurt her by cheating with Lily. But he's still my father. There's love I've always had for him; even though it was buried under a lot of resentment and anger for years, it's never really gone away. As good as what he just said makes me feel, there's still apprehension in the back of my mind. It almost feels like this might be too late. I might be going to prison in a few months. How are we supposed to work on our relationship then?

When I lift my head, my eyes are drawn to the left, where I can feel someone staring. There's an older couple seated two tables over. The wife quickly averts her eyes when she notices me staring back at her. I caught her in the act of whispering to her husband that she recognized me. I can't hear everything she's saying, but I'm sure whatever it is probably involves telling him that I'm the boy they think killed that white girl.

"You're mighty quiet," my dad says, pulling my focus back to him. "You had so much to say the other day. Didn't even let me get a word in. I know you're angry with me. I want you to be honest. I really want us to be better."

I sigh. "You and Mama have been saying all the right things. Everything I wanted and needed to hear but never thought I would. It's making me more worried than happy. Like y'all are telling me all this because you know in your hearts I ain't getting out of this trouble."

I'm probably overthinking it, but I can't help it. My life is on the line, and they know it. The possibility of Mr. Dillard proving that I didn't kill Chloe looks damn near impossible at the moment.

"All I've been able to think about today is the moment my

phone is gonna ring and it's going to be Mr. Dillard letting me know that I've been indicted," I say. "As much as I've wanted to hear you finally admit how fucked up you treated me, it's only making me think more about the possibility of going to prison. I don't want to think about that. That's why I came here. To think about anything else but what's happening today and how it's going to affect my family."

My dad sits back in his chair, taking a deep breath, then leans forward again and says, "Let's talk about you apparently knowing how to cook, then."

I frown at first, until his smirk reveals how he found out. Then I shake my head with an exasperated sigh.

Marcel.

"You're gonna learn that your brother can't hold water—unless it's *his* secrets, then suddenly you won't get nothing out of him," my dad says. "Now, *he* claims you really know what you're doing. I'm guessing your nana had you in the kitchen with her like she did me growing up."

An image of me helping my grandmother fills me with warmth. "She actually said I was a much better helper than you."

"Oh, so you think you better than your old man in the kitchen?" he teases, pursing his lips at me. "Boy, I'm a Michelin-starred chef."

The impending indictment slowly fades to the back of my mind as I sit up straighter. "I don't know nothing 'bout all that. *But* your own mother and son seem to think differently."

His eyebrows lift at my cocky grin.

"Get up," he says, standing.

"What?"

"Get up," he repeats, waving his hand at me. "You think you can throw down better than me, come show me what you got."

"Right now?"

"Yeah, right now," he says. "The lunch rush is over. I wanna see if you really know what you're doing. Come on."

After a beat I slide out of the chair and follow him through the swinging double doors into the kitchen. A smile teetering between awkwardness and curiosity planted on my face.

"Nicco, let my son at the grill," he calls out to an older Black guy chopping herbs on a metal counter to our left.

"My son is talking smack, thinking he can cook as good as me," my dad explains to Nicco. "Let's see if he can back all that talk up."

Nicco looks me up and down and smiles. "All right, youngster, show us what you got."

My dad turns to me. I'm standing off to the side, my hands jammed in my pockets.

"Don't get shy, now," my dad says. "Show me something."

I eye the pantry to my right and then the cooler in the far back. "Bet."

I hit the pantry first to see what ingredients I'll have to work with. I can feel my dad watching me as I pluck a bag of flour off the shelf. A feeling I've never felt before gets my adrenaline pumping. I want to make him proud.

31

Marcel

Mr. Dillard is right. There's gotta be *something* or someone who can link Jared to Chloe's murder. It's not enough Jared's getting dragged on social media for starting the slave game. The calls for his expulsion (justifiable) and the debate the game has sparked around cyberbullying (also important) are distracting everyone from what they should be focused on. That he killed Chloe to keep all this from happening, not realizing Chloe was already two steps ahead of him.

The chilling way he said *We'll see about that* to me that day in the hall after I threatened to prove what he did still haunts me. It's like he knows it won't matter if the world knows he's a racist piece of shit if it's my brother who goes to prison for the murder he committed. For people like him, time makes everyone forget. He doesn't have to work a day in his life and he'll still be okay. But going to prison for murder, that stain will stay with Amir forever. Change him. Destroy him. I'm not about to let that happen to my brother.

I could sit back and let Mr. Dillard do his job, like he told me to last night, but that won't be as gratifying as if it's *me* who uncovers the thread that will vindicate Amir and avenge Chloe. That's why I didn't go over to Amir's earlier when he called. I'd rather spend time today on taking Jared down instead of sitting around failing at trying to distract Amir from the thing that has consumed our family. I'm not wanting to falsely get Amir's hopes up again over something I'm not sure will pan out, so I've reached out for help somewhere else. And he's already waiting in the public parking lot on Magazine Street. His face lights up the second he sees my car pulling in.

Quincy called last night after the news story aired.

"Really appreciate you helping me with this," I say to him as I'm stepping out of my car.

"Don't even. Anything for my boy." His face goes serious. "How's he doing?"

"You know, putting up walls, but I know he's worried. Grand jury is meeting today. I think he's losing hope that he'll ever get out from under this."

Quincy nods. "You sure this is the way to go?"

"Q, it's all I got at the moment," I say. "Jared might have been able to sneak into Chloe's house undetected, but there has to be someone, somewhere who saw him that night. It was late, but it was still Mardi Gras. People be all up and through the Garden District on Fat Tuesday. We just need to find one of them who can place Jared in this area around the time of Chloe's murder."

"So the plan is to go door-to-door in a mile radius around Chloe's house?" he asks.

Canvassing residents around the Garden District, I suspect, is something the police didn't do, since they already assumed they had their guy in Amir. Or if they did, I'm betting any interviews they conducted were focused on gathering witness statements supporting their theory. Had I not been so focused on Trey for so long, I might have thought about doing this sooner.

I motion for Quincy to back up so I can open the rear door on the passenger side of my car. I reach inside to pull out the map of Chloe's neighborhood I printed. I hold it out so he can read it over my shoulder.

"Look, I know it may take us a couple days, so I thought we can take it together section by section," I explain.

"Yeah, we could do that," he says. "*Or* we could get it done a lot faster another way."

"How?"

He walks out into the middle of the lane I'm parked on and whistles, waving his hands toward the row of vehicles parked behind me. Car doors start opening and heads pop up all over the place. At least a dozen or so Black kids our age. Everyone gets out of their cars and starts toward us, led by Buster and Nick.

"What's going on?" I ask Quincy as everyone gathers around my car.

"These are some of our friends and classmates from Douglas Egan," Quincy explains. "I recruited them at school today. They wanna help Amir any way they can."

Buster pulls me into an aggressive one-handed embrace. " 'Sup, pretty boy."

"Hey," I respond, nodding in Nick's direction.

"They don't want to see Amir go down for this either," Quincy says, waving at everyone with a proud smile.

"Amir is our boy," a skinny dude wearing a backward Saints baseball cap says to me.

"We got you, boo, what'cha need us to do?" adds a girl with butt-length box braids and a pierced eyebrow.

I smile at her, tears pricking my eyes. *This* is what I wish I had at school. People supporting us, giving Amir the benefit of the doubt. If not for him, at least for me, who they've known for years. *This* is what friendship is supposed to look like.

"Don't look so stunned, pretty boy," Buster says, slapping my chest. "We ride or die. *Plus,* I owe Amir. I got him into that trouble they used to make him look guilty. I need to make this right for my boy."

"I really appreciate y'all," I say, blinking back my tears. "It's been a rough two weeks for my family."

"Don't even trip, man," Nick says. "We got you."

After nodding at Nick, I immediately start dividing everyone into pairs and coordinating the areas they'll cover. Instructing them to knock on every door and talk to every business owner and employee within their assigned area, keeping track of where they've been and who they talked to. I tell them to show people Jared's picture before asking if they recall seeing him Mardi Gras night.

"Everyone got iPhones? I can AirDrop y'all a photo of him," I say, opening my phone.

"Dude needs a beatdown for that game," says a boy in a Douglas Egan letterman jacket.

Once I've AirDropped a picture I lifted off Jared's Instagram page, I say, "Call me the second anyone says they saw him in the area that night."

"Bet," Buster replies.

Everyone breaks into their assigned pairs. Leaving me with Quincy, who I, of course, paired myself with.

The second everyone in our group has left the parking lot, I do the thing I've been wanting to do for a while now. I kiss him. Which he doesn't expect, because he's looking down at his phone when I do it. But once he realizes what's happening, he closes his eyes and pulls my body up against his. He tastes like spearmint and peace. Our first kiss starts tender, then becomes passionate and rougher. I reluctantly pull away as I feel my jeans getting tighter.

"Well," he says, licking his lips. "That was better than I've been imagining."

I grab his hands, wishing I could touch so many other parts of him. "Thank you for coming through like this."

"Anything for you Trudeau boys," he says with a smile that keeps my stomach fluttering. "Look, I didn't want to ask this 'cause you already got a lot going on. But after what just happened, I'm wondering if . . . why don't you let me take you on a date."

My gaze drops and my shoulders slack.

"Not any time soon," Quincy quickly says. "After things are better with Amir."

"That's the thing, Q," I say. "If we can't prove Jared killed her, I'm really scared things won't ever get better for him."

Quincy lets go of my hands to dismissively wave away what

I just said. "I don't even wanna hear that. We not letting my boy go down for this. You hear me? We can do this. *You* can do this. I believe in you."

"Why? You barely know me."

He scoops my hands back into his. "The one positive thing I ever heard your brother say about you is that you overthink anything you do, even did when you were little. So overthink this shit and let's bring this white boy down."

Quincy and me are going to hit up the businesses along the west side of Magazine Street between First and St. Mary Streets. The girl with the long box braids and her boyfriend are canvassing the neighborhoods on the east side of Magazine in the same block radius as us.

It takes more than an hour for Quincy and me to make it through half our section. Receiving mostly polite head shakes whenever we show Jared's picture to whoever answers doors or is walking the streets. Every "Sorry, I don't think so" or "Never seen the kid before in my life" causing my heart to shrink a little. There was a fleeting glimmer of hope when a housewife who was unloading groceries out of her minivan did a double take at Jared's face on my phone screen. Seeing her brow furrow as she leaned in to get a closer look started my heart racing. I thought, *This is it! She saw something. Saw him that night.* Only for her to lean back and shake her head. "No. He looked like someone else I know. I was sound asleep around that time. I go to bed at nine p.m., even on Fat Tuesday."

The farther we got from the Garden District, the less likely it felt we'd find someone who could have seen him that night.

"We're almost six blocks from Chloe's street," I say to Quincy as we're approaching St. Mary.

"This seems kinda far for him to park and then go on foot," Quincy says. "But you never know. If he really didn't want to be seen, he'd park as far away as he could."

I'm about to respond when I see the sign for Ma Bell's posted up ahead. It's the store where Mr. Dillard said they got surveillance footage of Mr. Braswell the night of Chloe's murder. I stop, rolling over in my mind again the possibility that our principal turned to violence to keep his job.

"Wassup?" Quincy says, looking confused.

"Let's pop in this store right quick," I say, explaining why as we cross the street.

There's only one customer inside. He's in the process of finishing his transaction with the older man behind the cash register as we enter. I use my phone to pull up the Truman Academy website as the customer is grabbing the brown paper bag filled with whatever he just purchased. As he turns to leave I step up to the register. There's a small TV monitor flanked by bottles of liquor that are for sale on the wall-to-wall wooden bookshelf behind the old man. A black-and-white version of me at the cashier's stand is on the screen. A warning to anyone attempting to rob this place that every move they make is being recorded.

"Can I help you, young man?" the man asks with a smile in desperate need of some dental work.

I read his plastic name tag. "Yes, Mr. Clyde. You wouldn't happen to have been working here late on Fat Tuesday? This place is open till three a.m., right?"

"We are, but I wasn't here," he says, pressing his thick wrinkled arms on the counter as he talks. "My granddaughter was. She already talked to your boss about some preppy-looking guy who was in here that night."

"My boss?" I repeat, confused.

"Yeah, you work for that lawyer who subpoenaed us for the footage from our surveillance camera that night, don'tcha?" Mr. Clyde says.

He's talking about Mr. Dillard. Who he's assuming I work for. *Cool. Let's go with that.*

"Yes, yeah. I'm an intern at the firm." I show him my phone, with Mr. Braswell's photo blown up from the school's website. "This the preppy-looking guy you mentioned?"

He leans in and eyes my phone and says, "Yeah, that's him. He's in here a lot—well, at least once or twice a week. Always late at night. My granddaughter told your boss he was in here around one-forty-five that night, all disheveled and sweaty like he usually is when he stops in here. Brought a bottle of Vitaminwater and a pack of gum and was gone."

Hearing that he comes in here a lot is a little soul-crushing. Makes it less suspicious that he popped in the night Chloe was killed.

"Was his clothes stained any?" I ask, placing my phone back in my pocket.

"We don't judge here. Everybody's money good," Mr. Clyde responds.

"What does that mean?" I say.

"That whatever a grown man does is his business," Mr.

Clyde replies. "He ain't the only gay man who comes strolling in here often, that time of night, after they've been doing who knows what in Coliseum Square Park. If law enforcement wants to turn a blind eye, who am I to judge? That's between them and God."

I struggle to keep the disappointment from showing up on my face. Another person I have to strike off my suspect list.

I'm still trying to process the bombshell Mr. Clyde dropped as Quincy walks up with two bottled waters he places on the counter. I know Coliseum Square Park. Nolan has talked about being propositioned by older guys to meet up there for hookups.

"Is that guy caught up in some nasty divorce?" Clyde says to me as he's ringing up the water. "Y'all work for the wife? That why y'all in here asking about him?"

"Something like that," I lie as Quincy is holding out his debit card to pay.

Quincy waits until we exit the store to ask, "What did he say that's got you looking like you just got slapped by Will Smith?"

"Coliseum Park—we passed it a little while ago when we were on Josephine." I accept the bottled water Quincy hands to me. "Our principal's been hooking up with randos in there late at night—that's why he was in the area. Also explains why he'd be freaked out that we knew."

Quincy's lip twists as he unscrews the top off his water. "I don't understand."

"He's married," I say. "Doubt his husband knows he's been creeping around."

"Damn," Quincy says after swallowing the big gulp of water.

My phone rings and my heart drops. It's almost five-thirty. The grand jury is surely done by now. Meaning this call could be my father, or even Amir himself, letting me know that we've run out of time to stop him from being indicted. I pull out my phone, but the lock screen isn't flashing to announce an incoming call. Quincy is in the process of answering his phone beside me when I look up.

"Yo, what's up, Dalton?" he answers, putting the call on speaker so I can listen.

I think Dalton is the guy who was wearing the Saints cap. He was paired up with his girlfriend. Can't remember the name Quincy told me.

"Q, get over here, man," he says in an energetic tone. "There's a woman Amir's brother needs to talk to. Like now. Hurry up. We're on Camp Street. I'll pin you the location."

"Bet," Quincy says before ending the call. "Come on."

We take off running. My heart racing. All I can think is *This is it; I got him!*

32

Amir

I take a deep breath, holding it in my lungs as I watch my dad bite into the buttermilk-lemonade fried chicken he challenged me to cook off his menu at Trudeau's. It's the second thing I've cooked for him today. I made a cucumber salad with fried oysters first, which he admitted was "pretty damn good."

He closes his eyes as he chews on the buttermilk-tenderized meat and crunchy, lemon-flavored crust. I used some of the recipe he shared with me and added a few seasonings of my own to punch it up a little.

His mouth gradually widens with an approving smile. "All right, you got some skills," he says after he swallows.

My chest pokes out as my lungs expand when I release the air I was holding in.

Nicco, who's nibbling on a drumstick, high-fives me with his free hand. "You showed him, young buck!"

"Told you, I'm a beast in the kitchen," I tease.

"Calm down, you still got a lot to learn," my dad says, taking another bite. "You made your nana, and me, proud."

Did he really just say . . .

I'm grinning so hard my face hurts.

"This boy got talent, Martin," Nicco says. "Might need to send him to culinary school. He'll give you a run for yo' money."

The last two hours were what I needed. I haven't thought about the grand jury once. But now I check my phone and see the time.

"Damn, Dad, I need to go." I start untying the apron he gave me to wear. "I gotta be home in forty-five minutes or this thing will go off," I say, lifting my right ankle.

"I'll drive you," he says, dropping the piece of chicken he was still nibbling on.

"But I rode my bike here."

"You can put it on the back of my truck," he says. "Nicco, will you do me a favor and clean up while I get him home?"

Nicco nods. "I got this. Young buck, keep yo' head up, all right? All men make mistakes. The good ones own up to them, and the great ones don't hold on to the past."

I know he's talking about me and my dad. I let his words plant themselves in my mind. My dad exhales when our eyes meet.

"I'll meet you out by the hostess stand, son," my dad tells me, pointing toward the front of the restaurant. "Give me a minute to lock up my office and I'll be right out."

I say goodbye to Nicco and punch through the double doors.

The dining area is starting to fill up again as the evening crowd wanders in. I purposely hold my head down to avoid being recognized. I pull out my phone. I missed a call from Mama. I don't know how to feel that there isn't one from Mr. Dillard. Maybe that means the grand jury decided *not* to formally charge me with Chloe's murder.

Why would they do that, though? I'm thinking when I hear my name as I'm nearing the hostess stand.

Trey Winslow is seated on the waiting bench to my left, looking as surprised to see me as I am to see him. He's dressed like he just came from the gym: basketball shorts, a loose tank top, and some fly-ass sneakers I wouldn't mind copping.

"Didn't know you worked here," he says, getting up and walking over to me.

"I don't. Was visiting my dad," I explain.

I realize this is the first time we've seen each other since our tiff in the hallway at school. Which is why I'm thrown off that he's talking to me and doesn't got his nose turned up like I smell like shit.

Marcel finally clued me in the other day about all the stuff about Senator Winslow's affair. Should have known he'd be as fraudulent as his son comes off.

"Had to stop by and pick up an order of the truffle fries for my moms," he says with an awkward grin. "She's addicted to them."

Do I look like I care? I think. Does this fool not remember accusing me of murdering his ex-girlfriend? He could really get up out my face.

I respond with a strained smile and then look back down at my phone. But evidently that doesn't give off the *Leave me alone* vibe I intended, since he's still standing here.

"I'm actually glad I ran into you, real talk," he says, his tone getting serious. "Look, man, I know things haven't always been great between us. Especially lately with all the stuff surrounding Chloe . . ."

His nervous look throws me off a bit. I ain't never seen dude *not* look confident.

". . . but after learning about Jared's game . . ." Trey rubs the back of his neck. "Listen, I think we have to stick together. It's still an Us versus Them situation. At the end of the day, we need to have each other's backs, since it's clear what some of my so-called friends think about me. All that to say . . . I'm sorry, bruh, if I've been acting like White Lives Matter Kanye. Like, for real."

I respond with an agreeable nod, not really knowing what to say. On one hand, good for him that he's finally acknowledging the reason I never had respect for him. On the other hand, there's something about dude that isn't authentic, making it hard for me to really trust anything he says. Now I know it runs in the family.

"My boy Patrick was one of the people in that thread," he says. "Now he wants to be apologetic. Says it was *just a joke,* he *really doesn't think like that.* I'm so heated."

"I bet things at school been mad tense," I say.

"I wouldn't know," Trey says. "All the Black and other minority students skipped today, and probably will the rest of the week, to protest how the administration handled this. My father is putting together a press conference to call for Mr. Braswell's firing and further corrective action."

Given what I know now about his father, that seems a bit ironic, but this is not the time or place to point that out.

"Things were so messed up between Chloe and me these past few months," he says. "I think me wanting to defend my father after she told me what he was up to made her feel like she couldn't trust me with what Jared was doing. If you hadn't found her flash drive, we'd still be in the dark. How did you even know where to look?"

"Lucky," I say.

Don't care if dude is acting all nice. If Chloe wanted him to know, she would have told him instead sending me that message.

I eye the swinging doors, hoping my dad will emerge.

"Those screenshots the only thing you found on there?"

There it is. The *real* reason this fool is in my face, trying to get buddy-buddy. In all the outrage over the slave game, I forgot what first had Trey at the top of Marcel's suspect list. He caught him looking through Chloe's bedroom for something. Maybe this fool's sister lied to Marcel and it wasn't some love notes he wanted back. He might *have* been looking for her flash drive. He must have thought she had pictures of his dad with that white woman saved on it. Let me free myself of this convo by telling him what he wants to know.

"Relax, bruh, we didn't see anything regarding what the *senator* has been up to," I say.

"For real?"

I sigh. *Guess I was right.* "We didn't really look through it," I tell him. "Just the file with the stuff about the game."

I knew his *we have to have each other's backs* was lip service. There will never be a scenario where I like this dude.

"He's doing good; for our community, for the city," Trey says, like he's practiced it many times in the mirror. "I'm not just looking out for my family."

"Uh-huh, whatever, dude," I respond.

"You ready to go, son?" my dad says, appearing beside me. "Oh, hey, Trey. Haven't seen you in here in a while. How's your father?"

Trey mentions the press conference again, naming several activists and Black city leaders who they've asked to attend but not extending an invitation to my dad. Why not? Has to be the Winslows don't want to be associated with us. Trey's father wouldn't even have a soapbox to stand on to gain reelection points if *my* family hadn't given it to him.

"Let's bounce, Dad, we ain't got time to be wasting on him," I say, charging out of Tru before I cuss Trey out for playing in my face to hide an affair while I'm fighting for my freedom.

33

Marcel

Quincy and I have broken a sweat by the time we reach Eighth and Camp, where Dalton and his girlfriend are standing on the corner with a middle-aged white woman and her golden retriever. It starts barking and hopping around on its leash as we're jogging up. The afternoon sky is eagerly making its transition into early evening. We're surrounded on all four sides of the intersection by Greek Revival–style homes with waist-high wrought-iron fences.

"Calm down, Trixie," the woman says, tugging on the leash while petting the dog's fluffy coat at the same time.

It takes Dalton's girlfriend kneeling to pet the dog and give it all her attention before it settles down.

"We got here as soon as we could," I say, catching my breath. My heart is racing from exertion and the possibility that this woman will tell me what I need to take Jared down for good.

"You really didn't have to rush," the woman says to me, shaking her head. "I saw a lot of people on the street that night."

"Mrs. Collier, this is Marcel and Q," Dalton says, giving me an exasperated look. "And you said it wasn't *a lot* of people. You told us it was *a few.*"

"Yes, yes, a few," she says, flicking her eyes toward the sky.

"Was one of them him?" I ask, showing her the picture of Jared I already have pulled up on my phone.

My breath gets knotted in my chest and sits there while I impatiently wait for her answer.

Mrs. Collier lowers her chin to look over the rim of her rose-tinted sunglasses. "I mean, I don't know, sweetie," she says while squinting at Jared's picture. "Like I told your friends, I can't be certain. That young man looks sort of like one of the boys that were traipsing up and down the street that night."

"He was by himself?" I quiz.

"No," she replies, shaking her head. "I think he was with another boy. Or maybe not. There were a few, actually—"

"White?" I interject. I push my phone closer to her face. "Can you look again? Did any of the guys look like him?"

Mrs. Collier backs away some, narrowing her eyes at me. "What is all this about?" She turns to Dalton and says, "You told me y'all were working on a class project. What *kind* of project?"

Dalton nervously looks at me, unsure how to respond.

"Ma'am, please," I say, softening my tone. "Think hard. This is really important. Was there a chance you saw this boy between one and two a.m. on Fat Tuesday?"

"It was Fat Tuesday. People turn this neighborhood into a thoroughfare during Mardi Gras," she says. "I wish the police would put a stop to it. I'm tired of drunk frat boys throwing up in my yard during carnival season. I've even called city hall—"

"Did you see him or not?" I snap.

Quincy lightly grabs my forearm, lowering my phone out of the woman's face. "Ma'am, sorry. He's just a little wound up. It's been a long day."

Mrs. Collier sighs. "Like I already said, I could have, but I can't be certain. There were a few people walking the streets when I took Trixie out. I definitely remember a couple; there was a young white boy, or two—"

"Did he look like he was in a hurry?" I interject.

"Maybe," she says with a shrug.

"Did you see *any*thing strange?" I ask.

"If you think a young girl catching an Uber that late at night on the street is strange, then yes," she replies with a little attitude.

Of course *that's* not strange, and she knows it. No one likes to drive around this city during Mardi Gras, not even locals.

"Strange to me is how your generation doesn't seem to care how they look when they come out in public," Mrs. Collier continues. "That girl had on some of the prettiest pink barrettes I've ever seen, and with what? Sweats. Looked awful. Girls in my day, we cared about how we looked when we walked out the door. What do y'all possibly see in these young ladies who have no class and no pride in their looks anymore?"

I cut my eyes at Dalton, who I now want to slap across the back of the head for calling me over for this.

"The *guys,* ma'am," I press. "None of them were acting strange that night—like in a hurry to get someplace?"

"Look, if they were, I really wasn't paying attention, sweetie," she says. "I was too busy wrestling a key out of Trixie's mouth. She will just pick up anything off the ground and think it's food. She nearly swallowed part of a tire once. Took fifteen minutes to pry it from her mouth."

"The tire?" Dalton's girlfriend quizzes, brow furrowed.

Mrs. Collier chuckles. "No, that key."

My heat drops. "Wait. A key? What kind of key? What did it look like? Was it purple and gold?"

Quincy's eyes stretch as wide as mine while Mrs. Collier, Dalton, and his girlfriend stare at us in confusion.

"Actually, yeah, it was," Mrs. Collier says while nodding at me. "How did you— Was that yours? I hope not. Once I got it out of Trixie's mouth, I threw it away."

"Where did she pick it up?" I ask, my pulse speeding.

"Near that storm drain over there," she replies, pointing across the street toward the rusting metal top of the drain by the narrow strip of grass edging the sidewalk.

"Bruh, they were on this street after . . . ," Quincy says.

My ears are ringing. My world spinning.

"What's going on?" Mrs. Collier says. "Whose key was that?"

With it starting to get dark, Quincy and I call everyone back to the parking lot where we started after we leave Mrs. Collier, whose number I got in case we need it later. We ended up telling her a half-truth to settle her curiosity: that we think Jared stole that key from a friend with the intent of hurting her. She was more than willing to help in any way she could to prevent that.

"Don't lose hope, a'ight," Quincy tells me, standing outside my car after everyone has left. "Why you look down? We know what happened to that spare key now."

"That's not enough to keep Amir from getting indicted," I respond.

"I know, but now we know Jared was on that street, in *that* area. We'll come back tomorrow and focus there. Knock on every door. That lady didn't say she *didn't* see him. She might have. Maybe someone else will have a better memory."

I just nod. Can't muster up the strength to say much. I know he's right. It's like we got closer but are still so far away from the truth. If that key was near that storm drain, Jared must have forgotten he had it because he was rushing to get away from Chloe's house. He must have been trying to get rid of it or it fell out of his pocket, maybe while he was tossing the steak knife he used to kill her into the sewer system.

After promising I'll call him later, Q and I say our goodbyes and I get in my car, sinking into the driver's seat. The world feels like it's gotten smaller. I stare out the front window in silence and jump when my phone buzzes. It could be my parents or Amir, texting me with the grand jury's decision. I'm relieved that it turns out to just be a weather alert. There's a chance of flash flooding overnight. Good. Maybe this entire city will flood and drown every person who thinks my brother murdered my best friend.

I shut my weather app while I reflect on what Mrs. Collier told us. She couldn't be certain she saw Jared that night, but she also mentioned seeing someone who resembled him with someone else, another guy. Maybe he didn't act alone. I think about Colin, and him being willing to get the jump drive for Jared to stay in the Lanfords' good graces. Could Colin have been with him that night?

I sit up straighter and open my Photos app and begin scrolling through pictures that were either sent to me or I took the night of my party. I haven't really looked at them, or posted any, since our lives blew up the following morning. Nothing about the images feels familiar anymore. It's like they're all snapshots of a life I used to have, surrounded by people I thought I knew.

Colin and Jared aren't the only ones who were in that thread. I remember Colin saying something about Patrick Rawlings also being at the party where the slave game began. I have to swipe to the fourth pic to confirm my suspicions. Patrick was at my party that night. I swipe through more photos, paying attention to the background. Colin said Jared threatened him by saying everyone in that thread would point fingers at him being the person behind it if it was exposed. Did everyone in that thread also know what Chloe was up to? Jared could have told them, and any one of them could have confronted her too at my party.

I need to get that list the news station had outing the individuals involved in the game. There's a possibility I haven't been casting a wide enough net to get to the truth. A chill walks up my spine when I pause on a pic of me standing on our staircase talking to someone. It was taken right after I caught Chloe and Trey arguing upstairs in Amir's old room.

The picture makes me think of what else Mrs. Collier said she saw that night. A girl wearing pink barrettes.

34

Amir

My phone starts ringing as my dad is exiting the interstate and we both tense up.

I eye my screen. "It's Marcel," I announce, relieved. *Not Mr. Dillard with news about the grand jury's decision.*

"'Sup?" I answer.

"You don't still need me to come over and chill tonight, do you?" he asks. It sounds like he's in his car.

I had forgotten about our earlier conversation. That feels like it happened days ago.

"Nah, I think my mama is home from work already," I say.

"And no word from Mr. Dillard yet?"

"Nope."

"Cool," he says. "There's . . . uh . . . *something* I need to look into."

I give my dad a sideways glance. I suddenly feel him watching me. Trying to figure out what we're talking about.

"What's going on?" I ask.

"I'll tell you later. Gotta stop by the Winslows' for a minute," he says.

"For what?" I ask, my residual irritation with Trey resurfacing.

My dad turns down our street with fifteen minutes to spare before my curfew kicks in. I really need to stop cutting it close like this.

"To holla at Tiffany right quick. Stay by yo' phone."

Then he ends the call.

"What's your brother up to?" my dad asks.

"I have no idea," I say, which isn't entirely a lie. Whatever he's doing, I know it's got something to do with me. Marcel wouldn't want our father knowing he's disobeying his request that we leave the detective work alone. That has me wondering what he thinks Trey's little sister might know.

My mom's car is parked out front. My dad blocks it in when he stops in front of our house.

"You gonna let me know as soon as you hear from Dillard, right?" he says as I'm opening the door.

I pause. "Yeah. I will."

"And, son, I enjoyed today."

I look back before sliding out of his truck. "Yeah, me too," I say.

He waits until I've gotten my bike out his truck bed and walked inside before he pulls off.

Mama's bedroom door is shut but the light is on. I prop my bike against a wall in the living room, then enter my room, still thinking about Marcel's call. My run-in with Trey needling in the back of my thoughts as well.

Right as I'm starting a game on *NBA 2K23,* Mama pokes her head in the doorway of my bedroom. She's wearing a terry-cloth robe.

"No word yet?" she asks.

I shake my head, never taking my eyes off my game.

"Maybe no news is good news."

"Maybe," I say with a deep sigh.

She quietly lingers for a few seconds, watching me as I pretend I don't feel her standing there. Right after she disappears, she pokes her head back in.

"Oh, did your friend Trey find you today?" she says.

"I ran into him at Tru," I say.

"Good. Mrs. Lee, next door, sent him to the hospital after he stopped by here looking for you and no one was home. He showed up saying he had something urgent he wanted to talk to you about, had to do with that slave game mess at school. I told him where you were."

I pause the game. "He made it seem like he didn't know I was there."

"He knew 'cause I told him after your daddy let me know you showed up there," she says.

Mama proceeds to ask how things went with my dad, but I tune her out as I rerun the conversation I had with Trey. Why'd he lie about running into me?

35

Marcel

It doesn't make sense. And at the same time, it could.

If the Colin situation taught me anything, it's that coincidences are rarely just that. At least when they concern my best friend's murder. Tiffany was wearing sparkling pink barrettes that night. Of course, that doesn't automatically mean she's the person Mrs. Collier claimed she saw catching an Uber on Camp Street. She's not the only person in this city who owns a pair of pink barrettes. Even though I know that, seeing that picture of Tiffany and me talking on the staircase at my party reminded me of something: she had beef with Chloe too. The friendship they had established when Chloe started dating Trey had ended by my party, I assumed due to Trey and Choe's breakup this last time. Looking back, though, Chloe never really gave me a concrete reason why she stopped talking to Tiffany. I never saw the need to press her about it since I know how it works when couples split. Tiffany was collateral damage.

Maybe something bad went down between her and Chloe,

separate from the breakup with Trey. *Or* could Tiffany have been lying about when she found out her father was having an affair? That's possible, given how close I know she and Trey are. I could also see a scenario where he didn't tell his sister about Vivian Crane, worried Tiffany might slip and say something to her mother. But if Tiffany did know about the affair before Chloe's murder, she could have had the same fears as Trey about Chloe knowing too. Folks love to shoot the messenger when they receive news they don't like. Tiffany told me she heard Trey come home that night and that at first she thought he might have murdered Chloe. What was she doing up so late, though? Had she just gotten home herself after—

Nah, this is Tiffany. Awkward, painfully shy Tiffany.

Being reminded of her pink barrettes has had my mind spiraling with all these dark thoughts. Planting seeds of doubt about a girl I could never see hurting anyone. That's why I'm going to the Winslows' to shut this down now. Eliminate all doubt.

It was definitely another girl, Marcel, I tell myself again as I'm pulling up to their eclectic two-story house. Trey's car is parked in the driveway. I reach into my back seat and grab my messenger bag, which contains the vital component I need to get inside and settle these doubts. My mouth feels like cotton as I'm walking up their porch steps. I ring the doorbell and wait.

I take a deep breath, straightening my shoulders as I prepare myself for the performance.

Tiffany opens the door barefooted, wearing black leggings and an oversized sweatshirt.

"Marcel? Hey," she says, frowning at me.

I wave at her with a smile that feels strained. "I felt bad about leaving you high and dry yesterday on the mock trial stuff, so I worked on our opening statement all today, and I feel so good about it that I decided to stop by and see what you think."

"Uhhhhh, *okay,*" she drawls, still eyeing me with an unsure look.

"I needed a distraction today. The grand jury is meeting to decide if they'll indict my brother," I say, feeling like a little honesty will land better.

Her expression shifts to what seems like empathy—or maybe guilt, if Mrs. Collier was right. *Chill, Marcel, you know her. She's a sweetheart, not a murderer.*

"Invite me in so I can keep my mind off all that a little longer . . . please?" I add.

She nods with a tight smile, stepping aside so I can enter. "You really shouldn't have even bothered to do it," she says as I walk past her. "I didn't go to school today, and probably won't for the rest of the week."

"Why not?"

"You don't know?" She shuts the front door. "We're all skipping classes, the minority students, in protest over that game. My father is going to call for Mr. Braswell to resign and the board of directors to take immediate action to suspend all the students who were involved. My parents are at his office now, pulling together all the particulars for a press conference tomorrow."

Hearing this an hour ago would have been everything. When I was still one hundred percent convinced that it was Jared, and possibly other people in that thread, who killed Chloe to keep everything that seems to be happening now from happening.

"You've had your mind on other things, so I understand why you didn't know," she says in an apologetic tone.

"Can I sit down over there and show you what I came up with?" I ask, pointing at their dining table.

"Yeah, that's cool," she says.

We walk over to the dining area together. My heart is pounding so hard I'm worried she can hear it.

I pull out a chair facing the window and set my messenger bag on it so I can take out my laptop. Tiffany watches from the other end of the table with a patient grin. Her face so innocent and light.

"Where's Trey?" I ask as I set my laptop on the table.

"Upstairs, probably playing video games," she replies with a nonchalant shrug.

I open my computer and pretend to press the power button. Then I wait a few seconds, frowning when the screen doesn't light up. "Fuck! The battery is dead." I look down in my book bag, knowing my charger isn't in there because it's still on the back seat of my car, where I put it after I pulled up. "You wouldn't happen to have a charger for a Mac, would you?"

I know she doesn't.

She shakes her head. "I'm a PC girl."

"Can I use yours? I can access my file through my Google Drive," I say.

"Sure. Let me run upstairs and get it," Tiffany says before darting off toward the staircase at the back of the room.

So far, everything is going exactly how I intended.

I replace my laptop in my messenger bag and set it down on the floor next to the chair after I sit. Every nerve in my body is tingling as I wait. The silence, deafening. I'm banking on two things: One, that Tiffany has her email account directly linked to her laptop access, just like I do, so that after she logs on, all I have to do is open the email app to get access to her inbox without needing her passcode. And two, that she has her own debit or credit card like me, and she receives all her Uber receipts via email.

Tiffany comes bouncing down the stairs, hugging her laptop to her chest.

"You're a lifesaver, girl," I say as she sets it down on the table in front of me.

"Oh please, you probably about to get us an A, 'cause I damn sure didn't know what I was going to say for this case," she says as it powers up. "Given what Jared did, I'm not feeling too keen on defending him, even if this is all fake."

Can't say that I disagree with her there.

After she keys in her password, her screen comes to life. I make sure to wait until it's completely powered on to give myself the time I'm going to need. I click on the icon to open the Google app. As soon as the landing page fills the screen, I turn and look up at Tiffany, who's standing behind me. "Y'all got something to drink—water, a Coke? I haven't really eaten much all day."

"Yeah, I'll grab you a water out the fridge," she says, scurrying off toward the kitchen, which is on the other side of their house.

She's far away enough for me to do this without her knowing.

"So, what precedent did you use to build our case?" she asks as she disappears down the hallway.

"I'll tell you in a sec," I yell over my shoulder as I quickly minimize the Google webpage and click on the email icon.

Tiffany's inbox blossoms on-screen. *Yes!* I shoot up straighter in my seat. It would take too long to scroll through the thousands of emails, so I click in the search bar and type *Uber.* Instantly the list morphs into nothing but emailed receipts from her rides. There are a lot of them. Judging by the days and times, she uses the rideshare service a few times a week for school. I'm guessing whenever Trey can't take her to and from himself.

I'm holding my breath as I scroll down, scanning for the night of Fat Tuesday.

Nothing.

I should be relieved. Tiffany isn't a killer. But my eyes are pulled toward the trash icon on the taskbar at the bottom of the screen. I bite down on my lip as I double click it.

If it's not there, then I know for sure.

I click in the search bar and type *Uber.*

Again . . . nothing.

I collapse in the chair with a deep sigh that releases all the tension that's been twisted up in my body since I got here.

"Marcel, you want ice?" she yells from their kitchen.

I sit up and say, "Yeah, sure," and begin hitting the delete button to clear *Uber* from the search bar one letter at a time. A file name pops up that causes a chill to twist my gut. A jpeg she recently transferred into her trash folder.

SlaveGame2224, it reads.

I click on it. It's exactly what I expected: the first screenshot Chloe had saved on her flash drive from Jared's slave game. The chill in my stomach expands. I close the image and scroll through the rest of the list. All the screenshots Chloe collected are here. I keep scrolling. The other folders I recall from the flash drive are listed as well.

How could she have this . . . ?

A video file labeled *Tiffany21124* catches my eye. Based on the file names for the screenshots, I have to assume the numbers are the date the video was recorded. That was two days before my party.

I click on it, my breath catching in the back of my throat as a black rectangular-shaped box pops up on-screen.

TIFFANY21124.MP4

Chloe is standing in front of her mirrored dresser, her phone propped at an angle that gives a partial view of her closed bedroom door and open closet in the background. Her long blond hair is wet and limply drapes onto the pink robe she's wearing.

She picks up a slim makeup brush with a black handle and a small eyeshadow palette and says, "Okay, the goal is to pull off this cool, blended smoky eye thing that Kim K had on the cover of *Vogue.*" She pauses, raising an eyebrow to the camera on her phone. "If I can pull this off, this will be the first makeup tutorial I'll post to my TikTok."

It's so weird, seeing her alive like this.

She starts applying light blue eye shadow to her left eye,

when her bedroom door violently opens, slamming into the nearby wall, causing her to yelp. Tiffany storms into the room.

"You sanctimonious-ass bitch!" Tiffany screams.

Chloe spins around and steps to the right, the lower left side of her robe the only part of her visible. Tiffany's now taking up most of the background within the video.

"How did you get in here?" Chloe says.

Tiffany hurls a key at her. Chloe cries out when it hits her.

"You wouldn't answer the door, so I let myself in," Tiffany says, her eyes angry and mouth tight.

"You had no right to hijack our spare key like some psycho," Chloe yells.

"Like you have no right getting up in my family's business! Why did you contact that journalist? You tipping him off about my father's affair?"

"How do you—"

"We know," Tiffany rails. "What did you say to him?"

"Nothing. That's not about your father. Now get out!"

Tiffany points at Chloe, her eyes feral. "I'm not my brother. I'm not begging. Keep your fucking mouth shut or you'll regret it, trust me!"

"Yeah, I'm the issue 'cause your dad is a fraud."

"Say something else slick about my father and it'll be the last thing that comes out of your mouth, girl." Tiffany takes a step closer to Chloe, who backs away, now completely off camera. "I'll make you the headline. Try me and see."

Tiffany's eyes shift to the right and stretch wide when she notices the camera.

"You recording me?" she shrieks.

Tiffany reaches for the phone, but Chloe snatches it up first. All that's visible now is the pink fibers of Chloe's robe.

Chloe screams, "Get out of my house, Tiffany! Now!"

"Consider this your first and final warning from me," Tiffany says. Then the video ends.

The creaking of a floorboard behind me causes me to look up just in time to catch Tiffany's reflection in the window in front of me. She's standing behind me, her hands raised in the air. Then a white-hot pain explodes in the back of my head and everything goes black.

36

Amir

My call to Marcel rolls over to his voice mail—for the tenth time in a row. I start pacing around my bedroom again. It feels a little bit smaller than it did before I made this last unanswered call. The back of my throat is so tight my breathing is labored.

Pick up the phone, bro! I try calling again. Six rings and then his voice mail picks up. Again.

"Fuck!"

Something doesn't feel right. Questions I can't quite connect are ricocheting in my mind: Why did Trey show up at my dad's restaurant pretending he had randomly bumped into me when he already knew I was there? What could Marcel be *looking into* at the Winslows' with Tiffany? Why isn't he answering his damn phone all of a sudden? A flash of Chloe's bloody body pops into my head. My mind showing me the worst possible answer.

A picture of fourteen-year-old me and Nana laughing together on her stoop looks back at me from inside the frame cluttered amid everything else on my dresser. Her voice echoes in my head.

Go!

The weight around my right ankle giving me pause.

Another phone call to Marcel. Another one that rolls over to voice mail. My stomach is in knots.

Go! Nana says again.

Trey was obviously worried Chloe might've had evidence on her flash drive about his father's affair.

Those screenshots the only thing you found on there? I remember him saying.

Relax, bruh, we didn't see anything regarding what the senator has been up to, I replied.

And then I said something about us only looking at the slave game files.

I stop pacing, a realization rolling over in my mind. *Why didn't he ask to see the flash drive after I told him Marcel and I hadn't looked at all the files on it?* I open the Google app on my phone, remembering something else during our exchange. Those fiya-ass sneakers he was wearing. They were purple, black, and white with pink shoelaces. I recall there being some kind of S-looking emblem on the sides. Probably some high-end designer brand, that's why I don't know them. I type everything I remember about them into the Google search engine. The ones Trey was wearing are the fifth picture that pops up.

I click on the link that will take me to the page where I can buy a pair. Not interested. I blow up the images that are attached, which give me a three-hundred-and-sixty-degree view of the shoe as I click through, the last being the one I'm looking for. It's a picture of the sole. I minimize that page to open my Photos app. The picture I took of the muddy shoeprint from the night of the break-in is the first image in my Recents photo album.

It becomes harder to breathe. *They match!*

I bolt out my bedroom and call out for my mama. She needs to get to the Winslows'. Marcel could be in danger. It was freaking Trey who broke into our house and stole that flash drive. That means it was probably him who killed Chloe too. Marcel was fucking right all along!

"Ma!"

Her bedroom door is open and the light off. I poke my head in, turn on the light, call out for her again. Nothing. I run down the hall, into the kitchen and then the living room. More silence. No movement.

"Ma!" I yell after stumbling out the door onto our front porch. My cry for help evaporating within the womb of the chilly, silent black night.

Where is she? I didn't hear her leave. And her car is still parked in the driveway. Could something have happened? Did Trey . . . because he thought I was lying about not seeing anything about his father's affair on Chloe's flash drive?

I spin around and run back inside. "Ma!" I cry out. Her keys are exactly where she always leaves them: on the counter near the basket where she keeps our mail. I pull out my phone and call her.

"Hello," she answers after three rings.

Thank God!

"Ma, where you at?" I ask, my heart still racing. *I have to get to my brother!*

"I'm down the street at Mrs. Johnson's house." I hear talking in the background. "I'm helping Shonda lift her mother back up on her bed."

"Stop!" I yell. "We have to get to Marcel, he's in trouble."

"Amir, hold up one sec. . . ." More scrambling and talking in the background. "Look, let me call you right back. Mrs. Johnson, I can't—"

The call ends.

"Ma, *no*!"

I'm about to call her back but pause, my gaze stopping on her keys. I snatch them up but pause again. Remembering my ankle monitor. Any apprehensions I have about breaking the rules of my curfew are pushed out of my mind the second a flash of Chloe's lifeless body enters my thoughts.

Fuck house arrest! I have to make sure Marcel is okay.

Him and I agreed to share our locations with each other after the break-in, in case . . . something like *this* happened. As I'm running out the house and barreling down our porch steps, I open the Find My Friends app. Once I'm in Mama's car I zoom in on the map. Marcel's avatar is settling on a house on Jefferson Avenue. That's only five minutes away.

The ankle monitor is going crazy. Its persistent beeping and flashing red light keeping up with my pounding heart.

It's GPS monitored. The police are probably tracking me

now. *Good.* They'll show up in case some foul shit has gone down and Marcel isn't answering his phone 'cause—

Don't think like that, bruh, I tell myself. I don't want to know what my life will be like without him in it. Not anymore. Not when I was finally starting to get comfortable with having him there. Having my back, like a real brother.

Once I'm in the 2000 block of Jefferson Avenue, I know where the Winslows' house is. Marcel's car is parked out front. I whip Mama's car right behind his and jump out. I don't even bother to take the keys out of the ignition or shut the door.

I run up the porch steps and bang on the front door, ignoring the doorbell. The thirty seconds it takes for someone to answer feel like thirty minutes.

When the door flies open, it's Trey staring back at me. His face blank, beads of sweat on his forehead. His T-shirt is damp. Like he's been jogging—or killing my brother.

"Where's Marcel?" I bark.

I catch his eyes quickly shift to the left before he gives me a strained smile. "Huh? H-he-he's not here. Said he was parking here to—"

"Get the fuck outta my way!" I yell, pushing past him into the house.

I stop as soon as I see his sister. Standing over Marcel in their dining area. A laptop opened on the table. My brother lying still on his stomach on the floor. The bush of curly black hair on the back of his head is matted and slick-looking. *Blood!* Tiffany glaring at me from across the room, her eyes wide and mouth slack.

"What did—"

A burst of wind charges toward my face. I turn toward the shadow, moving to my right. Ducking just in time to avoid whatever heavy object Trey swung at my head. The backward jerk of my body sends me stumbling into a table behind me. My back scratching up against its sharp edge.

"Bash his head in, Trey!" I hear Tiffany shout.

I don't get a chance to recover before Trey takes another swing at me. I manage to scoot out of the way in time, crashing to my side on the hardwood floor as he shatters the porcelain bowl that was centered on the table.

"Hurry up!" his sister screams from the dining area.

Using the armrest of a nearby chair, I'm able to pull myself up off the floor. Trey comes charging at me again with what I now see is an aluminum baseball bat. My eyes frantically bounce around. Looking for a weapon of my own. I can't find one before Trey swings again. But this time I duck and then charge forward, tackling him by the waist and sending us both flying across the floor near the dining area, where Marcel still isn't moving.

Please don't be dead!

My anger and adrenaline give me the strength to pop up quickly and start pounding Trey with my fists. He has to let go of the bat so he can use his arms as a shield.

"You killed him? *You killed my brother?*" I scream as I rain my fury down on him.

All I see is red. The same crimson red that started all this. The crimson Chloe's lifeless body was soaking in. But it doesn't have me feeling light-headed or queasy, like usual. It gives me strength. I punch harder. Ignoring the pain in my hands as I keep slamming my fist into his head. I can't let him get away with this.

"Get off of him!" I hear behind me.

Tiffany! I forgot his sister was here. She reminds me by digging her nails into my face. "Get off him!" she screeches, tearing into my flesh so hard my head whips back.

"Agggghhhhh!" I cry out in pain.

I have to stop hitting Trey so I can rip her hands away. Doing so allows her brother to reach for the bat. I have no way to stop him from slamming its handle into my chest, knocking all the wind out of me and sending me flying backward.

I'm too out of breath to recover in time before he's standing over me, pointing the bat in my face, his expression feral. "Don't fucking move," he says through clenched teeth.

"Bash his skull, Trey!" his sister screams behind him, her baby-doll face filled with a rage I've never seen before.

"Be quiet, Tiff!" Trey yells.

As chaos fades to silence, the beeping of my ankle monitor echoes louder. Trey looks down at my feet, realization entering his bruised face.

"What's that noise?" Tiffany asks.

"His ankle monitor—*fuck*!" Trey screams.

I sneer at them both. "Right. The police are already on their way."

Trey scrubs his head with erratic flair.

"Kill him!" Tiffany shouts.

"Shut up!"

Tiffany glares at her brother. "*You* shut up and do what I said."

"You've already done enough. How are we supposed to explain this?" he says, waving at me and Marcel, who's still motionless on the floor. "You're fucking out of control! First Chloe—"

Chloe? Wait. It was his sister?

"—and now Marcel. I can't keep cleaning up *your* messes!"

"Then do a better job keeping your hoes in check!" his sister screams, spit flying from her mouth. "Had you properly shut Chloe down, I wouldn't have had to step in."

Trey spins around toward Tiffany. "It wasn't even about our father. She reached out to that journalist about that fucking game!"

"We didn't know that!"

"Killing her wasn't the answer!"

"Dead women can't tell no secrets," Tiffany says, her eyes intense.

"I warned Dad to stay away from that woman," Trey replies, his voice cracking under the weight of everything he's been hiding.

"Oh please," Tiffany hisses, throwing her hands in the air. "Daddy is weak like you when it comes to women. He wasn't going to stop seeing her and you know it. I did what had to be done."

"And caused all of this!" Trey yells, waving the bat in my direction.

"I told you, I didn't know he was in the house," Tiffany shouts. "Had I . . ."

She would have killed me too. Oh fuck.

"Bruh, there's no way y'all are going to get away with this now," I say. I need to appeal to Trey if I want to get out of this alive. He's the sensible one. "The police are coming. I'm going to tell them—"

"You ain't telling them shit!" he screams.

"Kill. Him," his sister hisses.

"How y'all gonna explain that?" I say to Trey. "Why are you doing this? To me? To my family?"

Trey slowly turns to me, panting. "'Cause families like ours aren't allowed to make mistakes in this world. We have to be perfect. Or white folks will get our own people to turn against us. Look at what happened to your father. We're not letting that happen to ours. Our privilege don't work like theirs. Everyone is ready to tear a Black man down as soon as he makes something of himself." He kneels down so that he's in my face. "My family has to *always* come first."

"Wow," I sigh. "My father wouldn't let Marcel or my lawyer put the heat on you in the press for that same reason. He didn't want to tear down another prominent Black family. He ain't a fake-ass bitch like you."

I charge, tackling Trey again, but this time tilting all my weight to the left so that my push sends him crashing into the dining table. The side of his head cracks against its edge with enough force to daze him. The fall also knocks the bat out his hand.

I reach down and grab it before his sister can get it.

"I wish you would," I say to her, reaching back, ready to swing should she make any sudden movements.

Her eyes shift to the right, over my shoulder. Something moves in my periphery. There's a white police officer standing near the front door when I look over my shoulder. His gun pointed in our direction, his gaze trained on me.

"What's going on here?" he says to me. "Why did you leave your approved zone?"

"He's trying to kill us, Officer!" Trey yells, using one of the dining chairs to stand up. He backs away from me, grabbing the side of his head. "He charged into our house. Hurt his brother, and then tried to hurt us because we know what he did to my ex-girlfriend."

The officer looks like he's actually considering this bullshit, so I lower the bat. "Officer, that's a lie. They—"

"Officer, please, help us," Tiffany sobs.

The officer looks down at Marcel before he looks back up at me. "Drop the bat and get on the ground . . . *now*!"

I slowly begin to do what he says. My gaze locks with Trey's as I do. There's a sinister smile on his face. I know what he's thinking. What he's about to do. The floor vanishes from beneath my feet at the thought.

He's going to use this dumb cop to silence me, because his sister is right: he's too weak to kill me himself. He's gonna get someone else to do it for him.

"Sir, he's got a gun!" Trey yells, jumping back as if he's afraid I'm about to do something.

I take a deep breath. I can see the officer's grip tighten around his revolver. How could one of us use the police's inherent bias against Black men to kill me?

My mouth drops open, and I'm about to scream as I see the officer's finger start squeezing the trigger.

"Noooooooooo!!!!"

The scream doesn't come from me. It's Marcel, who has managed to push himself up off the floor, blood dripping down the front of his head. He's alive!

"Don't shoot my brother," he cries out, his voice weaker than it just was. "*She* killed Chloe Danvers! She killed him, not my brother."

What he said takes what little strength he has left. He collapses back to the floor. Up close I can see how deep the gash in the back of his head is.

"All right, *nobody* move!" the officer orders, waving his gun at Tiffany and Trey. With his eyes still on all three of us, he lifts his right shoulder up to his face, using his left hand to mash the button on the walkie-talkie receiver attached near the collar of his uniform shirt. "Unit 487, requesting backup to 2434 Jefferson Avenue."

37

Marcel

Everything feels like a nightmare. The scenes keep replaying themselves in a horrifying loop, starting with that video of Tiffany basically threatening Chloe's life. Then Tiffany sneaking up behind me and bashing me over the head. That police officer about to shoot Amir. Hearing Nana's voice telling me to wake up, giving me enough strength to stop that from happening before everything went black again. Then bright white lights. Hazy memories of doctors and nurses working near me in frantic conversations.

None of it feels real until the darkness fades and I see my parents standing over me, their faces a tense marriage of torment and relief. My head feeling as if it's on fire when I try to lift it.

"No, no, baby, don't move too much," my mother says, gently pushing me back down on the cloud of pillows propping up my head. "You have a fractured skull. They had to use eight stitches to repair the damage that little heathen did."

My tongue feels like cotton. My thoughts are a little wavy. Like I'm underwater. "Amir," I call out, wiggling my legs but not having the strength I need to get out of this bed. "Where's Amir? What happened to—"

"I'm right here, bro."

His voice comes from somewhere out of sight but close by.

It's when my parents look over their shoulder that I see him. Standing at the foot of my hospital bed with his mother, who gives me a warm smile. Both Monica's and Amir's eyes are swollen and red. Another shadow moves to the right of them. I turn toward it and see Mr. Dillard step forward, looking a lot younger in a polo shirt that's slightly untucked from his slim-fit jeans.

"He made me come straight here from the police station," Monica says, gently placing her hand on Amir's shoulder.

"You—you didn't get shot," I say, my voice rough and shaky. Like it doesn't even belong to me.

Amir grins. "Thanks to you."

The cup of water my mother tips into my mouth helps soothe the tightness in my throat. The time it takes for me to drink it all lifts some of the fogginess. It also lessens the dull ache in the back of my head. Everyone surrounding my bed looks tired. I realize it's almost two a.m. when I see the digital clock on the right wall, next to the whiteboard that lists my name, diagnosis, the nurse assigned to my room, and the time she'll be back to take my vitals again.

"You almost got yourself killed," I tell Amir, tears entering my strained voice. "You were on house arrest."

"Nah, *you* almost got yourself killed," he says to me. "You should have told me what was up with you going over there."

"No, you *both* should have told us what was going on," his mother interjects. "Thought we had a talk about y'all not playing detective."

"I tried to tell you, but you were too busy playing nurse," Amir says to her with a smirk. "I couldn't wait. I knew. Figured out it was Trey who broke into our house and hurt you to get that flash drive. Knew I had to get to Marcel before he hurt him too." He looks back at me and adds, "I'd do it again."

My heart swells. I've never seen him look at me like this before. Like he's grateful I'm alive.

Just as I'm about to ask how he knew it was Trey who broke into their house, my mother says, "I'm glad Amir did what he did, or those two hellions would have gotten away with worse."

My father reaches down to squeeze my leg through the blanket covering the lower half of my body. "We're blessed. And as right as both your mothers are, I'd like to think we still have the two of you here because you had each other's backs, the way yo' nana always wanted you to."

Amir lowers his head and starts grinning harder when our father grabs his hand and squeezes it. I take a minute to enjoy what's happening. Us feeling like a real family that found a way to love each other despite our messed-up backstory.

"What happened to Tiffany and Trey?" I ask.

"They're being booked right about now," Mr. Dillard says, reminding me of his presence. "We've been down at the station for hours sorting all that out. Police finally got them to crack, or rather, got *him* to admit everything they did."

"I don't understand why Tiffany killed her," Amir says.

"For the same reason I thought Trey did," I answer in a sad tone.

I tell them about finding that video of Tiffany bursting into Chloe's bedroom and threatening Chloe because she believed Chloe had contacted a journalist and was getting ready to out their father's affair with Vivian Crane. "Tiffany didn't know that was about Chloe wanting to out Jared's game," I explain. "Chloe's cousin Victoria even mentioned to me how Chloe reached out to that reporter."

"That's pretty much what Trey told the police," Mr. Dillard says. "Apparently the reporter is a close family friend of the Winslows, and he let them know that Trey's girlfriend had reached out to him about a story tip."

"I'm still trying to wrap my head around how vicious and evil Tiffany looked in that video," I say. "I've never seen her like that."

"Same," Amir follows. "Tonight she had no remorse about anything. She said if she had known I was in the house too that night, she would have . . ."

Amir doesn't have to finish his statement. Everyone knows how it would end.

I scoot up higher in bed, thinking back on that day I ran into her and Dustin in the hall at school. I mentioned Chloe's flash drive then; that's how they knew we had it.

"The DA's office plans to hold a press conference around

eight in the morning to announce the arrest of Senator Winslow's kids for Chloe's murder," Mr. Dillard says. "A press conference they had previously scheduled to announce the grand jury's decision to indict Amir, which obviously got thrown out."

Mr. Dillard looks at us both. "I know your parents aren't happy about it, but, Marcel, that was smart, canvassing that neighborhood like that. No one would ever have suspected Tiffany, especially since her brother had destroyed that flash drive."

I never would have either, if it wasn't for Mrs. Collier not liking how Tiffany paired her pink barrettes with the sweatpants she must have thrown on before going to the Chloe's house. Nana used to say the devil is *always* in the details.

"Why would Trey ruin his life like that over what she did?" my mother says.

"He was always protective of Tiffany," I say.

"Nah, he was protecting his family's status," Amir says. "When we were fighting, he told me he would never let people turn on them the way they turned on us after I got arrested. He basically said Black people who reach the one percent status don't get to make mistakes and stay on top. And for him, that was more important than any solidarity we thought we had."

I want to hate Trey for what he did. What he and his sister almost got away with. But that's hard when I understand his motivation. Scary too, 'cause there's a possibility I might have done the same. Look how far I was willing to go to save Amir.

38

Amir

Waking up and living in the world has gotten better. While everything else in the city seems to be unraveling.

A news report published a few days after Marcel was released from the hospital claimed that Senator Spencer Winslow will likely be resigning from office in the wake of the scandal surrounding the arrests of Trey and Tiffany. "He thinks his time will be better spent focusing on his family right now," the anonymous source in the article was quoted as saying. The day before that, a package of articles about the slave trade game dominated the front page. One informing the public that Mr. Braswell was forced to resign, and the school's board of directors is commissioning a "diligent search" for his replacement.

"Watch they hire someone Black to clean up that mess," my mother said as she was reading it. "That's what they do any time something like this happens."

Another article that day was an exposé into the Crescent

City Foundation, detailing a twisted web of dark money, bribes, and other questionable practices Jared's father had a hand in. He's been kicked off Truman's board of directors. Elected officials have publicly begun distancing themselves from Mr. Lanford and the foundation, the Lanford name now tarnished. The third article in the package was how Marcel and I found out that Jared and the other students in that game thread had been expelled from Truman. The article didn't name the other students, but some online hacker outed everyone who was involved and published their names in a Twitter thread that went viral in less than three hours. Some of the kids' homes have been vandalized in the aftermath. Their names now immortalized by the ordeal.

CNN reached out to my dad's public relations team this week, asking for an on-camera, sit-down interview with our entire family about the game and how it affected us emotionally. There have been similar incidents at other schools around the country. Since national news outlets got hold of the story, there's been lively debate between pundits, some of whom think these types of things have become a trend because slavery and the repercussions of systemic racism aren't being taught in schools. "Educators don't want white kids to feel ashamed for what their ancestors did, but it's okay for Black children to be shamed because of their ignorance," a race relations professor from Spelman College theorized during a segment Mama and I watched two nights ago.

"The school administrators turning a blind eye to stuff like this all see racism as innocent fun, or just a phase that white kids go through," the professor went on to say. "They don't want to punish a kid for being *funny*."

We agreed to do the interview. They're flying us to Atlanta to film our segment next week. Keeping this in the headlines as long as possible is Marcel's new goal in life.

As I'm wiping sleep from my eyes and staggering down the hall, I hear music blaring in our front yard. The clock on the microwave says 11:15 a.m. Mama didn't have to work last night, which explains why she's up this early on a Saturday. I step out onto the porch and find that she's not alone.

Mama is bent over our grill, and dozens of our neighbors and other people are setting up chairs and tables in our front yard.

"What's going on?" I ask.

Mama turns with a smile. "'Bout time you woke up." She drops the brush she was using to scrape off the grill and bops over to me, shaking her shoulders to the beat of the music blaring from the large speakers that have been set up on either side of our porch. "Go put on some clothes. We're having a little cookout today."

"For what?" I say.

"'Cause you alive, you ain't going to prison, and you don't have to sulk around this house anymore with that ankle monitor on," she says, looking down at my bare feet.

They took the monitor off before I left the police station the night Trey and Tiffany were arrested.

"How you wake up and decide to throw a party all random like this?" I say, waving back to Mrs. Lee and a few other people who are waving at me from our yard.

"That's what we do in New Orleans, bay-bee," she says, bumping her hip into mine. "We let the good times roll. Now go get dressed. We got lots to celebrate, boy."

By the time I shower and change, the music has gotten louder, and I can tell from the shouts and conversations I hear all the way inside that the crowd has grown.

As I'm entering the living room to head out, I hear, "Amir."

I turn, and there's Lily on our love seat. Waiting. For me. She stands up.

"Can I have a word with you . . . for just a minute?" she says, rubbing her palm with her thumb.

Instinctively I look around for a lifeline. None of my experiences with this woman have been good. She's only ever made me feel unwanted and unworthy. What could she possibly want to say to me? *Sorry for thinking you killed my dog.* What am I supposed to do with that? Act like all the other petty shit she did or said to come between me and my dad didn't happen? And for what? 'Cause she felt some type of way that I even existed? Or because she hated my mother? Thought that we came before her and Marcel in our dad's eyes?

"You have every right to hate me. I've been nothing but, for lack of a better term, an evil Disney stepmother," she says.

That sounds like something Marcel would say.

Lily slides her hand across the side of her head, as if a strand of her hair has popped out from her slicked-back bun. "I can't change the past, can't go back and erase all the times I made you feel like you didn't belong with us."

Where is she going with this? I don't need a recap of all the ways she's been a bitch to a kid that never did anything to her but show respect and try to stay out of the way in a place where I knew I wasn't welcome.

"The truth of the matter is, I knew very early on that Marcel was gay." She lets her arms fall to her sides and looks me square in the eyes. "After having so many gay friends and a fabulous uncle, I saw the signs. A mother knows when her son is going to be special. However, I was very afraid your father wouldn't feel the same. Black men, the toxic masculinity standards some of you live by . . . I didn't want Marcel to grow up to be the one thing Martin could never accept. Especially when he had another son who looked like him and was a typical boy in every sense of the word.

"So I lifted Marcel up while trying to tear you down," she says, her voice shaking. "Only to realize later that Martin was a man who truly loves unconditionally. And that I had played a part in preventing him from doing that with you, all because I built up this competition in my head that ultimately made you feel like there's no place for you with us."

She steps up to me and places her hands on my shoulders. "My apology to you is changed behavior going forward."

I lower my head as tears build behind my eyes. Lily gently lifts my chin with her hand and smiles at me. "We are the Trudeaus, honey. After everything you've been through, everything you risked to save Marcel, I'm proud to call you my stepson."

More emotions fold over the ones I'm already struggling with. I just knew whatever she was going to say would be depleting. Hearing her include me with them—*we are the Trudeaus*—

filled me up. My dad's other family doesn't feel like such an *other* anymore.

She straightens the backward cap I'm wearing and gives me a once-over. "Okay, let's get out there and enjoy ourselves before your father and mother think I've done who-knows-what to you."

As she's reaching for the doorknob, I say, "Hey, Lily?"

She stops and turns to me, brow furrowed.

"You keep this up, you might go from evil stepmother *toooooo* . . . kinda cool stepmother," I say, doing a so-so gesture with my hand when I say *kinda.*

The right side of her mouth gradually stretches into a smile. She flicks imaginary hair over her shoulder and says, "Now, *that,* I like."

People are spilling out of our front yard into the street and into the yards of our immediate neighbors. It looks like Mama invited everyone on our block and at least three blocks over. The smell of barbecuing meat awakens my stomach. I laugh at a cluster of folks who are line dancing to Beyoncé's version of "Before I Let Go."

"Took y'all long enough. Everything good?" a familiar voice says.

My dad is standing on our porch to my right, holding a bottle of beer in one hand. Lily walks over to him, slipping her hand into his other one. She starts cooling herself off with a fan that matches her flower-print sundress.

"Everything is gonna be all right, Martin," she says, winking at me.

"You being nice to my son? Alert the press," Mama says as she walks up the porch steps to join us.

"He is the only thing you've done right," Lily replies, pursing her lips.

Mama rolls her eyes, but with a faint smirk. This dynamic is weird. I don't hate it, but it's gonna take some time to get used to. Will they become friends? Doubt it. Respecting each other, if for no other reason than keeping peace between me and Marcel, is enough for me.

"You hungry? Your father has half the menu from Tru spread out over there," Mama says, pointing at the folding table near her car.

"Anything for my boy," my dad says.

"If that's true, how about you get him a new car so I don't have to cart him back and forth to school anymore?" Mama says.

Our parents have pulled me and Marcel out of Truman. Dad refused to give that place another dime. I'm going back to Douglas Egan to finish out my senior year.

"Woman, don't tell me what to do," my dad replies in a playful tone. "*But* if he wants one, all he has to do ask."

Now everyone is looking at me, waiting for a response. This is a topic I will be revisiting soon, just not today.

"Where's Marcel?" I ask, looking around.

Lily cranes her neck and points over my shoulder. "He's over there. Sitting a little too close to that young man. Who is that?"

I turn and find Marcel seated on the hood of his car with Quincy. I sigh. Might as well get this over with.

"That's Quincy. He isn't . . ." Whatever Mama was going to

say gets caught in her throat once she sees the body language between Q and Marcel. "Wait. Is Quincy . . . ?" she says to me.

I grin. "Let me go holla at them right quick."

It takes me ten minutes to make it out of our front yard. I keep getting stopped by people who want to tell me they're happy everything turned out okay. That they were praying for me all along. I don't know how much of it is true, but it feels good to hear.

Marcel sees me approaching before Quincy does. Quincy's too busy staring at Marcel like he's the most interesting thing he's ever seen. I've never seen him look at someone like that before.

"Can I talk to you right quick?" I say to Quincy.

"I'll give y'all a minute," Marcel says, getting ready to slide off the hood of his car. The air is warm, but Marcel is wearing a beanie to hide the stiches on the back of his head. He's been wearing one since he got out of the hospital.

"No. Stay," I say, holding up my hand. "You can hear this too. I mean, you clearly already know something my *supposed* best friend couldn't tell me."

"Amir, man, look—"

"Nah, Q, let me go first," I interrupt. "At first I felt some type of way 'cause I couldn't understand why someone who was supposed to be my boy, my brother, couldn't tell me he was gay. But you know what? You don't owe me shit. You do you. And whatever that is, you gonna still be my boy."

Marcel is smiling hard.

"It's not like that, man," Quincy says. "I mean, I'm not gay. I'm figuring shit out. I think I might be bi. It's hard to tell a person who you are, when you aren't even one hundred percent sure yourself. What I do know is that I really like your brother. And I wanna see what's up between us . . . if you okay with that."

I take a minute, my gaze shifting between him and Marcel. "All I'ma say is this: you hurt my brother, I'ma beat yo' ass."

"Noted," Quincy says with a chuckle.

Then I turn to Marcel and add, "You try and play my boy, we gon' fight. Got it?"

"Got it," Marcel says, still smiling.

"And you still my boy first, *period,*" I say, pointing at Quincy.

"Well, you gotta answer yo' phone and let me be, even when shit rough," he replies.

I bite my bottom lip, lowering my head.

"Touché," I say.

"And speaking of . . . ," Quincy says, pointing behind me.

I turn to see Buster and Nick approaching. Before I can say anything, Buster runs up on me and puts me in a headlock and says if I ever go ghost on them again, he's fucking me up. Then he lets me go and hugs me so tight I can barely breathe.

I try to hold back the tears, but I can't.

39

Marcel

A party isn't a party in this city until there's a second line.

As soon as the music cuts and everyone hears the energetic pulse of the trumpets, trombones, saxophones, and tubas, people start bopping into the street, gyrating to the rhythm of the snare drums as the second line band begins parading in front of Amir's house. Quincy pulls me out in the street to join some of his friends from school. I scarf down the barbecued hot dog I was eating so I can properly wave my arms in the air as I quickly shuffle my feet to the beat.

Beneath the canopy of the tangerine sky, everyone forgets their worries and frustrations as this impromptu cookout rolls into evening. I was dancing for at least fifteen minutes before I noticed Amir was missing. I start hopping around to see over the crowd and finally spot him sitting on the porch steps of the house directly across the street from his. He's by himself, watching the crowd with a faint smile, his face shadowed with melancholy.

"Hey, I'll be right back," I tell Quincy before maneuvering my way through the pulsating crowd to get to him.

From where he's seated, he can see his entire block, since his neighbor's house sits seven feet off the ground on concrete cylinders. Like many homes in this area after the massive floods Katrina caused.

"What'cha doing up here by yourself?" I say, nearly out of breath from climbing all the steps.

"Just thinking," he says, scooting over to make room for me.

I follow his gaze, which is pointed at my parents and his mother, who are all dancing near each other with a lot of other adults. To look at them now, you would never think there was any bad blood between them. I know it's simmering beneath the surface, but I'm hoping they can bury all that for my and Amir's sake.

"This may sound a little morbid," Amir says, his tone even, "but in a way, Chloe brought us together. You know what I mean?"

I do. And I'm sure he doesn't mean she had to die to do that.

"She was something else, meddling from beyond the grave," I say with a smirk. "Her and Nana."

"Yeah, you know how you said you heard Nana's voice when you were passed out at the Winslows'?" He waits until I nod to finish. "I heard her too. Telling me to get over there when you weren't answering your phone."

We sit in silence. Letting whatever that means fill us up with the warmth of her love.

"I honestly thought my life was over," Amir says. "When they put those handcuffs on me, I knew I would never have my freedom again. I stopped caring about everything. And look at me now. For the first time, I'm thinking about what my life is gonna be like after high school. I'm actually excited about it.

"If it wasn't for you, none of this would be possible," he adds, turning to me, his eyes glistening with tears. "You wouldn't let me give up, which got on my nerves at first."

I chuckle.

"You really showed me what having a brother could be like," he says, his voice trembling. "I know I didn't make that easy. If I was you, I probably would have let my ass go to jail the first time I cussed you out. But not you, 'cause you better than me, man. I'm not jealous of that anymore. I appreciate it. I appreciate you. I really love you, bro. You might be annoying, but you're *my* annoying little brother. And I'm gonna always have yo' back, no matter what."

I've waited so long to hear this. His words have me feeling weightless. He didn't really have to say it. I knew he loved me. I felt it even when he was angry. Only love would make him risk what he did to save me.

"I love you too, man," I say.

He snakes his left arm over my shoulder, pulling me into him. I let the warmth from his body wash over me. Why did it take us so long to get here?

"I'm glad you feel that way, 'cause I was hoping you wouldn't mind the news I need to drop on you," I say after we break apart.

" 'Sup?"

"Since I'm not going back to Truman, I told my parents I'd like to go to Douglas Egan with you."

He smiles. "Is this about me, or does it have more to do with Quincy?"

"A little of both, but more you," I admit. "I want us to really spend time together and get to know each other while we can. Before we go off to college, or in your case, culinary school, I'm guessing. I heard Daddy talking about it with my mother this morning."

"Man, he on it already," Amir says. "He has mentioned opening a restaurant together to people here at least six times today."

I laugh with Amir. "Y'all good?"

"We'll see," Amir says with a shrug. "We'll see." After a beat he continues, "You'll definitely get popular quick at Douglas Egan. You gonna be the richest kid there."

"*We* will be," I correct him.

"That's right. *We* are the Trudeaus."

"And don't you ever forget it."

I make eye contact with my mother, who waves at us, calling us both down to join them.

"We're getting called out," I say, nudging Amir with my shoulder. "Come on."

I grab my brother by the hand and guide him down the steps with me, leading him into the crowd. At one point, Monica grabs my hands and pulls me toward her.

"Thank you for keeping your promise," she whispers in my ear, and then goes right back to dancing with Amir.

We keep dancing in the street until the sky is pitch-black.

ACKNOWLEDGMENTS

Lots more people to thank this time around.

First up, my parents, who continue to unapologetically serve as my *unofficial* publicity team. 🙂

My agent extraordinaire, Alec. Couldn't ask for a better champion for my career. Two down, a lot more to go, buddy.

Krista, may we continue to set new standards in publishing by holding editorial meetings in places of cultural significance. And, Lydia, you're an asset of this team who I can't wait to cheerlead from the sidelines as you embark on your own publishing journey.

Monroe, you've truly been there from the start. When what's happening now was simply a thing I dreamed about but didn't really know if it was possible. Through all the self-doubt and minor setbacks, you never let me talk myself out of thinking I couldn't accomplish this, and for that, I'm forever grateful to you, friend.

To my BFFs, Lance and Mikey, I'm still working on the private jet. Until I can afford one, knowing that I love you both dearly will have to be enough. My "G.M.B." crew, thanks for making me laugh on the days when life comes at me fast.

Kita, you truly are the best sister in the world. Leah, Riley, and R.J., I appreciate all the prayers you sent up for your uncle. And to my extended network of cousins, aunts, and uncles, my sisters-in-law and all my "play cousins," my extended group of friends and coworkers (past and present): thank you for showing up in all the ways you did, whether that was attending book events when I was terrified no one would come, telling others to buy my book, posting about it on social media, or all of the above.

To the staff of Penguin Random House and Delacorte Press, y'all rock! Major shout-outs to my publicist, Joey Ho; Kristopher Kam, Katie Halata, Erica Stone, Adrienne Waintraub, Beverly Horowitz, Stephania Villar, Jenn Inzetta, Meredith Wagner, Elizabeth Ward, Alex Hernandez, Shannon Pender, Kelly McGauley, Kim Small, Barbara Marcus, Amanda Close, Becky Green, and Kimberly Langus.

Ellen Whitfield, Layne Mandros, and Jennifer Vance with Books Forward, the work you did to help push my debut novel was truly great. You ladies are one of a kind.

Sofia Bolido and Alessandra Birch, thanks for your efforts in getting my work into as many foreign markets as possible.

Kara Thomas, J. Elle, Alexa Donne, and Tahereh Mafi: your blurbs for *The Black Queen* not only made my year, but they also made me tear up. Thanks for reading and your support. Jess, you're truly special to me. Thanks for all your insight and pep talks.

To the author friends I picked up during in my debut year, thanks for welcoming the new kid with open arms. Extra thanks to Dhonielle Clayton, Karen McManus, Nic Stone, Terry J. Benton-Walker, and Taj McCoy and for all the cutting up, advice, and support through this crazy industry.

To the organizers of the North Texas Teen Book Festival, TeenBookCon, and the LA Times Book Festival, and to the staff of the Detroit Public Library: thanks for putting me face to face with the kids I'm writing for. Those interactions were truly the inspiring part in all of this.

Barnes & Noble, it was a real full-circle moment for me when I walked into a store and saw my book on the bookshelf. Thanks for spotlighting my debut book, allowing me to take over your Instagram account on more than one occasion. The support of the B&N network was unexpected and appreciated. Special shout-out to Michelle Laikowski for cheerleading me through it all.

Charisse Gibson, thanks for coming in at the last minute and making my launch event an experience I'll never forget.

And to all the independent bookstores, bloggers, reviewers, publications, and librarians and teachers who championed *The Black Queen,* I'll never be able to repay for your support.

And last but certainly not least, to the readers who DM'd me and spread the word about my debut novel, LOVE Y'ALL! LOVE Y'ALL! LOVE Y'ALL! I hope that I can continue to entertain y'all for years to come.

XOXO

JE

ABOUT THE AUTHOR

JUMATA EMILL is a journalist who has covered crime and local politics in Mississippi and parts of Louisiana. He earned his BA in mass communications from Southern University and A&M College. He's a Pitch Wars alum and member of the Crime Writers of Color. When he's not writing about murderous teens, he's watching and obsessively tweeting about every franchise of the Real Housewives. Jumata lives in Baton Rouge, Louisiana, and is the author of *The Black Queen* and *Wander in the Dark.*